ONE GOOD SOLDIER

BAEN BOOKS by TRAVIS S. TAYLOR

One Day on Mars
The Tau Ceti Agenda
One Good Soldier

Warp Speed
The Quantum Connection

The Science Behind the Secret*

with John Ringo:
Vorpal Blade
Manxome Foe
Claws That Catch

*forthcoming

ONE GOOD SOLDIER

TRAVIS S. TAYLOR

ONE GOOD SOLDIER

This is a work of fiction. All the characters and events portrayed in this book are fictional, and any resemblance to real people or incidents is purely coincidental.

A Baen Books Original

Baen Publishing Enterprises
P.O. Box 1403
Riverdale, NY 10471
www.baen.com

ISBN: 978-1-4391-3316-3

Cover art by Kurt Miller

First printing, December 2009

Distributed by Simon & Schuster
1230 Avenue of the Americas
New York, NY 10020

Library of Congress Cataloging-in-Publication Data

Taylor, Travis S.
  One good soldier / Travis S. Taylor.
     p. cm.
  ISBN 978-1-4391-3316-3
  I. Title.
  PS3620.A98O55 2009
  813'.6—dc22
                                                    2009037591

10 9 8 7 6 5 4 3 2 1

Pages by Joy Freeman (www.pagesbyjoy.com)
Printed in the United States of America

This work is dedicated to my personal hero and big brother, who has been deployed to Iraq twice, Afghanistan, Africa, and elsewhere around the world to defend my freedom to write science fiction books (among other things). Aim high, Chief Master Sergeant Greg Taylor, aim high!

PROLOGUE

October 31, 2388 AD
Earthspace, 100,000 kilometers above Orlando
Monday, 7:40 AM, Earth Eastern Standard Time
The Separatist Terrorist Attack on Luna City

"Goddamn, what was that?" General Elle Ahmi was tired of asking that question. The Separatist battle cruiser *Phlegra* rang with secondary explosions, and warning klaxons sounded throughout the ship.

"I think we were hit by the moon's mass driver," Captain Sterling Maximillian answered. The mass driver of the Oort Cloud facility's moon had fired on them just before they had entered the quantum membrane transport to Earthspace.

"Damage report?" Elle said impatiently. Still, Sterling was a competent captain and the terrorist general had every confidence that he would get them to their target.

"I'm still checking. The teleport is operating as planned." The buzzing and popping from the Quantum Membrane Technology (QMT) projection stopped, and the Moon filled the view of the bridge. Luna City twinkled brightly beneath them as the shining metropolis that it was. Glints from Earth and Sol glared off the Luna City domes, through the portals, and onto the viewscreens. The tens of millions of inhabitants of the domes had no idea what disaster was about to rain down on them from space.

"Well, shut those damned alarms off. We're here." Elle sat back at the empty station behind the captain's seat. She drummed her fingers against the console, waiting for Maximillian's report.

"Sublight engines are down. We're venting like mad from every seal."

"Tell me some good news."

"Uh, yes, General. The auxiliary drive is unharmed, and we can reroute to that one. I'm working it. Propulsion will be up in five, four, three, two . . . there." Maximillian smiled triumphantly.

"Good. If Aux is all that is left, she'll be going there. All security personnel are to report to that section of the ship and stop that bitch." Elle slammed her fist into the screen of her console, cracking the cover. The CIA agent who had managed to infiltrate the *Phlegra* had been captured and tied up down in sickbay, but somehow she had managed to escape and was causing all sorts of problems for the terrorist's plans. She had already managed to knock out several key power systems somehow. "Stop her! Is that understood?"

"Yes, ma'am."

"Full forward to Luna City. Ramming vector!" Elle ordered. The plan was to slam the ship into Luna City, killing millions of American citizens with one attack. Elle Ahmi's sole purpose for the attack was to kill off a voting district and thereby sway an election—an election for president of the United States of America.

"Damnit, Jack, I'm cut off. I don't think I can get around to you. That last blast closed off several sections between us," Nancy Penzington warned Commander Jack "DeathRay" Boland. He and his mecha wingman had followed the *Phlegra* through the QMT transport from the Oort Cloud combat in an attempt to stop the ship and rescue the CIA agent. The hallway Nancy had been going down was completely destroyed, and air was beginning to vent out of it. She had been lucky that whatever had just hit them hadn't crushed her in the process. So instead of being killed instantly, she was probably going to die slowly of hypothermia or from lack of oxygen.

"Roger that, Penzington. Can you get out of the ship?" Jack pushed his bot-mode Ares-T Navy mecha back up to its feet and looked out of the gaping tear in the ship's hull above him. The Moon loomed overhead, maybe a hundred thousand kilometers or so away. They were running out of time, and Jack had no real, good idea of how to stop the battle cruiser.

"I don't think so. I think I'm trapped in here." Nancy looked in every direction but could see nothing but crunched metal. The hull of the ship had collapsed all around her, and it would take hours to cut her out with a laser cutter. There was no way that one mecha was going to dig her out in a few seconds.

"Hold on, we're coming to you. I'll blast you out if I have to."

"Don't, Boland. I'm too deep in the ship. I did my job. I got some good info on the Separatists' plan. I'm downloading it to you now. I haven't even had the chance to read all of it. You read it and then figure out what to do with it. And don't share this with anyone that you don't trust completely, and be wary even of them. I mean it." Nancy sat down in the corridor, listening to the air hissing through the cracks in the wreckage. She had done her job.

"That's defeatist talk," Jack said. "Now get your ass up and find a way out of there."

"Sorry, Jack. I'm stuck here, and my air is running out." She paused for a brief moment in thought. "If you can't stop this ship, you have to get out with the data I just gave you. Now, go. That data is more important than I am."

"Come on, Jack." Fish pulled her mecha through the gash in the ship to the exterior hull. The Moon continued to loom closer. At their present rate of acceleration, they would hit Luna City in less than a minute. Fish rolled her bot over into fighter mode and throttled toward Earth. Then her blue-force system dinged at her. There were two supercarriers not far from their location. "Jack, I've got two supercarriers Earthward."

"I see." Jack thrusted his mecha up through the ship and outward into open space, where he toggled his bot back to fighter mode. He paused during the maneuver, only briefly but long enough to look back at the *Phlegra* solemnly. "Godspeed, Penzington, or whoever you are."

Jack? DeathRay's artificial intelligence counterpart (AIC) spoke into his mindvoice. The implant in his brain translated the computer's communication direct-to-mind, or DTM, through a quantum neural interface between the AIC and the user.

Yes, Candis.

Blue-force tracker identifies the nearest ship as the USS John Tyler. *Perhaps it can stop the battle cruiser.*

Right.

✧   ✧   ✧

"Captain! We've got a major electromagnetic disturbance Moonward, and a Seppy battle cruiser just appeared out of nowhere!" the CDC officer of the *Tyler* warned the captain over the command net.

"What the hell?" Captain Westerfeld looked confused.

"Sir, we're being hailed by the CAG of the *Sienna Madira.*"

"Can't be. Wally's ship is way out in the Oort somewhere."

"Well, sir, his security codes validate."

"Patch him through."

"CO *Tyler*, this is Commander Jack Boland of the USS *Sienna Madira.*"

"Commander, this is Captain Westerfeld. What can I do for you?"

"Sir, this battle cruiser is on a ramming vector for Luna City, and we can't seem to stop it! I thought you might be able to help us out."

"Captain," Alexander Moore interrupted. "I have an idea." He shoved the *Sienna Madira* robot onto the teleport pad. The corrupted AI inside the robot likeness of the great president from Disney World had been under the Separatists' control. But for now it was being jammed by President Moore's AIC temporarily, but that would only hold a few more seconds. When the robot AI broke through the jamming signal, it would most certainly detonate the multiple megaton gluonium bomb hidden within it. Gluonium bombs used the actual quantum mechanical force that held quarks together and were the most powerful weapons developed by man.

"Agreed." Westerfeld nodded. "Commander Boland. I recommend that you get out of there as quickly as you can. We'll take care of it."

"Trick or treat, bitch!" Moore said to the AI-driven Sienna Madira robot look-alike.

"General, the propulsion system is locked on. Even if it was knocked out, at this point our trajectory will still take us to Luna City," Maximillian said, nodding toward the bright silver and blue dome of the great metropolis in the Sea of Tranquility. The captain of the *Phlegra* tapped a few keys on his chairarm and moved several virtual icons around in his DTM mindview. Then he turned to Ahmi and said, "We should go now, ma'am."

"All right. Very good. Activate the QMT projector snap-back routine," Elle ordered.

"Yes, ma'am. Recalling all personnel to original Tau Ceti QMT projection in three, two, one . . ."

Nancy Penzington, or Kira Shavi, or . . . well, her real first name had been Nancy, at least . . . sat with her back against the collapsed bulkhead of the *Phlegra*, hugging her knees and waiting for the end. The air hissed by her, and it was getting very cold in the corridor, and she was shivering uncontrollably. None of that really mattered at this point since the ship she was trapped in was about to crash and explode in seconds. She didn't want to die, but she was making her peace with it.

Nancy, we did our job, her AIC consoled her.

Yes, we did. And hopefully it will save some lives or do some good.

It will. Boland will figure out what to do with it. Allison had had the time to read the data when she had finally decrypted it. There was some very interesting information in there, and some contacts that went all the way up to the White House. The data was more important than Nancy or Allison themselves. *The data was worth the sacrifice.*

I hope it isn't too big for him.

He'll figure it out.

Nancy?

Yes, Allison?

I've really enjoyed being your friend.

Me, too, Allison.

The ship started popping and crackling around her, and then white light filled her vision. Through the light, she caught faint glimpses of the ship exploding all around her. She braced herself for the pain of the exploding hot ionizing plasma rushing toward her. And she braced for death. . . .

But death didn't come. A distinct sound of hissing and popping like frying bacon filled her ears, and the exploding ship seemed to freeze in place. Nancy's mind raced with her life's story as she knew that these would be her last seconds to reflect on her thoughts.

Nancy! I'm receiving an All Hands AIC ping!

So?

It is for a recall to Tau Ceti!

Can you hack it!

It didn't require a hack. It was an open handshaking call to all AICs on the ship, but you need to be prepared for escape and evade.

Damn right!

The exploding ship on the other side of the bright light filling Nancy's vision vanished from her field of view as bluish flashes of stars popped in and out of her sight. The high-energy cosmic rays from the QMT transport passed through her body mostly without any interaction, but occasionally one of them would affect the electrodynamic properties of the atoms in the aqueous-humor liquid of her eyeballs at speeds faster than the speed of light in the liquid and therefore generating Cerenkov radiation. The characteristic flashes of blue light then impinged on her retina, with the outcome being as if she were "seeing stars."

Then, as quickly as the exploding Separatist battle cruiser had vanished, it was instantly replaced by the inside of the QMT transport facility in orbit around Tau Ceti just inward of the orbit of the planet Ares. The electromagnetic whirlwind around her subsided abruptly, leaving Nancy sitting and hugging her knees on a large pad with over sixty Separatist battle cruiser crew members including the captain of the ship, a dead doctor, and several dead, mangled, and injured crew members. Near the center was Elle Ahmi in her trademark stars and stripes ski mask. The sight of the evil Separatist general refreshed the fear of the torture Nancy had gone through less than a half hour before. The remembered feel of those cold black leather gloves caressing her naked body and then slamming into her face made her shiver with spite and hatred for the woman. The residual pain and memories of the torture drugs they had used on her fueled a rage deep insider her. Oh, yes, Nancy was going to get that bitch one day. One. Day.

The crew quickly started scurrying about and dispersing, and Nancy stood and rushed purposefully off the pad amidst several soldiers who had materialized near her on the QMT pad. Two men just to her left were battered and bloody, and one was applying an organogel patch over the other's missing arm. There were several cries of pain across the pad. The mass-driver round that had struck the ship, the two mecha pilots, and Nancy herself had inflicted some damage to the battle cruiser before it was evacuated, and clearly there had been casualties. The teleport pad was in chaos, and that worked to her advantage. Nancy still hadn't figured out how they had teleported all the way back to Tau Ceti without bringing the ship. But there were more urgent thoughts on her mind—like getting the hell out of there and staying alive.

"Hey, you!" A bloody man in orange coveralls lying on the deck pleaded for her attention.

"What?" Nancy turned to see more clearly that the man was holding his stomach, which was ripped completely open. Blood trickled from his mouth.

"Help me," he said faintly. "Oh God, help me."

She paused for a moment and scanned around her. Someone would help him eventually. *Shit,* she thought. *That might be too late for him.* Some other time she might have to put a bullet between the guy's eyes, but right now wasn't that time. The right thing to do was to help. *Shit!*

"Medic!" Nancy yelled and then tore the bottom half of her shirt off and stretched it out in her hands to see if it would be long enough for a bandage.

Allison, what do you suggest? Her AIC used the visual information from Nancy's eyes as recorded through her brain from a DTM link and analyzed the damage to the man. His large intestines were clearly loosened and falling out. There was a bloodied red and dark gray jagged metal shard penetrating through his left side and out his back.

Other than getting the hell out of here, Allison started, *don't touch the metal object in him. Let a doctor remove that. Carefully put his body parts back in and bandage it off.*

Hell, I knew that. Got anything more?

Not much you can do without the proper equipment and supplies.

Okay.

"Hold still." Nancy undoubled the torn piece of shirt and slid it underneath the man's back. The slight movement made him scream in agony and fear. "Focus. Try to relax your breathing. You're gonna be okay. I'm Nancy. What's your name?"

"Alan," the man said faintly. Blood gurgled from his lips each time he tried to speak.

"Nice to meet you." Nancy reached into his abdomen and began placing his intestines back in gently. At one point she had to actually push hard to arrange them in place. Alan screamed again. "Listen, you have to help me here. Hold your hands here until I can tie this off!"

Alan did what she told him, but he had lost so much blood that he was almost too weak to apply any pressure. He was bleeding out pretty fast, and if he didn't get the right attention in a matter of seconds he wasn't going to make it. Nancy pulled at the jagged tear in the man's skin and then placed the makeshift bandage over his entrails. She tied it as tightly as she could and then pressed down with the palms of her hands. Blood oozed out through the bandage and between her already blood-red fingers.

"Where's that goddamned medic? Medic!"

"Here." Nancy felt a tap on her shoulder as a Seppy soldier with a red armband knelt beside her. He instantly slid an injection into the side of the man's neck and then popped open a large pack of organogel. "Good job, soldier. Now, don't move your hands until I tell you to."

"Roger that." Nancy held fast to Alan's abdomen as the medic squirted the organogel over her fingers and the large jagged gash. Then he applied more of the gel to the metal shard protruding through Alan's side. The injection must have been immunoboost and stims, because Nancy could tell that the coloring in Alan's face was already better. The medic pulled another small pouch from his bag and tore a seal-tab on it. The clear pouch expanded and turned a deep blood red.

"Sir, I'm giving you some instaplasma that should help alleviate the stress of so much blood loss. You're gonna make it, so just hang in there." The medic taped the pouch down to the wounded man's arm and jabbed the sharp tube into a vein at the wrist. The tube hissed and made a completely hermetically sealed connection between the plasma container and Alan's circulatory system.

"He needs a gurney," the medic stated. He whispered quietly to Nancy, "He's not out of the woods yet." He reached in his bag again and this time pulled out a roll of dull green material about three quarters of a meter wide and then rolled it out beside Alan. The material was a good two meters long once it was rolled out. The medic then pressed a membrane button on the top of it, and the material hardened and formed handles on each end. "We're gonna move him right up on the gurney. On three!"

"Got it." Nancy nodded that she understood him and adjusted her position in order to help move the injured man onto the gurney.

"One, two, three!" They both carefully dragged Alan onto the gurney. Nancy couldn't really do a lot as her hands were solidifying to Alan's midsection. The clear organogel was turning an opalescent pale pink, almost skin color.

"Okay, slowly, very slowly, pull your hands out. Don't worry about the bandage. The immunoboost and organogel will eventually eat it."

"Right." Nancy slowly retracted her hands with a sickening *squish* and *pop* as they escaped the viscous bloody goo. Her hands looked and felt as if she had been soaking them in a vat of petroleum jelly, and she was covered in blood up to her elbows. Her face was still swollen and battered, and several times during her first aid on the wounded man blood had squirted her in the face and on her clothes. She was a mess.

"Grab that end." The medic pointed and got a grip on the other end. Nancy did as she was told, but began thinking about an exit strategy.

Any suggestions? Nancy thought to her AIC.

Go about your business, Nancy, Allison warned her. *As far as they know, the CIA agent died with the* Phlegra.

Got it.

Nancy heaved her end of the gurney and continued on with it for several meters, letting the medic lead. They were several very long meters, to a passageway on the edge of the teleport pad. The pad was in a cavernous room the size of a professional basketball coliseum. It had clearly been designed to transport many troops and a lot of heavy equipment in a single teleport. Nancy also knew that the facility could teleport ships hovering over it as well. The Seppies had a serious technological advantage with this facility, and somehow the U.S. needed to be prepared for the types of attacks it would enable. But Nancy didn't have time to really focus on strategy at the moment. Survival tactics were about all she could manage. She had to get away from here to the planet below, where she could disappear into the population.

"Thank you, Nancy." Alan looked up at her and managed as much of a smile as he could. He was looking a lot better than he had just seconds before, but he still looked like leftover Hell twice warmed over.

"Just hang in there," she replied.

How did they develop all this? Allison thought to her, referring to the teleport facility.

Worry about it later. Let's get the fuck out of here and get lost somewhere a long damned way from Elle Ahmi. Nancy's first thoughts were survival. She couldn't believe she'd let herself get wrapped up helping the wounded. But it might work out for the best.

Agreed.

"Ma'am, are you all right?" the medic asked her.

"Sure. I'm fine. Superficial stuff—nothing to worry about." Nancy had already taken mental steps to put out of her mind the torture that she had endured just minutes before. While she realized that it must be still apparent on her face and body that she had recently been through physical torture, the simple fact of the multiple wounded around her was cover enough for it. She could feel the immunoboost working, the one she had been given by the man—Scotty, she recalled—who had helped her escape. It had removed some of the swelling and had started to close the various abrasions. She was wearing what was left of the commandeered clothing, which was way too big for her, and she had no shoes. Her battered look fit in with the surviving battered Seppy troops, but her clothes, well, didn't. She stood out. But hopefully, the other sixty soldiers scurrying about with their own frantic agendas wouldn't notice. Her bloody nose and mouth and Alan's blood covering most of her upper torso and arms actually worked to her advantage as a disguise. The first chance she got, she planned on commandeering herself a better one.

I'm picking up a hangar bay around the corner. I'm trying to handshake with some of the transport-manifest AICs. Maybe we can stow away to Ares, Allison said.

Right. Good plan.

CHAPTER 1

July 1, 2394 AD
Earthspace, Sea of Waves, the Moon
Friday, 7:40 AM, Earth Eastern Standard Time

"Watch the Gomer on your three-nine line, Dee! He's gonna lock you up!" Deanna Moore heard blasting in her ears on the tac-net. Her wingman, Jay Stavros, held as close on her ass as he could and continued to nag her about the crossfire, but it didn't faze her. She had to be cool in order to close the energy gap on the enemy mecha Stinger in front of her.

"You just cover my ass, Jay! I'm staying with this Gomer in front of us." Deanna stomped on her left pedal and pulled back on the stick with her right hand, all the while trimming the throttle with her left hand to maintain a steady energy relationship between herself and the enemy fighter. "Come on, goddamnit, make a mistake!"

She pulled into as tight a turn as the Marine mecha could withstand, and when she did the g-suit constricted on her legs and abdomen like a giant anaconda squishing its prey. Deanna grunted and cursed against the extreme gravity loading but held her course on the tail of the enemy Stinger.

Bree, give me some alternatives here! she screamed in her mind at her AIC.

Roger that, Dee, the AIC responded and placed several red lines and blue lines in her DTM mindview. The lines were alternative aircraft trajectories of her and the enemy's fighters spiraling around each other in a corkscrewing sinewy ballet of angular momentum

11

and propellantless propulsion energy application. *Too close for missiles—gotta go to guns!*

The yellow targeting X blinked and jumped around in Deanna's mindview but couldn't quite lock on to the Stinger. The X blinked red then yellow and then hopped off the enemy fighter again. No matter what type of juke or jink she tried, the damned enemy mecha managed to squirm, bob, or roll its way out of her targeting solution.

"Shit! Come on you bastard. Hold . . . fucking . . . still." She grunted against the overwhelming and crushing load on her chest. The g-suit squished her breasts flat as pancakes and her abdominal muscles were squeezed so tight that she wasn't sure she'd ever be able to unsqueeze them.

Then the enemy mecha did something. Dee wasn't sure if it was brilliant or stupid. The mecha, in fighter mode, flipped over forward and began to transfigure to bot mode. The transfiguration took only a fraction of a second and left the mecha standing upside down on its head and facing Dee and her wingman with both arms pointing forty-millimeter cannons in their general direction.

"Warning—enemy targeting lock established. Warning—enemy targeting lock established," the Bitchin' Betty of Dee's mecha chimed. Times like this the mecha's automatic warning system was more distracting than helpful.

Tracers tracked out of the right-arm cannon of the enemy fighter across her nose and into the empennage of her wingman's plane. Dee could see Jay jinking and juking his fighter around inside the firing solution of the enemy weapons, but there was little he could do at the time. The rounds continued to rip through his mecha, throwing bits of armor plating off into space with an orange and white spray of plasma.

"Pull out, Jay! Pull out!" Deanna, with her hands-on-throttle-and-stick (HOTAS), slammed the throttle full forward and the stick all the way forward against the stop, rocketing her fighter-mode mecha into a horrendous dive toward the deck.

"Shit, Dee, I'm hit! Eject, eject, eject!" Jay shouted.

Just as her mecha nosed down, her wingman's mecha exploded behind and to the right of her, and brilliant orange tracer rounds zipped by her canopy, only centimeters away. She didn't have time to see if an ejection couch cleared the fireball or not. The Gomer off her three-nine line to the right was closing in and firing. Then several rounds from the bot-mode mecha that she had been tailing zipped through her tail section but only caused minor damage. While Jay had been with her it was two against two and she had an enemy in her sights. Things had been looking up. Suddenly, in less time than it takes to blink an eye, the situation had switched in favor of the enemy. It was now two against one, and both of them were targeting her. Dee continued down at alarmingly increasing acceleration until it was clear that the mecha behind her and to her right were going to follow.

They're on you now, Dee! Bree warned her.

Roger that!

Dee toggled the transfigure button on the HOTAS and stomped the right, lower foot pedal all the way down to give her more slip as the Marine FM-12 transfigurable strike mecha rolled and flipped over and then transformed from a fighter plane into a giant armed and armored robot.

Let's see if what is good for the goose is good for the gander! she thought.

Dee, watch your altitude! Bree warned her. The landscape of the small moon they were fighting over filled her entire field of view and was rapidly approaching. It looked a lot like Pluto's moon, Charon.

She gripped the throttle and pulled it full-force backward with her left hand while controlling the flight path with the stick in her right. The standard HOTAS controls mimicked most fighter-control systems that had been developed for centuries with the innovation, of course, of the DTM-control links between the plane and the pilot and the AIC. There had been experiments where mecha had been piloted by AICs alone, and those mecha could make maneuvers that human bodies couldn't withstand. But there was a certain art to combat flying that only humans in the cockpit could bring. The experiments always showed the same results. Human and AICs together in the cockpit always came out on top when flying against a plane with just one or the other in it. The DTM connections between pilot, AIC, and mecha enabled modern fighter mecha to do things that no others in history could have done, and Dee was pushing the combination to the limit.

The bot-mode mecha now stood on its head, which was upside down in relation to the other fighters, and backward, facing the pursuing mecha. The g-loading of the full-force reversal caused

Dee to vomit dryly into her helmet, and her vision began to tunnel in around her. But she fought through it and held on to the HOTAS.

"Aaarrhhggg, woo!" She grunted and flexed her abdominal muscles again, trying to hold off blacking out long enough to lock up her pursuers. Two yellow Xs filled her mind, bouncing around the fighter-mode Stinger to her right and the bot-mode mecha on her tail. The quantum-membrane sensors locked up on the fighter-mode plane, and a lock tone sounded in her mind. "Fox three!" she shouted as she loosed a mecha-to-mecha missile. The missile spiraled out toward the enemy fighter, leaving a very faint blue ion trail through the almost nonexistent atmosphere of the small moon.

"Warning, surface collision imminent. Warning, surface collision imminent," her mecha's Bitchin' Betty announced.

"One more . . . second . . ." Dee grunted as the yellow targeting X turned red. "Guns, guns, guns!" she shouted as she triggered the cannons on both arms. Tracers tracked out and blew the enemy mecha into a fireball of orange and white debris.

Pull out, Dee! Pull out!

"Warning, surface collision imminent. Warning—"

Dee tried to pull the mecha over into a horizontal run with the ground but didn't make it. Her mecha slammed into the surface just as she began to black out.

"Apple didn't fall far from the tree, if you don't mind my saying so, sir," Thomas Washington commented to President Moore as they watched the president's eighteen-year-old daughter, Deanna, on the large viewscreen at the Mecha Combat Training Simulations Center located at the south end of the Sea of Waves near the limb of the Moon.

"I was never a mecha jock, Thomas." Moore smiled back at his bodyguard, only briefly taking his eyes off the simulation displays. Three other Secret Service agents stood behind them and didn't flinch or make a sound. The president's daughter was in a large metal box suspended on repulsor fields. The box whirled and bounced and twisted madly in place, simulating a combat scenario. Inside the box was a replica of a U.S. Marine FM-12 transfigurable strike mecha fighter cockpit.

Deanna had logged thousands of hours in the sim over the

last five years and had reached a point where her proficiency was approaching that of a seasoned Marine mecha pilot. Of course she hadn't gone through all of the basic Marine training, as it was against the law to enlist before the age of twenty-one. Deanna was only eighteen, and for more than a century, as life expectancies had increased, the age to enter active duty as soldiers, firemen, policemen, and a few other dangerous professions had been set to the legal adult age. So Dee would just have to wait a few years, but Moore could tell by watching how she handled the simulations that she had the skills to be a good mecha pilot. She just needed the benefit of age and training. And train she had. Since she had been thirteen, Dee had studied and trained and competed in any and all mecha jock activities she could. She had been accepted into the most prestigious military academy in the Sol System. And while there were plenty of skeptics out there, Alexander had never once needed to use their family's political pull to help her. Moore hated that Dee had been living in a dorm at the Sea of Waves Powered Armor and Mecha Academy for the past four years instead of at the White House with him and Sehera.

But Dee had put in the work and Alexander was proud of her. Fortunately, Air Force One often made trips to the Moon. He wished that Dee would have taken up lion wrestling, or football, or shark baiting, or chainsaw juggling, or anything less dangerous instead. But she hadn't. For the past six years, since that incident in Orlando, she had thought of nothing but being a goddamned U.S. Marine mecha pilot. When she saw those marines tromping around Disney World in bot-mode mecha, bringing all kinds of hell to the robot AIs that were trying to capture the First Family, her life changed. U.S. Marine Major Alexander Moore wanted to say "Oorah!" President of the United States of America Alexander Moore wanted to say, "Good work, and your country would be proud to have you serve!" But for just plain old Alexander Moore, hick from Mississippi, daddy to a little girl, it was *his* little girl, his princess. He didn't ever want to see her in harm's way.

But Alexander knew that Dee was gonna be Dee, and the best he could do was support her and try to make her as damned good a marine as he could manage. That might just keep her alive in the future. He still had three years to talk her out of it. He wasn't giving that much of a chance—snowballs and Hell came to mind.

"Goddamned gutsy, if stupid," USMC retired Colonel Walter

"Rat Bastard" Fink III stood at ease behind the president, with his hands behind his back.

"I agree." Moore turned to the mecha pilot instructor and frowned at the former marine. Of course, Moore knew well and good himself that there was no such thing as a former marine. "She is no good to anybody dead. And she can't move on to the final rounds of the competition, either."

"Permission to speak freely, Mr. President?" Colonel Fink asked.

"Go ahead, Rat."

"She isn't thinking of life and death at all, only about killing her opponent to win a competition. She still thinks of this as a game, sir. A game with a reset button. Oh, she is damned good at it, and with her and her wingman there we'll probably snag the trophy at Ross 128 next week. But I'm here to train marines, sir, not just simulation-competition winners. And like you said, she's no good to anybody dead, sir," Fink said without moving a muscle or changing the expression on his face.

"I think somebody should make her . . . aware . . . of her problem, Colonel Fink. Don't you?" Moore smiled at the instructor.

"Yes, sir," Fink replied as a large toothy grin covered his face. "And I think I know just the person, sir."

The "box," as it was affectionately referred to by mecha trainees, or "nuggets," drifted to a resting spot on the floor of the sim center, and the side opened up by folding over into steps. Two instructor techs rushed into the box to help Dee out of the pilot's couch. The box for her wingman a few meters to the left of hers had already been opened. Moore could see the young man's face was pale, and when he stood his legs were shaky.

Deanna managed to walk upright down the ramp but only with the support of the instructor techs under each arm. Once she made it to the bottom of the ramp she motioned that she could support herself and then twisted off her helmet. Alexander could tell by the look on her face that she was physically exhausted but proud of herself for having killed her pursuers. Fink was right. She still didn't understand the life and death of the predicament that she was considering getting herself into—the predicament of being a United States Marine.

"Cadet Moore!" Rat shouted with a rough, gravelly tone at the "First Nugget," as Dee was known.

"Sir!" Dee snapped-to tightly, her exhaustion showing through her expressionless face. She and her flight gear were soaked in sweat from her shortly cropped Martian-dark hair to her toes, which were a long, athletic, and curvy one hundred seventy-six centimeters down.

"How do you think you performed on that mission, Nugget?"

"I killed the enemy, sir." Dee didn't move or flinch or even blink.

"Your wingman is dead!"

"Yes, sir."

"You are dead!"

"Yes, sir."

"The entire nation is going on a week of mourning because the First Nugget has died uselessly, if heroically, in combat! Sorry, Cadet Stavros, but only your family will be mourning for you, as you are dead as hell as well!"

"Yes, sir," Dee and Jay answered simultaneously.

"You think this is a goddamned game, nuggets?" Fink stood looming over Dee, his nose only inches from her face. Then he glanced and glared at her wingman.

Again, simultaneously, Dee and Jay responded. "No, sir."

"Then what the hell was that! Your mission was to go in and support the recon unit infiltrating that facility, and you ended up getting yourself and your wingman killed. Now, what if those heart-breaking, goddamned life-taking, and God fearing AEMs down there needed some more air support? Huh? Just what in the flying fuck were you thinking? Those marines had a mission, and now, because you were too busy up there goddamned hotdogging it out like some goddamned virtual world goddamned gamer, this mission has a larger probability of failure. That is failure with a capital fuckin' F! Do you understand me, Nugget? Failure!"

"Sir!"

"And fucking failure, with a capital fuckin' F, is one thing that I WILL NOT accept from my nuggets! Do you two hotshots under-fucking-stand me?"

"Yes, sir!" Dee made the mistake of letting her eyes glance at her father standing in the background, but only for a fraction of a second. But that was a fraction of a second too long.

"Cadet Moore! Do you think just because your daddy is Alexander Moore, one of the most decorated marines in the history of the universe, and also happens to have gotten himself elected president of these here United States of America three times in a row, that you are gonna get some sort of preferential treatment? Huh?"

"No, sir!" Dee's eyes fixed, and glowered, at Fink. Alexander watched his daughter's body stiffen, and he could tell that Fink had hit her main nerve. He seemed to be enjoying himself a little too much. But Moore wouldn't do anything. If Dee wanted to be a real marine, she would have to make it on her own from here on out with no preferential treatment. He absolutely hated his little girl having to go through this. But, God, he was proud of her.

"Then why don't you turn around and crawl your asses back into those simulator boxes, and let's do this mission goddamned right this . . ." Fink continued to yell at the two nuggets for a few minutes as they were loaded back into the simulators by the techs standing by. The two pilot trainees were physically exhausted, but that was all part of the job. A good marine marches when told and trains harder than everybody else no matter how tired he or she is.

"Well." Alexander turned to his bodyguards. "This is gonna take some time, so why don't we go find the First Lady and grab some breakfast and shake some hands and kiss some babies."

"Yes, sir." Thomas nodded at the president and then to the other agents. He sent a DTM order to Dee's bodyguard that they would see them at the departure platform in a couple of hours.

"No, I didn't really get to talk to her at all." Alexander smiled across the table at his wife. It amazed him how much Dee looked like her mother and frightened him how much Sehera looked like her mother. The three women could be confused as triplets if Dee let her hair grow back out and if Sehera and her mother timed rejuves appropriately with a family photo. But one thing that both Alexander and Sehera knew for sure was that they never wanted their daughter close enough to Sehera's mother to ever have such a photo take place. After all, Sehera's mother, the famous one hundred eleventh president, Sienna Madira, a.k.a. Separatist terrorist General Elle Ahmi, was, in their minds, the craziest and most evil human being in the history of mankind, though Ahmi would argue that she had done what she had with the future of mankind and the United States of America at the heart of it all. But the Moores thought differently.

"Alexander, what is it?" Sehera asked. Moore had given up trying to hold out on his wife years prior. He must've been giving something away with his expression.

"Nothing really, I just . . . hate thinking of her in a fighter in some horrific space battle somewhere. It . . . kills . . . me."

"Ha. The big tough marine," Sehera said. Alexander had stared enemy mecha down and practically beaten them with his bare hands, and once he had killed over ninety of the meanest Separatist thugs all by himself, but his one weak spot was Dee. "She's your daughter, all right."

"You're kidding. She's more and more like you every day." Moore fiddled with the blood-red steak tips on his plate and pushed at the scrambled eggs with his knife and fork. He took a brief moment to glance out across the moonscape from the window at the Armored E-suit Marine training grounds and staging area in the distance. He knew that place all too well. The reflection of the holoview in the window also caught his attention. The Earth News Network (ENN) ticker-tape at the bottom of the reflection was about his tariff plans for the colonies and how the governor of Ross 128 was complaining of unfair taxation. The window of the restaurant held views to the things that had engulfed his life for a very long time. Moore tried to ignore the view and focus on his wife. She was a much more breathtaking vision anyway.

"Well, then she should be fine, shouldn't she?" Sehera goaded him again as she reorganized a strand of her long black straight hair out of her face and tucked it back behind her ear where it belonged. "What time is her flight again?"

"We've got time. It's in an hour. She jaunts from here to the QMT facility at Mars orbit, from there she rides the *Sienna Madira* to the Oort gate, and then she'll teleport to the Ross 128 system on a passenger transport. The competition isn't until next Tuesday. We should be able to make it with no problem. I need to spend some face time with the governor there, anyway."

"That all sounds fine. I'm sure she'll enjoy her ride on the supercarrier."

"Oh, yes, she'll be fine. Several ships of the fleet are engaged in war games there, and she'll get to see them loading up the mecha afterwards before jaunting out to the Oort. Nothing to worry about. Besides, Clay will be with her all the way. And she's in good hands with Colonel Fink."

"You're right," she said. Sehera sipped at her coffee slowly and then had an afterthought. "You do recall that you have a meeting with the ambassador from Ross 128 over lunch in the Rose Garden, right?"

How could I forget, he thought. But Moore was amazed at how his wife kept up with him—and without an internal AIC to boot. She had an AIC in an earring but wouldn't allow an implant or DTM connection with the AIC. Her earring used a subaudible signal projected to her eardrum to transfer information. It was slow but safe. Alexander knew that Sehera had a built-in fear of internal AICs and DTMs after watching her mother use them to terrorize the minds of her captives during the Martian Desert Campaigns. Perhaps she would get over it someday. In fact, Sehera had told him that she would get over it when she had to. And to date, she hadn't had to.

ABIGAIL? he asked his AIC.

Yes, sir. Air Force One is standing by, and we have everything going according to schedule for today.

Right then, he thought.

"Don't worry. Abigail will keep me on track. The ambassador will be QMTing from Ross 128 to the Oort and then from there to Mars. The *John Tyler* will bring him in from there and QMT him directly to the White House." He pushed his plate away from him. He didn't want the eggs anyway. "If you're finished, we've got just enough time to walk around the city a bit."

"Suits me."

"Approval ratings for President Alexander Moore today are the lowest they have been in the history of his three terms as President of the United States," stated Walt Mortimer, one of the so-called expert panel members for the *Round Table of News* and lead White House columnist for the *Washington Post,* almost too enthusiastically. But then again, the media icon had made his political position quite clear over the course of his illustrious career, and the news of the latest polling data fit right in with his agenda. Mortimer had long been considered one of the "graybeards" of reporters on Washington, D.C. and systemwide politics helping the populace, but it was quite clear that he was just another of the Beltway Bandits making a living by feeding shit to the American public. But it was a good living. Or at least it had been until Moore came along.

"His campaign promises following the attack on Mons City and the Martian Separatist Exodus led him to a whirlwind landslide election, and his policies following the attack on Disney World and Luna City led to high approval ratings systemwide, which in turn led him to reelection," Mortimer continued. "But heavy spending on defense against *potential* terrorist attack from outside the solar system at the expense of systemwide economic growth, not to mention protectionist policies against intersystem competition of market goods and commerce due to cheaper products from the colonies seems to have turned the American voters lukewarm on the president." Mortimer leaned back in his chair and scribbled some notes on a pad in front of him. He maintained a smug look of triumph on his face.

"The latest polls do suggest that is how the American people feel about it, anyway," replied Britt Howard, the show's host and anchor for ENN at the New York City anchor desk. "It would appear that the 'defend the system at all costs' policy is beginning to wear thin. Especially since the manufacturing base has yet to fully recover since the Separatist Exodus almost twelve years ago. It turns out that the 'Buy American' policy of the previous Democratic administration of President Alberts has been adopted by this Republican administration, but for a different reason. Indeed, the president has lobbied extremely hard to increase the tariffs on all imports from the four extrasolar colonies, same as his predecessor. However, where President Alberts used Sol System economic stimulus as the reason, President Moore is using the cost of defending the three heritage colonies and the two new start-ups from the rogue Tau Ceti Separatist system as his reasoning. This policy once seemed to be broadly accepted by the American public, but the latest polls show that the public is overwhelmingly for reducing the burden on the extrasolar colonies in order to increase the number of colony-manufactured goods available within the Sol System. Prices have gone up and availability has gone down," Britt Howard summarized and then nodded across the round table at the only female on the panel.

Alice St. John of the *System Review*, the more radical voice on the panel, said, "Well, I have to say that I think this will cause the wedge to be driven even deeper between the actual states here in Sol System and the colonists at Proxima Centauri, Ross 128, Lalande 21185, and the start-ups at Gliese 581c and Gliese 876d."

Alice never showed any restraint when calling one of the "elder reporters" on something that she thought was utter bullshit, and she particularly agreed with President Moore on most things. Originally, and fortunately, for Alice, she was smart and pretty, and therefore she appealed to what little bit of radical viewership the Earth News Network had and so was able to keep her job secure. That was until Moore was elected and the Republican viewership of ENN more than quadrupled overnight. Between her and the primetime anchor Gail Fehrer, who was also bent toward Moore, ENN had found a new niche to cater news to and thus improve their ratings.

"The colonies have shown little interest in getting involved with the military buildup that President Moore has called for, especially since, on the surface at least, they appear to be purely Sol System defense oriented according to the governor of Ross 128," she continued.

"I agree, Alice," Britt said. "That does seem to be the present view of the colonists as well as the Dems in both houses of Congress. The colonists' argument is that they are of no threat and therefore no interest to the Separatists and therefore are being taxed, without representation, unduly. An ambassador from Ross 128 is coming here today to speak to the president and to Congress about waiving the tariff on them, as it is pushing them into a recession."

"In fact, Britt, the president is talking out of both sides of his mouth on this issue. Though he will not waive the tariff on the colonies, he is asking Congress to approve an economic-stimulus package for them. I'm not certain I can see the logic in that," Walt interjected with a raised eyebrow.

Britt laughed. "That sounds like an oxymoron at first glance."

"Well, it isn't, though," Alice replied. "The president's economic advisors all seem to agree that the downturn in the colonial economies is a temporary effect of the increased tariffs that should be well overcompensated for in the future once they pick up the manufacturing pace and fill the void left by the Exodus and the secession of Tau Ceti. The stimulus should enable them to play catch-up."

"Ha, ha. Alice, sounds good on paper. But I wouldn't hold my breath waiting on Congress to approve his package. All of the scuttlebutt on the Hill is that President Moore's stimulus package is dead on arrival, and there are not enough loyal Republican seats in the House to sway that." Mortimer nodded his head approvingly as he responded.

"Well, be that as it may," Britt interjected with an attempt to maintain an even tone, "the main issue for today is that the Separatists took away a major manufacturing source for the country. The citizens in the remaining colonies do seem to have little desire to support this administration or its policies. In fact, the governors of all three of the remaining original colonies have issued statements that their executive branch and judicial branch lawyers believe that President Alberts' and then President Moore's tariff packages to the Congress were and are in violation of the Inter-System Free Trade Agreement and that they have been seeking appeals of the policies through the Supreme Court."

"Well, I think that is the right course of action, or perhaps the only real course of action, that could be taken from a colonial standpoint," Walt Mortimer said.

"And one would hope that the remaining colonists don't take a play from the Separatists' playbook here," Alice added. "After all, they are just territories without representation in the House or Senate."

"Oh, come now, Alice. You really think in worst-case scenarios, don't you?" Mortimer said.

"I'm just saying that I hope the colonists don't feel the same way the original Thirteen Colonies felt when King George upped the tariffs on them to protect them from France. You know what happened then. . . ."

CHAPTER 2

July 1, 2394 AD
Mars Orbit, Sol System
Friday, 7:40 AM, Earth Eastern Standard Time

"Admiral on the bridge!" Navigation Officer Commander Penny Swain snapped to as USMC Brigadier General Larry "EndRun" Chekov saluted without slowing his full Marine marching pace by the nav to the executive officer's (XO) station of the USS *Sienna Madira*, the flagship of the U.S. Naval Fleet. The rear admiral of the Outer Fleet followed behind his XO.

"At ease, folks." USN Rear Admiral Upper Half (RADM) Wallace Jefferson paced a little more slowly to the captain's chair to give Captain Wiggington time to get up and go to her usual seat at the air-boss station. Wallace nodded to her and had a seat. "Thanks, XO. Get me a status on the ground troops." The two-star admiral wiggled into his seat and made himself comfortable while giving his bridge crew an approving nod. They were good sailors, all of them—even the groundpounders. Wallace took a brief instant to look out the viewscreen as well as the battle-scenario DTMs going on in his head.

By now our tankheads and fighters ought to be wearing down the John Tyler, he thought to Captain Timmy Uniform November Kilo Lima Three Seven Seven, a.k.a. Uncle Timmy, who was both the commander of the AICs and ship's captain's AIC. Wallace and Uncle Timmy had been together for over four decades and made such a good AIC-human team that they could predict each other's responses and thoughts in most situations.

Roger that, Admiral. The clock is at four hours and seventeen minutes. The Warlords, the Utopian Saviors, and Ramy's Robots have pushed through the Martian National Guard units and the support from the John Tyler *and the* Abraham Lincoln. *And the Gods of War have pretty much cleared the upper ball of enemy fighters,* Uncle Timmy replied DTM.

DeathRay is giving them hell, huh?

Aye, sir. He and Fish already have a confirmed seven kills apiece. The Gods of War far outmatched both fighter groups from the Tyler *and* Lincoln.

Damn.

"Air Boss!" Chekov shouted.

"Aye, XO?" Captain Michelle Wiggington responded as she settled into her seat at the commander of the Air Wing station.

"Status of the support wings?"

"Utopian Saviors and Demon Dawgs are on the bounce dirtside, and the Gods of War have cleared the ball and are crawling the hull, sir!"

"Good. Ground Boss, status!" The XO turned to the station adjacent to Captain Wiggington.

"Yes, sir!" U.S. Army Brigadier General James Brantley replied. "Warboys' Warlords are on the move and have surrounded the target. Colonel Roberts reports his Robots are with them."

"Good, Roberts and his marines will get the job done. ETA to target, Larry?" the RADM asked his longtime XO and friend.

"Hold on, Admiral." Wallace could see his XO stare blankly into space for a brief moment. Clearly, he was getting a datafeed DTM from somewhere or was having a discussion with Uncle Timmy. Wallace often had a similar stare, and it was so commonplace the crew never paid it any attention. Hell, most of them were doing the same. "Aye, sir. Robots look like they will be in the end zone in seventy-three seconds."

"Roger that, Larry." Well, there was nothing really to do but sit back and enjoy the rest of the show in his DTM. His crew had done their jobs, and the rapid-deployment exercise was going well. It had taken just a bit more than four hours for the blue team to deploy and attack. In less than two minutes the end result of those four hours would be that the *Madira* would have full control over a useless patch of Martian desert that had been designated as a target coordinate. But what Wallace and his XO (and of course their AICs) knew that the rest of his crew did not was that the USS *Anthony Blair* was about to drop out of hyperspace on top of them and QMT teleport an entire contingent of AEMs, hovertanks, and fighters right into the mix of his tiring soldiers. Those fighters would be a fresh attacking red force. And they would be ready for some payback, since the *Madira* had beaten them hands down in a previous war-gaming engagement.

"COB, how's my boat?" Wallace asked his Chief of the Boat (COB) Command Master Chief Charlie Green. Charlie had been Wallace's COB for more than a decade, and the rear admiral was certain that even bad Navy coffee wouldn't get the man to retire, ever. Wallace looked around the bridge and realized that he had the most senior bridge crew in history and wondered if *any* of them would ever retire. At least the COB was looking spry and youthful since his recent body rejuv procedure.

"Well, Admiral, she's in top form. Top form."

"Roger that, COB." Wallace took the coffee cup from Charlie and halfheartedly toasted him. The COB nodded and raised his cup and then took a long draw from it. The COB was famous for his Navy stories and his blacker-than-black, stronger-than-strong Navy coffee, and Wallace could tell from the bite of his cup that CMC Green was still making the meanest cup'a joe in the fleet. He tried not to grimace at the taste or at the fact that the COB was about to start up one of his stories.

"Sorta reminds me of that time—"

"CDC, CO!" The Combat Direction Center a couple decks below pinged the bridge and interrupted what Wallace was sure would be a riveting and humorous story.

"Belay that, COB." Wallace held up a palm to Charlie. "CO, go, CDC," the RADM replied.

"We've got a hyperspace-conduit signature opening up thirty thousand kilometers port and ten thousand down, sir!" The voice on the other end trailed off a moment. "It is squawking as the *Blair*, sir."

"Roger that." Wallace hesitated a few seconds to give his crew the time to respond. He didn't want to give the exercise too much advantage with his prior knowledge. But at the same time he didn't want to look like he was intentionally stalling.

"Sir." Captain Monte Freeman, the ship's science and technology officer (STO), looked up from his console.

"What is it, STO?"

"I'm getting a red-force icon for the *Blair*, and it looks like she's simulating a power-up of her DEGs. And there is something else—" the STO's explanation was cut off as alarms blared throughout the ship, indicating that they had been targeted by radar and hit by directed energy guns (DEGs).

Sir, the simulated attack is under way as planned, Uncle Timmy stated into Wallace's mind matter-of-factly.

Roger that, Timmy, the RADM thought to his AIC.

"CO, CDC!"

"Go, CDC."

"We just had a massive increase in the number of troop signatures detected on the ground, and they are all squawking simulation red, sir!"

"Roger that, CDC."

"CO?"

"Go, Ground Boss!"

"The Robots report outnumbered and being attacked by a force that just appeared on them from nowhere!" Army Brigadier General Brantley reported.

"Well, General, I'd suggest they fight back," the XO added with the most gruff Marine sarcasm he could muster. It just sounded gruff—Chekov wasn't that good at sarcasm.

"Roger that," the ground boss replied and then began issuing commands DTM to Colonel Roberts and Colonel Warboys on the red surface below. The air boss took the orders given to the ground boss to heart immediately and started signaling the fighters to attack any new vehicles entering the mix.

"Structural Integrity Fields at maximum and start shooting back, folks! Let's move," the XO shouted and rerouted simulated power to the SIFs.

"Nav!"

"Aye, sir?"

"Put us between the *Blair* and the surface. Don't want them taking potshots at our troops down there, do we?" Wallace tapped some virtual icons around his head to plan where to make his next move. Simulations of potential battle-scenario outcomes ran quickly in his mindview. With the advent of the new Seppy teleportation tech, the fleet needed to practice fighting against it. And since a few of the fleetships had been equipped with the tech as well, the U.S. military had been war-gaming with it. Both the *Tyler* and the *Lincoln* had teleported troops in and out and around the battlescape over the past four hours, forcing the *Madira*'s groundpounders, tankheads, and mecha jocks to learn to quickly adapt tactics and think more four-dimensionally in their battle reactions. Wallace was becoming proficient at battle tactics and strategies involving troops and equipment appearing and vanishing and reappearing at different locations throughout a conflict. But they had yet to be in an actual engagement with the technology. *Practice makes perfect,* he thought.

Captain Benson Harrison, the chief engineer, a.k.a. CHENG, for the USS *Sienna Madira*, watched silently over his crew from the privacy of his office. His door was locked, and he was "indisposed" at the moment. In fact, he was both an observer and—as prearranged by the admiral—a red-team spy. He kept a very close eye through DTM on the ongoing battle simulation and how his second-in-command, Lieutenant Commander Joe Buckley Jr., was handling the situation of being in charge. To Harrison this was more than a test of his second-in-command of the engineering nexus of the mammoth supercarrier: it was a job interview for his replacement. But Joe didn't know that.

Benny, as he insisted his team call him, had watched Joe closely from day one. In fact, on Joe's first day of duty on the *Madira* he had performed amazingly as a main propulsion assistant in order to make the ship's hyperspace jaunt projectors give the ship one last and badly needed jaunt out of the line of fire of an enemy railgun. Amazing and timely performance, yes, but his—the then-new lieutenant's—actions led him and an engineer's mate to be fried through and through with high-energy gamma rays. The two barely made it to sick bay before their organs ceased functioning. Fortunately, they survived, were both rejuved, and even commended for their actions. Both were promoted. The engineer's mate resigned as soon as his four years were up. But Joe stayed on as a career man like his father had been. Benny appreciated that, especially after having put in his thirty years for the Navy. And since that day a couple years before, he had been grooming Joe to be his successor whether Buckley wanted the position or not.

Melissa, he thought to his AIC. *Sim a malfunction in the Damage*

Control Assessment System. With that shut down, he won't know what is working and what isn't.

Aye, Benny, Melissa Four One Four Eight Mike Juliet Oscar replied. *Done.*

"Okay, Buckley, let's see you get out of this one." The CHENG leaned back in his seat and smiled.

"Joe! We just lost the DCAS!" Lieutenant Mira Concepcion shouted from her console at the damage control assistant's station.

"Roger that, Mira. Get that thing back up. And get someone visually checking Aux Prop, Main Prop, SIF Generators, DEG power, and catapult-field power systems every thirty seconds until that thing is fixed!" Lieutenant Commander Joe Buckley Jr., acting CHENG, ordered in response. Like the CHENG, Joe had worked by the first-name-basis protocol in engineering. It had originally taken him time to get used to the approach, but after a few years of it he found he liked it. On the other hand, Joe was more likely to slip into official Navy protocol in crisis or heated discussions than Benny was.

"Joe, we've got reports from CDC and the STO that the *Blair* has popped into realspace and is QMTing troops and mecha dirtside left and right! They want to make sure the SIFs are set to block a teleported boarding party!" Technology Officer Lieutenant Commander Janet Wilbanks barked her report as she frantically typed in commands on her console.

"Yeah, I see that, Janet. Keep the structural-integrity field frequencies shifting on a random pattern. Any structure to it will allow some weisenheimer with a quantum computer to crack it. Set an AIC-to-AIC connection between your station and the air boss to allow any approved boarding to briefly run a standard SIF encryption pattern." Joe thought about it as he replied. As long as the SIFs were allowed to vary in frequency at random, there would be no way anybody could hack the sequence and slip through. The shields would simply be impenetrable as long as they held—theoretically, of course. However, there wasn't any guarantee that the SIFs would prevent a QMT teleport. The quantum-membrane technology used in the teleport projectors was still very new and not well understood. Even though the U.S. Navy hadn't figured out a way to use a QMT teleporter to penetrate a ship when its SIFs were activated didn't mean the

Seppies hadn't. And who knew what kind of bug the sim was going to throw at them?

"Roger that, Joe." Janet turned about the work, and Joe didn't give it a second thought.

"Mira! Where are my main systems visual confirmations? Are we sure everything is working?"

"First visuals are coming in now, Joe. Everything is clicking hot! The bells are ringing and the whistles are blowin'."

"All right. Don't make me ask next time. Every thirty seconds until you've got your station fixed!"

"Aye."

"Aha! I've got you now, Buckley." Benny laughed to himself and tapped in a ship-to-ship personal communications link.

"CHENG *Blair*. CHENG *Madira*."

"Benny?" The Chief Engineer of the USS *Anthony Blair*'s face popped up on Benny's holoscreen.

"Hey, Susan. How's your second doing?"

"Good, so far. What can I do for you?"

"Tell your captain that if she were to focus on our SIFs, we wouldn't know if they were down or not for about thirty seconds. They might be able to QMT a raiding party through the back door," Benny smiled at his counterpart.

"Really? I'll pass that along. Appreciate the info, Benny."

"Anything I can do for you, as always." Benny leaned back in his chair a bit and relaxed his back muscles. The holoview shifted to compensate for his change in position.

"Well, if you put it that way." Susan paused briefly and stared blankly into space. "My second has a tendency to ignore secondary power conduits. In about three minutes Main Prop is gonna overheat and blow out a main power-transfer conduit. I want to see how long it will take him to find an alternative route while he's under duress. We'll be dead in the water for several minutes probably."

"Got it. I'll pass that along to the bridge. They might be able to prolong your overheating problem."

"Thanks, Benny. Knew I could count on ya."

"Roger that, Suze. Benny out."

Melissa, send a message to the CO that we're gonna be boarded in a few minutes and that the Blair *is gonna be stuck in place about the same time,* Benny thought as he looked over his ship through the DTM interface. Even though there was simulated damage, he was still keeping an eye on the *real* status of his beloved supercarrier. At least, it was still his for now. He hoped he'd have good hands to leave her in.

Roger that, Benny, his AIC replied.

CHAPTER 3

July 1, 2394 AD
Tau Ceti Planet Four, Moon Alpha, a.k.a. Ares
New Tharsis, Capital City of the United Separatist Republic
Friday, 7:40 AM, Earth Eastern Standard Time
Friday, 3:40 AM Madira Valley Standard Time

"The QMT facility is fully operational, Madam President." Admiral Sterling Maximillian of the United Separatist Republic Navy looked in at Elle Ahmi through the long-range quantum-membrane communication link.

Elle only halfheartedly paid the highest ranking officer in the Separatist military any mind. Just then the brilliant colors of the gas-giant planet's rings were cresting over the horizon and casting a brilliant purple and blue hue over the valley below. She looked through the partially transparent holoview and out the floor-to-ceiling windows on the other side at the beauty of the Jovian system. Moons Beta, Gamma, Epsilon, and Iota were clearly visible, although Iota had never really qualified as a moon in Elle's mind, but astronomers will be astronomers. The sunlight reflected from the gas giant onto Epsilon in just the right way so glimmers from the man-made albedo changes could be noticed. The mining facility there was growing every day, and soon they would be exporting that to the other colonies—all of them but the Sol System, of course.

"President Ahmi, ma'am?" The admiral interrupted the Separatist leader's tranquil moment.

"Max, what does the governor say?" Elle walked barefooted

33

across to her desk and sat in her oversized leather desk chair. Other than her desk, the room held only the Martian oak four-poster bed and a formal sitting area with a modern Ares-style honey leather couch, love seat, and straight chair combination complete with area rug and coffee and end tables. The formal furniture was rarely used, as Elle was always too busy running a brand-new country, world, star system, and multigeneration-long plan to overthrow the Sol System government. Entertaining guests was something that she had little time or use for, unless it suited some part of her ingenious, intricate, and, as history has shown, murderous and bloody plans. Along those lines she had high hopes that soon, very soon, she would be hosting a foreign dignitary from Ross 128.

"He has agreed to your proposal and has promised action today. He is waffling on us a bit, though. I think he is waiting for his one last shot at Moore." Sterling paused for a second and, Elle thought, was discussing something with his AIC. "I'm having the recording of our conversation uplinked to Copernicus now."

"Waffling! Waffling! You tell that weasel slimy shit that if he even thinks about waffling on me, I will personally gut him from asshole to cerebrum while keeping him alive to watch as I eat his fucking insides! You got that?" Elle's hands trembled and her eyes widened with anger. Ross 128 was critical to her plans. She rose from her desk chair, turned, and grabbed the wooden guest's straight chair from beside her desk and beat it into the floor several times while screaming violently. "I will smash that sonofabitch! Do you fucking understand me?"

"Ma'am. Uh, I will—"

"Do you fucking understand me?" she tossed a piece of the chair's leg at the viewscreen, cracking it on one corner.

"Yes, ma'am. I'll take care of it."

"Good, Max." Her mood and personality seemed to change almost instantly to her more calm and calculated persona. "When do you snap back?"

"We are loading personnel now. It was a good R & R for my crew, but we're ready to come home. As soon as we get loaded up and our package arrives, we'll be under way."

"Good. That package is precious cargo, is of the utmost importance to our cause, and will be treated as such. You understand me? You see it to it that no harm comes to it. Personally, Max."

"Yes, ma'am."

"I mean it. Any harm comes to that package and I'll personally kill the person or persons that allowed it—after I torture, dismember, and kill their family and force them to watch. You get me?" Her fists clenched tight as she glared at her top admiral.

"Yes, ma'am. Understood."

"Good. Let me know the instant it arrives and then get it and my ship back here to New Tharsis. I feel . . . vulnerable . . . without it." Elle smiled at Sterling in a very unaffectionate way. The thinness of her lips and the deep, thoughtful stare in her eyes were more than enough to give away that she felt a piece of her plan falling into place. "Admiral, see you soon."

"Good day, ma'am."

Elle shut the holo off and exhaled softly. She pulled the red, white, and blue ski mask off her face and undid her ponytail. The long, dark locks of hair fell loose about her shoulders as she shook her head about from side to side to relieve her stressed shoulders and neck.

"Ah, that's better," she sighed and looked at the broken guest's chair scattered about. "Better get somebody up here to clean up this mess." Her desk chair creaked obtrusively as she leaned back in it. She gave herself a moment to prop her feet up on the light brown Queen Anne-style oak desk and rest her eyes. She had been plotting and scheming for *so long* behind that mask. And she had been isolated in her penthouse sanctum for *so long*. Oh, sure, she went out often to run operations or oversee projects or to show her people she was still there in person, which usually meant an execution, but since her longtime friend, co-conspirator, and father of her last child had died, she was lonely. She missed Scotty. She had loved him since the day he, Supreme Court Chief Justice Scotty P. Mueller, swore Sienna Madira into the office of president of the United States of America so many years ago. Scotty had always added a bit of humanity and morality to the plan. And then he had to go and help a damned CIA agent escape. Of course, she had been the one that had killed him. There was no other choice: she had to. So she was solely to blame for her loneliness.

Oh, Sienna Madira had had family, two daughters and a son, a multitude of grandchildren, great-grandchildren, and great-great-grandchildren. Sienna Madira had long since been dead and she would never know that part of her life again. Although a small few of them, a very select few, were in on the Separatist plan and helped her subtly from within the Sol System.

But Elle Ahmi had only had the one daughter, Sehera Ahmi Moore. Sehera grew up in hiding with her mother and father during the early years of the Separatist terrorist movement. She was in her early teens during the so-called "thought police" era. Elle never thought history was fair to her for calling it that. She had only used a modern technology to find people within her fold who were disloyal to her. Of course, she had them thrown out into the Martian desert without an environment suit, but she had to protect the integrity of her terrorist-cell structure.

Elle had watched Sehera turn into a tough but beautiful woman before her eyes and hoped that she would be right there by her side all the way to the new, better, and truly free humanity. But that was all destroyed by one soldier. One really good soldier who had managed to survive the surprise offensive of the last Martian Desert Campaign and then withstand the Separatist torture camp, and had somehow managed to get under her daughter's skin. And that is when Sehera did the unthinkable and betrayed the Separatist movement, her father, and Elle herself for that one goddamned Marine. Sehera had helped him escape.

But that hadn't been good enough for that son of a bitch! Any sane man would have cut his losses and run, bounced, crawled, or whatever he could do across the Martian desert to the nearest American outpost. Any sane idiot would have bounced away from the very torture camp in which he had just spent years watching his fellow Americans tortured, wilting and dying around him, but not him. Hell, no, not Major Alexander Moore. Against all odds, that SOB spent five weeks inside his armored e-suit planning, plotting, and scheming just so he could come back to the torture camp and kill every last one of Elle's soldiers. He had been too late to save any other of his fellow prisoners, because Elle had killed them in a fit of rage following Moore's escape. When he returned there was nobody left for him to rescue, so he killed everybody. Everybody. He killed everybody in the encampment but Elle and Sehera. Elle would never forget that day as long as she drew breath. Had she shot her daughter for the treason of helping Moore escape—the way she had executed Sehera's father, Scotty—she wouldn't have had Moore to deal with all these years.

It ended up in a big Mexican-style standoff. Moore had discovered Elle's secret identity, so there was no longer any alternative but to take him out of the picture. Elle was certain that he had to die, and then at the last moment Sehera stepped between her mother and the bloodied, enraged Marine. Sehera tried debating with them and pleading with them to cease, but Elle and Moore were each ready to die as long as they managed to kill the other one in the process. Elle had, for a brief instant, considered killing her daughter, or at least wounding her, but she couldn't do it. That was when the unthinkable happened. Then Sehera, Elle Ahmi's only child, chose Moore over her.

Elle had been so brokenhearted that she let them go without a fight. And Moore seemed, at that moment, content to leave with Sehera and his life. After all, he had killed over ninety of her men and women in his surprise rampage. Elle always wondered if Moore had thought that by taking her daughter from her, he was torturing her or paying her back. It didn't matter. Sehera was still alive and, as far as she could tell, was happy with Moore.

Ever since that day, Elle had been accounting and allowing for the two of them in her plans, for decades. Oftentimes, that damned Moore would do some random act of heroism that couldn't be accounted for that would ruin years of scheming, arranging of events, and planning, not to mention major resources. But she still couldn't bring herself to take them out of the picture. She just couldn't bring herself to ruin Sehera's happiness. Sehera was indeed the final love of her life. In fact, she even prodded and directed their paths every now and then without them knowing it. Elle had learned long ago how to manipulate a popular vote and was instrumental in Moore winning his first race as a Mississippi senator. Moore had no idea—or at least Elle had no reason to think he did. Neither did Sehera, for that matter.

And she didn't really regret not having killed them. They somehow seemed to keep her connected to her own humanity. Scotty had often told her that she had become so logical and calculating that he wasn't certain she had any emotion left in her soul. Maybe the Moore family was the only spark she had left of that. One day, she also hoped to see her granddaughter. So far, Moore and Sehera hadn't allowed that. But Elle had a plan for that, too. If all went according to plan, she'd meet her granddaughter in a matter of hours.

And there was always *the plan*. The Separatist plan that she had been developing, tweaking, forcing, and maintaining for decades, and no matter how many simulations she and her AIC Copernicus ran, it always ended the same way. That Mexican standoff between her and the Moores had to be played out to the finish.

Maybe you should get some sleep, ma'am, Copernicus said into her mind, snapping her out of her racing memories and thoughts.

Perhaps I will, Elle thought as she sighed again, sliding her feet to the floor softly so as not to disturb the quiet of the room and the tranquil view of the rings of the rising gas giant. Call her emotionless or even evil, but Elle still enjoyed the absolute beauty and wonder of the universe. Then she, Elle Ahmi, the most notorious and murderous terrorist known to the Sol System, the leader of the Separatist movement, the once great United States Army General Sienna Madira, the one hundred eleventh president of the United States of America Sienna Madira, felt the weight of her years on her shoulders pressing her like Atlas must have felt. But Atlas had only held up the Earth. Elle was trying to hold up the Tau Ceti star system, trying to coerce the Ross 128 system into jumping on, and planning to overthrow the Sol System. At that point, the other human colonies should follow suit. No, Elle wished she only had Atlas's problems.

Turn out the lights and bring the transparency of the windows down to about fifty percent, she ordered Copernicus. Her loyal AIC complied instantly, forcing Elle to blink a few times and stand still as her eyes adjusted to the darkness. She dropped her clothes on the floor at the foot of her bed and dragged herself under the sheets. She allowed herself a few moments to view the panorama from her office, her home, of the domain of the Separatists. *Not a very full home,* she thought. *But great plans require great sacrifice.*

What's that, ma'am?

Just mumbling, Copernicus. Good night.

Good night, ma'am.

Her mind still raced a bit, so she focused on the view through the windows. The arched windows of the penthouse stretched four meters tall and three meters wide, with only a few centimeters of semitransparent metal structure between them. The giant windows sat side by side, completely around the office. The lack of opaque materials in the three-hundred-and-sixty-degree view would frighten sufferers of agoraphobia beyond their wits. Those afraid of heights wouldn't do much better, either. The penthouse sat atop the capitol building, looking to the north across Madira Valley at the spaceport several tens of kilometers away. The dome at the vertex of the Separatist leader's home allowed for not only the three hundred and sixty degrees of view through the transparent armored walls but upward in a full hemisphere at the sky as well. Sitting in the quarters gave the impression of sitting on top of a very tall building on top of a high mountain peak with no walls or ceiling. The walls could be blacked out if needed or even have false images displayed on them to represent wood, concrete, or any other building or decorating material. But Elle liked the open view. She liked seeing the stars and the lights of the Tau Ceti capital city below and around her.

Her four-poster bed sat near the east side of the penthouse, so she could watch the Jovian rise several times a day and Tau Ceti rise in the mornings. She also could look out in any direction and see across several states of the Separatist nation. It wasn't the cold, dry desert of Mars, where she had grown up. In fact, it was a far superior planet, with oceans and an atmosphere and climates ranging from subtropical to cold mountainous regions. Ares was beautiful, and the Separatists would make the Tau Ceti system their home away from home. New Tharsis was the capital city, and she lived at the capitol building above the Senate floor.

Elle laughed at that thought. The Senate was nothing more than a gathering of powerful women and men who were her governors and generals overseeing certain regions of the system or large-scale projects. She didn't trust a one of them, and if something ever happened to her total dominating control over them, she feared that they would begin fighting amongst themselves, turning Ares into a world of separate regions controlled by powerful warlords. Elle didn't want the United Separatist Republic to turn into something akin to twenty-first century Africa. She rolled over onto her left side and looked out across the valley at the occasional spaceport traffic flying out of the city as her mind slowly drifted off to sleep and her eyelids grew too heavy to keep open. Elle needed her rest because she had a big day ahead of her, whether she knew it or not.

CHAPTER 4

July 1, 2394 AD
Sol System, Mars
Friday, 7:40 AM, Earth Eastern Standard Time

Ramy's Robots 3rd Armored E-suit Marines Forward Recon Unit had bounced alongside the Army tankheads for more than three hours since the war games had started. They had done some fighting along the way against the red-team AEMs, Army Armored Infantry (AAI), and Army tankheads that had dropped on them from the *Lincoln* and the *Tyler*, and they had come out on top with only minor losses. The sky was jam-packed with Marine and Navy mecha zigging and zagging through the thin atmosphere, leaving ion trails. Simulated tracer rounds and explosions continuously filled the sky. Modern-day war games looked a lot like the real thing, minus the blood and the terror. For tried and true soldiers who had tested their mettle in real combat, war games generated little more than the urgency to learn new skills or to sharpen old ones. They were so far from the real thing simply because the possibility of death was absent. But war gaming did make the soldiers more proficient in the case of real war, and each and every time they were given the opportunity to war game they brought their A-game. What a soldier might learn in a war game might just pay off in some real situation and save a life or two.

First Sergeant Tamara McCandless and Staff Sergeant Tommy Suez had seen the real thing, and both of them fully expected that the real thing was coming again sooner than most people wanted to admit. The two marines felt compelled to take the games seriously because neither of them wanted to end up a casualty of the real thing when it came. Besides that, there was team pride at stake. The flagship crew couldn't let themselves be defeated by other ships in the fleet.

Suez and McCandless led two small squads of AEMs ahead of the blue team by a couple of kilometers to feel out the enemy attack plan. They had bounced point across the red, dusty, cold desert of Mars mostly through overwhelming odds all day. But that was just the way that Colonel Roberts always liked it and was probably the reason that he had volunteered the Robots to be the tip of the spear. The colonel was at the rear of the forward recon unit. Warlord One of the tankheads guided the attack from a better sensor vantage point mostly because he had lost a game of rock-paper-scissors with the first sergeant as to who got to lead the attack.

It wasn't uncommon for Colonel Roberts to be out in front of his Robots charging into hell, but this time strategy—and the rules of rock-paper-scissors—dictated that he bounce in with the second wave. As soon as the forward teams figured out where the enemy were, Roberts would lead the tankheads in to overwhelm the red-team forces holding down the objective. Sensors showed a static force already occupying the hill, but they had yet to offer any resistance at close range. The original plan was to break through the perimeter front lines, which they did about an hour earlier, and then take and hold the objective.

Tommy understood the attack plan well. They really didn't even need to go over it in detail during the mission prebrief since it was a simple take and hold. The simulation scenario was that there was an important square half-kilometer on a very small and rocky hill in the Hellas Basin just north of the Southern Polar Cap, for no particular reason designated to be the end goal of the war game. If Tommy Suez had anything to say about it, the blue team, which included only the crew and soldiers from the *Sienna Madira*, was going to win. Tommy and two other Robots took the right side of the hill while Top had taken a squad up the other side. Tommy bounced ten to thirty meters and took cover. Corporal Danny Bates would leapfrog him and take cover. Then Private First Class Rondi Howser would leapfrog them both, and the process would start all over. Unless they encountered resistance, the plan was to continue the cover advance until they landed on the central coordinates of the objective zone.

As far as the staff sergeant could see, there was nothing but rocks, some red dirt, and occasionally some Martian hybrid grasses adding a faint splash of green to the landscape. No trees grew that far south, which meant that, unfortunately, the only cover was the rocks or going underground. What concerned him most was the fact that his QM sensors in his e-suit visor were showing enemy troops all around them, but he couldn't find them visually. There was no motion, no enemy fire, no traffic on the wireless, nothing. Tommy got a bad vibe from that, and he didn't like getting bad vibes.

"Top, where the hell are they? You see 'em?" he asked McCandless through the QM communications tac-net. He hoped the senior enlisted soldier would have a better viewing angle from her location farther up the hill and to the left. Tommy did a belly slide up to a boulder throwing a red dust rooster tail up behind him. He quickly rose up to a knee with his hypervelocity automatic railgun (HVAR) scanning the horizon. The dust settled slowly in the Martian gravity and threw sparkles of sunlight around them in a brilliant display of flashes. The green targeting X in his visor scanned from rock to rock across the desert, looking for a target, a hostile target, hell, anything to shoot at.

"Got anything, Sarge?" Private First Class Rondi Howser slid in behind him, quickly rising to her knees with her weapon at the ready. "I can't see shit with all this dust and smoke scattered about from the fireworks and the smokers."

"I don't see a damned thing," Corporal Bates added as he slid in beside them. He lost his balance and fell visor first into the ground. Dust flew up around them as they came to a halt. PFC Howser tried not to laugh.

"I don't see them either, Private. Keep the QM, IR, and lidar sensors pinging away. They're out there. We just have to find them and kill them. Nothing to it." Tommy continued to scan visually and compare what he was seeing to the sensor overlays, but he still had no better information than any of the other marines on that hill.

"Where the shit are they, Tommy?" Danny asked. The two of them had served together since the Oort and had become friends over the years. PFC Howser was new to the team, and they had yet to determine how good she was. But so far, Danny had been having a hard time keeping up with her. Tommy thought that was funny and dangerous and had warned Bates a few times that any chauvinistic attitudes could get him killed if they were in the real shit. Danny wouldn't admit to the bravado, but the fact that Tommy had to warn him of it was hopefully enough to shake him out of it.

"Keep it frosty, Suez," First Sergeant Tamara McCandless warned him. "I don't have them on eyeball, but my sensors are dinging like crazy, too. They're here. Be ready for an ambush."

"Bates, get your ass up and keep your head on. Top can't see them, either, but they're here and about to invite us to a party we didn't care to join." Tommy looked back at the young private. "Stay alert, Howser."

"I'm frosty, Sarge," she said. And as far as Tommy could tell the young marine was as frosty as a beer mug. She had the makings of a really good AEM. But only the test of real combat could determine that.

Tommy looked across the landscape and then again at the sensor overlay. The sensors showed return signals from potential targets just ahead of them and scattered about almost randomly. There was no method to the distribution that he could see. There was no front, no perimeter, no flanking positions, nothing that made any military sense. The signal locations looked to him almost like the blue-team troops were just peppered into place on top of the little hill with no defense plan. It didn't make any sense, because Tommy had war-gamed with other crews before and had actually fought with them at the Battle of the Oort, and he knew that American troops are so well-trained that this wasn't the type of stand they would make.

Any ideas? he thought to his AIC.

I'm just as confused as you. I will say that an analysis of the signals since we started detecting them shows them as not having moved a centimeter in the last thirty minutes.

Weird, Tommy thought.

"Suez, we can't just wait this out. I just got word from the colonel that the *Blair* has just popped into orbit from hyperspace. We're gonna get in the shit really damned quick," First Sergeant McCandless said over the net. "I think it is time to take the fucking hill, marines."

"You got it, Top," Tommy replied. Tommy motioned to his squad to fan out and move forward. Then he stood and slapped his jumpboots against the ground for a bigger bounce. The boots of the armored suit pounded against the ground, storing energy in the repulsor fields in the soles, and then released the energy, slinging him sixty meters forward and twenty meters high. From that vantage point he could see the enemy AEMs spread about the hill. All of them were lying down. Some of them were in prone position, others on their backs, and some of them were on their sides rolled up. Tommy rolled over into a forward flip, landing on his feet and coming down to his right knee. Bates and Howser landed nearby, and he could see Top and her squad hitting ground to the left, synchronized with them. Tommy rushed one of the suits, firing a few simulated rounds into it. As he approached it, he kicked it over onto its back and realized that there was nobody in the armored e-suit.

"What the fuck?" he grumbled. "Top, the suits are empty!"

"Same here, Suez," Top replied.

"Tommy, all of them are empty," Bates informed him as he bounced from suit to suit rapidly with his rifle swinging madly about looking for live targets.

"What does it mean, Staff Sergeant?" PFC Howser bounced beside him and sounded a bit nervous.

"No clue, Private. Somebody is trying to be clever here. But clever how, I'm not sure." Tommy would have scratched his chin to ponder had he not been in an e-suit and had years of training in them not removed such habits from his repertoire. "Better stay alert."

"Top, what's your status?" Colonel Roberts asked over the tac-net.

"We have the objective, Colonel." Tamara answered him with a hint of uncertainty in her voice. "We've met no resistance so far, sir."

Tommy bounced his team twice to meet the first sergeant in the middle of the objective coordinates. They had the hill, but for some strange reason it was littered with empty AEM suits from one of the blue-team ships. If there was some tactic or strategy being played, Tommy didn't get it. Then it hit him almost at once as there was a strange hissing sound rattling his suit and then a brilliant flash of light all around them. A brief instant later they were surrounded by a hundred or more blue-team marines with their weapons drawn.

We're surrounded, Tommy! his AIC shouted into his mind.

Holy shit! They've got us and will take the hill. We have to do something now!

What?

"Staff Sergeant Tommy Suez authorizing suit autodestruct now, now, now!" Tommy shouted over the net not for his squad or Top's squad to hear because they would be dead. He announced the order over the tac-net so Colonel Roberts would know what happened and how to react. Tommy just hoped that his sacrifice would do enough damage to the enemy force that had just appeared from nowhere to give Colonel Roberts and Colonel Warboys enough advantage to hold the hill.

"Suez, what the fuck are you doing?" McCandless turned to him with a horrified look on her face and shouted at him. But it was too late; Tommy had already given the order to his suit to detonate.

"Sorry, Top. I didn't see anybody else thinking of anything brilliant, so I took action." Tommy more than half expected the first sergeant to tear into him. He braced himself for the onslaught and verbal defilement, but it didn't come.

"Well, fucking shit!" is all Tamara managed to get out, and then she kicked at a boulder with her jumpboots. Tommy watched her as she realized that all the blue-team forces around them were cursing and kicking at boulders as well and realizing that their weapons had been locked out. Then the top sergeant seemed to settle down. Tommy almost thought he heard her laugh.

"Top," Tommy dared to add, thinking the entire time that he should just leave well e-goddamned-nuff alone. But his brain was slower than his mouth, so his mouth just kept on talking though his brain knew better. "That'll teach 'em to attack Ramy's Robots outnumbering us more than ten to one. Oh, the carnage."

"Oh, the humanity," Corporal Bates added. He had never been smart enough to keep *his* mouth shut as long as Tommy had known the marine.

"You two, don't try my fucking patience." Tamara shot them a stern look they could barely make out through her visor.

"Got it, Top."

The simulation referee AICs officially announced to all attack teams in the simulation that all troops within a two hundred meter radius of red team's Staff Sergeant Tommy Suez were all dead. Tommy could just imagine how the captain of the *Blair* must be reacting to the sim refs' announcement. The troops who had teleported down from the *Blair* never had a chance to fire a single shot before their weapons were locked out and they were reported as killed in action.

As far as Tommy could see it, he had done his job. He had kept the blue team from taking the hill under overwhelming circumstances, for now. It would be up to Roberts and Warboys from here on to hold it. Tommy found a big rock and sat down on it.

"What do we do now, Sarge?" PFC Howser asked him.

"Nothing, Private. We're dead."

CHAPTER 5

July 1, 2394 AD
Mars Orbit, Sol System
Friday, 7:59 AM, Earth Eastern Standard Time

"Aw shit!" Lieutenant Commander Buckley said as Engineer's Mate Petty Officer First Class (EM1) Andy Sanchez screamed from behind a control panel. "What now?"

"Caught a little extra current flow in my elbow, Joe. I'm all right," The EM1 replied while rubbing at a new burn mark on the left elbow of his orange coveralls.

"You've been trained on that shit, Engineer's Mate Petty Officer First Class. Don't make us have to write some incident up." Joe laughed at his senior enlisted man on the team. Hell, Andy looked young, but he had at least fifteen years in carriers. He had transferred over from the *Lincoln* just after the Battle of the Oort. Joe liked him, mostly because he was a very proficient engineer's mate. He planned to do everything he could not to fry this petty officer with hard X-rays like he had done his last one. He turned to his main propulsion assistant for an update on the jaunt projector.

"All looks good, Joe."

"Engineering! Bridge!"

"Go Bridge," Joe replied. He could tell by the voice it was the Air Boss.

"CHENG, I don't know what you people are doing down there, but I've got two squadrons of Ares mecha stuck on the lower cat bay! When do we expect to have that back up?"

49

"We're on it, Bridge!" Joe turned to his DCAS operator. "Goddammit, I thought I was gonna get verbal updates on the main systems until the Damage Control Assessment System was back online!"

"Joe?" Damage Control Assistant Lieutenant Concepcion gulped. "I'm checking that, sir. I sent two firemen to watch that but haven't heard a thing."

"Mira, get them on the speaker. And check out what other systems are down!" Joe turned to check on the engineer's mate as he was crawling from behind the DCAS control panel on his hands and knees.

"I've got the diagnostic for Aux and Main Prop hardwired directly to the readouts now, Joe. We should be able to keep continuous watch on them until the DCAS is fully up again." EM1 Sanchez took Joe's hand as he offered it and hauled himself up.

"Good work, Andy. Do me a favor and follow the power flow to the cats and see where they are shut off."

"I'm on it, Joe." The young engineer's mate took off through the hatch, down the hall, and out of sight.

He'll find it. He's a good sailor, Joe thought.

I'm tracing it, too. I see a disruption two decks down and one over between here and the hangar bay. There is something else interesting there, too, his AIC, Debbie Three November One Uniform Zulu Juliet One, added with a very animated tone in her mindvoice.

What? Joe tried to keep himself cool and focused. *It's just a sim.*

That corridor is very close to the exterior hull, and the air pressure reads as though we are venting.

You mean a sim, right? There is a simulated leak?

No, Joe. I mean there is an actual venting taking place. The air handlers had to kick in. Wait. It just stopped. Debbie sounded perplexed, but Joe wasn't. Joe had loved every aspect of the modern-day hyperspace supercarrier and enjoyed pouring over the blueprints, designs, and construction plans almost as much as he enjoyed sex. Sometimes, he thought, even more. And he knew immediately where that corridor led and how many maintenance hatches there were along the way. If the SIFs were down, somebody could QMT inside the outer armor layer inside the bulkhead. There was no atmosphere in the outer hull sections to prevent fire from transferring from the armor to the inner pressure walls, but that wouldn't stop marines in armored e-suits.

"EM1 Sanchez! This is Buckley. Stop dead in your tracks! I repeat.

Stop dead in your tracks. Communicate DTM only and hide your ass! I think we've been boarded, and they are right on top of you!" Joe turned toward two firemen at the aft edge of Engineering near the hatch who, in a real fight, would have been putting out fires, pounding damaged metal back into shape, and scurrying about with heavy tools or repair parts for some senior NCO or officer. As it was, they were standing around watching with nothing to do but stay out of the way and keep their thumbs in a neutral posterior location.

"You two! Go out the passageways from both Engineering Room exits three hatches deep and secure them. Dog them down and step back each level dogging the hatch doors from the inside with lock-down protocol. Then get back in here and secure that hatch. Watch out for enemy boarding parties and get yourselves some firearms!"

"Aye, sir!" they responded eagerly. They were probably just happy to remove their thumbs from where they'd been and to get busy doing something useful to help the ship win the war game.

Debbie, patch me through DTM to Sanchez.

Patched! Go, Joe.

Andy! What do you see?

Nothing yet, Joe, he replied in a somewhat shaky mindvoice.

"CO, CHENG!"

"Hold on, CHENG!" the CO replied. Joe hated having to wait. Every second could matter here. In the meantime he turned to his technology officer, Lieutenant Kurt Hyerdahl. "Kurt, I think the structural integrity fields are down! Get on it! And Goddammit, Mira, get that DCAS back online or get me a work-around!"

"CHENG, CO. Go!"

"CO. I think we've been boarded, sir. I've got someone trying to confirm visually, but we have real venting in the aft section that suddenly stopped. It's in the same corridor near an exterior maintenance hatch, sir," Joe said quickly.

"Understood, CHENG! Keep your man under cover."

"Aye, sir!"

"Kurt! Tell me about those SIFs!" Joe shouted with urgency.

"I've got it, Joe! There is a power inverter blown out on the main control panel of the SIF-generator distribution assembly. It is, uh, hold on . . ." Kurt clacked away at his panel keys and at the same time was talking DTM with his AIC, but it didn't matter. Joe knew the answer.

"Never mind, Kurt. I know where it is." Joe whipped his head around to look across the room at the SIF control panels. They should have been lit up like a damned Christmas tree, but instead they looked normal. Then he shook his head and glanced to his left at the DCAS panel. That damned diagnostic system was a single-point failure in the major systems. They weren't there six years ago, before the fight at the Oort. During the repair, updating, and retrofitting of the ship afterward, the damned engineers at the Luna City shipyards had seen fit to upgrade to the new, approved all-in-one Damage Control Assessment System. If you asked Joe, it was a piece of shit.

To calm himself, he let his gaze settle for just a second on the Main Prop system—the true love of his life. The power couplings between the vacuum fluctuation energy collectors and storage system and the hyperspace projector and fluctuation-field shields were intact, and the spacetime metric modification projector tube was swirling a perfect pink and purple hue. That meant that the Main Prop was in tip-top shape and humming beautifully.

It's just a sim, Joe reminded himself. Joe had seen the real thing up close, personal, and almost deadly for himself. Sims were a piece of cake. Hell, there was no violent ship motion and gravity lurches that nearly made you vomit. There were no horrendous *thwangs* against the hull plating from enemy missiles. No constant and never-ending fires, blowing circuit panels, fused breakers, overheating power couplings, and, best of all, no goddamned liver-toasting hard X-rays! It *was* just a sim. Hell, the firemen and other lower-rank sailors might as well have been playing checkers for all they could add. In a fight, they'd be working their collective asses off. At least now they were getting to stand guard and dog down the doors. Maybe there was more they could do. But Joe decided he'd just have to get back to that one.

Right, it's just a sim, Debbie agreed with him.

The sentiment brought Joe's heart rate down a good fifteen beats per minute. That enabled him to focus on winning the sim. After all, winning was what the crew of the flagship of the fleet was best at. Under all types of unbelievable, overwhelming odds, they had come out on top time and time again in war games *and* in battle. Joe was sure that the admiral wasn't going to let up without a fight, so he wasn't about to let up now, either.

"The problem here is, folks," he shouted to his engineering team as he tried to keep a calm demeanor and look each of them in the eye, "we have a blown fuse between the power to the SIFs, Aux Prop, Main Prop, Directed Energy Guns, et cetera. And that fuse is the goddamned DCAS piece of crap. We need to unhook that thing and bypass it without shutting down the major systems. I'm sure if the admiral were to out of the blue lose his DEGs just because we are monkeying around with shit down here, he would be a bit, uh, unnerved. Any suggestions?"

Joe looked around and scratched at his head for a brief instant. He was perplexed. *How the hell did he bypass that damned DCAS panel without wrecking the ship?*

The problem was that there was no way to get the energy from the storage units on one side of the DCAS to the power inverters across the room on the SIF panel. That was a distance between the two panels that might as well have been light-years. Besides, that damned DCAS was tied into everything. Joe was beginning to feel like he had been in this situation before. It was déjà vu all over again for him.

"Joe." Lieutenant Mira Concepcion snapped her fingers. "Who cares about the DCAS? If we bypass each system to the appropriate control panel, the DCAS will just read that they are not working. But we're using visuals anyway, so who gives a shit?"

"All right! Good plan. Everybody, we're breaking into teams. I'll take the SIFs. Fireman's Apprentice, you're with me." Joe pointed at a sailor behind the Aux Prop panel and motioned the young enlisted woman to follow him. "Keri, take the Props. Kurt, the DEGs. Mira, get the cats going."

"Aye, Joe!"

Joe! Eighteen AEMs just passed by me. They're headed you're way! EM1 Sanchez reported through the DTM link.

Thanks, Andy. Good job. Unless you've got a weapon and want to tangle with a bunch of jarheads, just stay out of it. My guess is that the cat bay has been taken also, so don't go that way, either. Best to stay put and wait it out. If you see something nearby that needs fixin', and you can get to it, go ahead. Otherwise, sit the bench for a little while. Joe hated not having one of his well-trained, more-senior enlisted sailors where he needed him, but that was just the way it was.

"We've got company headed our way, people! Everybody grab a sidearm!"

CHAPTER 6

July 1, 2394 AD
Mars Orbit, Sol System
Friday, 8:07 AM, Earth Eastern Standard Time

There was just no way in hell that Andy Sanchez, United States Navy engineer's mate petty officer first class, was going to sit in a wiring closet and hide while enemy marines, simulation or no, marched around on his ship. But first, he needed a plan.

How can one EM1, unarmed and unarmored, take out a squad of armored-to-the-damned-teeth e-suited hardassed fucking marines with weapons, and explosives, and lidar, and radar, and infrared, and QM sensors, and no telling what other shit that I ain't been trained on? he thought. *I'm not about to let the* Madira *lose this wargame if I can do anything about it. But what . . .*

Joe said to stay put, his AIC, Petty Officer Third Class Bebe Six Four Alpha One Sierra, reminded him. She had always been an AI that liked to follow orders to a tee. But she had no choice except to go where Andy took her, being inside his head and all. So she had learned, all the way back to Andy's fireman-apprentice days, to not push the spit and polish too much.

He said to fix something if it needed it. So we just need to find the right thing to fix. Andy started running scenarios in his mind about how he might be able to slow down a bunch of marines. He had been repairing and upgrading parts of the ship for the better part of six years now, and he understood it well. Not quite as well as Joe and Benny, but well. There had to be some repair trick he'd learned over the years that would let him set up some sort of catastrophe at the right time. But just what was the right thing to do?

Bebe, pull up the repair and upgrade schedule for this part of the ship. And can you track where those marines are? he asked.

Schedule up, Andy. Hmm . . . track the marines. Using the internal environment controls, I have been able to track a grouping of heat signatures travelling in a pattern that would suggest they are moving carefully and covertly. Also, using the internal sensors I can track them because there is a region of sensors being jammed that seems to be moving. Must be them. There is another group behind us several hundred meters, and one on the other side of the ship.

Good. Andy thought about it for a moment and then started reading through the maintenance schedule in his head. *Bebe, plot that track on a deck-overlay map for me and keep it up in my visual. Might as well start heading toward the ones going for Engineering. Pass this map along to the bridge.*

Aye, Andy. Though I'm not sure we'll make it to Engineering in time.

We'll see. If we don't, we don't.

Andy crawled out of the wiring cabinet and adjusted his orange coveralls. His tool belt hung on the cabinet door's handle, slamming the door against his back.

"Shit." Andy cursed at his clumsiness and told himself to be quiet. Then a thought hit him.

Bebe, those marines are in armored e-suits. They'll be bumping into hatches and shit all the way. They'll have to take the outer and larger corridors to get where they want to go without damaging the ship. And we know they don't want to do that—after all, they are U.S. Marines, right? So can you extrapolate from the motion you are detecting which likely big hatches and passageways they would be taking to potential targets?

Sure, Andy. Here. Then his AIC highlighted three new paths in his mind. The three groups weren't going for different locations. Well, one of them was going for Engineering and was already knocking at the door. Nothing he could do for Joe and the rest of the Engineering team. But the other two were headed to the main elevator shaft internal to the upper deck tower located midship, which led to the bridge. Then he noticed one small line on the maintenance schedule that he had almost missed. The line read:

MAIN TOWER ELEVATOR REPULSOR-FIELD GENERATOR
RECALIBRATION, UPGRADE, AND CHECKOUT.

The main tower elevator shaft was the only internal passage
to the bridge and the command crew. Andy didn't have to think
about what to do any longer. He had to shut off that elevator
shaft somehow. He started running as fast as he could go in the
direction of the forward main elevator. He made a point to stay
in the tighter hallways. He also made it a point to beat those
red-team marines to that damned elevator.

Patch me through to Joe.

Done.

The Engineering team had managed the patches around the
confused and failed damage diagnostics hardware of the DCAS,
and just in time as a squad of red-team AEMs started knocking on the doors three levels out. At first they tried hacking the
protocols on the locks. When that didn't work, they went to high
explosives—simulated high explosives. The sim boxes that attached
to the door made a pop like a firecracker, and if the box was set
to simulate the right level of HE, then the AIC referees running
the simulation would open the hatch. It took the AEMs several
tries on the first hatch. Joe knew that they wouldn't make the
same mistakes a second and third time.

What the hell can we do? he thought to himself, not necessarily to his AIC.

Too bad they're in suits or we could gas them, Debbie added.

*Hey, do it anyway! Maybe they don't have their faceplates down.
You know how AEMs are about breathing real air anytime they
can. That might buy us some time.* Joe thought more about that
approach. They didn't have much heavy firepower, but they did
have the power equivalent to a miniature neutron star trapped
in the Main Prop hyperspace-jaunt projector tube.

"Everybody on me!" Joe said in his voice of command. The
full complement of the Engineering team and the supporting
seamen and firemen and fireman apprentices converged on him
as he made his way to the center of the room underneath the
four meter in diameter pink and purple swirling tube that ran
the length of a major portion of the ship. He reached up with
his hands and tapped the bottom of the conduit to the projector

tube. Then he addressed his team with a somewhat wacky idea. Hell, it wasn't that wacky—he'd actually done it before. Last time he did what he had in mind, it worked, but—and there was always a "but" in these situations—it had nearly killed him and his first engineer's mate.

"Listen up, everyone. We haven't got but a few minutes maybe. We're going to pull a cable from that power coupling on the jaunt drive projector here"—he pointed at the now-infamous Buckley Junction—"tie it around the junction housing, and then drag it to both exit doors and then over here to the power unit for Aux Prop. Get to it!" The team scurried about to set up the makeshift power conduit rerouting. The enlisted men and women began pulling the heavy flex-conduit that was several centimeters in diameter and heavy as hell. The senior techs and engineers began rerouting power flow and making certain things were connected, they could get a power-flow circuit that would work, and that every breaker in the ship wouldn't blow.

"Keri!" Buckley grabbed his main propulsion assistant (MPA) by the shoulder. "Listen—when this thing is triggered, the backup systems and breakers will try to shut it down. You have to make certain that they don't. You and your AIC have to stay ahead of the ship's backup hardware long enough for this to work."

"Everybody has studied the Buckley Maneuver, Joe. They teach it at the Academy nowadays, I hear." Keri smiled at him. "Besides, I was actually there, if you recall. Good thing I wasn't actually in Engineering when it happened."

"Well, I'm just saying."

"Understood, sir!" Keri snapped back at her acting CHENG with another smile. "I've got it under control." Joe didn't say anything more. Keri *had* been there at the Battle of the Oort when he did this before, and he had ordered her out of the room before he and EM1 Shah triggered the Buckley Junction and cooked themselves. He knew that she had seen him and Shah in the hospital with their bodies cooked through and through. She understood.

"Good. Now let's move." The sound of a firecracker popping one level out went off. The AEMs were on them.

It only took the AEMs about a minute to get through to the Engineering Room hatch. But that minute was all the Engineering team of the U.S. Navy flagship needed to set up a nice surprise for them. The team hunkered down behind a makeshift X-ray shelter that several of the enlisted sailors had stacked up. There was a stack of cabling spools, spare power couplings, sheet metal and armor plating, chairs, computer stands, and anything else of high density they could find.

"I hear them at the hatch, sir!" one of the firemen standing guard at the door shouted.

"Then get your ass over here under cover, Fireman!" Joe turned to his MPA. "Keri, you know, we really ought to consider install-ing an X-ray shelter in here somewhere."

"Not a bad idea, Joe."

"All right, as soon as that door opens, snap the trap on our mice."

About that time another popper went off just outside the hatch. The lock cycled and the hatch swung open. An infinitely long second or two passed, and then another popper went off on the aft hatch. Both passageways were opened and simultaneously AEMs burst through the doors with their rifles drawn.

"Wait," Joe whispered to Keri. "We need them all in here."

Several more AEMs filed into the large Engineering Room in cover formation. They were getting ever so close to the makeshift redoubt. It was now or never.

"Do it!" Joe said. "Everybody down."

There were no fireworks this time. There were no lightning bolt–sized arcs jumping around the room from deck to bulkhead. There were no vapor clouds from ionized metal being thrown about. And most importantly, in Joe's mind, was that there were no *real* hard X-rays cooking his liver and brain! But as far as the sim refs were concerned, it was all there, and the AEMs from the *Blair* were right in the midst of it.

The AEMs must have been told of their predicament as there was a chorus of "What the . . ." and "Goddamned motherf—" and other such colorful and untranslatable AEM lingo drowning out the hum of the jaunt drive and the other high-technology components of a state-of-the-art supercarrier's Engineering Room. The AEMs had their masks down, probably because of Joe's gas trick. That hadn't helped with the X-rays. A moment more of the cursing continued as the marines started popping up the antireflection-coated visors one by one. One of them actually twisted his helmet off and tethered it down the back of his armor.

"Goddamned needed some more sack time any-fucking-way,"

the AEM lance corporal said. He started to sit down, but his NCO was on top of him and in his face in a heartbeat.

Debbie?

They're dead, Joe. All of them!

Hot damn! And us?

The sim has given us fifteen minutes of effectiveness, and then we will be listed as casualties. The pile of stuff helped, I guess.

I guess. Joe smiled to himself then stood up.

"Welcome to the *Sienna Madira*," Joe said. One of the AEMs instinctively pulled up his weapon. Joe just smiled and raised his left eyebrow at the man. "Dead marines have a hard time pulling the trigger on those things. Now, if you folks wouldn't mind standing over by the port bulkhead out of our way, we have more work to do."

"Son of a fuckin' bitch!" One of the marines kicked at the deck with his armored foot, making a loud *clank* as he did.

"Fuck it!" one of them replied. "We're dead. You fucking move us."

"If that's the way you want it, I'll have one of the firemen pull a repulsor lift in here and have him push you up against the bulkhead. Be advised, we haven't really trained him on that thing yet, and he's as likely to squish you into the bulkhead as he is to run over you. But if that's what you want."

"Stow that shit, Private!" The same NCO turned to Joe. "Lieutenant Commander, we're out of the game. No need in us causing a ruckus between the two best crews in the fleet."

"Thank you, Staff Sergeant." Joe turned back to his work. The damned AEMs had taken precious time off his fifteen-minute clock.

"You heard the lieutenant commander. I want your dead asses against that bulkhead out of the way." The staff sergeant clanked his armored boots across the deck to the far side of the room, glaring at one of his privates.

"Mira, Keri, make sure to get the Main and Aux Props back on line. We have about fourteen minutes before the sim refs take us out of the game." Joe thought about their predicament. He'd kept the AEMs from taking Engineering, but he had also wrecked a whole bunch of systems. They had work to do.

"You did it, Joe!" Keri slapped him on the back.

"Not yet. There's still two teams of AEMs trying to get to the bridge."

"Let our marines take care of that, Joe. We did our part," Keri said to her longtime friend and colleague. "We just need to make sure the ship is in the best shape it can be before we die."

"Right. Maybe." Joe thought for a few brief seconds as the rest of the team set to work on undoing the damage they had just caused to the ship's propulsion hardware and software.

Joe, EM1 Sanchez is trying to DTM you, Debbie said.

Patch him through. Joe gave her a second to turn the link on. *What's up, Andy?*

Joe, the AEMs are trying to get through to the main elevator up the tower. I need you to help me shut the thing down.

I don't know if you can, Andy. Even if you turned the elevator off, the AEMs could still climb the shaft.

I was afraid of that, sir.

Yes, other than welding the damned doors shut, I don't know how else to stop them, so you might as well let our Marines fight it out with them.

Weld the doors? I could do that sir. I'll start with the floor they're on.

Andy! Absolutely not. We will not weld the doors, do you understand me?

Great fucking idea, sir! Weld the doors. Got it.

Andy! Andy?

Sorry, sir, having trouble hearing you. Just in case you can hear this, I'm gonna go on over to the main elevator and weld the doors shut so nobody can go up or down them. Then I might look and see if there are some repairs to do while I'm there.

That's it, Andy! A repair job.

Sir?

Routine maintenance of the repulsor-field generator and the upgrade and regularly scheduled maintenance on the braking system we've been putting off. Do that.

Uh, you serious, sir?

Yes. In fact, that's an order, EM1. Then Joe had it. He had the plan that would stop the Marines from getting up the tower, period. He wasn't sure he had time to explain to the EM1 what he had in mind.

Okay, sir, Andy replied.

The safety regs for upgrading any elevator repulsor systems on the ship required that the elevator shaft be sealed from the inside physically so that nobody could be below the system in case the repulsor-control system went nuts and started slamming the elevator car randomly up and down the shaft. There was a cubbyhole for the repair team to hide inside the shaft and out of the way of a stray elevator car if such an emergency occurred. The team had to physically cover the entire shaft afterward and remove the interlocks by hand. Joe didn't envy the task that he was giving the EM1. The best part about it, though, was that once the repairs started, nobody could enter from the outside for any reason. Even the simulated explosives couldn't override crew-safety protocols. The logged repair start would shut down the elevator until the CHENG signed off on the elevator's operational safety.

Andy, as soon as you start the diagnostic of the elevator, the shaft will lock down.

Aha! I get it, Joe. I'd better run, sir. These repairs just keep piling up. It's gonna be tight, sir. So be prepared to approve the repair protocol rather quickly, Andy replied, and Joe could feel the urgency in his mindvoice. Andy must've realized the red-team AEMs were getting close to the main elevator. *You're a clever son of a bitch, if you don't mind my sayin' it, sir.*

As soon as you get inside that shaft, you let me know, and I'll dog it down for the system upgrade and maintenance. If this shit works, I'm crawling in the first door you open and promise to help you do the unlock sequence myself.

ETA two minutes, sir.

Go!

Two teams of the *Blair*'s boarding party converged on the main elevator shaft from opposite directions. Major Frances Jones pinged the corridor with her suit's sensor suite and mapped out the area. Her suit showed only her team and the other one approaching them from head-on. There was no resistance. This was going to be far easier than she had thought. Oh, there had been a team of firemen and a few MPs armed with handguns here and there, but there had been nothing along the lines that a team of AEMs couldn't handle. *Too easy. All too easy.*

"Ma'am, we're here. Want me to check it out?" her NCO asked.

"Nah, I got it, Jack." Frances bounced in front of the main elevator with her HVAR at the ready. The metal blue-gray bulk-heads and the recessed lighting panels as well as the oversized passageway were exactly like the one on the *Blair* and other supercarriers she had been on. It always made her feel a little weird to be attacking one of her own ships.

You could damn near get a hovertank in the supercarrier tower elevators. The double-wide doors had to be five meters across when they were fully open. Frances had her AIC hack the electronic lock for the elevator, but nothing happened. Then she noticed a yellow and black striped warning sign taped to the door where it joined. The sign read:

NOTICE:
MAIN ELEVATOR SYSTEM IS DOWN FOR REGULARLY SCHEDULED UPGRADES AND MAINTENANCE AND IS TEMPORARILY OUT OF ORDER PENDING RECERTIFICATION OF THE SYSTEM'S SAFETY BY THE CHIEF ENGINEER. NO ENTRANCE TO THE ELEVATOR SHAFT IS TO BE APPROVED UNDER ANY CIRCUMSTANCES WITHOUT PRIOR APPROVAL FROM THE CHIEF ENGINEER. THANK YOU.

"What the fuck?" the major said. "Jack, get your ass over here!"

CHAPTER 7

July 1, 2394 AD
Mars Orbit, Sol System
Friday, 10:40 AM, Earth Eastern Standard Time

"So then Staff Sergeant Suez says to First Sergeant McCandless that he is standing on the target coordinate spot, right?" Private First Class Rondi Howser held up her hands and shrugged her shoulders at the others around her in the shower. The movement of her arms exaggerated her brilliant red, black, and blue cobra high-resolution laser-printed tattoo. It curled around her left leg three times from the knee, up between her legs from behind, across her rippled abdominal muscles, and around both breasts with its open mouth and fangs showing on the left side of her midsection. The red and blue were fluorescent and glowed brilliantly in the low lighting of the showers. "Then the first sergeant tells the colonel that we had secured the spot."

"Yeah, we were there. We heard it, Private," Army Specialist Karla Hammermill responded, almost annoyed by the PFC's story. But the two of them had been running partners for more than a year, since they had both been deployed to the *Madira*, and the army specialist had gotten used to the marine's tall tales.

"Sure, you may have heard it on the QM wireless, but you didn't see it," Corporal Sandy Cross, who was in McCandless's team, added. "I was there. Goddamned FUBAR if we ever get attacked like that in real life."

"The next thing you know," Howser continued, "we—well, shit, we're all standing on the hill looking around at all these empty

65

e-suits and all of a sudden just five of us plus the two sergeants were surrounded by like two hundred fucking marines from the *Blair*. Snap! Just like that we were outnumbered and surrounded."

"Don't undersell it, Howser. We were waaay-the-fuck outnumbered," Cross added.

"Right. We were waaay fucking outnumbered. There was no way in hell that we were gonna hold that hill with those kinds of odds against us barring some kinda fucking miracle."

"So?" One of the Army pukes shrugged her shoulders at her.

"So? Don't you see? What the staff sergeant did next is what was so brilliant. He self-destructed his suit! Now if that ain't a big fuckin' 'oorah,' I don't know what is. The simulation refs said the blast took out everything in a two hundred meter diameter." Rondi stepped away from her showerhead, and it turned itself off. The dryer blasted her for about five seconds, and then she began rummaging through her bag for her other personal hygiene sundries.

"We thought that was an accident," Karla said in disbelief. "I was told that there was a suit malfunction caused by damage from the fight."

"Nope, you can read the sim logs. He blew it himself." Rondi pulled her female-specific compression undergarment into place and stood tall in front of a sink and mirror as she pulled and squirmed into her Marine-issue compression short-sleeve top. "It was all Staff Sergeant Suez."

"Goddamned crazy fucking jarheads think it was cool that their NCO sacrificed them all to take a fucking hill. Glad he ain't my NCO," another Army puke added.

"Hey, fuck you! The sarge followed orders and took the hill," Rondi snapped back while she adjusted her top.

"Hey, stow that shit!" another Army woman Rondi didn't know shouted from farther down the shower stalls.

"Yes, Sarge!"

"No shit," Karla said in a calmer tone to cool the discussion back down. She stepped through the dryer and turned to her running partner. "Don't pay them no mind. They're just mad that there was nobody left to kill after you Robots blew your top."

"Hey, that would have been funny had it been First Sergeant McCandless that had blown her suit. Ha, ha, blown her top, get it?" Corporal Cross laughed. Nobody else thought it was funny.

"Damn." Rondi just shook her head and ignored the corporal.

"Suez's suit blowing took out all of us Robots except for Colonel Roberts. That's when he, the Warlords, and the rest of you Army pukes swarmed in and held the hill. Hell, at least we had front-row seats for it." She was a good-looking corpse, though. The fireproof fabric conformed to her Marine-hardened midsection and pushed up her breasts into a supported position. The compression shirt had been designed to fit skintight as a lightly armored fireproof paper-thin layer. And it did. The shirt not only wicked away sweat and moisture, conformed to most environment color schemes, would repel low-order shrapnel, resist fire, and compress the muscles, improving the wearer's performance, but it did it in a way that made the person wearing it look damned good. The new universal combat uniforms (UCUs) looked great on recruiting posters. Rondi smiled at herself in the mirror approvingly and tapped the membrane panel under the neckline to display bulkhead blue-gray, which was the standard uniform color for onboard a ship. She slapped the 3rd AEM Recon patch onto her left shoulder. The patch and shirt fabrics meshed together and hardened into a seamless decoration. She then slapped her name tag atop her right breast, with similar results, and then donned her digicam pants. The pants tracked the color scheme of the top and changed to the same blue-gray base colors. Marines always wore base color camo that matched their environment. The Navy always wore a darker blue camo base, and their tops were different colors, depending on their job. There was never any chance of mistaking a marine for a Navy sailor—that is, unless a marine was trying to be camouflaged as one. Rondi adjusted her short-cropped blond hair and then tucked her cover in her pocket.

"And here I thought you poor marines had simply managed to get all yourselves killed and us 'Army pukes' had to come charging in and save your asses." Karla smiled at her friend. She adjusted her UCU for Army digicam with the standard Army green base colors. Her green base color top was just as form-fitting, protective, and flattering. "Hoowah!"

"First Sergeant McCandless, did you give Staff Sergeant Suez the authority to self-destruct and take out my platoon of Robots?" Colonel Ramy Roberts, the commander of the 3rd Armored E-suit Marines Forward Recon Unit, looked solemnly at his longtime friend and staff noncommissioned officer (SNCO). He had fought with Tamara all the way back before the Martian Exodus. The two of them were friends and had no problem completely entrusting their lives to each other in the direst of situations. In fact, there had been any number of times when the two of them played rock-paper-scissors to see which one of them got the honor of staring the lion in the teeth first.

"No, Colonel. I had no idea." Tamara stood at attention and stared blankly ahead. "On the staff sergeant's behalf, sir, I must say that he did take out a shitload of enemy combatants, sir."

"Taking that into consideration, First Sergeant, is the only reason I haven't busted his balls further down. However, he did take out my entire platoon!" Colonel Roberts turned his attention from Tamara to Tommy. "Well, Staff Sergeant Suez? Just what in the flying fuck makes you think you have the authority to self-destruct not just yourself but an entire platoon of marines? I mean, there I was all by myself with nothing but a bunch of damned Army pukes to help me retake and hold our objective. Do you realize how much money Uncle Sam has invested in a platoon of AEMs? Well?"

"Sir, I, uh, was pretty sure we were dead anyway, and our objective was to take that hill, sir," Tommy replied nervously.

"Take it! Take it!" Roberts shouted. "Take it, hell. You took it all right! You took it and blew it to fuck and gone. Had it been the real world and not a sim, you would have blown that hill halfway to the Oort Cloud. What if there was something special about that hill that we needed? A decision like that is above your pay grade, soldier. Hell, it's above my pay grade!"

"Had no intel on the hill, sir. Just that we were supposed to take it. So, rather than die to railgun rounds, I decided to go out taking as many of the enemy with me as I could, sir," Tommy said, still standing stiff as a board and looking forward.

"Staff Sergeant." Colonel Roberts paused and lowered the tone in his voice. "Next time, try to come up with a less costly solution. You are dismissed. Go get some lunch and meet the dignitary if you can. From what I hear, she'll likely be hanging out with the mecha jocks. Now get. I've got to think on this situation more. And stay out of my sight for a little while or you might find that I lose my temper again."

"Yes, sir!" Tommy spun on his heel and marched out of Roberts's office.

Once the younger SNCO had closed the door behind him, Ramy motioned to Tamara to have a seat. He sat down and could no longer contain himself; he burst into laughter. Tamara followed suit. They laughed for several minutes, until tears filled their eyes and their sides hurt.

"Goddamned if that wasn't the quickest damned exercise I'd ever been in." Roberts pulled a bottle from his desk drawer along with two glasses. "I mean, hell, why not just blow everybody up each time we get in a fight? Makes it all go by rather quickly."

"Well, sir"—Tamara nodded in acceptance of the shot of brandy—"we'd kinda start running short on Marines after judicious use of that tactic, sir."

"Goddamned right, Tammy." He held up his glass and silently toasted with his first sergeant. "So what are we gonna do about our staff sergeant, huh? That was amazingly quick-witted. When you saw all of those damned enemy AEMs pop into reality in front of you, what did you plan to do?"

"Mostly shit my suit, sir. Then I thought I could take one or two of them with me before I was killed. I was reaching for a grenade, but by the time I had thought of that, Tommy had killed all of us." Tamara finished the shot of brandy and sat it back down on Ramy's desk.

"He's up for E-7. Been a while since we had a 'gunny' around the Robots—since Nicks took the job at the Island." Roberts laughed out loud. "I'd love to have seen the look on the *Blair*'s ground boss when he had to tell Admiral Walker that she had just lost over two hundred of her marines about one second after they hit the ground. Goddamn, I'd love to've been a fly on that bulkhead."

"Damn right. I'll keep on Suez about it. He's a damned fine marine, sir. You know that. Hell, I've thought so ever since we got him before the Battle of the Oort. I recall him sweatin' like a mother needing a chill pill more than any marine I ever saw. But Tommy wouldn't take the drugs. And then he did the damndest thing after we loaded our gear. He unwrapped a piece of Halloween candy with his e-suit gloves on. I've never seen such suit control before. And green as hell and on his first mission he managed to take out several enemy haulers with that commandeered Seppy mass driver. The kid has a gift at being an armored e-suit marine, sir."

"Good. Let's don't razz him too much and give the poor kid a complex of some sort. And let's hope and pray that we ain't never stuck with him in a situation where we are instantly, amazingly outnumbered." Roberts swiveled his desk chair and pulled a drawer open. He pulled out a folder and handed it to her.

"What's this, Colonel?" Tamara took the manila folder from him and opened it. It was a personnel file of new recruits. By the looks of it, the Robots were getting a few new faces. The face in the top file was of a new second lieutenant on his first tour. Tamara was certain that was just what they needed—a goddamned fresh-out green lieutenant.

"Well, after Major Noonez retired to the Pentagon, we have finally gotten, or should I say are getting, a brand spanking new second lieutenant. We pick him up at the Oort station this afternoon. Read up on him. Otherwise, take some time for yourself.

"I think I'm gonna have some lunch. You interested?" Ramy shoved the desk drawer to and stood up, adjusted the waistband of his blue-gray digicam pants, and tucked in the utility cover in his back pocket just in case he went outside. In space that wasn't likely, but trained habits die hard. And who knew? With the advent of these new QMT teleporters, any damned thing could happen.

"Colonel Fink, Mr. Stavros, Ms. Moore, welcome to the flight line." The young-looking lieutenant who was assigned to them as a tour guide held out his arm as the elevator doors slid open. After a quick introduction to the bridge crew, senior staff, and the CO, RADM Jefferson, they had been handed off to a liaison officer for special dignitaries and were being toured around the ship. Dee didn't mind so much as she was getting to see the most awesome behemoth of firepower the United States military had ever managed. They had seen the bridge at the top of the tower, and the admiral had even let her sit in the captain's chair.

Under other circumstances the three civilians wouldn't have been as much of a sore thumb sticking out amidst the crew of a U.S. Navy warship other than the fact that they were constantly shadowed by a very large, dark-skinned man wearing a black suit and Secret Service visor. Dee had gotten so used to not going anywhere without an agent following behind that she paid him no attention. But her dad had insisted that Clay Jackson, the giant former AEM turned presidential bodyguard, go along with her on this planned out-of-system trip. Clearly, Clay made Jay uncomfortable, but if Colonel Fink even noticed him, she couldn't tell.

The hangar bay was filled with activity, as ingressing SH-102 Starhawks brought in the last cargo from Mars before the *Madira* would QMT to the Oort. Navy VTF-32 Ares-T class aerospace fighters filled the hangar from one end to the other, and the technicians, flight deck officers, and pilots were scurrying all about in T-shirts or coveralls of solid reds, greens, blacks, yellows, or oranges, depending on their particular jobs. Automated robot forklifts on preprogrammed routes or that were AIC-controlled were zigging and zagging in and out between vehicles and people carrying loads to and fro. The yellow and black–striped vehicles almost looked like giant mutant mechanical insect menaces from early science fiction movies. Having grown up in Mississippi, the scene most reminded Dee of a fire-ant mound that had been kicked over. She knew what happened when you pissed off a fire-ant mound, and she was curious what would happen if you pissed off this bunch of deadly fire ants.

On the starboard side of the supercarrier's hangar bay were the Marine FM-12 strike mecha fighters. Most of them were in fighter mode and were being loaded into their appropriate hangar location. A few of them were in bot or eagle modes and were being reloaded or serviced. Standing around the mecha were two Navy officers and one marine that Dee had seen at the White House over six years ago after that nightmare at Disney World. There was another female Navy officer, two female Marine officers, an Army colonel, and a few other marines, soldiers, and sailors that she didn't know.

"Captain Boland, Commander Fisher, nice to see you again. Major Strong." Dee nodded and shook their hands. She had seen them a few times around the Beltway the year she had turned twelve and felt some familiarity with them. She wasn't in any branch of the military yet anyway and was only a student in a private military school, so military protocols didn't exactly apply to her. Also, she *was* the First Daughter of the country and could bend protocols every now and then and get away with it.

DeathRay and Fish had sat by her at her father's address to the nation just after the incident in Orlando. And the U.S. Marine FM-12 mecha jock with the long blond hair beside them was none other than Delilah "Jawbone" Strong. Jawbone had literally singlehandedly saved her and her family as they were trying to get away from wild, menacing terrorist-controlled dinosaur robots in Orlando. Dee had really liked Jawbone the few times she had met her, and looked up to the marine. In her eyes, there was only one other marine that was cooler: her dad. She did wonder what the marine was doing here since last she had known Jawbone was stationed in Florida. Dee also noted that she had been promoted to major. Her dad had seen fit to have her promoted from lieutenant to captain after the Orlando thing. Now, six years later, she was a major. Dee was proud of her. Her guess was that the hotshot mecha jock wanted to be where the action was, and everybody knew that there were only two ships in the fleet for that: the *Blair* and the *Madira*. Dee hoped one day she'd get the *Madira*.

"Oh, this is my instructor Colonel Walt Fink, and my wingman at school, Jay Stavros." Dee could tell that Rat didn't like her taking the lead of the conversation, but she *was* the President's daughter, and if he didn't like it . . .

"Colonel, Ms. Moore, Mr. Stavros." DeathRay stepped forward as if he were not sure if he should address the Secret Service agent or not. Dee could see that he hesitated slightly and then decided against doing so. After all, Dee and everybody else noticed the big man had no change of expression on his face after Boland glanced at him. Dee had always thought Clay was hilarious ever since the first day she had met him.

"Let me introduce a few folks to you," DeathRay continued. "This is U.S. Army Colonel Mason 'Warlord One' Warboys, leader of the Warlords M3A17-T tank mecha squad. These two here are U.S. Marine FM-12 strike mecha fighter pilots Lieutenant Colonel Caroline 'Deuce' Leeland and Major Connie 'Skinny' Munk of the mecha squadron called the Utopian Saviors. Major Strong there just joined them a few months back. And this is U.S. Navy Commander Wendy 'Poser' Hill, the commander of the VTF-32 Ares-T mecha squadron Demon Dawgs. I'm Captain Jack Boland, they call me DeathRay, and this is my wingman Commander Karen 'Fish' Fisher. We're from the navy squadron known as the Gods of War." Dee liked the way Boland spoke and stood and, well, everything about him. She could find it real easy to do more than just "like" the man. Not only was he a tried and true bona fide hero and super mecha jock, he was also easy on the eyes in an action-hero sort of way. She instinctively adjusted her long, straight black hair behind her ear the way her mother so often did.

"It's nice to see you again, Ms. Moore," Delilah added and shook her hand and then shook Jay's as well. Dee could tell by the way her wingman was eyeing the Marine major that he thought she was easy on the eyes or hard on something else, and she wasn't quite sure which was distressing her cohort the most. Dee had to admit that Jawbone was worth looking at twice. Hell, all of them, men and women alike, in that group of transfigurable mecha pilots were rock-hard super athletes, but there were a few that had more than just the killer physique. There were a few that had the "it" factor. And Jawbone and one of the other female mecha jocks there had "it." Dee looked twice at Poser and Jawbone and wondered why they weren't in another line of work. Of course, that is exactly what people said about her. But she understood exactly why the two women were there. They were there to fly state-of-the-art fighting mecha!

"Ms. Moore." Colonel Warboys stepped forward and offered his hand. "You may not realize this, but we met very briefly when you were about six years old on the precipice of a bluff at Mons City on Mars. I was leading the tank squadron that met you and your family there that horrible day. Then I met you a little later on in the afternoon as well, when I got to meet your father for the first time. He is a great man."

"Oh! Yes. You are Warlord One! I remember you like it was yesterday." Dee turned to her bodyguard and pointed a thumb at him. "Clay Jackson was there right beside me in that foxhole, Colonel. He was a sergeant AEM at the time. It is good to finally put a face to the giant metal monster I remember. I'm sorry I don't recall meeting you out of your armor."

"Ma'am. You were very tired and had had a very long day. It's understandable." Warboys smiled a very personable, warm grin at her that reminded her of her father.

"Colonel." Clay shook the hand that Warboys offered. "It was a damned good thing the Warlords and those mechaheads from the *Blair* arrived when you did that day."

"Sergeant." Clay nodded solemnly as Warboys shook his hand. "That was a bad day for certain."

"One day on Mars that I wouldn't want to relive, Colonel," the bodyguard replied.

"Amen to that," Fish said. "I think everybody but Jawbone here was there that day."

"Ms. Moore and I had our fun elsewhere, didn't we, ma'am?" Jawbone added.

"I don't recall thinking of any of it as fun," Dee replied.

"Me, neither," Jawbone agreed. "Lost a couple good friends that day."

"I read about that on the Web," Lieutenant Colonel Leeland added. "We've all somehow or other been in it together. The Saviors, including Skinny and myself, were crawling around on that enemy hauler that was trying to crash on top of you during the Seppy Exodus. We tore that rust bucket to shreds but couldn't stop it."

"Right." DeathRay stepped in to change the subject. "Who wants to go for a ride in some mecha?"

"Can we?" Dee tried her best not to grin from ear to ear like the little girl the soldiers remembered from that day on Mars or from watching her grow up on television.

"Well, I'll have to ask the CAG first," DeathRay said almost a bit too smugly not to notice.

"Oh, Jesus! You're a corny ham, sir." His wingman laughed at him, not with him.

"For those not in on the joke," Commander Hill said with a smirk, "Captain Boland here *is* the commander of the Air Group and has been for more than a decade. Of course, what he probably wouldn't tell you is that he was the CAG before that once, but he managed to get himself busted out of it for blowing up a civilian terraformer dome in the southern Martian desert."

"All right, all right, you don't have to go bringing up that, *Poser*." Boland smiled his best action-hero smile. There must've been some funny and embarrassing story behind the marine's call sign. Dee was afraid to ask.

Bree, any idea how Poser got her call sign? she thought to her AIC.

I'll see what I can dig up. Hold on. The AIC paused briefly. *I did find that Wendy Hill appeared in a men's magazine in a article titled "Women of the Military." Perhaps that is the reason?*

Dee laughed to herself. She got the joke. She wondered how Captain Boland had gotten his call sign, and kept her attention on his smile. She really liked it. A lot.

"Just so happens I have three trainers set up," DeathRay said. "Two Ares-Ts and one FM-12. I thought we might play a little three-on-three dogfight if you're up for it?"

"Up for it?" Dee almost shouted. "Jay and I are more than up for it. Right, Jay?"

"You bet!" Stavros replied eagerly.

"Well, we're gonna play this game a little differently than you two might be used to. One of you will be my wingman in the Ares-T, with Fish riding backseat for you, and the other will be Deuce's wingman, with Jawbone riding backseat. Skinny will fly with the Marine team. Poser can fly Colonel Fink with her if the colonel is up for a ride."

"You bet, Captain," Fink responded.

"So, who wants to be the navy aviator and who wants to be a jarhead?" Boland looked at Jay first. Then he rested his gaze on Dee. Dee almost volunteered to ride with him.

"Should we flip for it?" Dee asked, although she really wanted to be in the FM-12. She was almost torn, because she wouldn't mind being DeathRay's wingman—among other things—but flying a Marine FM-12 would be the shit. So, she was only *almost torn* about the decision. She was certain Jay felt the same way about flying with Major Strong, but he'd have a win-win situation there being in an FM-12 with the hot marine that seemed to be getting his hackles up.

"Flip for it, Dee," Jay replied and was clearly as excited as she was.

"Ms. Moore, I'm not so sure that would be a good idea, ma'am," Clay stepped forward and warned her. "There would be no protective services there."

"Oh, Clay, you're just a nervous old lady. You can't always be with me. I can take care of myself, and the fine mecha jocks will be right there with me the whole way. I'll have America's finest to protect me in your absence. That is, unless you want to ride in one of the fighters." Dee gave him a look that she borrowed from her father that he used with them to say without words that the discussion was over.

"Like father, like daughter," Clay mumbled to himself. Dee ignored it, mostly. She also loved it when people said that.

"What's that?" She smiled at the giant bodyguard.

"Since I can't talk you out of it, ma'am, please be careful."

"Bah. These great pilots will be right there with me, Clay. And so will Colonel Fink. You really need to consider trying to relax." Dee knew that careful was for old ladies and not for upcoming young hotshot fighter pilots.

"I will one day, ma'am, but not while I'm with you." Clay smiled at the President's daughter. Dee ignored the comment.

"So let me get this straight, Wally." Rear Admiral Lower Half (RDML) Sharon "Fullback" Walker towered over the two-star admiral and smiled. "You mean my marines were trapped and sitting ducks because some petty officer—"

"Petty officer first class," Admiral Jefferson corrected his long-time colleague, friend, and recent simulated enemy.

"Uh, petty officer first class, right. Because some petty officer first class was doing a regularly scheduled maintenance on the main tower elevator and it was therefore locked down because of safety regs?" Sharon finished her rhetorical question.

"That is absolutely right, Fullback. Care for a snort?" Wallace sat down behind his desk and motioned at the one-star admiral and CO of the *Blair* to have a seat.

"Don't mind if I do." Sharon sat down and crossed her legs all ladylike. But Wallace knew better than to think of her as anything but tougher than nails and then some. Fullback had been her call sign because way back in her Navy Academy days, she had played fullback for the Navy, which was not a position that many females played. It was especially not a position that many females played with the expertise and drive that Sharon had. Sharon was built more like a stack of bricks, a big stack of very big and mean bricks, and had a face that her mother might say was "handsome." More recently, Wally had been hearing rumors that her COB, Command Master Chief Petty Officer Bill Edwards, might think of her as more than handsome, but rumors never bothered Wally as long as they didn't bother the people they were about and didn't impact the performance of the sailors involved. And, besides, it wasn't any of his damned business. Good for Sharon, was his opinion.

Besides, what Sharon lacked in the beauty department she more than made up for in the brawn and brain department. She could have been a champion bodybuilder at the Academy, but she was more ambitious and way smarter. And on top of that she could run a four-point-one second forty-yard dash and do it over and over for four quarters while being hit hard by big, mean Army linebackers. She was definitely Navy Fleet Officer material. Wallace had played lineman a couple of the years with Sharon running behind him. The two admirals had been teammates for a very long time. That's what made this situation so damned funny.

"So, do you have a problem with a ship's crew keeping up with its routine maintenance schedule, Sharon?" Wallace had to grit his teeth to keep from laughing while he handed his friend two fingers of scotch he poured from the bottle in his desk.

"Hell, no, Wally. But if you asked me, and I know you didn't, it was kind of like cheating or gaming the system." Sharon smiled, her whiter-than-white teeth contrasting against her ebony skin. She took the drink and took a tall pull from it.

"Now, you aren't gonna start claiming the refs made a bad call and that's why the *Blair* lost the game, are you?"

"You know me, Wally. I'd never use a bad call as an excuse. We should have had a better battle plan, or my marines should've improvised better when they got trapped. I must say that your crew was quite creative with their improvisational skills."

"Yeah, I don't know whether to reprimand or promote them. But it did sure as hell work." Wallace refilled his glass then stretched across his desk to do the same for Sharon. "I do have some concerns, though."

"Such as?"

"Well, sure we won the war game, but to win it we treated it like a game. On both sides we were just gaming. What would your marines have done if it were a real firefight?" Wallace leaned back and exhaled in an attempt to relax.

"They would have done what marines do, what soldiers and sailors always do, Wally. Improvise, fight, die, succeed. And not necessarily in that order," Sharon replied.

"Sure, but think of it a bit more fleet-wide. We haven't been in a real shooting engagement for nearly six years now. How ready are we going to be when the president finally decides to take it to the Seppies in their own star system? You know that is coming soon. You can't just secede from the Union. Wasn't it Zachary Taylor that said something like he would personally lead the Army against persons taken in rebellion against the Union, and that he would hang them with less reluctance than he would spies?"

Uncle Timmy? He double-checked with his AIC.

Aye, sir. It was Zachary Taylor, the twelfth president and a military man to boot, Uncle Timmy quickly responded. *Do you need more, sir?*

That'll do, Tim.

"You were the military-history major, not me," Sharon replied.

"Something just doesn't set right with the way things are right now," Wallace continued. "We haven't seen hide nor hair of the Seppies since the Battle of the Oort. President Moore has been doing his best to fight the idiots in Congress to build up the fleet, but that has been slow and marginal. You know that Ahmi hasn't had the same problem dealing with her constituents."

"If she did, she'd have them killed. Or do it herself. She's a bloodthirsty bitch, that one," Sharon agreed.

"We better get ready. I think America is in for the culmination of the last hundred years of strife between the Martian working class, the colonists, and the manifest-destiny explorers."

"Yeah, I believe it is coming sooner than we realize, but who knows? God help us is all I can say. But the Seppies haven't been in a shooting war for the same amount of time, either." Sharon finished her drink and sat it back down at the edge of Wallace's desk.

"Good point. Want another?"

"No, Admiral, I'm on duty. I've got to get back to the *Blair* and get ready for our jaunt in a few hours."

"Yeah, me, too. Did you want to meet the First Daughter while you're here?"

"No, thanks, I just don't have time. And stop being such a Wally-worry-wart, Admiral, it'll give you heartburn, headaches, and hemorrhoids. We've got good troops, you and me. They'll do what has to be done to get the job done." Sharon stood up and saluted the two-star admiral. "As always, a pleasure, Admiral Jefferson."

"Right back at you, Admiral Walker." Wallace returned the salute. He was slightly startled by a crackling and sizzling sound and a bright flash of white light, and then Sharon vanished from right in front of him. "Goddamn, I'm never gonna get used to that."

CHAPTER 8

July 1, 2394 AD
Mars Orbit, Sol System
Friday, 11:05 AM, Earth Eastern Standard Time

"Lieutenant Commander Buckley and Captain Harrison are here, Admiral." The XO stood at ease in the hatch of the admiral's office.

"Come in, Larry, come in."

Joe wasn't sure what all this was about other than the fact that he had been ordered to report to the CHENG and the XO as soon as he got the "goddamned elevator back on line." That had been the XO's exact words.

"At ease, gentlemen." RADM Jefferson stood with a deadpan expression and his arms behind his back. Joe tried to relax just enough as not to look too at ease. Joe knew that the admiral liked him. Well, at least he thought he did. He had given the admiral every reason to like him. Hell, Joe's dad had sacrificed himself to save the ship for Captain Jefferson years ago. And then Joe had done nearly the same damned thing on his first day on the job. Hopefully, if there was some ass chewing about the elevator trick, then his past performance would soften it. And there was always the nagging fact that his antics helped them defeat the *Blair* in the war game. Being on the winning side was always better than being on the losing one, especially when it came to ass chewings.

"Sir." He and Benny responded almost in harmony with each other. Benny's voice was a little more baritone than Joe's, and couldn't neither one of them carry a damned tune in a bucket.

"Benny, I have to tell you, your presence in the Engineering

Room most certainly was missed today. Did you hear about all the crazy things that went on down there in the Engineering Room of my ship?"

"Aye, Admiral, I did," Benny replied.

"Lieutenant Commander Joeseph Buckley Jr., what are we supposed to do with you?" The admiral turned from Benny to Joe. "That trick with the elevator you pulled today, son, well, it was underhanded, and dirty pool. Let me tell you, Admiral Walker ain't none too happy about it, either. And the audacity of putting up the notice sign . . ."

"Sir." Joe looked straight ahead and tried not to let his voice crack. "Just following procedure for the elevator maintenance, Admiral."

"Benny, what do you think about it?" the CO asked.

"Admiral, if you ask me, I'd say it was clever, sneaky, and I never would've done it in a million years. The sign was a nice touch."

Oh, great—Benny is selling me out, Joe thought. The sign had actually been Andy's doing, but Joe wasn't going to cause his engineer's mate any undue strife by giving up that information. No, sir, he'd take the lumps for that sign. Hell, Benny was right—it *was* a nice touch. And it *was* funny as hell.

Relax, Joe. Debbie tried to calm his nerves, but his heart rate was through the roof. *You know that Benny wouldn't sell you out.*

"And what about wrecking a perfectly good piece of hardware on my ship just to win a sim, and then go about sabotaging the propulsion systems because he didn't want to have to fight off a few wussy marines—"

"Ahem!" USMC Brigadier General Larry Chekov grunted.

"No disrespect intended, EndRun, just making a point." The admiral grinned at his XO. The XO muttered something about squids, but not loud enough for any of them to make out.

"What's that, XO?"

"Nothing, Admiral. Just clearing my throat."

"Benny?" The admiral turned back to the CHENG.

"Again, sir, I never would have done it in a million years." Benny repeated the same answer.

"And why is that, Captain Harrison?"

"Well, Admiral, I hate to admit this, but I just don't think I'd have ever thought of it, sir." Benny let a thin smile cross his lips briefly.

"Never would have thought of it?" the XO interjected. Joe was afraid the vein throbbing on the side of the Marine's neck was going to burst at any moment. "Am I to believe that you are telling us now that Buckley Jr. here is smarter than our CHENG?"

"I'm afraid so, XO."

"Pardon my French, Admiral, but that just will not fucking do, sir. Goddamnit, it will not fucking do, Admiral."

"Why is that, Larry?" It was clear that the admiral was quite used to the fact that in order to properly function his XO seemed to have the need to profusely spout expletives several times a sentence, or he might keel over. After six years on the *Madira*, Joe was quite aware of that fact himself. He had learned a little too closely a few times. Everybody on board knew that the admiral and the XO had served together for decades, and so the admiral always seemed completely unfazed and mostly immune to the colorful expletives.

"Sir, we are the USS-by-God *Sienna Madira*. The flagship of the fleet. Our marines are the goddamned toughest sonsabitches ever to shit between shoes. Our mecha jocks fly like no other and eat their own vomit for lunch on a regular basis all the while begging for fucking more. Our Army pukes puke better than any. So our by-God CHENG had better be able to out fucking CHENG any other goddamned CHENG in this wonderful fleet of ours, sir."

"And your point, XO?" The admiral looked back and forth between the XO and Buckley. Joe stood motionless, not understanding at all what this was about. He felt the best plan was to stand still and keep his damned mouth shut until he was told to speak.

"Well, sir, if'n our CHENG has done gotten so damned old and outdated that even he admits that Buckley Jr. here can out-CHENG him, then maybe he ought to be thinking about some damned greener pastures somewhere else, sir." The XO sighed. "No offense, Benny."

"None taken, XO." Benny was clearly now straining not to laugh, but Joe was still left out of the joke.

"Well, Benny, just what do you have to say about the XO's comments?" The admiral cocked his right eyebrow.

"Well, sir, I guess he's right. I'll just have to retire, sir."

"Well, damned if that sure doesn't leave us in a bind here, CHENG! We are to ship off to the Oort in a couple hours, and my CHENG is up and quitting on me? When do you plan to leave us?"

"Uh, Admiral, my bags are packed and I plan to make shore

before the *Madira* breaks orbit, sir. I've got several weeks leave I put in for. I'm gonna take that, and then my final date is next month, sir. Of course, you already approved my leave, Admiral." Now Benny couldn't control his laughter.

"Well, goddamn, that had slipped my mind. One other thing, sailor—you'll be missed around here, Benny." The admiral held his hand out sincerely and shook Benny's hand. Joe still didn't get the joke.

"Thank you, sir."

"Same goes for me, Benny. You always kept us running while we were in the shit," the XO added and shook hands with the CHENG. "Can't ask for more than that of any CHENG. So, you're not having a party or nothing?"

"I just want to go home to Luna and spend some time with my great-great-grandchildren, sir. Apparently, I have thirty-seven of them." Joe wasn't sure, but he thought he actually saw a tear in the CHENG's eye. "I hate retirement parties."

"Well, by damned you *will* have one, sailor, and that is an order. We'll make a point of it when we get back from the outer system." The admiral slapped Benny's shoulder. "But you are still leaving us in a serious bind."

"No CHENG, sir." The XO nodded in agreement. The gruff Marine went straight back to his normal gridiron hardassed self. "Got to have a CHENG."

"I'm aware of that XO. But who could do the job?" the admiral asked no one in particular.

"If you ask me, sir, I think Buckley here would make a good CHENG someday," Benny said and turned to his assistant chief engineer with a big smile. "Maybe if he were put to work being the CHENG, he wouldn't have enough time to go about tearing up the Engineering Room every time he turns around. And it might make him a little more reluctant to fry himself with X-rays every chance he has a decent excuse to."

"Buckley, you up for it?" The admiral looked Joe square in the eyes, but Joe didn't falter a bit. Well, his mind was racing, his heart was racing, and his stomach was in knots, hard U.S. Navy knots, but he didn't hesitate to answer.

"Aye, aye, sir!"

"Wait a minute, Admiral. There is a problem with that," the XO interrupted again.

"What's that, Larry?"

"The *Blair* has an O5 as their CHENG. We can't have a lower-ranked officer as our CHENG than she does. That just wouldn't be fitting, Admiral." Joe glanced at the old marine only slightly, since he didn't want to take his eyes off Admiral Wallace, but he couldn't tell from the glance if the XO was serious, joking, or just being an ass. But that was usually the way it was with General Chekov.

"You're right, Larry." Rear Admiral Upper Half Wallace Jefferson turned and picked up something from his desk and handed it to Joe. "Open it, son."

Joe opened the little box and found a silver leaf and two melding fabric patches. Each of the patches had three gold stripes at the bottom with a single gold star above them in the middle of the patch. The smaller of the patches was for the collar of his UCU jacket and the larger for his shoulder. Joe didn't say a word.

"Congratulations, Commander Buckley." The admiral offered Joe his hand.

"Take care of her, Joe." Benny slapped his protégé on the back. "Or should I say CHENG?"

CHAPTER 9

July 1, 2394 AD
Ross 128, Planet Five, a.k.a. Arcadia, 40,000 Kilometers
above New Megalopolis
Friday, 3:09 PM, Frontier City Standard Time
Friday, 11:09 AM, Earth Eastern Standard Time

The Separatist flagship wasn't like the previous warships of the Separatist fleet. The ships used in major battles at the Martian Exodus and at the Battle of the Oort had been retrofitted cargo haulers. The haulers were large, even bigger than the U.S. supercarrier class ships, but they were still old reconfigured cargo ships that had been turned into makeshift warships. The fact that the old haulers were, well, *old* is what led the U.S. forces to refer to them derogatorily as "rust buckets."

The Separatists had been updating and building new weapons since they had moved from Mars to the Tau Ceti system twelve years ago. There was some intelligence that suggested that the Tau Ceti colony had been in on the Separatist movement all along and perhaps had been developing mecha, weapons, and even the new line of battleships for them. It was unclear who had retrofitted the previous generation of ships for them, although Tau Ceti was the most likely candidate. It was possible that the Separatists had retrofitted the ships in space somewhere deep in the outer parts of the Sol System. After all, they had managed to build a small moon-sized QMT teleport facility in the Oort Cloud right under the U.S. military's nose. And then they managed to plan an exodus of over thirty million citizens from the Sol System to the Oort facility and then on to Tau Ceti.

In twelve years, the thirty million Separatists, along with the thirteen million colonists at Tau Ceti, had managed to manufacture a brand new fleet that was just now coming on line. Four of the new supercarrier-class ships and five new battle cruisers had gone through their checkout flights and were prepping for their maiden voyages. The four supercarriers were equipped with a second generation of Stingers, which were copies of the U.S. FM-12s; new transfigurable Gnats, comparable to the U.S. VTF-32 Ares-Ts; and a new version of Orcus droptanks that had a bot mode similar to that of the U.S. M3A17-Ts. The battle-cruiser class ships carried Gnats and armored troops and were smaller, more maneuverable ships. The haulers and previous generation of ships still existed, but the question was if there were enough personnel available for them to have crew.

The flagship of the United Separatist Republic was the USR *Deborah Sampson*. The *Sampson*, no matter what star system's technology one considered, was a state-of-the-art warship fully equipped with modern SIF generators, directed-energy weapons, missile tubes, a fast hyperspace-jaunt projector, catapult bays for mecha and drop tubes, two hundred kilogram projectile rail cannons, and QMT teleporters with personnel snap-back capability.

The *Sampson* was over three kilometers long and about half that in width and depth. The general design was very similar to the U.S. supercarrier designs. Since that is what she had been designed to fight, the design was perfectly logical. Rumors were that Elle Ahmi had designed the flagship herself, right down to the Mars-red color scheme of the interior décor. The color scheme was most likely the reason for that particular rumor. Every citizen of the U.S.R. understood that Elle Ahmi had a nostalgic soft spot for Mars in her heart—though they also realized that was probably the only soft spot she had anywhere.

The *Sampson* had been on line for several weeks and had a full crew complement. It had made several deep-space hyperspace jaunts as well as several QMT jumps between Tau Ceti and Ross 128. On two separate occasions she had simulated an attack on one of the outer planet moons of Tau Ceti. All of the flight wings were deployed as well as the droptanks and armored troops. The ship and crew combination was a well-oiled machine and definitely deserved the title of flagship to the U.S.R.

Flagship flight-wing crewman Ensign Bella Penrose sat near the viewport in the starboard galley picking at her food and staring out at the large QMT facility. The facility hung in a non-Keplerian orbit hovering over the capital city of the U.S. colony of Arcadia. The Ross 128 colony was as beautiful as Tau Ceti and was far more developed. Tau Ceti had over fifty million people and had been established for a few decades. Ross 128, on the other hand, was nearly a hundred years old and had over one hundred million colonists. The colony was old enough to have several generations of native-born Arcadians.

Penrose looked at the large octagonal structure and towers of the small moon-sized facility just beneath the warship. The facility reminded her of the ones she had seen at the Oort Cloud in the Sol System, and the one above New Tharsis in the Tau Ceti system. The times she had seen those facilities her name had been either Kira Shavi or Nancy Penzington.

Since her return to the Tau Ceti system it had taken the CIA agent almost six years to create a cover that would allow her to get aboard the flagship of the U.S.R., Once before she had infiltrated one of the Seppy ships, but she was discovered and barely managed to escape with her life and some very useful intelligence data. She had managed to get that data back to the Sol System mainly by happenstance. But she did get it back.

Unfortunately, the byproduct of her successful espionage had been that the Seppies had stepped up their efforts to prevent a spy from infiltrating their military infrastructure ever again. Things had become even more difficult for spies, and that was mainly because of her. Twelve years before, she had managed to infiltrate the Seppies, and after that no other agents who had attempted to do so had ever reported back to the CIA. Bella, at the time she was Nancy, had managed to infiltrate the Separatists most likely due to the mass confusion involved in the Seppy attack on Mons City on Mars followed by the exodus of the Separatists.

Allison, any idea what this package is that is of such importance? she thought to her AIC. Her flight group's orders were to be on standby to support the delivery of a highly important package to the capital city and directly to Ahmi herself. Bella knew that meant trouble. But just how much trouble, she wasn't certain.

Your guess is as good as mine, the AIC responded. *We'll just have to be patient. It isn't scheduled to arrive for a couple hours.*

It had taken Nancy Penzington six months to completely cover her tracks after her return to the Tau Ceti QMT facility six years prior. Once she had managed to get away from the facility by stowing away aboard a troop carrier dirtside to Ares, Nancy spent several weeks considering going native and giving up the spy business. She had made plenty of personal sacrifices for the United States of America. She should have died on the Seppy battle cruiser *Phlegra* when it had tried to make a kamikaze run on Luna City. But, luckily, she hadn't. She still had several covers she could use if she needed them. So she did. Like any good undercover agent who is in country and cut off from home, she had multiple bank accounts, money and weapons caches, and a couple of safe houses under various names throughout New Tharsis and the Madira Valley. She cashed in on some of them and spent several months on the beach outside the spaceport working on her full-body tan.

After the second month of mental recovery, a.k.a. lounging on the nude beaches of Madira Valley, it dawned on her that with the *Phlegra* destroyed near Luna, Elle Ahmi would want a new favorite mode of space transportation. Nancy began formulating a hypothesis that the new supercarrier-sized battleships under construction at the base at the beach might fit that need. After a few fun and not-so-fun nights, with off-duty sailors and contractors, she managed to get enough word-of-mouth information to back up her hypothesis. Elle Ahmi actually spent a significant amount of time visiting one particular ship that was under construction. There had to be something special about that ship, because according to rumor that was the only one Ahmi visited regularly.

Nancy didn't necessarily have a specific mission she needed to do; her general mission orders were to gather intel on the Seppies. Gathering intel on the Seppy military capabilities seemed as good a plan as any to her. But she had other plans, too. After Ahmi had tortured her and the way that she had tortured her, Nancy had decided one thing. Someday, she would make Ahmi pay, dearly.

Then one night at the nightspot for the military types just outside the base adjacent to the beach spaceport she met a young naval cadet in her last year of college. The young cadet had hopes and dreams of being a mecha jock. The cadet was in the Naval Reserve Officers Training Corps (NROTC) and had a good chance of making it into the flight-training program upon graduation. Nancy had the beginnings of a plan at that point. She befriended the young cadet and gathered as much information about the young woman as possible. She learned everything she could about becoming a cadet and getting into the NROTC. Then Nancy cashed in some assets and paid for a new rejuvenation that left her appearing as young as or maybe a bit younger than the cadet. She never spoke with that particular cadet again.

The next three months took patience. Nancy laid low on the beach and stayed away from any recent friends she had made—her appearance had been changed pretty dramatically, but she didn't want to take any chances. She simply lived the life of a beach bunny and gave herself the time to rest, relax, and enjoy life for a while. She stayed in shape by running ten to twenty kilometers a day up and down Madira Beach and by taking some yoga and martial arts classes at a local gym.

Slowly and carefully, she gathered emotional and cultural information about getting into the U.S.R. Navy flight line. She researched all the pertinent logistics, admissions, and paperwork information she needed. Three months passed before she finally got the break she was looking for. An earthquake occurred in the middle of the ocean, causing a tidal wave. The tidal wave struck an archipelago called Campbell's Islands on the southern region of the Amazonia continent. Amazonia was a large landmass about the size of China, and the archipelago region was analogous to the Philippines on Earth. There were casualties numbering in the thousands. Nancy immediately gathered herself up off the beach, hopped aboard a plane stored at one of her caches, and was in southern Amazonia only a few hours after the news broke. She managed to board a rescue boat as a volunteer a few hours after that. Soon after, she had managed to get herself lost in the aftermath of the tidal wave impact zone of East Plantation Island.

East Plantation Island, according to public data records, had thirteen hundred inhabitants and more than three times as many tourists at any given time. Needless to say, Nancy found plenty of casualties to work with. Allison scanned for other AICs broadcasting casualty locations. The CIA super-AIC hacked those AICs for personal bio information, looking for just the right profile. After a couple of hours of this she found one that fit her needs on the far side of the island. The casualty had lived on Tau Ceti since before the Martian Exodus and was about sixty years old. The lady had no known relatives on Tau Ceti, although she reportedly had family still alive on Earth. And, to top it off, she had recently been rejuved to a very young appearance. Nancy and Allison found her drowned and broken body trapped inside what was left of her home. Allison had no problem copying the data files from the commercial AIC that poor Bella Penrose had in her skull, even in its nonfunctional, damaged state. Then Nancy removed the AIC from the lady's brain and crushed it. The unlucky artificial intelligence was just a casualty of war, and Nancy had little remorse about it. Allison had long since given up such emotional hang-ups about killing other AICs as well. They had a job to do—for the betterment of the United States of America. They disposed of the body and AIC remains with a couple of incendiary chemicals that Nancy had brought along with her, and then she went about addressing her appearance and plan for being rescued. She scratched herself up with some broken glass and changed into the clothes that the real Bella had been wearing. She climbed atop the roof of Bella's small beach house and waited for help as Allison mimicked the AIC help broadcast. Eventually, she was rescued by a group of volunteers and was flown to a makeshift hospital for treatment.

Following her rescue, Bella Penrose moved to the other side of the planet Ares to Madira Beach and quickly made it through NROTC and college with a double load of courses that she, along with her super-AIC, had no problem with. After two years of college and NROTC, she was selected—with a little hacking help from Allison—to the Aviation Preflight Indoctrination (API) program. After fourteen weeks of API she did six weeks as a student naval flight officer, and then she had twenty-two weeks of training at the Navy Flight Officer Training Command at the Madira Valley Beach Spaceport Armored Mecha Flight Training Grounds, and then another thirty-six weeks in mecha combat tactics training.

Following that she had a pip "pinned on," and she became U.S.R. Navy Ensign Bella Penrose. Although the process and military structure was very, very similar to that of the United States military, there were some cultural differences. One difference was that call signs didn't stick with the person, they stuck with the job. And as soon as she was assigned to the USR *Deborah Sampson* Flight Wing 1, Group 2, Tiger Squad, she became "Tiger 5." Of course, the other cultural difference was that everything was done in praise of Elle Ahmi. Although Ahmi's tactics had been extremely bloody to the American people, the Separatists were now free of the U.S. government and had a planet of their own, a very nice planet. The Separatist people viewed that fact as being solely due to Ahmi herself. It wasn't hard to understand why they followed the charismatic terrorist. But then again, most of the Separatist people had never met the crazy bitch. It took all of her training to mask her hatred for the Separatist leader and to appear as a loyal servant of the U.S.R. Navy, but Bella managed. After all, that is what she had done all of her adult life—pretend to be somebody else.

So, after escaping from the QMT facility over six years prior and lying low for several months, after about six months of gold brickin' on the beach, after a few weeks of rehab from a natural disaster, after two years of college and NROTC, and about another two years of mecha training, Ensign Bella Penrose found herself staring out the viewport of the USR *Deborah Sampson* while trying to stomach the galley food, figure out just what Elle Ahmi was up to, and how she was going to kill her. Well, killing Ahmi hadn't been part of her original orders, but Bella was going to do that one for herself. It would be good therapy.

As Bella let her mind wander, something caught her eye. Actually, it caught the eye of everybody on the ship, as it was hard to miss a QMT. A ship approached the center of the teleport-pad towers, and then a large green and blue sphere of light began to grow, centered directly over the central tower. The sphere grew to several kilometers in diameter and looked like a giant plasma ball resting atop the tallest spire. Then the giant ball of plasma instantaneously collapsed to a flat disk of light with blue and white lightning shooting across the surface. A ripple, like waves on a pond, traveled in a circular wavefront from the center of the disk, and then the ship vanished into the event horizon of the disk. As soon as the ships appeared in local space, the disk collapsed inward on itself and vanished with a final flash of white light from the center.

It was a scene that humanity throughout the colonies was beginning to become accustomed to. The intel that the Seppies were getting from the colonists of Ross 128 was that the U.S. had built teleport platforms now at each colony and one near Mars. The only route to the inner Sol System, though, was still through the original Seppy-built QMT pad in the Oort. From there, ships could teleport to Mars and then hyperspace jaunt inward to Earth. As far as the Seppies knew, the American scientists had not yet figured out how to hack any of the systems to go from any pad to another. Elle Ahmi had often laughed at the Americans in public broadcasts for that—of course, she knew how to do this. There was even rumor that the new battleship fleet didn't need the pads. Bella hadn't confirmed that yet. But if that was the case, the U.S. military needed to know.

Ensign Penrose hadn't seen the *Sampson* do a QMT without a facility yet, but she had seen it go back and forth between Ross 128 and Tau Ceti. And she also knew that the U.S.R. had the QMT schedule for the Ross 128 facility, because they often would hide behind one of the moons and run in silent mode to avoid being seen by incoming teleporting ships.

"General quarters! General quarters. All hands, prepare for hyperspace jaunt in one minute. Prepare for battlestations call and silent running," the *Sampson*'s AIC said over the ship's 1-MC intercom.

Allison? Bella asked her AIC.

Regularly scheduled jaunt behind one of the moons, it looks like. We must be expecting an incoming QMT from Earthspace, Allison replied.

Well, it's my day off. Let's do some snooping, shall we?

About time.

CHAPTER 10

July 1, 2394 AD
Mars Orbit, Sol System
Friday, 11:40 AM, Earth Eastern Standard Time

DeathRay finally decided that he had to flip a coin to be fair. Dee won the toss and chose to fly in the FM-12 mecha with Jawbone. The other cadet was with Fish in the Ares-T trainer. DeathRay led the other two Navy mecha out of the cat bay and into a standard patrol orbit a safe distance from the supercarrier. The three mecha flew in a staggered V formation with DeathRay in the lead, Stavros and Fish in the trainer on his left wing, and Poser and Fink off his right, but farther back.

I've got the marines just coming off cat and into the engagement zone, Jack, his AIC, Candis, alerted him.

Yeah, I've got them. Let's see how long it takes our nugget to spot them. DeathRay relaxed his grip on the HOTAS and adjusted his position in the pilot's couch, something he wouldn't be able to do if they went to high-g maneuvers. He centered his mind by breathing deep a few times and relaxing his body from head to toe. Soon every muscle in his body from head to toe would be wishing it could relax.

Right.

"DeathRay, DeathRay, this is Navy2," Stavros said over the net.

"Go Navy2." DeathRay rolled his helmet from shoulder to shoulder. *Shit, not bad. Get ready, Candis. Here we go.*

Aye, sir.

"I've got our Gomers at eight o'clock at five kilometers! Three

93

Marine FM-12s in fighter mode," Stavros replied. From the sound of his voice, DeathRay was pretty certain that the kid was about to squeeze the HOTAS into oblivion. Fish would calm him down.

"Good eyeballs, Navy2. Hold our present vector until I say otherwise. Colonel Fink, when I say 'break,' I want you to go solo and try to make a nuisance of yourself. Navy2, you stay on my wing like stink on a skunk's ass."

"Roger that, DeathRay," Fink confirmed.

"Uh, roger that," Stavros replied a little hesitantly. Fish must've had to remind the kid to key the tac-net.

Jack went to full battlescape view in his DTM. The interior of the little snub-nosed mecha became transparent, allowing him to see space in every direction. He looked below to keep a bearing on where the *Madira* was and had his AIC plot the trajectories of the three inbound in red. They were coming fast. Damned fast.

Plot me some strategies, Candis.

Roger that, his AIC replied. Multiple traces of reds for the Marine team and blue for the Navy team spiraled around each other in his mindview. DeathRay studied them briefly until he found one he liked and then thought the others away.

That one looks good. Pass it on.

Roger that.

"All right, folks, the party is starting. Wait for my signal," DeathRay announced. "Now!"

DeathRay pulled his stick back and pushed the throttle full forward into a full g-loaded climb. He could tell through his DTM that Navy2 followed him and was right on his wing. Colonel Fink and Poser in Navy3 had banked left and down and away from them. The three Marine fighters stayed with DeathRay and Navy2.

"They're on our six, DeathRay, and closing fast as shit!" Stavros grunted against the g-suit.

"Hold it with me, Navy2. When I say 'now,' you hold your vector for a count of three and then toggle to bot!" DeathRay ordered.

"Roger that."

"Three, two, one, now!" DeathRay immediately toggled the mecha from fighter to bot. He could see his wingman streak by him in a red blur. "Fox three!" he shouted as the Ares-T fighter tossed a mecha-to-mecha missile simulator at the oncoming Marine FM-12s. His fighter rolled over and reconfigured itself to an upside-down bot. The maneuver flung DeathRay through multiple direction changes pulling anywhere from minus six to plus eight gravities. He grunted, squeezed his abs, and stomped the left pedal, spinning the bot around to face the incoming planes and went to his forearm cannons.

"Guns, guns, guns!" He fired. There had been no time for targeting, but the computer scored several hits against the onrushing planes. None of them were kill shots. DeathRay kicked the thrusters in the feet of the giant armored bot downward and out of the path of the rushing Marine fighters. Two of them zipped past to Stavros while one of them pulled out and rolled over into bot mode.

"Shit, I've got two of them on me!" Stavros shouted. "I need some help here."

"Fox Three!" came a third voice from the net. It was Fink. The colonel might be a retired instructor, but he could still fly, and he was doing just what DeathRay had told him to do. Fink broke right across the three-nine line of the Marine fighters pursuing Stavros and put a kill shot right on Skinny. The icon for her plane turned orange, showing eliminated status.

"Thanks, Colonel!" Stavros shouted. "I've still got one on my six!"

"Go to guns, Navy2!" DeathRay shouted at the cadet. Then he kicked his bot-mode mecha into a roll and back to fighter going full throttle just in time to get out of the way of the Marine trainer in bot mode on his ass. It was Dee. *Shit. She is either good, or that's Jawbone doing the flying.*

I've confirmed with Jawbone that it is her, Candis assured him.

Well, how about that. Let's take her out. DeathRay grunted as he grinned to himself, actually grinning would have taken too much effort, as he was currently pulling about nine gravities.

"Watch it, Marine2, that Navy Gomer is gunning for you!" Deuce warned Dee over the Marine channel.

"Roger that, Deuce. I see him." Dee rolled over from bot back to fighter, stomped the right pedal and gave full left on the HOTAS. The FM-12 went into a near-flat spin and went around full circle twice before she hit the throttle to hold her in a reverse-pointing trajectory. The nose of her fighter was pointing toward the Navy fighter that was on her tail now, while the ship flew in the complete opposite direction. She was flying backward with respect to her trajectory. "Guns, guns, guns!"

"Watch the guns, Marine2. We're too tight to each other!" Deuce shouted at Dee.

"Shit, Deuce, get out of the way—I've got a shot!"

"Dee, I suggest you get some separation with the Navy and let's regroup," Jawbone chimed in from the backseat. "And don't forget who the squad commander is."

"Got it. Deuce is the lead. Not used to that." Dee jinked and juked but couldn't get anything clear on DeathRay, so she flipped her plane back around in normal flight vector. "Deuce, I can't get a shot, and he's coming hot! Any suggestions?"

"Thought you'd never ask." Deuce would have laughed had DeathRay not been keeping them both grunting and squeezing every muscle in their bodies. "We have to stay together, Dee. We've lost Skinny, so that leaves us outnumbered. Just stay on my wing and take shots if you can get them."

"Roger that." Dee barrel-rolled over to Deuce's wing. She decided to trust the Marine lieutenant colonel ace for now.

Bree, give me some ideas, Dee asked her AIC.

Got it. A second later, several trajectory solutions popped in her mindview. *Dee, Navy3 has broken from the pack again.*

Shit. Colonel Fink is gunning for us.

"Deuce, Deuce, Navy3 has broken from the pack! I've got him projected as trying to loop around on us!"

"Roger that, Marine2. Stay on my wing!" Deuce replied. "Stay on my wing."

Dee held tight to the squad leader's wing, but she didn't get her tactic at all. She stayed on Stavros's tail, trying to get a shot while he and DeathRay rolled and bounced around each other, trying to shake them. The effect of the Navy planes' dangerous ballet left the targeting computer confused, and neither Dee nor Deuce was going to get a shot anytime soon. But Fink was coming in off their four o'clock very quickly. They had to make a choice soon or he was going to pick one of them off.

"Navy Gomer just behind our three-nine line, Deuce, closing fast!" Dee didn't like waiting on a shot at a plane in front of them that they were never going to get while an enemy mecha was closing in on them from the side. Then tracer simulators zipped across the canopy and into the front of her fighter. "Shit, Deuce! I'm taking fire."

"Stay on me, Marine2!" Deuce ordered.

"What!" Dee didn't like that order.

"Dee, stay with your wingman!" Jawbone warned her as she grunted through the maneuvers from the backseat. "She knows what she's doing."

"Fox three!" Deuce shouted. "Bank up, Dee! Bank up!"

The mecha-to-mecha missile simulator twisted out in front of them and into Navy2 with a confirmed kill. There were fireworks simulating a fireball, and the computer animations didn't show an ejection of the pilot. That meant there would have been no time for Jay to eject.

"Shit!" Dee banked up, pulling the HOTAS back with her right hand and full forward with her left. Her stomach stayed somewhere about two hundred meters behind her when she did. Tracer simulators rocked her hull, but the computer scored it as minimal damage to the aft armor plating. Her SIFs were holding.

Pulling up the way the two FM-12s did put them above Navy3, who was now undershooting them rapidly and would have to burn off speed to loop back to them. This left the two remaining Navy planes separated from each other by a good distance and in a situation where they would be vulnerable in a two-on-one attack for a few seconds. Fink was closest. Dee liked that.

"Pitch reverse and guns, Dee!" Deuce shouted at her, meaning for her to flip over, pointing her nose in the opposite direction as that she was traveling, and go to guns while flying backward and upside down. Of course, she was in space, so upside down was really meaningless and only relative to the pitch angle she had been oriented in.

It took Dee only a microsecond to understand what she was supposed to do. Years in the simulator had honed her senses for just this sort of maneuver. But Dee had to admit that the simulator, even with gravity compensators and full mindview simulation, was nothing like the real thing. She pulled the stick all the way back and kicked both lower foot pedals. The ship flipped over. Dee could see through her canopy that Deuce was doing the same. Stars spun around her head, bringing the *Madira* and Mars behind her back into view. Now both of the Marine mecha were flying upside down and backward and were pointed at Fink's plane.

"Guns, guns, guns!" Deuce shouted. Not to be left out, Dee followed suit.

"Guns, guns, guns!"

"Let's go, Marine2. You take the lead!" Deuce shouted.

"My pleasure!" Dee slammed the throttle full forward a bit eagerly and abruptly. When the propulsion kicked in against the backward velocity vector, she hit about twelve gravities for a few seconds. "Whoooaaah, shit!"

"You might wanna tell somebody next time," Jawbone coughed from the backseat of the trainer.

"Ungh, no shit." Dee held back her stomach from lurching out of her throat by biting down as hard as she could on her bite block. When she did, the mouthpiece shot fresh oxygen and stimulants into her system that snapped her quickly back to life. The high-g thrust reversal's effect on her quickly vanished, and she pushed on her pursuit of Fink's ass.

"I'm on the Gomer!" Dee kept her targeting X in center, trying to lock it on to the Navy fighter, but the old Marine colonel was real good at managing his energy.

The Navy fighter pushed at top acceleration upward and back directly toward Dee and Deuce. That was a brilliant, yet gutsy as hell, maneuver. Had Fink pulled down and away, it would have allowed the marines to get on his six and lock him up. Pulling into Dee's vector put the Navy fighter's and the two marine's vectors criss-crossing at near equal energies. The key to modern space combat was controlling the energy of your three-dimensional position vector and trying to make the other guy overshoot you. Then that would put their ass in your sights. The other key was not to get killed.

As it currently stood, Dee and Deuce were now barrel-rolling around each other and Fink, and all three pilots were cutting and adding throttle in a three-way dance to see who slipped up first. Dee had every intention that it was going to be Fink.

"Deuce, you got DeathRay on eyeball?" she grunted.

"Negative, Marine2. You watch Navy3 and I'll keep an eye out for the CAG."

"I've got him DTM coming in behind us. He'll be in range in ten seconds, so we better get on with this!" Dee added.

"Roger that, Marine2. Stay on Navy3. I'm with you."

"Do you see him anywhere, Jawbone?" Dee asked. *Why have a backseat driver if she couldn't help?* she thought.

"He's back there. Trust your DTM and your wingman, Dee. And hurry up and lock this Gomer up!" Jawbone replied.

Dee rolled and jerked the Marine mecha trainer round and round but couldn't get a lock. At one point the two fighters were cockpit to cockpit with each other. If it weren't a simulation with good guys on each side, Dee thought she could go to eagle mode and punch the pilot through the cockpit, but they were all friends here playing a game. One hell of a game. Then an idea hit her. She would do just what DeathRay had done to them in the first round of the engagement.

What's good for the goose . . .

"Deuce! When I say bank right, do it!" she shouted to the squad commander. Rank didn't really apply to covering wingmen in a tactical scenario.

"Roger that, Marine2," Deuce replied.

"Three, two, one, now!" Dee slammed her throttle full forward hard into the stop, shooting her way out in front of the dance she had been in with Fink. She could see in her mindview that Deuce had banked away.

Now I've got you, Colonel, Dee thought. She then toggled the mecha into bot mode.

The g-load on Dee's body from the mode change was over thirteen gravities for the entirety of a second or less, and then it lurched her the other way to minus seven, but under that much gravity time slowed and it seemed like it took an hour and a half. Dee screamed and grunted and fought blacking out as best she could and kept presence of mind to stomp her left pedal to spin her bot around, pointing at Fink's plane. She had just enough strength left to pull the trigger.

"Guns, guns, guns!" she growled. The yellow targeting Xs from each arm bounced around, and then both of them locked onto Fink's snub-nosed fighter plane and turned red. The tracer simulators pinged him and generated a fake fireball. There was no simulated pilot ejection, either.

"Great shot, Dee! Now go to fighter! Hurry!" Jawbone shouted loud enough that she could almost actually *hear* her through the cockpit and not just over the internal net. But Dee was stunned by the maneuver and didn't respond quickly enough.

"Dee, break out of there at top throttle, go!" Deuce yelled at her as well.

"Full throttle up, Dee!" Jawbone continued.

Dee shook herself to and saw DeathRay's fighter looming at

her fast. She was certain that she was a goner, but at the last second tracers came in off his three o'clock. Deuce engaged him just in time to give Dee the second she needed to recover and get the hell out of there. But then the damndest thing Dee had ever seen happened.

The Navy Ares-T fighter started swirling about its center of gravity point while still traveling along the same trajectory it had been on. The Navy fighter twisted and spun in a mad whirl in all directions. Tracer simulators came out of it each time it tracked around to hers or Deuce's position. The little fighter whirled so fast Dee could barely see it or manage to respond quickly enough. Finally, the thought hit her just to get the hell away from there. So she slammed the throttle forward.

"Move, Dee!" Jawbone shouted, and then she sighed. "Shit. Fucking, goddamned DeathRay."

"You have been confirmed killed in action," the computer-simulator referee voice chimed.

"What the hell?" Dee could tell by Deuce's icon turning orange in her DTM that she was KIA, too.

"Pukin' Deathblossom," Jawbone said between breaths. "Good flying, Dee. DeathRay is, well,·DeathRay."

"A puking *what*?"

CHAPTER 11

July 1, 2394 AD
Sol System, Earth, Washington, D.C.
Friday, 12:31 PM, Earth Eastern Standard Time

"Ambassador Spellman, welcome to Washington D.C. I appreciate your joining us today," Alexander Moore stood from behind the *Resolute* desk and made his way across the Oval Office to meet the ambassador from Arcadia. The Ross 128 governor should have made the trip himself, but President Moore saw this as power posturing by the leader of that colony.

"Mr. President. It is an honor, sir. Please, call me Alonzo" The ambassador looked nervous to Moore. That was just the way that the president wanted him. Moore knew he had to convince the colonists to back down on this revolt against the tariffs. Without the money from those tariffs, there was just no way Congress would continue to fund the large military buildup and presence being planned for the U.S. colonies and territories. Without protection, they would be sitting ducks for the Separatists to move in and take them.

"Well, Alonzo, I know it is a damned hot July day, but why don't we take a walk through the Rose Garden and chat man-to-man before the press gets hold of us, huh?" Moore clapped the man on his shoulder with his right hand and pointed him toward the door with his left.

"Certainly, Mr. President. Whatever you would like."

"Thomas." Moore turned to his ever-present shadowing Secret Service agent. "We're gonna go for a little walk." The Secret Service man just nodded and followed.

101

Abigail, he thought to his AIC.

Yes, sir?

Is Sehera waiting for me out in the Garden?

Yes, Mr. President.

Good. We'll good-cop/bad-marine this flunky.

Amateurs.

My sentiments exactly, Abby.

Alexander and Sehera did their best to take turns charming and then threatening the ambassador at the same time. It was a First Family effort for the history books that applied both soft-spoken diplomacy as well as the big stick. Alexander thought at times that they were getting through to the thick-headed and dull-witted politician, but he wasn't sure.

"Alonzo, my good man, if the Separatists decide to bring their terrorism into your star system, there is very little that Governor Brown could do about it. The Arcadian Naval Guard is little more than a rescue service. You would be at their mercy." Alexander argued his point. "It takes a lot of resources to keep a defense force there, and how do you expect we'll pay for that?"

"Nevertheless, Mr. President, we have a major ground force. Do not forget that our planet has been inhabited for over a century and we have a million-man Armored Guard fully equipped with M3A16 transfigurable tank squadrons. Granted they are not the more modern version used by the U.S. Army, but they are still a considerable force. Governor Brown feels, and I concur, that we can take care of ourselves, sir."

"Even if you are blockaded from space?" Sehera asked. "We only have your protection and best interest in mind, Alonzo."

"Much appreciated, madam, but I'm not certain it is necessary. The governor would like to take steps to insure that no Seppy attack from space would occur, though." The ambassador seemed to be talking out of both sides of his mouth or in circles, and Alexander couldn't tell which. *What the hell did he mean by that?*

"What steps? The only steps on the table are to accept the tax structure as it is, at least temporarily." Sehera sounded puzzled and for damned good reason. Alexander was beginning to believe that the Arcadians had made a deal with somebody in Congress to hold over the president. But for what gain? He had yet to put his finger on it, but there was most definitely a rotten apple somewhere in this deal, and Alexander was afraid he was going to end up with it.

"Alonzo, Alonzo, my friend, you have got to make Governor Brown see reason on this issue. What little intel we are able to get from the Separatists is that they are conducting a major buildup. I'm not a warmonger. Hell, I've been there, and I hate, with a capital *H*, war of any type. But I fear it is coming, and we'd better be ready for it, all of us. And we'd better figure which side we're on before it is too damned late!" Alexander emphasized his concerns, though he had very little intel from Tau Ceti to tell them anything. He hadn't spoken to Ahmi in over six years. That was the last they had gotten intel from the CIA, also. Moore was partly bluffing and partly going on a gut feel. He wasn't sure which one he was going on the most.

"You must acknowledge the importance of protecting yourselves from space, Alonzo," Sehera added. "If the Separatists manage to jaunt or QMT in to Ross 128, the first thing they would do is bombard the technology centers and bases across the system. Millions could be killed from space before there was ever an enemy foot set on Arcadian soil."

"Perhaps, but it is merely speculation that there is something at Arcadia the Separatists want. We have no reason to believe this. To the Arcadian people, it sounds fabricated to impose improper taxation upon us." Alexander was incredulous. For some reason, the big stick of the U.S. Fleet didn't seem to have as much impact on the man as it should have. Either he truly didn't believe that the Seppies were a threat, in which case he was an idiot, or he didn't think the U.S. Fleet would do anything about it, in which case he was an idiot. But Alexander had a hard time believing the solution was that simple. Alonzo's visit seemed more calculated, more strategic, and a hell of a lot more obfuscated than it would have been if the man were simply the idiot bureaucrat he first appeared to be.

The three of them talked and talked for the next hour or so and seemed to keep going in circles and couldn't reach a conclusion. After tea in the Rose Garden and a tour of the White House led by the president and First Lady, and the occasional stop for photo ops, enough of their time had been wasted. It finally felt to the three that there could possibly be some conclusion and resolution between Earth and the Ross 128 system, but the president was

going to have make good on promises to cut tariffs and have a
Navy supercarrier in the system. And larger contracts would have
to go to the manufacturers of Arcadia.

The larger contracts part only made sense after the secession of
the Tau Ceti system, anyway. Tau Ceti and the Martian Reservation had been the primary manufacturing base for humanity. After
the Exodus, all that had changed. Moore couldn't understand why
the Arcadians weren't jumping for joy because of the prosperity
this new arrangement was going to bring them.

The talks bogged completely down somewhere near the Kennedy
Room, so that was when Moore finally called them to an end.
He thought they had reached a logical stopping point for now,
anyway, and the dead horse had been beaten, rebeaten, and then
beaten again just for good measure. Also, they were slated for a
public press conference on the outcome of the meeting around
two in the afternoon, which was drawing pretty close.

"Next discussion, Alonzo, I want Governor Brown to be present. You should make that quite clear to him upon your return,"
Moore told him.

"Well, sir, I will take your proposal back to the governor, but
he will not be happy with the tariffs still being in place. After
all, my primary mission for this long trip was to have them at
least temporarily suspended to enable our economy to catch up
with the demands that the U.S. military buildup is putting on it.
We are having to reinvest into our infrastructure at too great of
a pace to afford these taxes, Mr. President."

"Just tell Donnie to hang in there, and maybe we can get
Congress to sway on them in the next session," Moore promised.

"I see, sir" was all the response the poker-playing ambassador
would say. Moore and Sehera led the ambassador back to the
Oval Office for some final discussions and preparations for the
press conference. They decided to tell the press that discussions
were positive and ongoing. Or at least that is what Alonzo had
led Moore to believe.

"Ladies and gentlemen of the press, of the country, good afternoon," President Moore said as he looked into the camera and
then at Ambassador Spellman. "Our friends from the colony at
Ross 128 have been patient in their understanding of the current
need to post tariffs on the imports of goods and services into

the Sol System in order to maintain our strong national resolve in protecting this colony as well as all other colonies and territories of the United States of America from outside attack by the Separatist rogue system at Tau Ceti. I have assured Ambassador Spellman that although Tau Ceti citizens may feel that they are no longer part of the United States, they are merely being misled by a few mad people who are fueling the Separatist sentiments and the entire movement. At no time in the past twelve years, now, or in the future, will the United States government accept the secession of Tau Ceti. And hopefully, with the resolve of all of the colonies, territories, and states of the Union, we will soon resolve these difficult times. I have asked the ambassador to speak to you today on behalf of his people at Governor Brown's request and approval. Ambassador."

Moore held out his arms, gesturing to the colonial ambassador at the podium next to his on the lawn of the White House. Photos were snapped continuously, and video and holo streams were being fed across the Sol System and out to the stars. President Moore clapped his hands, signaling to the press corp to do the same, and once the applause settled, Ambassador Alonzo Spellman cleared his throat and looked down at the podium briefly as he started to speak.

"Mr. President, First Lady, I thank you for your most gracious efforts today." Spellman raised his head, turned, and nodded to the president and offered him a gracious smile. Then he set back into a solid pose behind the podium and looked as if he were waiting for his AIC to post a speech in front of his vision in his mindview. Then he began again.

"Ladies and gentlemen of the United States, after a long negotiation with President Moore today I must relay the following as the status of the colony at the Ross 128 star system and all citizens there. I'm here for the purpose of announcing to you all, Congress, the Senate, the White House, and to you citizens, that I have satisfactory evidence that the Ross 128 colony and the citizens of Arcadia, by a solemn ordinance of her people in a convention assembled of systemwide representatives, has declared our demand of tariff cessation or separation from the United States." Spellman paused briefly for his words to sink in.

Moore had known that the representatives had granted the governor wide discretion to seek tariff relief, removing virtually all of the usual congressional oversight. But separation? Was the governor overstepping here, or had things really gotten that bad on Ross 128?

"Under these circumstances, of course, my functions are terminated here as an ambassador for the governor of the United States Colony of Ross 128, and I appear only as an ambassador for the governor of the free star system of Ross 128. It has seemed to Governor Donald Brown of Arcadia and myself only proper to give the president of the United States one last chance at holding our allegiance. After our negotiations today, it is clear that this is never going to happen. Therefore, the governor and I feel it necessary for us to say something on the part of the people I here represent, on an occasion as solemn as this, for our colony has been a part of the United States for over a century.

"Governor Donald Brown and I desire to make certain that it is known to the people of the Sol System that Arcadia has always advocated, as an essential cornerstone of political sovereignty, the right of a state to peacefully secede from the Union. On the other hand, we would be quite naive of history were we to think peaceful secession is usually the end result. Therefore, if I had thought that Arcadia was acting without reason, or without a history of debate with the Sol politicians of the improper taxation of our people and without a history of time and again undue taxation without representation, I might hesitate to be party to this act. Since history has shown us that this is not the case, under my theory of government, because of my allegiance to the system, planet, and people of which I am a citizen, Governor Brown and I have been bound by her people to take this action. Action in a clear and concise direction has never been more warranted in history than it is now. We debated long and hard over this decision, as we knew, as with the forefathers of the original Thirteen Colonies and those who orchestrated secession from the Union before the great Civil War, that our actions would lead us to only one of two paths: success or death in trying. In the historical words of Patrick Henry, "Give us liberty or give us death." With this secession, with over one hundred million people following over fifty million people from Tau Ceti and Mars who have already seceded from the Union, each and every one of you should rethink your policies and politics."

Moore began to feel his anger rise. He wanted to take the

microphone and shove it down the ambassador's throat. But he had to let the man finish. Then Spellman would go to prison and Moore would have his turn to speak.

"There was a time, in the beginning of America, where people believed that secession was both legal within the Constitution and purposeful within the needs of a state governing entity. Secession belongs in the Constitution as a peaceful solution to grandiose-scale predicaments. Our current predicament is, indeed, grandiose. It should be justified following the basis that all of the states, territories, and colonies of humanity are sovereign and of sovereign people. There was a time when none denied it. But this was before the great Civil War set precedent against this theory of government. I hope the time may come again, come again in fact today, when a better comprehension of the theory of our government exists than it did just twelve short years ago, and the inalienable rights of all of the people of humanity will prevent any one from denying that each state of many is sovereign, and has a peaceful means to that end. Thus, any sovereign should be able to reclaim the grants of freedom from any government entity which it has made allegiance, again, peacefully.

"Arcadia must therefore concur in the action of the people of the Martian Reservation and of Tau Ceti, believing their actions were indeed necessary, legal, and proper. And that the military response of the United States was not legal within the Constitution as it was no longer the laws of the Separatist people. In fact, the acts of the United States were none other than those of waging war against a separate sovereign country.

"We must recall the very nature, design, and birth of the United States of America and to the historical pact, if you will, which binds us all together, and has for so many centuries, even as mankind stepped out to the planets and now to the stars. The principles upon which our government was founded were that all men are created equal and that liberty above all is of utmost priority. This, I dare say, is what led the forefathers to rebel against King George III. I say then to the United States, would you deny your brethren in other star systems the right to the liberty of which they choose? Would you deny them the same rights held so dear by our historical forefathers?

"By the very act of denying us the right to withdraw from a government, that has become perverted and unsympathetic to the needs of the colonies disconnected by light-years of the coldness of space, you ignore and remove those rights of the colonists.

"As Jefferson Davis said, 'We but tread in the path of our fathers when we proclaim our independence, and take the hazard. This is done not in hostility to others, not to injure any section of the country, not even for our own pecuniary benefit; but from the high and solemn motive of defending and protecting the rights we inherited, and which it is our sacred duty to transmit unshorn to our children.'

"People of the Sol System, we are at an impasse in history. We are at that proverbial rock and hard place where I fear David must stand tall against a Goliath. Please recall that the United States was once that David against the British Goliath, and it stood fast and succeeded against complicated and unnerving odds. You must understand that we citizens of Arcadia and the Martian Separatists and the citizens of Tau Ceti have not been in league other than to say that we share a type of the general feeling of 'us against you.' This doesn't have to be hostility toward you but rather a sense of adventure and competition. Choices made today by you will determine if that competition is in friendly business or in the ugly business of conflict. I hope not the latter, as you are our brethren and we are yours. I therefore must express our desire for peaceful future relations with the United States even though the time has come for us to part political ways.

"In the event that you feel we cannot coexist peacefully and that you must bring disaster on us, then note that every portion of Arcadia—every man, woman, child, and artificial intelligence—will stand up to you to the very last drop of blood and the very last electron if that is what it takes to defend our sovereign rights. Unlike Jefferson Davis, who threatened to, and I quote, 'invoke the God of our fathers, who delivered them from the power of the lion, to protect us from the ravages of the bear; and thus, putting our trust in God, and in our own firm hearts and strong arms, we will vindicate the right as best we may,' *we*, the citizens of the star system known as Ross 128 of the governing body of the free people of Arcadia, will instead invoke the trust and friendship of President Elle Ahmi of Tau Ceti and the might of the United Separatist Republic. May God forgive us all. And may all humanity live in freedom, liberty, and happiness."

Once it was clear that Spellman had finished speaking, Moore nodded to his Secret Service team to take the man into custody. The press corps was both dumbfounded and teeming with questions and shouts of "Mr. Spellman, Mr. Spellman!" But none of the questions were answered. And the Secret Service didn't manage to get him into custody.

Spellman tapped at his wristwatch, and suddenly Moore could feel, hear, and see a very familiar buzzing, hissing, crackling, electric wave of light forming around the man, who then vanished into thin air.

Sehera immediately rushed to Alexander's side even as Secret Service agents surrounded them, trying to whisk them inside the White House.

"Alexander, we must stop Dee!" Sehera said urgently.

"Thomas, get Air Force One ready now!" he told his head bodyguard and friend.

Abigail, get the Sienna Madira *CO on the horn now!*

Yes, Mr. President. I'm already trying, the AIC replied.

"We're on it," he said to his wife, nodding for her to go with the Secret Service. But he shrugged off the hands trying to guide him and stepped up to the microphone where seconds earlier the ambassador had delivered his bombshell and disappeared. President Moore raised his hands to silence the crowd, then waited for the clamor to die down. Even after the crowd quieted, he paused, reflecting upon the gravity of the moment.

"My fellow citizens of the United States, including those in Ross 128, I wish I could say this came out of left field, but these seeds of sedition were planted years ago. The fact that the *former* ambassador not only deceived this administration as to the nature of our talks today but then hijacked this press conference for his own Separatist purposes—well, that was a bit of a shock. But we've come to expect this kind of underhanded behavior from the adherents of the terrorist Elle Ahmi. When it comes to Ahmi, we must expect the unexpected.

"I may just be a simple marine from Mississippi, but I can tell you this much—as much as Mr. Brown from Ross 128 and Ahmi in Tau Ceti would like to portray themselves as the good guys, they aren't. They aren't the revolutionary colonists who were grossly taxed by a tyrannous England without representation. And they sure as heck aren't after states' rights like Jefferson Davis, no matter how many times they quote him.

"No, my friends, my fellow Americans, if they want to compare themselves to rebels of years long past, they are not Americans, they are the French. They use the rhetoric of American freedom to disguise a return to tyranny, tyranny headed by a terrorist, Elle Ahmi. By their actions, shall ye know them.

"Do we target civilians? No, but the Separatists were willing to destroy an entire city on Mars just to cover their escape. And they were willing to kill tens of millions of citizens in Luna City.

"Do we put their people in concentration camps? No, but they do. I know, because I escaped from one of their death camps. I was the only survivor of that camp. The victims were tortured and murdered by Elle Ahmi, literally by her hands.

"As Abraham Lincoln said, 'Those who deny freedom to others, deserve it not for themselves; and, under a just God, can not long retain it.'

"You might be worried. *Can* we fight this war Elle Ahmi has brought to us? The Separatists and their pawns seem to have all this wonderful new technology. How can we possibly match them? Wouldn't it be easier all around just to let them go?

"And the answer is not just no, but hell no!

"It was George Washington who said, 'If we desire to avoid insult, we must be able to repel it; if we desire to secure peace, it must be known that we are at all times ready for War.' Those words are as true today as they were more than six hundred years ago.

"For the past two terms, we've done everything in our power to cut the size of government and return authority to the local level. We've sought to shrink government intrusion into individuals' lives and decrease the outrageous regulatory burden Americans had fallen under, while striving to keep our borders safe and our military strong and well-trained.

"How does this prepare us for war, you ask? It means that not only do we have the most professional, intelligent, and prepared military in the galaxy, we have the economic strength, public vitality, and flexibility of manufacture to support a war.

"And I can promise you one thing—with the new jump technologies, that war will be prosecuted so fast it will make those Seppies' heads spin. They may think they sprang a surprise on us here today, but they haven't.

"My friends, the forces of the *Sienna Madira* and the rest of our fighting men and women are *even now* taking the fight to the Separatists. And this is a fight we will win. For the sake of all humanity.

"Again, it was the very first Republican president, the great Abraham Lincoln, who said, 'Those who won our independence believed liberty to be the secret of happiness and courage to be the secret of liberty.' All I ask for, my fellow citizens, is your courage, and your belief in liberty. God bless you all, and God bless these United States."

Alexander took a deep breath and checked to make certain Abigail was already giving the orders to put the vast American military machine in gear.

Then he said, "As you can guess, I have important things to do today, so please forgive me for taking no questions at this time." Moore turned to his Secret Service contingent and his wife and motioned for them to move out.

CHAPTER 12

July 1, 2394 AD
Sol System, Oort Cloud
Friday, 2:17 PM, Earth Eastern Standard Time

Dee sat in the copilot's seat of the passenger shuttle and watched as Colonel Fink handled the controls like the seasoned Marine pro he was. She was still ecstatic from her short stay on the nation's flagship and getting to fly in real mecha with real ace pilots. The day couldn't get any better as far as she was concerned. Well, it would've been better if she had shot down DeathRay, but that little maneuver he had done was amazing and was tempting Dee to sway toward the Navy ROTC program instead of the marines. Her mind raced with the torment of such a decision. She didn't have to make it for two years tops, so she tried to put it out of her mind and focus on the wonder that was her trip thus far.

"You should have seen her, Clay," Jay said to her bodyguard. The two of them were sitting in the two seats behind the pilot and copilot's couches. "She was all over the place, thinking she was all badass. But I'll tell ya one thing, that Captain Boland really stuck it to her and the other marines." Jay laughed just a bit. Dee knew her wingman loved it if he ever could manage to get under her skin. She seldom let that happen. Dee had learned from growing up watching her father that being calm and collected when people were trying to get at you was one of the best defenses in deflating their attacks. When people saw that you didn't really care about their verbal abuse, they tended to quit wasting the effort.

"Yeah, Clay, you should have seen it." Dee turned back toward them with a sly grin. "Jay lasted at least forty seconds or so. He was so awesome right up until that marine blasted him out of the sky." She smiled at her wingman. Had she been six or twelve she might have stuck out her tongue, but the smirk she gave him was quite sufficient.

"Knock that chatter off, you two dead-ass nuggets," Fink grunted at them. "I'm trying to fly to another star system here."

"Passenger Shuttle *Hermione* all clear for QMT in ten seconds," the QMT facility-control AIC announced to Fink.

"Roger that, tower. We're ready when you are."

The four of them sat silently for the countdown and watched as the quantum membrane of the universe was tugged together between stars that were nearly fifteen light-years apart. The large light sphere appeared and then rippled into a two-dimensional illusion. The view of the Oort Cloud below blended and then swapped with a different view of an almost exact duplicate QMT facility, but this one was orbiting a plush blue-green world just below it rather than out in the cold depths of deep space.

"Welcome to the Ross 128 Colony of Arcadia, U.S. Passenger Shuttle *Hermione*," the Arcadia tower AIC announced.

"Thank you, tower," Fink replied and then turned to Dee. "Cadet Moore, why don't you take it from here. I'm gonna stretch my legs a second."

"Roger that, Colonel." Dee took the controls and had her AIC tap her into the DTM link to the traffic-control AIC. She paid little attention to the colonel as he made his way between Stavros and Clay to the back.

Dee followed the flight corridor she was given by the tower AIC, with little concentration required. After all, it wasn't like dogfighting with ace mecha pilots. The tower told her to pull into a parking orbit momentarily and hold for further instructions. Then she heard a muffled *spitapp spitapp* and then another one behind her followed with grunts and the sounds of a scuffle. Dee swiveled the copilot's chair around just in time to move out of the way as Clay and Fink slammed into it. The two men were scuffling over something that Fink had in his right hand.

Dee twisted past the two men and barely managed to avoid a clawing grasp from Fink's right hand. She lunged her body backward to avoid his grab just as Clay brought his forehead into

Fink's face twice. Fink leaned back and shook his head as if to clear his vision just in time for Clay to follow up with another head-butt to the bridge of his nose, cracking it and sending blood streaming down his face.

Dee lost her balance and landed in her wingman's lap. As she recovered and pulled herself up, she said, "Sorry, Jay." But then realized that Jay felt not only quite limp, but wet. She looked over her shoulder at her friend. He had a blank stare in his eyes, and the right side of his head was blown completely out with gray matter and red blood streaming down his face and neck onto his shirt. Jay was dead. Dee screamed in horror and jumped up from his lap only to slam back into the two men fighting over a railpistol. The impact flung her back between the two rear seats, down on all fours.

Get a grip and protect yourself, Dee, Bree screamed in her mindvoice.

Right, Dee thought and shook herself.

The scuffle continued in a flurry of hand-to-hand jabs, knees, head-butts, and elbows between Fink and Dee's bodyguard. *Spitapp, spitapp, spitapp,* she heard again and stood to rush Fink.

"No, Dee!" Clay yelled at her. "Stay out of this."

"No way," she yelled back at him as she leaped forward in a bicycle roundhouse kick, bringing the top of her right foot hard against Fink's back. The kick stunned him only slightly, but it was enough for Clay to twist inside his grip, backward head-butt him in the face, and then pull Fink's elbow down against his shoulder. There was a loud *crack*. Fink's right elbow hyperextended the wrong way, and he let out a scream of pain.

Dee jumped up at him again and slammed her left knee into his ribs, brought her left elbow down on his collarbone but missed it, and then she gave him a right knee into his back as hard as she could.

"Get off my back, you little bitch!" Fink, bloodied and with his right arm broken at the elbow, somehow managed to squirm out of Clay's grip and pushed off his back, sandwiching Dee between him and the bulkhead. Dee's head slapped against the viewport so hard she saw stars and wobbled to her knees.

Dee was dazed but managed to make out that Clay had blood trickling from his lips. Then she realized that he had a red spot on his chest. He had been shot, too. Dee forced herself to her feet and shook the stars out of her eyes with the hopes of another assault on the crazed Fink. But even though Fink had a broken arm, he still managed to hold them off with blocks and kicks, and then out of nowhere came a knife. Clay managed to avoid it once by falling backward, but he had just lost too much strength from his wound, and Fink was soon on top of him.

Clay met Fink's lunge with both his arms, but Fink put all his body weight behind the knife. Clay couldn't hold him off much longer.

"The gun, Dee!" he managed to say as the blade of the knife inched closer to his throat.

Dee turned and scanned the deck of the shuttle wildly for the gun, but it was on the other side of the two men. Instead, she threw her body into Fink, knocking him over onto his right side. His broken arm rammed into the pedestal of the pilot's chair, and he screamed in agony. Clay managed to push him the rest of the way off him and kneed him in the groin. Unfortunately, Fink fell right on top of the railpistol. Seeing this, Clay pushed Dee backward into the bulkhead and rose between her and Fink just as the madman raised the weapon and fired. *Spitapp, spitapp.*

There was absolute quiet for a brief second. Dee looked into Clay's eyes, and he smiled at her with his big, toothy smile. Red poured from the corners of his mouth and off his tongue.

"Sorry, Dee . . ." He collapsed dead on the floor at her feet.

"What did you do?" Dee screamed and started at Fink but then quickly froze as she was staring at the barrel of the railpistol.

"Quiet!" Fink shouted at her while waving the pistol in her direction. "Don't you make a fucking move, or it *will* be your last. Now sit down! Turn back around in that chair and keep your hands up where I can see them."

Dee did what she was told. Fink carefully approached her, then grabbed her left arm and pulled it behind her chair with his good arm. She briefly thought of trying to overpower him, but Fink jammed the barrel of the railpistol into the side of her head. He winced in pain when he did it, but there was no doubt he could still pull the trigger.

"Don't even think about it." He then zip-tied her hand to the railing of the chair back and continued to do the same with her right hand.

"Why are you doing this, Fink? What do you hope to gain? You killed them. You killed Jay for no reason. You, k-k-killed Clay!" Tears ran down her cheeks. She and Jay had been classmates for years. They were wingmen, and at one point there had been some sexual interest. Now he was dead. She had known Clay since she had been six years old, and the man was one of her heroes. And for some reason this madman had just killed them both!

"Casualties of war, Dee."

"Don't call me that. You don't have the right to call me Dee or anything else, you fucking monster! My father will hunt you down to the ends of the galaxy if you harm me. He will rip your fucking eyeballs out!" Dee screamed at him uncontrollably. But Fink only laughed at her as if she were a silly little girl.

"It won't be me that he will go after, girly. I'm just a middleman. And in about ten minutes I'll be a very fucking rich middleman." Fink double-checked that Dee couldn't move. He pulled the ties tighter, and Dee could feel them cutting into her wrists.

Fink stepped back behind her and began rummaging through something in the back of the shuttle. Dee managed to swivel her chair, but as she did Fink brought the pistol up with his left hand. Once he realized she wasn't going anywhere, he set the pistol down and went about digging through the locker in the side panel of the shuttle. He finally found what he was looking for, apparently, and pulled it out with his good arm.

Bree, what do we do? Dee thought. Fink was preoccupied with something; now might be a chance to come up with a plan, or something, anything.

I'm searching for help, Dee, but we are a long way from home. I've contacted the governor's mansion, but got an odd response.

What do you mean?

They claim to no longer recognize U.S. authority.

This ain't good. Keep broadcasting my emergency signal. There has to be somebody out there that can help.

"Aha!" Fink pulled out a first-aid kit and popped the latch on it. "This will do."

He found an emergency hypo of immunoboost and peeled the plastic wrapper off with his left hand and his teeth. Holding the hypo up, he turned and glared at Clay's body and then jabbed the hypo in his neck. There was a quick *hiss*, and then he tossed the empty medicine tube on the deck. Then he felt about his right elbow with his left hand.

"Shit, at least it ain't broken. Just dislocated." He muttered to himself and then yanked his arm outward, popping the bones back in place. "Fuck!" he screamed.

"Well, come over here and I'll break it for you, if you like," Dee spat at him.

"You've got spunk, kid. I give you that much. Most kids in your position could be spoiled little worthless brats. But you're not. Oh, well, sometimes life is a meat grinder."

"You are a disgrace, Fink. A murdering goddamned disgrace and for certain not a U.S. Marine." Dee struggled against the chair briefly, until she realized that she wasn't going to pull free and was only cutting her bonds more deeply into her wrists. She screamed again in anger.

"Hey, haven't you heard the saying, 'Once a marine always a marine'?" Fink gave her an evil look.

"Yeah, well, apparently, it's just an expression, you piece of shit."

Daddy ain't gonna get a chance to kill this motherfucker, because I am so gonna rip his goddamned head off and shove it up his ass!

I hear you, Dee. You hang in there.

CHAPTER 13

July 1, 2394 AD
Sol System, Oort Cloud
Friday, 2:17 PM, Earth Eastern Standard Time

DeathRay finally had a few minutes to himself to relax. Fish had asked him if he wanted to hit the galley and get a drink or two, but it had been a fairly long day already. He pulled his boots off and slid out of his flight suit down to his underwear and crashed onto his rack.

"Long day," he said audibly. When he was alone he liked to talk to Candis through the speakers in his cabin. Jack had been in the Navy for more than twenty years and didn't see family much. In fact, he only kept in touch with his grandfather, who lived in Texas. Otherwise, he was pretty much alone other than his military family. Candis was as close to a wife as he had. If a small sunflower-seed–sized plastic-coated artificial-intelligence computer installed in his brain counted. He closed his eyes and did a few relaxation breaths. "We should go on a vacation sometime. Maybe skiing, or to a beach somewhere."

"You got that right, Jack. You've been saying we were gonna do that for about five years now." His AIC changed the subject. " How about that First Daughter?"

"Not bad. Sure not what I'd have expected had I not met her father and mother on a few different occasions. That apple sure didn't fall far from the tree."

"I think she was kind of, well, interested in you, Captain."

"What? You're out of your mind, Candis."

"I'm not so sure, sir. She eyed you pretty closely and hung on every word you said." Candis had a slight hint of goading in her voice.

119

"She was in love with the FM-12s, Candis. Not me."

"Whatever you say, Jack."

Jack kept his eyes closed and let his mind wander. He'd been controlling his thoughts all day; driving the quantum mechanics of the DTM links of fighting mecha took a heavy toll on the mental faculties. Most good pilots learned to relax after flying to let their physical body recuperate while letting the mind rest as well.

"No, she sure didn't. I thought she was going to get you for a second there."

"Not a chance. Just letting her feel that false sense of security before I squashed her." Jack laughed with a purposeful tone of arrogance. The tone was only for show, as he had lost all sense of arrogance on the battlefield decades earlier. His true persona was the cool and level-headed confidence of a seasoned veteran. He just considered himself good at his job.

As Jack's mind flowed from thought to thought in random order, he came to the memory of when he had met President Moore for the first time. It was just after the Battle of the Oort, when he and Fish had teleported back to Earthspace, fighting the Seppy ship hell-bent on doing a kamikaze header into Luna City. The president had invited the two pilots to the White House.

At that time Jack hadn't had a chance to read through, much less to understand, the data the CIA agent he knew only as Nancy Penzington had transmitted to his AIC, but she had warned him not to trust anybody. Well, Jack had considered that she couldn't have meant the president himself. So while he and Fish were shaking hands and passing pleasantries with the man, he had his AIC send the data to the president's AIC, along with an explanatory message. Moore never even changed his facial expression during the exchange. He'd make one hell of poker player was what Jack thought after that meeting.

He had also met the entire First Family at several other political events as he had become a poster boy for the president to parade in front of the press at major public addresses. Moore had apologized to DeathRay about doing so, but Jack just assured the president that it was an honor for any Naval aviator. Jack and Moore never did speak of the data he had transferred, but Candis assured him that his AIC had gotten it.

The data itself was nothing short of incredible. Apparently the U.S. had developed a prototype design for the quantum-membrane teleportation technology decades earlier in a top-secret program.

There were even drawings of the big QMT facility design, personnel QMT pads, and mention of projecting a QMT forward from a facility to a place where there wasn't one. These thirty-year-old documents even had the math predicting that a device could be built that would allow projecting small masses, like people, back and forth between the stars without a large QMT pad on either end. Neither Jack nor Candis was a quantum physicist, but they understood enough of the math to make some conclusions from the data. It looked to them like a wristwatch-sized device could collect enough vacuum energy to perform one human teleport as far as twenty or thirty light-years.

Somehow all of the QMT information had been transferred to the Separatists but managed to be lost from history as far as the U.S. military was concerned. The entire concept of QMT seemed to have been erased from any databases—only to reemerge after President Moore had taken office. Moore had managed to dig it up somewhere and started putting it to use. Jack was curious what had happened to the scientists that had developed these concepts. Had they just vanished? Had they been murdered or kidnapped by the Seppies?

Finally, Moore got two prototypes constructed on the USS *John Tyler* and the USS *Abraham Lincoln*. Then, at about the same time the technology was about to go on line, it was leaked to the press. Moore originally had gotten the blame, Jack recalled, but it turned out to be some sort of coincidence that the Seppies and the U.S. had developed the tech simultaneously and perhaps independent of each other. And it was all part of some FBI sting operation to catch some Seppy spies that were congressional staffers. Yeah, that was bullshit if Jack had ever heard it. Clearly the Seppies had managed to develop the Stingers, Gnats, and Orcus mecha independently, and they just accidentally looked like their U.S. military counterparts, too. And if you believed that one, Jack could pull on his left ass cheek and play the Navy fight song out his sphincter. Something stunk somewhere—something other than Jack's sphincter.

Jack had been thinking on that data for more than six years, and he wasn't anywhere closer to figuring out exactly what it meant than he had been the day he had it transmitted to him. He had decided that there were serious moles within the U.S. government infrastructure that must be sympathetic to the Separatists. In order for them to get such highly classified information, they had to be pretty well-connected. Perhaps there were congressmen and women or senators on the intelligence or defense committees that were Separatists at heart. Jack wasn't sure. And spinning it over and over in his mind only got him all worked up.

He focused his mind on the blackness of space. Then he began to slowly drift off to sleep.

"General quarters! General quarters. All hands, all hands, report to duty stations immediately. Prepare for battlestations call," the ship's AIC said over the 1-MC intercom and through QM wireless to all AICs aboard the *Sienna Madira.*

"What the hell?" DeathRay jerked himself up via the built-in reflex to the general quarters call. "How long was I asleep, Candis?" He stretched and rubbed at his eyes.

"About thirteen minutes, Captain. I guess there is no rest for the wicked."

"Goddamned right," Jack muttered as he shook himself to and then threw on his UCUs and put a toothbrushing cube in his mouth. "Got any idea what this is about?"

"No, Jack. But the admiral has ordered all the senior officers to the briefing room."

"That doesn't sound good. Start scanning the news feeds for me." He spat out the cube into the sink and wiped his mouth with his sleeve. Jack slipped his boots on and pressed the seal tab. They suctioned in place, and the color scheme of his uniform set itself to Navy blue. He slapped on his name tag, insignia, and wings, and stuck the black beret typically worn by mecha jocks in his back pocket. Then he was out the hatch in a mad rush toward the main briefing area.

Ross 128 just seceded from the Union, Jack! Candis thought to him.

"Down ladder! Make a hole, seamen." Jack turned the corner of the corridor into the mostly full stairwell. The enlisted men in his way hugged the bulkhead or flattened their backs to it.

Oh shit! Dee! he thought. *They'll shut the QMT gate down first thing. And you know they'll try to nab her.*

She is with a bodyguard and a seasoned marine, the AIC said.

Yeah, against an entire damned planet. Those ain't good odds for Dee. DeathRay didn't like this situation at all. He really liked the First Daughter and hated to see her get caught up in the middle of bad shit, again. *That kid just has some bad luck, doesn't she?*

It's not her fault. And this all seems timed too coincidentally to me, Candis added.

Good point. Dee just happens to arrive at Ross 128 just moments before they secede from the Union and shut down the teleporter. Yeah, bullshit. This was another one of those coincidences where the Separatists were concerned. Who knew what that crazy bitch, Elle Ahmi, had up her sleeve. This could be the start of a full-scale invasion. He hoped like hell that Ahmi didn't get her hands on Dee.

"Hold the elevator!" he shouted as he rounded the corner to the main tower elevator. It was filling fast, and there were several officers piling in.

"Captain Boland, you barely made this one." Colonel Warboys held the door for him. Warboys never smiled as far as Jack could tell. The Army man was all business. Even when he cracked a joke, it was sometimes hard to tell if he was laughing or grimacing.

"Thanks, Colonel." Jack caught his breath. "Any idea what's up?"

"Did you hear about Ross 128?" Warboys asked.

"Yeah, and the First Daughter just passed through the QMT."

"Sounds too coincidental if you ask me." Warboys reached into his pocket and pulled out a pack of stimgum. "Want a slice?"

"Hey, do I look that bad?" DeathRay grinned and took the gum. Almost as soon as the stick hit his tongue he felt a wave of energy rush through his body, and he was as wide awake as he'd ever been in his life.

"It's been a long day already. And I suspect it is about to get a hell of a lot longer." Warboys looked blank for second. His AIC was telling him something.

"Shit, gonna need something stronger than gum, then, Colonel."

"Me, too, Jack. Me, too."

A matter of minutes later, very short minutes, and the main briefing room one deck below the CDC filled in and the doors were pulled shut. More than a thousand officers and SNCOs filled the room. The more senior ones were seated forward of the room and the lower ranks filed backward. There were hundreds standing against the rear and side bulkheads of the auditorium. Jack and Warboys sat next to each other in the front row. General Chekov marched across the stage and stood at attention.

"Rear Admiral Wallace Jefferson!" the XO grunted. Everybody stood to attention. The admiral walked across the stage and nodded to the XO, who then turned and marched off the stage and stood by a seat in the front row of the auditorium.

"At ease. Be seated," RADM Wallace said calmly. "At fourteen-seventeen Earth eastern standard time, the ambassador from the Ross 128 colony known as Arcadia announced from the White House that the colony was seceding from the United States of America and that they were aligned with the Tau Ceti separatists and their terrorist leader, Elle Ahmi. The ambassador made his statements and then subsequently vanished into thin air in the same manner as is indicative of a top-secret technology to teleport a single individual from one star system to the other without a QMT pad known by mathematicians as a 'snap-back algorithm.' We have no idea where he teleported to at that point. And now we have been ordered to muster rapidly and QMT into the Ross 128 system and take the government and National Guard units by force. The Outer Fleet is mustering here at the Oort Facility as rapidly as possible and will hold here under the direction of Rear Admiral Walker aboard the USS *Anthony Blair*." The admiral paused briefly to get his breath and gather his thoughts then continued with the briefing.

"The colonists on the other side of the QMT bridge have shut down communications with us. We will have to do a QMT forward projection from our facility with no way of returning home unless we retake the QMT facility there or take the long eighteen-month hyperspace jaunt. Either way, we are going, and we are going to take that system. You senior officers are having all the pertinent mission goals, data, and battle strategies available at this time transmitted to your AICs. You have thirty minutes to put your teams together and prepare your battle plans and tactics, because we QMT for Ross 128 at fifteen hundred hours precisely and will come out on the other side shooting. We are the tip of the spear of this attack. Thirty minutes behind us will be the USS *Abraham Lincoln*, the USS *Theodore Roosevelt*, and the USS *John Tyler*. The rest of the Outer Fleet will hold here unless we need them. We will have a team of couriers on board each ship equipped with top-secret snap-back transmitters that will enable them to bounce back and forth between systems to give status reports until we take the QMT facility and turn the long-range QMT communication systems back on.

"Now, there is someone else who would like to speak with you." RADM Jefferson turned to the big screen behind him and stood at attention. "Mr. President?"

The big screen blinked on, and a three-dimensional projection of President Alexander Moore and the First Lady standing in front of the *Resolute* desk in the Oval Office jumped out on the stage.

"Thank you, Admiral Jefferson. Ladies and gentlemen." Moore nodded at the senior crew of the flagship of the U.S. Navy and appeared to be looking at each and every one of them. "What we are asking you to do today is to go to war. We cannot let another colony effectively secede from our great nation. You, the brave men and women of the U.S. military's ultimate might, the USS *Sienna Madira*, must go forth and take back that system. If we fail today, I fear that we will fall into a horrible war, one that will be far worse than all the previous civil wars combined. We must put a stop to this separatism today! I know that I am asking you to leap into the unknown without a clear path home. But we are faced with a task that must be accomplished, or our way of life as we know it may fade into history. We have to take the fight to these Separatists before they bring it home to the Sol System. Good luck, God bless you, and may God bless the United States of America." The president and his wife stood motionless and looking solemnly at the officers. The admiral and the XO turned and waited for the auditorium to come to attention, and then over a thousand men and women saluted. President Moore stood stern and returned the salute. Then the holo projection blinked out.

"All right! You heard the president. Let's get to work." The XO turned and shouted to the crowed. "DeathRay?"

"Sir!" Jack shouted from down front and to the right of the stage.

"Put Deuce on CAG duties right now, and you stay put."

"Yes, sir." Jack stayed put. *Candis, transmit the orders to Deuce to get the battle plan set up and the pilots ready to go.*

Yes, sir.

Jack, the XO, and the admiral waited for the crowd to clear the auditorium, which took about five minutes, five precious minutes. And DeathRay had no idea what this was going to be about. Finally, the auditorium was clear and the hatches automatically shut and locked themselves. The three of them stood on the side of the stage.

"Stand at attention and face the screen, Jack," the admiral said in a voice so low it was almost a whisper.

"Aye, sir." Jack turned and faced the screen at attention. Then a voice came through the speakers.

"Are we clear, Wally?" It was President Moore's voice.

"Yes, Mr. President," the admiral replied. Then the screen blinked back on, and the three-dimensional projection popped out, and the Moores were standing right in front of the supercarrier officers.

"Good. Captain Boland, good to see you," the First Lady said. "Deanna sent me a message about how wonderful a host you were to her. Thank you very much for that."

"Any time, ma'am. And it's good to see you too, ma'am." Jack wasn't sure how to respond.

"Okay, this is the deal, Captain," President Moore said. "We've got a problem that only DeathRay can handle. Can we depend on you, Captain?"

"Yes, sir. Anything I can do for you, Mr. President."

"Well, Jack, you see . . ." Moore paused as if he had to gather himself. Jack had never seen him like that. "They've got our daughter. The goddamned Separatist bastards kidnapped Dee, and we don't know what they plan to do with her or where they've taken her. As you know, she teleported into Ross 128 for a cadet mecha competition right after she left you. Well, she teleported there just moments before those bastards seceded and shut down the QMT pad on their side. But just before they shut down the long-range comms, the Secret Service received a transmission from her bodyguard's AIC that he and the other student with Dee had been killed and Dee was being kidnapped by Colonel Walt 'Rat' Fink. You met him, I gather?"

"Yes, sir. Sorry to hear this, sir. Whatever I can do, you can count on me, Mr. President."

"That is just what I wanted to hear, Captain Boland. Take whomever you want, whatever you want, and go get my daughter back safely! You hear me, Captain? You do whatever it takes!" Moore's face was furiously red, and the veins on his forehead were throbbing. The man looked ready to explode. And Jack didn't blame him at all.

"Yes, sir. I'll get her back, sir."

"Jack," the First Lady interrupted. Tears formed in her eyes. "She may act all tough, but she is still just a kid. Don't let her do something stupid. And bring her home, please."

"Yes, ma'am. I understand, ma'am."

"And DeathRay," Moore added. "The fewer people that know what's going on, the better chance we'll have. We sure don't want the press in on this."

"Of course, Mr. President."

"Godspeed, Jack. Good luck."

Holy shit!

CHAPTER 14

July 1, 2394 AD
Sol System, Oort Cloud
Friday, 2:41 PM, Earth Eastern Standard Time

"Tommy, why don't you try this on for size?" First Sergeant Tamara McCandless handed the soldier a new insignia patch as they made their way down the corridor heading to the drop-tube hangar bay. All the AEMs had been ordered to battlestations. "Congratulations, Gunnery Sergeant Tommy Suez."

"Thanks, Top." Tamara watched as he pulled the staff sergeant patch from his shoulder and stuck it in his pocket. He smiled thinly as he slapped the new rank insignia onto the shoulder of his UCU top. The patch melded with the fabric and then became seamless with the shirt. "Now I'm making the big bucks," he said with a laugh.

"You and me both, Tommy," Tamara agreed.

"Any idea what is going on?" Tommy asked.

"Yes, the Ross 128 colony just seceded from the Union, and we're going to stop them," Tamara replied with a calm, matter-of-fact tone to her voice. She didn't want to excite her new gunny.

"Holy shit! The president's daughter just went there." Suez had briefly met her before she got all tangled up with the mecha jocks earlier in the day. He had followed Colonel Roberts' orders and went down to the hangar bay to meet the dignitary. He even got her autograph. Suez was a full-blooded true marine through and through, but he was also a Republican at heart. It had been a big thrill for him.

"You would imagine that the most powerful man in the known galaxy would get a little pissed if his daughter were put in harm's way." Tamara hadn't thought of that until now. She had been so busy all morning that she hadn't had any time to think of the dignitary visitor. But the President's daughter was trapped at Ross 128. She hoped somebody was going to go get her.

"Are we going to get her?"

"No, Gunny. We are going to take the QMT facility, transition it to a reserve team, and then drop to the planet below and take it." At least that was how the colonel had described their mission.

About that time a young-looking Marine officer in UCUs rounded the corner in a hurry, headed in the opposite direction. He was the new second lieutenant the Robots were expecting. Tamara and Tommy stepped aside and saluted as he walked by; the new gunnery sergeant gave his best salute to the new second-ranking officer of the Robots.

"Excuse me." Second Lieutenant Zachary Nelms nodded and kept on his way, not returning the salute. He looked very preoccupied to Tamara, but she didn't give a shit. The second lieutenant continued on in the other direction as Tamara and Tommy stood there holding their salutes and looking shunned. Tamara could see that Suez wasn't sure what to do in response, and, in fact, he was probably feeling a bit belittled by the lack of gesture. There were varying protocols for indoor and outdoor salutes, and there had been protocols for them on naval vessels throughout history. But with the advent of mixed forces on the mammoth supercarriers, the philosophy or rule of thumb of "when in doubt, whip it out" had become the standard for saluting. It was a form of showing respect. And Suez and McCandless had just been disrespected.

"Well, that goddamned little shit," Tamara fumed. "Excuse me a moment, Tommy," she told Suez and headed back down the corridor after the young officer.

"Excuse me, Lieutenant, I'd like a moment of your time," Tamara said as she hurried up beside the second lieutenant and looked down at him. She was nearly two meters tall and athletic as hell. She had played both basketball and volleyball in college and probably could have gone pro. She might still after she retired and got her next rejuv, but for now she was happy being the SNCO of Colonel Ramy's Robots of the U.S. Marine Corp 3rd Armored E-suit Marines Forward Recon Unit. She was tall, muscular, and a trained heartbreaker and life-taker. *Intimidating* would be a good word to describe her.

"Not now, First Sergeant, I'm in hurry," he replied.

Oh, no, he didn't, Tamara thought.

"Well, sir, then I'll walk with you, but you are going to hear what I have to say, sir," Tamara said sharply and right to the goddamned point. *Goddamn fresh-outs,* she thought.

"All right, First Sergeant, uh, McCandless." He looked at her name tag as if making a mental note to report her later to the CO of the Robots.

"Well, sir, what do you see as the role of senior NCOs, sir?"

"The NCOs are to keep my marines and their equipment functioning as a well-oiled heartbreaking and life-taking machine," the second lieutenant said with a whole lot more than just a hint of annoyance in his voice. He almost sounded perturbed to Tamara. She didn't give a flying rat's ass.

"Yes, sir. That is half of the NCO's job. The other half of it is to act as an experienced advisor and mentor to junior officers, sir. You are a second lieutenant, sir, and have been active duty at best not even a year, sir. Most of the NCOs will have been in service for several years and even decades. Myself, I've been in twenty-one years, and Gunnery Sergeant Suez back there has eight years in, sir. I served at the exodus on the ground at Mons City at the battle for the main dome and at the Battle of the Oort. Gunnery Sergeant Suez back there was absolutely key in the victory at the Battle of the Oort. Saluting is a common courtesy and a show of mutual respect, sir. *Mutual respect.* And not saluting is a damned piss-poor way to slap the face of an enlisted person, whom you've never met and don't know from Adam, sir. Now, I'm most definitely not saying this out of vanity or need for you to salute me or to toot my own horn, sir. I'm saying this as your first mentoring session. We are about to stick our goddamned heads into the mouth of the lion in a matter of minutes, Lieutenant, and you sure as shit don't want to start off by letting your soldiers think that you think you are above the common courtesy of saluting seasoned veterans of the United States Marine Corps, Sir!" Tamara gave the second lieutenant her best drill-sergeant glare and half expected him to jump down her throat and go tattle to the colonel. But the young officer's facial expression changed in a way that she didn't expect. And he stopped walking toward the elevator.

"Thank you, First Sergeant McCandless for pointing that out to me," he said and turned the other way in an even bigger hurry.

"Huh?" she said, surprised. *What, no argument? That just takes all the fun out of this.*

Maybe he's a good marine and just needed that lesson, her AIC added.

Well, his file looked good. And the colonel handpicked him out of his class.

Tamara followed him back down the corridor but stayed far enough back to not look like she was following him. She simply kept him in view. Then the young lieutenant did the damndest thing. He chased Gunnery Sergeant Tommy Suez down and apologized to him. Then he shook his hand. And then he saluted him as crisply as any marine could.

Oorah, she thought.

Indeed, her AIC added.

Better send a note to the colonel that the new lieutenant and I had a run-in so it doesn't blindside him if he complains.

Affirmative. Memo sent, First Sergeant. I bet he never brings it up. Might be too embarrassing for him. The colonel is talking to Colonel Warboys, and they have worked out a sketch of a battleplan. He says to get the Robots ready and to quit harassing his new officers. I'm DTMing you the battleplan now.

I see it. Looks awful familiar to me, Tamara thought.

Reminds me of six years ago when we took another QMT facility, the AIC said.

Yeah, and it was a meat grinder then.

"Again, thank you, First Sergeant. Feel free to keep those mentoring sessions coming." The second lieutenant hurried back by her, and she saluted him as he passed. Second Lieutenant Zachary Nelms stopped and returned the salute.

Now we better get our asses in gear. Tamara hurried back in the direction of the hangar bay to catch up with Suez and the rest of the Robots.

"What was that all about?" Tommy asked her.

"Just breaking in the new LT," she replied. "Tommy, get the Robots on line and ready to drop with the Warlords. The colonel is talking to Colonel Warboys right now about our strategy, but we will be dropped on the QMT facility with them, and our mission is to take back that pad. Assuming all that goes well, then we'll most likely be teleported to the planet to hold or take some ground there. We go in hot and loaded with everything we can carry. Got it?"

"Got it."

"All right, all right, let's listen up," Lieutenant Colonel Caroline "Deuce" Leeland shouted from the nose of her FM-12 mecha. She stood there above all the pilots assembled in the aft cat room. Marine and Navy mecha filled the room as far as the eye could see hundreds of meters in either direction and several mecha deep above them. The floor was filled with pilots surrounding her plane. Behind them techs and robots scurried about, loading planes with missiles and ammo and recharging or repairing some component at the last minute. "We have about fifteen minutes before we deploy. Fish!"

"Hooyay!" Lieutenant Commander Karen "Fish" Fisher—Death-Ray's wingman—shouted.

"You have the Gods of War. Your mission is to protect the ball with the *Madira* in the center," Deuce told Fish, meaning that the plan was for the Gods of War to protect a sphere around the supercarrier and keep enemy planes off the hull of the ship.

"Roger that, Deuce!" Fish shouted.

"Poser!"

"Hooyay!" the Navy commander shouted back.

"You take the Demon Dawgs to the bottom half of the ball and keep any resistance off the Utopian Saviors as we go to ground on the QMT facility. Keep those Seppie bastards in the ball and off the ground, got it?"

"Affirmative, Deuce!"

"Okay, Saviors, we are to create a bowl over the Warlords and protect those Army pukes. The Warlords are gonna take a squad of AEMs through enemy lines and take the control room of that facility. Make certain that those AEMs get there, got it?" Deuce shouted.

"Oorah!" was the response from the Marine mecha jocks of the Utopian Saviors.

"The other flight groups are deploying after us and will take on any target of opportunity. Once we have the QMT facility secured, we will then turn our attention to taking and holding that planet." Deuce pulled the zipper tab of her flight suit up and slipped her helmet on with a twisting motion. "All right then, let's mount the fuck up and get it done!"

DeathRay had decided that his best plan of action would be to go through the teleport already deployed from the supercarrier with the hope of slipping off without being noticed. Hopefully, the supercarrier, the flight wings, the drop tanks, the AEMs, and the AAIs would distract the Arcadians enough to not notice one lone Ares-T fighter. Theoretically, Dee's AIC would be broadcasting a QM signal that would in turn enable him to locate her. The signal was spread spectrum on an encoded hopping frequency that wouldn't be detectable without the key code. It would look like noise otherwise. But Jack, Candis actually, had the key code, so he would know where Dee was. That is, assuming that Dee was still in the Ross 128 star system. The beacon only had a range of probably a light-year at best. If Jack didn't find her at Ross 128, he would go to Tau Ceti next. Somehow.

DeathRay had devised—thrown together at the last fucking minute, actually—a plan, and that plan was to rocket in at maximum speed to whereever the hell Dee was, kill everybody around her, and get her the fuck out. Okay, it wasn't a very detailed plan, but DeathRay was good at making up shit as he went along, especially when it came to blowing stuff up. He had two personal QMT projector devices on his wrist. The jump coordinates had been set for the Oval Office. As soon as he managed to grab Dee, he planned to trigger the teleporters, and then the two of them would be out of the shit and safe in Washington, D.C. The trick was going to be finding Dee and probably killing a whole bunch of Seppies along the way. DeathRay worked his mind around what he was about to do. Not just anybody would be crazy enough to put themselves in such situations.

So here he went again into the shit. After six years of uneasy peace, it looked like the time he had been expecting soon had finally come. It was time for war with the Separatists, and all bravado aside, they didn't call him DeathRay for nothing. He was good at war. He hated it with a passion, but he was good at it. Jack and two crew chiefs had loaded his fighter with every piece of gear, sensors, hand-to-hand, and survival equipment that he could squeeze in. He had originally considered taking a trainer, but with the QMT personal projection device, he wouldn't be needing to fly Dee out. He crawled into his fighter off the ladder and sat down.

"Good hunting, DeathRay!" The deck chief in a red shirt snapped a salute from the top of the mecha-support scaffold. He didn't say a thing about all the firearms, grenades, knives, and other weapons stowed in the webbing of DeathRay's armored flight suit. Jack's mission was classified, and the chief knew better than to ask a bunch of questions. He just did his red-shirt chief job, which was to make sure the plane's ordnance was loaded and in proper functioning status. He did make one final comment. "Sir, hope you get to eat that bear you plan on scrapping with, and not the other way around."

"Roger that, Chief. Me, too. I could use a new rug for my quarters." Jack saluted back, and the chief quickly climbed down and was joined by a purple shirt and a fireman in orange coveralls with blue kneepads. They unhooked the power and com umbilicals then moved clear of the launching pad.

Jack locked his helmet and then settled into the cockpit—the one place he felt most at home. He felt the familiar hiss of the cool, dry air rushing into his suit as he plugged the hardwire connection from the universal docking port (UDP) of his fighter into the thin little rugged composite box on the left side of his helmet, which made a direct electrical connection to his AIC implant via skin-contact sensors in his helmet.

"Hardwire UDP is connected and operational. Lieutenant Commander Candis Three Zero Seven Two Four Niner Niner Niner Six ready for duty," Jack's AIC announced over the open com channel and in the cockpit speakers. Then directly to Jack's mind, *Let's go get 'em, Captain!*

Roger that, Candis!

Jack saluted the yellow-shirt flight-deck officer and started the take-off process. The canopy cycled down and the harness holding the fighter dropped it the last twenty centimeters to the deck. Jack both loved and hated the *squishing* feel from the landing-gear suspension, because it always reminded him of what he was about to do. He hated the lump in his throat and butterflies in his stomach that had become his natural reflex to the landing-gear squish. Too many times in the past it had meant hurtling out the ass end of the supercarrier into a storm of raining and streaking hell flying from all directions. But there was nowhere else he'd rather be.

Jack swallowed the lump, ignored the butterflies, and followed the launch sequence, as he had hundreds of times before. The green arrows on the deck lit up and pointed the taxiway directions for him to follow to the cat line. He moved his fighter in line for takeoff. He was presently the only one taking off before the QMT teleport of the supercarrier, but he was pressed for time. The jump was expected in just a couple of minutes. Jack caught a glimpse of his wingman, Fish, to his left. She saluted him, and he returned it. He hated leaving her alone. She was talking to Ensign Zeke "Dragon" Franklin. He was new to the Gods of War, and it looked like Fish was going to take him on her wing.

"This is double zero," Jack called over the tac-net to all the pilots in the hangar getting ready to go as well. "This is probably gonna be a mess of a furball, folks, and I want everyone covering their wings and following the plan as usual. Y'all listen to Deuce. Good hunting and good luck." He thought his faceplate down and pulled his mouthpiece closer with his teeth. His DTM mindview kicked in, but he ignored it for now.

"Fighter zero-zero call sign DeathRay, you are cleared for egress. Good hunting, Commander Boland!" the control-tower officer radioed. "Handing off to cat control."

"Roger that, tower." Jack went through his ritual as he had since the first actual combat mission that he'd come back from. "Y'all just keep the beer cold, and good ol' DeathRay will be back soon enough." Jack taxied to the "at bat" slot and braced himself for the "ball," chewing at the bite block and soaking in the fresh oxygen and stimulants.

"Fighter double zero, you are at bat and go for cat! Call the ball."

"Roger cat, double zero has the ball," Boland responded. The little gold catapult field alignment sphere blinked on in his DTM view, overlaying the projected launch window circle in the cat field before his fighter. He sighed a deep breath and focused on relaxing his body from head to toe. He closed his eyes for a split second as he prepared himself.

"Good hunting, DeathRay!" the catapult-field AI announced. Jack throttled the Ares-T forward and switched to hover as the landing gear cycled and extracted. It was always the same when he knew it was a real fight. He was nervous. He bit down hard on the temporomandibular-joint mouthpiece and eased the throttle just a little more forward so that the fighter slipped into the catapult field.

"Roger that. Double zero has the cat! WHOOO! HOOO!" Jack let out his ritual battle yell, and as usual it was muffled through the mouthpiece. The support tube for the bite block started pumping oxygen and stimulants in his face and mouth more rapidly to account for the g-load of the cat field. At over twelve Earth gravities of acceleration, for a brief instant the cats always gave Jack the exhilaration of being on one hell of a ride.

The stars filled his field of view, and the Oort facility was behind him. He pulled his fighter over and looped back along the same vector as the *Madira* but above it relative to the QMT pad. He pulled into a matching hover orbit about two kilometers above the bridge of the supercarrier. The plan was to QMT in at about a thousand kilometers from the Arcadian QMT facility, and then the supercarrier would accelerate across it dropping troops, tubes, and mecha. Jack would be scanning with his sensors and with his AIC's wireless QM transceiver for Dee. Hopefully, he would find her.

"CO Madira, DeathRay," he called over the net.

"Go DeathRay," RADM Jefferson's voice responded.

"I'm in position, Admiral. Whenever you're ready, sir."

"Roger that, DeathRay. And Jack?"

"Sir?"

"Good luck."

"Thank you. You, too, sir. DeathRay out."

CHAPTER 15

July 1, 2394 AD
Ross 128, Arcadia Orbital QMT Facility
Friday, 2:41 PM, Earth Eastern Standard Time

Ensign Bella Penrose, a.k.a. Nancy Penzington or Kira Shavi or a hundred other classified cover aliases, decided the best place to pick up gossip on the U.S.R. flagship was either in the galley or down in the hangar bay. She had been in the galley earlier, and it was dead in there, so she tried the hangar bay. She could always use the excuse that she was checking on her mecha. Hell, she was an officer of the flight wing, so she really wouldn't have to offer any excuses to the enlisted crew in the hangar.

Bella casually sauntered out of the main shaft elevator that led from top to bottom of the supercarrier as it opened onto the large open corridor leading to the hangar about ten meters across from it. There were crews in multiple colors of uniforms, shirts, or coveralls running to and fro. The hangar bay wasn't unlike any other she had ever been in. She followed the taped off pathway toward her almost brand-new second-generation Gnat. She had only been out in it maybe twenty times. According to the flight records, she was the first pilot assigned to it. She came to a stop at the nose of the fighter. The little fighter was a knockoff of the U.S. Ares-T mecha. The Seppy engineers must have gone to great lengths to reverse engineer a downed Ares-T, or they had stolen plans or perhaps a little of both. The result was a new generation of transfigurable and very fast fighting mecha. One thing that Bella was interested in was the fact that nobody during her training

137

process had so much as mentioned, much less trained her on, the U.S. Navy pilot maneuver where the vehicle would spin about in every direction madly killing everything in sight. Perhaps the targeting system for that capability hadn't been reproduced by the Seppy engineers. Perhaps they just hadn't thought about it because few Seppy pilots ever returned from such attacks.

"How's it hanging down there, sailor?" she asked a man in a purple shirt crawling around under her fighter. "Something up with my bird?"

"Uh, no, ma'am. Just doing the hundred-hour inspection." The petty officer first class crawled out from under the mecha and stood. "What can I do for you, Ensign Penrose?"

"Nothing. I just thought I'd get some air and couldn't think of a better place." She smiled her best girl-in-heat smile. That was always a good technique for greasing the lips of young male soldiers.

"I dunno, I could think of better places," the petty officer said as he unscrewed an umbilical from the empennage and started to drag it across to the next plane on his list.

"Need a hand?" Bella grabbed the umbilical farther behind him and tugged on it and helped him drag it.

"Uh, thanks, ma'am. Did you see all the hubbub a few minutes ago?" he asked her.

"No, what hubbub?" Now she was getting somewhere.

"Well, we had this shuttle come in just a bit ago. Some guy in a U.S. military school outfit led some young girl in a cadet uniform of some type around at the end of a pistol. She was zip-tied, and her mouth was duct-taped. Several fully armed grunts met them and marched them up to the elevator. Fireman Tibbs claims the elevator didn't stop till it went to the top, but she could just be making that shit up."

"That is interesting. Any idea who they were?" Bella had missed that somehow.

Must be the package that we were waiting on, Allison added.

The package is a person. Curious.

"Nope. Somebody said they thought the girl looked like somebody famous, but nobody could put their finger on just who." The sailor turned back to the umbilical and plugged it into the Gnat beside Bella's. "If you don't mind, ma'am, I better get this shit done before the chief rains down on my ass, ma'am."

"Sure, sorry to bother you, Simms," she read off his name tag. "Thanks for the gossip."

"You're welcome, ma'am."

Allison? She turned from the hangar and headed to the elevator.

I'm scanning for images of the two, the AIC replied.

What about AICs?

Wait a minute. I've hacked into the security-camera systems and have a couple of images coming in now. Allison displayed the images into Bella's mindview.

Holy shit! they both thought simultaneously.

That's Deanna Moore! Where is she, Allison?

Right now she is being held under armed guard in the CO's quarters. They had been stationed on the supercarrier long enough that Allison had learned her way in and out of most of the ship's less sensitive functions with simple hacks and without leaving a trace she had been in them.

Shit. Bella thought about it for a few moments. *We have to stay with her. See if you can figure out a way to contact her. Can you handshake with her AIC?*

I'm trying, but she has firewalled herself off from anybody sending data in.

Shit again.

How about the speakers of the CO's quarters? Allison asked.

Good. Can you take my mindvoice and project it on the speakers?

Yes, I can.

Then we need to get her to talk to us. Do it now.

Go when you are ready.

Will we be able to hear her?

Yes, I'm taking the input from the security sensors placed in the CO's quarters to keep an eye on her and rerouting that back to you. I'm also monitoring the sensors outside of the quarters, just in case.

Okay. Here goes. Ms Moore, I am an undercover CIA operative that just by coincidence is aboard this ship. I just discovered you are here. I will do what I can to help.

Bullshit! Bella heard in her mind.

Yeah, I wouldn't believe it, either, she thought. *That doesn't matter. Just do as they tell you and don't provoke them. I'm working on a plan to get you out of here.*

There was no response. Bella was pretty sure that the president's daughter didn't believe her. She at least hoped that in the back of the girl's mind it would give her hope and help prevent her from giving up.

What do we do? Allison asked.

I don't know. I'm working on it, she thought. She was startled almost out of her skin by the bosun's pipe.

"General quarters, general quarters, battlestations! All hands, all hands to battlestations. Prepare for incoming fire and immediate evasive QMT jump."

"What the hell?" Bella said out loud. She reflexively turned back toward the hangar, her Seppie pilot kicking in. But right now she had to be a U.S. CIA agent. She paused to think for a second.

Allison, give me a full DTM battleview from my mecha.

Okay, here goes.

The supercarrier became transparent, and she could see space in any direction. Several thousand kilometers out beneath them was the QMT facility, and below that was Arcadia. Then she saw it. Just off the QMT facility and coming in fast was a supercarrier. It looked like it was about to do a drop run on the facility.

I'm getting IFF pings from AICs everywhere, Bella. It's the Sienna Madira!

Goddamn. Talk about timing. Is Boland out there?

I've got him! He is.

Connect me to him now!

The QMT jump into Ross 128 went as planned. Jack squinted against the brilliant sphere of light he found himself engulfed in and readied himself for whatever might be on the other side. The view of the Oort faded out and a much brighter view of a blue and green planet beneath him burst into sight. The *Madira* was below him as planned, and the Arcadian QMT facility was out ahead and a little beneath them. How the Navs that ran the QMT jumps figured out just where to put a ship on the other side of a quantum mechanical event like the membrane jumps was beyond him, but it didn't matter. What did matter was that the jumps worked. And there he was.

"Warning, enemy contacts bearing seven thousand kilometers, two degrees theta, and nine degrees phi," his Bitchin' Betty dinged at him.

Candis, what is that out there?

Looks like a supercarrier, Jack.

When did the Seppies get a goddamned supercarrier?

I don't know.

Any sign of Dee's beacon?

I'm scanning. Just a moment. Candis paused briefly. *I have good news and bad news.*

Okay?

Dee is here. She is on that supercarrier.

Shit! What are we waiting for, then?

DeathRay slammed the throttle all the way to the stop, accelerating the fighter to top speed. The g-load pushed him into his seat at nine gravities. He rocked the HOTAS left slightly to line him up with the enemy carrier. It was moving toward the QMT facility very fast and would reach there long before the *Madira* made its run across it.

Jack! I'm getting a DTM hail from Nancy Penzington!

What? Can't be. She's dead. Jack had seen the ship that she was in blow up. *How the hell could she still be alive?* he wondered.

Well, then it is her ghost, because her verification code pans out. It is her.

Patch her in.

Boland? Are you there?

I'm here, Penzington. We thought you were dead six years ago.

Yeah, well, I'm not. Listen, Deanna Moore is aboard the enemy supercarrier here.

Yes, I know. I'm here to get her.

Well, you better goddamned hurry, because we are QMTing back to Tau Ceti in seconds!

Shit! Can you get to her?

No, not in time. Try to get here, fast!

Roger that, Penzington. You do what you can to keep her safe. I'm coming.

Hurry then.

"CO *Madira*! DeathRay!"

"Go DeathRay!"

"Sir, our missing package is on that supercarrier! I also have confirmation that Operation Bachelor Party is in play! Repeat, Bachelor Party is in play, and our package is on that enemy supercarrier! Bachelor Party has made visual confirmation."

"Understood, DeathRay!"

Jack pushed at the throttle more, but it was already against the stop. He wasn't sure he could take the g-load much longer anyway. He sure as hell couldn't keep talking and do it. Any further communications would have to be DTM or from his AIC only. Then he started taking on anti-aircraft fire from the Seppy supercarrier.

"Warning, enemy radar targeting signal detected. Warning, take evasive maneuvers," the Bitchin' Betty chimed.

"No shit!" he screamed back at it. Jack killed the throttle and yanked the HOTAS left and down and then in a corkscrew inward toward the ship. Orange tracer rounds the size of racquetballs tracked all around his flight path, but he managed to keep out of the targeting solutions. The AA rounds kept coming. His best chance to keep from getting shot down would be to get inside the range of those things. The only way to do that was to get really, really close to that enemy ship. That fit into his plans perfectly. The problem was that the enemy ship was a long goddamned way off, and he was running out of time.

As the enemy ship drew closer and closer to the QMT facility, Jack continued to struggle against the AA fire while trying to keep the most time-efficient vector to the QMT jump-intercept point. Jack was still way outside range of the QMT sphere that would appear.

"Fuck the AA. We either make it or we don't!" He pushed the throttle back down to the forward stop, picking the acceleration back up. At that high thrust, the evasive maneuvers put extreme g-loads on him—upward of thirteen gravities at times. But Jack had to persevere and beat that QMT before it was too late. He had no idea how he was going to slow down and not slam into the enemy ship if he got there, but first things first. He had to make it through the gate, or slowing down was a moot point.

"Come onnn!" he shouted. Several AA rounds hit the forward hull armored plating, but the SIFs held. The impact rocked the fighter's nose upward slightly, and Jack fought to correct the pitch. More AA tracked him, and he jerked the HOTAS left and right, tossing the mecha around like mad. His stomach retched several times, and he heaved into his faceplate. Only bile managed to make it out. He choked his stomach back down as best he could and fought against the wild ride. The fighter spun and pitched and yawed, with each evasive maneuver putting him under near bone-crushing pressure. Then a big sphere of light formed over the QMT pad and rippled inward.

"Mooove, damnit!"

The Separatist supercarrier accelerated into the QMT gate that opened and vanished in front of him. Jack held his throttle against the stop while he grunted and squeezed every muscle, fighting as best he could against blacking out.

We're not gonna make it! Candis shouted in his mind.

We're gonna make it! Jack thought.

Jack, we're not gonna make it!

We're gonna make it!

His vision began to tunnel in front of him, and everything went dark around him briefly. Jack grunted and fought blacking out as best he could. He squeezed his legs and abs. The pressure suit constricted around his body like a prey-crushing anaconda. It was all he could do to breathe. He forced his breath like a woman in labor with triplets. He bit so hard on his TMJ bite block that he thought he would bite through it. The biting action triggered more fresh oxygen and stimulants into his mouth. The stimulants helped him hold on to the tunnel vision a second or two longer.

"Aaarrrggghh!" he grunted in a most guttural scream. He would have pissed on a sparkplug if it would have helped and he could've actually moved to do it.

Kill the throttle, Jack! Kill the throttle!

Two things immediately went through Jack's mind. The first was that the rings of the giant gas planet filling the sky out in front of him were beautiful. They reminded him of Saturn. The second thing was that the supercarrier rapidly rushing against him was way too fucking close.

Reverse throttle, Jack!

"Warning, collision imminent. Brace for impact. Warning, collision imminent. Brace for impact," his Bitchin' Betty chimed.

"This is gonna hurt!" Jack yanked the throttle all the way to the reverse stop and then pitched the fighter over tail first toward the supercarrier. The propellantless drive of the mecha pushed him in the opposite direction of the relative speed he had with the supercarrier. But it wasn't going to be enough to prevent a catastrophic collision. And the maneuver made him vomit into his helmet. "Fuck!"

He gurgled and heaved a few times more as his suit cleared the faceplate by absorbing the stomach material into the organogel layer. He put his left hand on the eject handle but didn't pull it.

Give me a countdown to impact, Candis!

Roger that! Nine! Eight! Seven . . .

Jack kept the fighter's ass end to the ship right up until the last second. The supercarrier was all he could see, even though he was still several hundred meters away. At those speeds that was only seconds. He pitched the nose back over, placing the cockpit away from the supercarrier's hull. The seconds ticked slowly since the gravity load was well above ten gravities. Time crunched by slowly, but the deceleration was working.

Three! Now!

Jack brought down the nose of his fighter and shouted "Eject, eject, eject!" as he pulled the handle. The ejection couch fired its thrusters just as the fighter slammed into the hull of the Seppy supercarrier. Jack's fighter spread out into an orange and white ball of hot vaporized metal plasma. Then the ordnance and the powerplant blew, making the explosion even more spectacular.

Jack hoped the thrusters of the ejection seat would give him just enough deceleration to survive the impact. That didn't mean it wasn't going to fucking hurt like hell. Shrapnel from his mecha's impact against the hull spread out in a hemisphere in all directions and slapped into the backside of the ejection couch. Jack held his breath and prayed that none of it hit him. Statistics were on his side, though, since the impact was at such a high speed most of the big chunks stuck. Anything that escaped was small or vaporized, and the relative velocity wasn't extremely fast. His armored flight suit and the ejection chair should protect him.

How long to impact? he asked Candis, but it was too late. The couch slammed into the hull plating with an impact that would have broken his teeth were it not for the bite block in his mouth. The couch was designed to absorb a lot of impact, but Jack could still feel the vertebrae in his back crunch, fracturing his tailbone and rupturing several discs in his lower back and his neck. The pain was overbearing, and he passed out for a few seconds.

Jack! Captain Jack Boland! Captain Jack Boland! Wake up, Jack! DeathRay, DeathRay, wake up!

CHAPTER 16

July 1, 2394 AD
Ross 128, Arcadia Orbital QMT Facility
Friday, 2:45 PM, Earth Eastern Standard Time

"DeathRay and the enemy ship have vanished, Admiral!" the STO shouted from the science and technology officer's station. "Sir! We've got missiles launched from the planet and the facility!"

"Plot the trajectories for me, Captain Freeman," RADM Wallace Jefferson ordered his STO. "And see if you can detect what type of warheads they are."

"Aye, sir! Coming to you now. They're nukes, Admiral."

Wallace had the entire sphere of the battlescape in his mindview and could see the missiles firing up from the planet at near the speed of light. They were only a second away and not a lot he could do about them other than hope and pray that the ship's SIFs and armored hull plating held in place against the tactical nuclear warheads about to detonate against them.

"Full power to the SIF generators!" he shouted. There was no time for a hyperspace jaunt. "All countermeasures fire! Nav, evasive maneuvers! And keep the facility between us and the planet below!"

"Aye, sir!"

Sound it, Timmy!

Aye, sir.

Uncle Timmy sounded the bosun's pipe over the ship's 1-MC intercom. "All hands, all hands, brace for impact and incoming fire. All hands, brace for impact."

"Larry!"

"Sir!"

"See if you can get me some analysis of that ship that was just here! I hope they don't have more of those." The first wave of missiles hit before the evasive maneuvers and countermeasures could have any effect, and Wallace gritted his teeth.

A handful of the missiles slammed against the starboard hull structural integrity fields with multiple tens of kilotons each. The explosions rippled the SIF barrier fields with an opalescent blue wave of light. Seven smaller missiles hit random locations across the belly of the supercarrier. But unlike a turtle or an alligator, the belly of the *Madira* was as hard as any other part. The SIFs held, for the most part, but multiple systems were overheated, and there were a few hull breaches in some noncritical locations. There were no casualty reports or systems failures as far as the admiral could tell, and the attack was merely annoying. But you could never be too sure about how badly something was damaged by simply depending on diagnostic sensors.

"COB, check on my ship!" the admiral ordered the chief of the boat. The impact of the missiles rocked the ship upward and to port. The internal inertial dampening fields kicked in and reduced the effect of the missiles' impact. The crew was still tossed about a bit, but they had seen worse, much worse. These missiles had merely caught them off guard. The countermeasures should take care of the next wave.

"Aye, Admiral." Command Master Chief Charlie Green finished his coffee and was out the hatch in double-time. The COB would take care of the ship; that was his job, and he was good at it. Wallace had to focus on the fighting and taking that QMT facility.

"XO! Get the troops deployed!"

"You heard the admiral! Air Boss, why ain't the Gods of War already out? Ground Boss, get those drop tubes moving. I want the AEMs, AAIs, and the Warlords on the ground five seconds ago!" the XO shouted in his gravelly voice at the appropriate bridge crew members. It was his job to make certain that things got done right the first time so the admiral could focus on what to do next.

"Aye, sir!"

"Gunnery Officer of the Deck!" the admiral called out. The youngest member of the bridge crew looked a little nervous.

"Sir!" Lieutenant Junior Grade Guy Hall replied.

"Fire at will at any potential targets. But do not, I repeat, do not destroy that QMT facility!"

"Aye, sir!"

"Nav!"

"Aye?"

"Take us in closer than we had planned. If we scrape the surface of the facility, then maybe that'll keep those missiles from the planet off of us." RADM Wallace Jefferson sat back into the captain's chair and tapped at some of the sensor controls on the chair arm's console. He widened the DTM view of the battlescape in his mind all the way out to beyond the moons of Arcadia. There were three moons of appreciable size, not counting the QMT facility, though it was mostly artificial. Or, if he recalled right, it was half an asteroid that had been tugged there from the rings of the gas giant that Arcadia orbited. The artificial moon looked like a jagged half sphere with craters all over. The moon was standing on edge with respect to Arcadia. On the flat surface there were many concentric octagonal rings. At each point of the outer octagon were towers reaching several hundred meters up into space. The largest such tower was right in the middle of the thing. The facility looked pretty much like the one at the Oort Cloud in the Sol System, without the extra moons and scrapped ships moored to it for structural integrity. This system looked newer and better thought out. It had been built by the U.S. military, not the Seppies on a shoestring budget.

He scanned as best he could for any other surprises. The Seppies were known for using clever guerrilla tactics, booby traps, and kamikaze ships loaded with gluonium bombs, and they had used mass-driver guns at the Battle of the Oort very successfully. He hoped they didn't have any of those here. The problem with mass drivers, though, was that the damned things were usually kept underground and were hard as hell to find until after they had been fired. With all the American traffic in and out of the Ross 128 system, it would have been difficult for the Arcadians and/or the Separatists to build mass drivers in the system without anybody spotting them. Wallace doubted they had them here, but he wasn't taking anything for granted or making any undue assumptions. When in doubt, check it out.

"CO!" The air boss, Captain Michelle Wiggington, turned from her console. "Gods of War are out, sir! The Demon Dawgs and the Utopian Saviors are deploying."

"Good, Michelle."

"Drop tubes away, CO," the ground boss, Brigadier General James Brantley, added. "The Warlords and the Robots are out. The AAIs are right behind them."

"Good. We are stuck here without that facility." RADM Jefferson could do little more than wait at this point. The battle plan had been put into action. There was no gauge of the enemy's real strength until they started using it. Were there mass drivers? Did they have any ships? How many troops were on the QMT pad? "And I don't want to spend the next eighteen months in hyperspace."

"Sir! We're taking in some serious AA fire from the QMT facility," the XO said.

"I've got it, XO," the air boss replied. "I'm putting the Utopian Saviors on it."

"Ground Boss, any sign of enemy troops on the facility?" Jefferson asked.

"No, Admiral. Only automated defenses," Brantley replied. "But, sir, there are apparently a hell of a lot of the automated defenses. A lot more than were originally installed on that thing, according to our records."

"That's not what I expected to hear. They have been planning this for some time, it would appear. Who knows what modifications the damned Seppies have made to this facility? There could be traps, ambushes, and minefields. Better tell the ground forces to dig in and cover until we take out the automated systems from the air." The admiral was happy to see there were no defenses to speak of at the facility moon, but that also gave him a queasy feeling in his gut. The Arcadian ambassador had claimed to have a million man–strong Armored National Guard. Where were they?

"All right Saviors, listen up." Lieutenant Colonel Caroline "Deuce" Leeland bounced her USMC FM-12 strike mecha around to avoid the QMT facility AA fire. Her mecha in fighter mode screamed across the surface at just over fifty meters high. Her wingman, Captain Timothy "Goat" Crow, was off her right wing at five o'clock, and the rest of the Utopian Saviors were in pairs spread out behind her. "We've been given new orders from on

high, and those are to take out the surface defenses and that
AA fire. Skinny and HoundDog, Golfbag and Volleyball are on
me. Jawbone, you and Popstar split off with Beanhead, PayDirt,
Romeo, and Freak. My team will hit the AA and, Jaw, your team
takes the ground defenses."

"Roger that, Deuce," Jawbone replied.

Deuce pushed her throttle forward a bit, tapped her right top
pedal slightly, and crabbed her fighter to her right a few degrees
to line up on the enemy AA cannons. From what she could tell,
the cannons were dispersed on the towers of the facility at each
of the points. There were eight points across each of the octagonal
concentric rings. The outermost ring had half-kilometer–tall towers on each, and there was an even taller one dead center. The
three-dimensional image in her mindview was fused together by
QM, IR, lidar, radar, and optical sensors into an extremely detailed
view of the targets. The cannons looked like large gray metal
cubes with a gun turret sticking out of each of the five faces that
were not attached to the ground or tower or other structure the
thing rested on. Deuce picked the first one in her general flight
direction and locked it up with a QM guided missile.

"Fox three!" she shouted. The missile twisted out across the
surface of the Arcadian QMT toward the AA box on the tower
nearest her. She guided her mecha low to stay out of the AA firing solutions so she could watch the impact of her missile. The
missile never got close to the target before it turned upward and
tumbled wildly out of control, landing somewhere beyond the
engagement zone and never exploding. "What the hell!"

"Fox three!" Goat shouted. Her wingman followed up her attack
the same way. The second QM guided missile spiraled out of control and went dead as well. "Shit, we're being countermeasured."

"Roger that, Goat. Shit." Deuce pulled away from her current
run and out of the AA as best she could. "Saviors! Abandon
present mission approach and pull back to angels ten. The facility is Gridiron. I repeat, the facility is Gridiron and fox three is
ineffective."

"So why don't we just go to guns, Deuce?" Skinny called back
over the net. Just because they were Gridiron—meaning electromagnetic countermeasures were taking out the missiles—didn't
mean that guns would stop the AA boxes.

"Negative, negative, Skinny. We can't take the chance of damaging any part of the tower. If we can't hit the boxes, we don't hit them at all." Deuce thought about the problem for an instant and then had an idea and switched channels to the AEM command-net frequency. "Colonel Roberts, this is Lieutenant Colonel Leeland."

"Go ahead, Deuce."

"Colonel, the locals have us Gridiron and zapped, making our missiles useless against the AA boxes mounted on the towers. I'm DTMing you my sensor data of their locations now." Deuce thought to her AIC to link up with the AEM commander's AIC. "We need someone to burn them for us so we can go to laser-guided seekers."

"Hell, Deuce, we were getting bored down here anyway. I think my senior NCO is taking a nap. I'll see if I can wake her up and get it done for you."

"Roger that, Colonel. We'll see if we can't help keep the ground defenses preoccupied while you do it. Keep us posted on the status of the burn."

"Roger that. Robots are on the move, Deuce."

"All right, Saviors, watch for the AEMs making a move for the towers and let's see if we can't give them some cover," Deuce ordered her flight squad.

Ramy Roberts's Robots, also known as the 3rd Armored E-suit Marines Forward Recon Unit, had made it a policy, strategy, crazy-assed tactic, or whatever you'd like to call it, of riding down the drop tubes with the Army tank mecha. They had first done it at the Battle of the Oort with great success, and it had been adopted as standard operating procedure. Most of the other AEM squads thought it was a great idea. Most of the Army armored infantry squads thought that the marines were bat-fucking crazy.

"Warlord Five in the tube and ready for drop!" Army Captain Sam Cortez announced as he brought the tank to a stop inside the tube and locked it down. "Hang on out there, Jarhead, we go in five, four, three, two, one . . ."

"Shiiiitttt!" Tommy growled as the tube was launched. His suit was magnetically locked down to the tank so he wasn't going to fly off. But it was still one hell of a ride.

Nearly three dozen drop tubes were launched toward the QMT facility by the *Sienna Madira*'s underbelly catapults. Traveling at over four thousand kilometers per hour, only ten of them actually held the tanks and their unusual attachments. The rest were decoys in case the fancy electronic and quantum membrane countermeasures failed to confuse all of the enemy fire.

As AA rounds peppered against the exterior armored hull of the drop tube, Suez thought it sounded a lot like the ringing of the bells of Notre Dame. He hoped like hell the tube's SIFs held up. They only needed to last for thirty seconds or so, since the flight of the drop tubes cut an unusually short ballistic trajectory. Tommy had been through this before, but it was still the most unsettling half-a-minute of any fight.

Since there was nothing he could do about it while magnetically locked to a tank inside the tube, he did his best not to think about the harrowing drop through flying shards of hot burning incendiary armor-piercing rounds outside. One way or another, it would be over soon enough. He went over in his mind exactly what he planned to do when he hit the surface. He was going to take cover and shoot any fucking thing in front of him without a blue force tracker beacon on it.

It was a good plan.

A few more seconds passed, and Suez had to grit his teeth against the jar of the tube retrofields firing and the demo blowing apart the tube, leaving him riding atop the tank-mode mecha in open space with the ground rushing up at them extremely fast and enemy AA rounds flashing about. The orange tracers from the enemy cannons seem to fill every part of the sky as far as he could see in front of him. So, like a good marine, he was headed toward where the shit was thickest.

"Thanks for the lift, Warlord Five!" Tommy gave the command to pop the superconductor magnet free, and he pounded his jumpboots against the hull of the tank, launching him wide and clear of the mecha. He rolled in a forward flip, and then he slammed into the ground with his left knee creating a crater and slinging up dust. He pulled his HVAR at ready and scanned it around, looking for targets of opportunity. There were no enemy soldiers, but there were automated ant hills with antipersonnel defenses splattering out railgun rounds as fast as they could. The fifty-millimeter railgun rounds tore through chunks of rock and dirt all around the LZ and all around him. He recalled the taking-cover part of his plan.

The Robots spread out to cover the landing zone for the

tankheads, and then, to confuse the ant hills, they spread across the ridgeline a couple of klicks up in front of Army mecha. PFC Roger Willingham and PFC Hicks pounded down not far on either side of him, and Tommy could call them up in his DTM blue-force tracker if he needed to. The rest of the Robots were on the move as well, and it was clear that they had to move forward fast and randomly or those damned automated snipers were going to tear them apart.

"Kent, keep your fucking head down!" Tommy heard Top shouting at the female lance corporal. McCandless's voice sounded as if she could chew the lance corporal's head off.

"Goddamn, I'm hit!" Kent shouted over the Marine unit's tac-net. Tommy couldn't tell by the sound of her voice how bad it was.

"Top, Kent is down," he communicated.

"Got her, Gunny. She'll survive, but out of play. Keep moving," Tamara replied over the net.

"Roger that, Top. This fucking ground fire is thick as shit! I'm open for ideas." Tommy ducked behind an outcropping of rocks.

"How about we get the fuck out of it?" Corporal Sandy Cross said. "I mean, I could think of more fun places to be."

"You kidding—ain't this right where all the action is? You gotta love it, Sandy," Corporal Bates threw in his two cents' worth.

"Knock that shit off, Danny," Tommy ordered. He kept his position behind the rock pile for the moment. He couldn't tell if they were a man-made refuse pile of boulders or if they were part of the asteroid that had been dug out to make the QMT pad or if they were a natural phenomenon. He didn't really give a shit, either. They offered cover from those goddamned fifty-millimeter railguns, and that was all he was looking for at the moment.

The automated snipers were not very accurate, but they put down a shitload of antipersonnel rounds in a goddamned hurry. The Robots were gathering around the valley at the bottom of the ridgeline as best they could, and they could see the tankheads back behind them setting up a line. Several of them fired volleys into the ant hills atop the ridge and managed to take out a couple of the automated snipers, but there were hundreds of them per linear kilometer, which was way too many for ten tanks to take on.

Tommy, PFC Willingham, PFC Howser, and Sergeant Dallon Hubbard had bounced point to the rock pile he had found. There were more of the piles farther up the ridge that would make good cover and get them almost in range where their grenade launchers would be effective against some of the closer ant hills. He motioned to the two marines on him.

"Come on, we're moving up to that next pile. It's bigger and will give us a better vantage point," he told them. "On me in leapfrogs. And remember to adjust for the lower gravity. Go!" Tommy bounced first as far as his jumpboots would bounce him. He hit the ground on his belly, sliding uphill in prone position like a baseball player sliding into second base headfirst. He held still with his weapon pointed in the general direction of the ant hills. Several rounds from the automated railguns threw dust up around him, but he held still and the automated systems of the snipers didn't lock on him.

PFC Howser bounced twice. Her first jump was shorter than Tommy's, putting her about fifty meters behind him. Then she bounced as far as she could up the hill. She was still not even a third of the way to the next cover point. PFC Willingham followed the procedure, putting him somewhere near halfway to the rock pile. Then Sergeant Hubbard made it almost to the two-thirds distance before he slid to a stop and covered himself. Tommy crawled to his hands and feet and then bounced all the way up to the sergeant before he stopped. The two of them held still, planning to make it to cover last.

"Okay, Howser and Willingham, this time go and don't stop until you get there," he ordered them.

"Got it, Gunny."

As they bounced up the hill and over the two sergeants, Tommy noted that PFC Howser wasted no time on the bounce as she hit the ground. She bounced flawlessly. Willingham, on the other hand, seemed to be having trouble with his footing on one of the landings, forcing him to hesitate a second too long. His hesitation cost him. It cost him his right leg from the knee down.

One of the automated rifle rounds hit home, punching through his armor just below his right knee. The round trajectory tore upward through the knee joint, blowing out the back and scattering red blood on the asteroid regolith. The red was less pronounced in the red light of the red dwarf star.

"Oww fucking goddamn hell!" he screamed over the net. "Shit, shit, shit!"

"Gunny! Willingham is hit!" Howser shouted.

"Keep bouncing to that cover, Howser. I've got him on my bounce!" Suez ordered her.

"Need help, Tommy?" Sergeant Hubbard asked him.

"No. You get up there and make sure Howser doesn't do anything stupid."

"Got it, Gunny." The marine bear-crawled his armored suit up the hill a few meters to get up speed. Then he kicked off, looking like a four-legged armored menace leaping into the air. He rolled forward into a front roll and put his jumpboots down just in time to maximize his bounce went he hit. Two more bounces and he was behind the rock pile with Howser.

Before Tommy could decide exactly how he wanted to handle Willingham, out of the periphery of his vision to his right he caught a glimpse of two other AEMs bouncing in from somewhere farther down the valley behind him. His blue-force tracker showed the blue dots in his DTM mindview to be the second lieutenant and Corporal Bates. Tommy didn't like the angle they were bouncing at, but they had made it that far without taking a hit. Shit, you couldn't tell Bates anything anyway, but the SOB was lucky. Tommy had to give him that, because just as the two AEMs reached a point that should have been in a firing solution for the ant hills, four FM-12s streaked across the hill, plowing the ridgeline to nothing but dust and smoke. The autosnipers were blown to vapor and dust that scintillated and sparkled quite beautifully in the red sunlight. Tommy stood and bounced fast, coming down beside the second lieutenant and Corporal Bates.

"How is he, Danny?" the lieutenant asked the corporal. Bates had taken on the role of squad medic since the Battle of the Oort. Tommy figured it was because of all the wounded they helped load and unload onto troop shuttles in the aftermath of the battle. It had driven Bates to want to help more than just load and unload screaming and battered soldiers. So he had trained on being a medic in his spare time. The colonel had encouraged it, and it was part of what got Danny promoted to corporal.

"His knee is gone. The suit sealed off the wound. He can still bounce in it, but he won't be winning the AEM Olympics, I bet." Danny looked him over and had his AIC talk with the wounded marine's suit. The wireless health-monitoring system indicated that Roger was not in any near-term danger from his wound and in fact could function with somewhat diminished capacity.

"Roger, how you doing?" Tommy leaned in to the PFC and took a closer look at the suit. He would be fine. Hell, the adrenaline and the immunoboost were probably already healing the wound, but he didn't have a knee in there. He was going to have to have a replacement knee printed up for him back at sickbay. Until then, the knee-joint mechanism of the suit would move for him. He wouldn't really notice a big difference until he tried to take the suit off.

"I'm good, Gunny. It hurt like goddamned hell at first," Willingham said.

"Do you wanna evac out or can you keep going, Marine?" Tommy asked.

"I'm good, Gunny. I'm stayin'."

"If you start dragging on me, we're getting you out of here, got it?"

Tie into his health-monitoring system and keep me updated, Tommy thought to his AIC.

Affirmative.

"I'm good, Gunny."

"Gunny, I think we should get to cover," the second lieutenant ordered.

"Good call, sir." Tommy and Second Lieutenant Nelms helped the private up and then bounced twice up the hill to the rock pile.

"You know," Danny Bates started, "these damned rock piles are all over this valley and up this ridge. What the fuck are they?'

"I don't know, Danny," Tommy replied. "But right now they sure are handy as hell to have around."

"Spoil piles," Second Lieutenant Nelms said. The tone of his voice couldn't have been more indifferent if he'd tried.

"Sir?" Tommy asked.

"These piles are the rocks they dug out to make those ant hills, Gunny. They're called spoil piles."

"Of course, sir. I didn't see that." Tommy looked left and right and could see the piles as far as his sensors could see, which was to the horizon of the facility. The facility was built on an asteroid that had been blown in half, so it was basically flat on the QMT side and round on the other. That meant that the suit sensors could see many kilometers in either direction, barring hills and ridgelines and spoil piles and artificial structures, which there were plenty of.

"Woah," Bates moaned. "If that means there's an ant hill for each one of these things, then we are in some thick-ass shit!"

"I'm afraid you're right, Corporal," Nelms replied. "Way thicker than we can manage with the firepower we have with us."

"So, do we dig in or keep moving, sir?" Tommy asked the lieutenant.

"For now, that is above my pay grade, Gunny. Hold on and I'll check in with the colonel."

"Yes, sir." Tommy liked the fact that the new lieutenant wasn't trying to figure out everything himself, but he also hoped he didn't think he'd have to ask the colonel about everything. Giving the new guy the benefit of the doubt, Tommy thought the second lieutenant did okay going after Willingham the way he had. He must've either realized the air support was coming or was lucky as hell. It worked out all right for him in the end. If you thought that being on an excavated enemy teleport facility in space under heavy fire was lucky. Tommy wasn't sure his perspective was in the right place. After all, they had all volunteered to be there.

The Robots were hunkered down not too far from where the drop tubes had spat them and the Army tankheads. The tankheads had set up a reverse perimeter while the Robots pressed forward. At first it was just a jog in the park, but as soon as they crested the first hill in view of the outermost structures of the QMT pad, they were picked up by QM sensors and the automated ground-defense systems started plinking away at them. The automated snipers along the ridgeline had them pinned down. The mecha jocks kept making run after run on them, which was creating gaps in the autosniper's coverage, but they were having their troubles, too. They were under heavy AA fire while trying to take out the ant hills. Apparently the FM-12 squad trying to take out the AA couldn't because of some type of electronic warfare. The only way to knock out the AA cannons would be with laser guiding the missiles to them. And that meant that somebody on the ground had to get close enough to the damned things to light them up with a laser designator. A shame they couldn't just raze the rock from space. . . .

"All right, Zack, the mecha jocks and the tankheads are gonna focus on this section of the ridgeline here." Colonel Roberts highlighted a piece of the ridge on a three-dimensional map projected into all their heads DTM. Though they were spread out behind the spoil piles across the valley and up the ridge, they could still have a fully interactive conference with visual aids via their AICs and DTM connections. "That ought to knock out the autosnipers long enough to create a pass through this line. Take Gunny Suez and PFC Howser and bounce like hell across this AO to that ridgeline."

"Yes, sir."

"Zack, don't worry about shooting anything unless it gets in your way. Find a covered vantage point and start burning those AA cannons with the designator, got it?" Colonel Roberts ordered his new butter bar. Tommy hoped like hell that the new second lieutenant *got it*.

"Yes, Colonel. Got it. But from that angle I don't think we could get good line of sight with more than five or six of the tower batteries and a few of them on the ground, here, here, and here." He highlighted potential threats.

"Top and I will take the rest of the squad up the ridge farther around to our left and burn the boxes you can't get to."

"I see, sir."

"Good. Robots, let's get ready to move out."

Jawbone looked over her left wing at her wingman, First Lieutenant Dana "Popstar" Miller, then around the battlescape. There were no enemy fighters as far as her eyeballs or her sensors could see across the long, gray, flat surface of the QMT-facility asteroid. They had made several runs across the ridgeline where the groundpounders were pinned down, but they still hadn't done enough damage, and the AEMs weren't moving very rapidly. Those damned autosniper ant hills were every-fucking-where.

"Major Strong, you understand the plan?"

"Yes, sir, Colonel. We're gonna focus our attack and punch two holes in the line at your designated coordinates. We're ready when you are, sir," Jawbone replied.

"Well, don't wait on us. Roberts, out."

"Roger that, Robots." Jawbone turned her mecha back around for another strafing run while trying to stay as far out of the view of those AA cannons as she could. Since the damned surface of the facility planetoid, or asteroid, or whatever the hell you'd call it, was so fucking flat, well, that made it difficult to duck the AA.

As easy as shooting flying elephants at Disney World, hey, James? she thought to her AIC.

Maybe. At least the ant hills aren't flying.

"All right, marines, on my wing, and let's hit the deck. We need to clear the way for the groundpounders." Jawbone's mecha skimmed dangerously close to the surface, and she had to keep a close eye on the topography ahead just so a hill or a structure wouldn't manage to take her by surprise. "Deuce, you be ready to hit those AA cannons as soon as we get those AEMs in place, because this shit is thick!"

"Roger that, Jaw. Been there, done that," Deuce replied.

The plan seemed to work just fine. The Marine FM-12s hit the ant hills no-holds-barred. Then Tommy and company bounced up the hill quickly and professionally. One sniper system managed to survive the strafing run, but a few well-placed grenades from Bates's left forearm grenade launcher took care of it nicely. Tommy and the platoon leader crested the hill, giving them perfect line of sight of five of the eight towers. Both of them lay prone and started lighting up targets with the designators built into their HVAR sighting systems.

Once the AEMs tagged the AA cannons with laser markers, the second wave of FM-12s swooped in, going to missiles. Two of the mecha fighters screamed overhead, bobbing and weaving through the hailstorm of orange tracers out of the automated AA systems. A missile fired from underneath the wing of each of the fighters and corkscrewed through the cannon rounds right onto the laser spots designating them.

"Hot damn! That's two of those mothers." Tommy cheered and then slid his elbow a few centimeters to his right to find another target to designate. Then several missiles were fired on the other side of the ridgeline, where Top and the colonel had gone. Those missiles hit home as well. Things were looking up.

CHAPTER 17

July 1, 2394 AD
Tau Ceti Planet Four, Moon Alpha, a.k.a. Ares
Separatist QMT Facility
Friday, 2:53 PM, Earth Eastern Standard Time
Friday, 7:53 PM Madira Valley Standard Time

"Owww, goddamn that hurt!" Jack came to screaming in pain as he tried to shake himself back to consciousness. There was severe pain everywhere in his body. He could still wiggle his toes and fingers, but his neck and back and ass hurt so bad there was no way he was going anywhere for a while. He carefully, very carefully, brought his right hand up to a breast pocket and pulled out a medipen. He slid the armored access panel up on his neck and then activated the pen. The needle slid out, arming itself, and then he jammed the thing through the seal layer of his armored flight suit into his neck. That hurt, too.

Candis, how long was I out?

Three minutes and fifty-one seconds.

Oh, well, not as bad as I thought. How am I? He could feel the adrenaline, pain meds, and immunoboost rushing over him. The pain had almost completely vanished.

I wouldn't try to move for about five more minutes. The immunoboost should be getting you back on your feet safely by then.

Roger that. What about Dee?

I'm not sure how she is, but I can still detect her AIC's emergency signal. You should try contacting Penzington, perhaps.

Good idea.

159

Jack was afraid to move his neck yet, but he could survey his predicament fairly well with his peripheral vision and by having his DTM mindview rotate about the axis of his head. His suit and helmet had limited sensors without his fighter, but he could still get simple optical and IR imagery.

He had come down about ten meters from where his mecha had hit and exploded. The gravity on the hull of the Seppy supercarrier must have been along similar protocols as that of the U.S. fleet ships. He felt like he was sitting on about one half of an Earth gravity. That's why his ejection couch hadn't simply bounced off and floated away. He could tell that he had bounced several times until his couch finally lodged itself into a niche in the hull plating. He had barely made it through the QMT gate in time, had barely managed to slow down enough, and had barely managed to eject at just the right time to not get himself killed. He'd have been of no use to the president's daughter dead.

As it was, he needed to let the immunoboost do its job for a few more minutes, figure out where Dee was, and then figure out how to get inside the ship. He was hoping that his CIA buddy on the inside could help him out with that one.

Candis, connect me to Penzington.

Hold on, Jack, she said into his mind. *Okay. Got her.*

Penzington?

Boland, you made it! Where the hell are you?

I crashed into the hull of the ship. I'm sitting in my ejection seat somewhere, uh, I'd guess near the aft end about midway up the port side.

We've got to move fast. They are about to teleport the president's daughter to the New Tharsis Capitol building.

What? Why there?

Elle Ahmi lives in the penthouse. You want to make a guess?

No. Shit. We've got to get off this ship and down there. Any ideas? Jack would have rubbed his chin in thought if he weren't still afraid to move and in an e-suit on the exterior hull of a spaceship in space.

Well, it's worse than that. We were just given word to go to battlestations and prepare to QMT back to Arcadia. I hope more than just the Madira is gonna be there, because the entire Seppy fleet is headed there!

Shit, I've got to get off this ship and to the planet, fast. Jack hadn't gone through damned near killing himself just to end up getting teleported back to where he started. He had to think of something. He had to get to Dee.

Well, with the SIFs up, you are not gonna get inside. Your best bet would be to get to the QMT facility and go from there. Maybe steal a ship, sneak onto the QMT pad, or something.

Jack decided he felt good enough to move, so he did. He unstrapped himself from the ejection-seat harness and stood up. The Tau Ceti QMT facility was directly over his head about five kilometers. The ship had moved off center of the QMT pad, probably from standard protocol to get out of the way in case some other ships came in from elsewhere. He looked at the ejection chair briefly and scrambled through the inventory of things he had in his suit's webbing. At one-half gravity there was no way he could jump and reach an escape velocity to get off the ship. Hell, that would put escape velocity somewhere around five kilometers per second. In other words, it would be like standing on the surface of Mars and trying to run and jump off the planet into orbit. That wasn't going to happen. He'd need a rocket. On the other hand, the gravity only lasted a few meters above the hull on most ships. Maybe the trick would be to just manage to get above the artificial gravitational metric of the ship and then somehow push himself toward the QMT facility. Slowing down before he hit the surface of the QMT facility would be another problem to deal with. But first things first.

Can you get off the ship, Penzington? Can you come and get me?

I don't know. I think I can get onto a shuttle that is leaving in a few minutes for the QMT pad, but that is about as good as it gets. Maybe from there I can get out to you. But you'd have to get off the ship first.

Shit, that ain't gonna work. I've got to get above the ship's gravity well somehow. Any way he thought about it, he was screwed. Jack couldn't think of anything to get him off the ship. He'd need some sort of propulsion system to manage that.

He went through his webbing and again took inventory of his gear. He had some HE, a handful of grenades, ammo for his rail-pistol, a couple knives, first-aid gear, about a hundred meters of nanotube filament rope, a few carabiners and clips holding things to his webbing, some duct tape, and whatever he could scavenge from a slightly used ejection couch. He looked the seat over and figured there was little there he could use. The propulsion system for the seat was dead because he had used it all up to keep from plummeting to his death a few minutes before. The QMT facility was right there. It hung just five kilometers or so above his head. If he could get there, he'd figure out a way to the planet.

Jack, I'm on the shuttle, and we are leaving now. You've got maybe five minutes before the ships get here and they all start moving into position to jump. If you're gonna think of something, do it quickly, Penzington warned him through the DTM link.

I've got no idea. Can't you take the shuttle by force and come get me?

Well, no. Not yet. I'm in an e-suit in a storage compartment stowed away on it.

I see.

By the time we land and I can get back to you, it would be too late.

I get it.

Good luck.

You, too.

There was a way to do everything, Jack had always told himself. He jumped twice to get to his crash site. His ship had done minimal damage to the hull. There were no material pieces of his fighter left that were larger than a meter long. Sooner or later they would just fall off into space. Maybe a work crew would get out to remove it on the next exterior-hull maintenance shift. But for now, he had a few chunks of armor-plated fighter plane that he might be able to use for something. He wasn't sure just what.

Time is ticking, Jack.

I know, Candis. You have any bright ideas?

No.

We need propulsion somehow. What could give us that? Jack thought about it, and then he had a very, very bad idea. *I got it. Maybe.*

What?

Run some sims for me. How much HE would I need to lift the ejection chair with me in it out of the gravity well of this ship with a little extra velocity left over?

How far does the gravity well extend? The Madira's goes ten meters.

Okay, use that. This ship looks like a knockoff of her anyway.

All right then. According to spec the chair has a mass of five hundred kilograms. You in your suit and gear are another one fifty. To get to a height of ten meters you would need a minimum energy of thirty-two point five kilojoules. The HE is ten megajoules per kilogram, so you need a minimum of three and a quarter grams to reach escape height with no velocity left. You need less than four cubic centimeters. Like four dice worth.

Okay, got it.

Jack pulled three chunks of the scorched armor plating and piled them beside the ejection seat. Then he rummaged through his webbing and pulled out a bar of the HE. The bar was basically the size of a stick of butter and was sealed in a vacuum package. He guessed at about five cubic centimeters and then added a little extra just in case. He stuck a wireless detonator chip into it and then set the two armor fragments from his destroyed fighter on top of it. Then he began kicking and tugging at the ejection seat until he managed to free it from a piece of loose hull plating on the ship. He dragged the seat on top of the armor fragments—he was glad there was only half a g, or he might never have gotten the couch moved.

Jack looked up. The QMT facility filled most of his overhead view. There was no way he could miss it. He'd more likely kill himself with the HE than drift off into space. And by that time, if he did miss and was floating off into space, Penzington might be able to come and get him.

While Jack was looking up, four supercarrier class Seppy ships materialized out of hyperspace out in front of the ship he was on. Then several new battle cruisers and a couple of older haulers came out of hyperspace.

"Holy shit! The *Madira* is gonna be in it deep," he muttered.

You got that right, Candis agreed with him.

Jack adjusted the seat angle to what he hoped was somewhere near the edge of the QMT pad and not into the jump region. He needed to get moving. The ship could start moving into jump position at any moment. He sat down in the chair and strapped himself in. He made sure his feet and arms would be inside the shadow of the chair so no shrapnel or plasma from the explosion could damage him or his suit.

"This is really gonna fuckin' suck!" Jack pushed his body into the couch as best he could and tucked his chin into his chest.

Okay, Candis, trigger this thing.

Are you sure, DeathRay?

Yes, that is an order Lieutenant Commander!

Yes, sir. Going in five, four, three, two, one . . .

The high explosives went off from the wireless trigger signal Candis sent to the detonator chip. The stored chemical energy inside the solid material converted to kinetic energy in the form of heat and a plasma moving upward at over three thousand meters per second. The shockwave vaporized the first armor plate and slammed the second one upward into the ejection chair. The ejection chair blasted upward away from the hull of the Seppy supercarrier with about twice the force of a standard ejection seat. In other words, it went up pretty damned fast—fast enough that Jack was slammed into the chair with a force of about ten gravities for about a second. But DeathRay was used to high-g maneuvers that rattled his bones. It didn't hurt as much as he had expected, but that was probably because he had just taken a shitload of immunoboost and pain meds.

The chair crested the ten meters that he needed in order to clear the ship's gravity well, and it kept on going. It kept on going pretty damned fast. The acceleration was over within microseconds after the blast, and any deceleration was finished once they escaped the Seppy ship's artificial gravity well. DeathRay was in microgravity at this point and was floating freely along a constant velocity vector straight at the QMT facility. Jack could see the surface of the QMT moon starting to get slowly closer. The planet Ares filled his field of view off to his right. The Jovian planet Ares orbited was behind him now.

What is relative velocity, Candis?

Using objects on the surface for angular-size reference, I can approximate that we are moving at about fifty kilometers per hour with an error bar of about five kilometers per hour.

Okay, the seat was designed to take a fall at fifty-five kilometers per hour with no problem.

Yes, but that assumed it landed first. Jack, you do realize you are staring at the surface?

Holy shit! Is this fucking nightmare never gonna stop? Okay, we have to rotate the seat.

That would be advisable.

What can we use for a thruster?

You could always throw things.

How about my railpistol? There is a certain amount of recoil to it. Jack had blasted himself out of one predicament into another. But at fifty kilometers per hour or so and the surface five kilometers away, he had about six minutes to figure out what to do.

That might work.

He pulled his pistol out of the thigh holster and held it straight in front of him with both hands. The safety grip received the safety code from his AIC and unlocked the trigger and safety. Jack thumbed the safety and then pulled the trigger. He waited a few seconds to see if he could tell a difference in his angular orientation. He was moving at about a degree per ten seconds. He needed to move at one hundred and eighty degrees in less than six minutes. Doing the math quickly in his head, he decided that he was rotating five times too slow. So he quickly pumped out four more rounds. He and Candis both worked at calculating his angular velocity and decided that the chair would be as close to the proper orientation as they were going to get with the tools they had in hand. Jack reholstered his weapon and just waited.

Penzington?

Boland?

I'll be on the surface of the QMT facility in five minutes.

Really?

The Seppy supercarriers, battle cruisers, and haulers all moved into position directly over the center of the QMT pad. The big sphere of light formed and then turned into the two-dimensional–looking ripple in space. Then all the ships and the light show vanished. The *Sienna Madira* was about to catch hell.

Hang in there, Madira! Watch your six, Fish, DeathRay thought.

Amen, Jack. Amen, Candis agreed.

CHAPTER 18

July 1, 2394 AD
Tau Ceti Planet Four, Moon Alpha, a.k.a. Ares
New Tharsis
Friday, 2:53 PM, Earth Eastern Standard Time
Friday, 7:53 PM Madira Valley Standard Time

Dee had for the most part kept her mouth shut and done her best to ignore her captors. She had her AIC firewall itself and then lock itself down from any inputs other than hers. Apart from the initial rough treatment by Fink, she had been held at arm's length by every other Separatist soldier involved. They did remove the zip ties and put electronic cuffs on her. She was cuffed behind her back, and nobody could get the things off unless they had the wireless encryption key. She wasn't sure which of the two was more uncomfortable, the zip ties or the cuffs.

Fink shadowed her every move and was flanked by four regular Seppy soldiers, two on either side of him. They first were led through the ship to a teleport pad near the hangar bay, and then they were QMTed to the Seppy capital city of New Tharsis to somewhere inside a building that she couldn't see out of. The architecture of the building was very much like that in the Capitol Building in Washington, D.C. and similar to the White House, although the decoration style was a mix between ancient Greek and modern. It was quite an unusual mix that still gave Dee no clues as to where exactly she was. She only knew she was in the city of New Tharsis from having overheard the captain of the Seppy ship make mention of that. She guessed by the fact that

167

she had QMTed from Ross 128 that she must be in the Tau Ceti system, planet Ares, somewhere in New Tharsis.

Dee watched as best she could every detail of her path and any and all security sequences and processes, hoping to gather some tidbit of information that would allow her to escape when the opportunity struck. There was still that strange communication over the intercom while she had been held on the Seppy ship. Was it possible that there was really a CIA agent that close to her? Dee found it hard to believe. It didn't matter, because she knew her father and her mother were not going to let something like this happen to her without taking action. And she also knew that she was not going to wait for somebody to save her. She was, by God, Deanna Moore, the daughter of Alexander Moore, and she was going to stand tall and get herself free as soon as she got the chance. Somewhere along the way she hoped for the opportunity to put a couple bullets into Fink, too.

The guards and Fink led her into an antechamber outside a single elevator. The lights on the elevator showed that it was on the way down and that she was on the second floor. That meant that the teleport pad was somewhere on the second floor. She'd have to remember that, for certain. She thought that she could find her way back to it, but she had gone through three different AIC-negotiated security doors. That would prove difficult to overcome, but she'd figure it out. Hopefully, if she got back to the teleport pad she could use it to teleport herself to safety. Dee had no idea where safety inside the Tau Ceti system might be. She also had no idea how to operate a teleport pad. She'd blow that bridge up when she came to it.

The white elevator light dinged and lit up, indicating that the elevator car had arrived at their floor. The Seppy soldiers moved to an attention pose, but Fink didn't seem to change that much. Dee could tell that he subtly shifted his balance on his feet to a slightly more alert stance. She wasn't sure what that meant, but it left her feeling a bit uneasy.

The elevator doors slid open. There was a lone figure inside. The figure was a tall, slim woman wearing black military UCUs, boots, leather gloves, and a red, white, and blue ski mask. She had long, straight black hair pulled up in a ponytail and out the back of the mask. Every human alive knew who *she* was.

Dee swallowed a lump in her throat and then felt the barrel of a railpistol press against the back of her head. The four soldiers immediately shifted and pointed their weapons at Fink.

"That is close enough, Madam President," Fink said.

"What are you doing, Fink?" Elle Ahmi asked calmly.

"Just wanting to insure my investment makes a profit. Transfer the money, or I'll simply kill her." She *had* to kill this SOB. Jay and Clay deserved at least that much. Fink would pay.

"Your money has been transferred, Colonel. Now step aside and walk away. That is the only opportunity you will get to leave here alive." Elle Ahmi didn't mess around, and Dee felt certain that she could come through with her threat if she so desired.

"Begging your pardon, Madam President. My AIC tells me the money has been transferred as promised. It was a pleasure doing business with you. But there is one more thing." Fink kept the barrel of his pistol against the base of Dee's skull.

"Don't try my patience, Colonel." Ahmi stood calmly in thought. "Very well, what is it?"

"I want in on this revolution of yours. I've played my part bringing her here. Now I want to be one of your generals." Fink lowered his weapon and backed up slowly between the Seppy soldiers. The four of them kept their weapons trained on him.

"You're a funny man, Fink." Ahmi grinned. "And either really brave or really stupid."

"I would be of use to you, ma'am."

"Let him go," Ahmi said and waved the soldiers off Fink. "Escort him out of the building and let him go for now. Become accustomed to our way of life here, General Fink. I'll call you soon, when I need you."

"You're welcome, ma'am. Good day." General Fink of the United Separatist Republic turned and walked away, with the soldiers shadowing him. As soon as the soldiers were out of sight, Dee caught some motion from her peripheral vision, and then a holowall turned off across the room. What had looked like a normal wall with a bust of some old bald guy in front of it wasn't. The wall and bust vanished. Five men in black armored uniforms stood with their weapons drawn. Clearly, they had been there all along. Dee realized that Ahmi kept her bases covered and for some reason wanted her to know that.

"At ease, gentlemen," Ahmi told them.

"I'll get you, Fink," Dee muttered to herself. Ahmi didn't pay any attention to her mutterings.

"Come with me, Ms. Moore." Ahmi held out a hand, leading her to the elevator. "I can remove those cuffs if you promise to behave yourself."

"I'll behave for now. But I'll make you no promises about when I'll decide to change my mind," Dee tried to say calmly, but her clenched teeth gave her anger and stress level away.

Ahmi laughed. "Indeed, you are your father's daughter."

"You're goddamned right I am." Dee almost spat the words.

"No need to be so crude, dear. I wouldn't have wanted you to be anything less." The terrorist mass murderer smiled through the ski mask at Dee. The smile unsettled her horribly. There was something both vicious and familiar about it.

The cuffs unlocked themselves, and Dee pushed them off and rubbed at her wrists. She had been either zip-tied or cuffed for more than a couple hours, and it was getting old. Her wrists had red marks. Dee wasn't sure what if anything to say, so she quietly stood there for the time being. What do you say to the most wanted mass murderer in history once they have kidnapped you for uncertain, but most likely sinister, purposes?

"It is an honor to meet you, Deanna. I would love to know more about you. Please tell me more about yourself." The elevator reached the top floor, and the doors slid open. Ahmi led her across a foyer and to another security door. The door slid open, and they stepped into a second elevator. This elevator was a transparent cylinder that only went up one floor. The door to the elevator was half of the cylinder, which slid around inside the other half. The two of them stepped out of it into a very large cylindrical room. The elevator door closed once they stepped free, and then the elevator itself sunk into the floor and disappeared.

"Lights please, Copernicus. Make them sixty percent. And make all the windows transparent. Our guest has never seen the rings rise over New Tharsis," Ahmi said out loud. Dee assumed that she was talking to her AIC.

Suddenly the walls turned transparent, as did the dome overhead. Other than a few structural members here and there, Dee suddenly felt as if she were standing atop a very tall building that was sitting on top of a very high peak. It was breathtaking, and she nearly lost her balance at first. To the east, the multicolored brilliance of the rings of the fourth planet of the Tau Ceti system filled the horizon. Two other moons were visible on the horizon as well. They were fairly bright. Dee wondered if either of them was the QMT facility she had seen earlier.

"Please, have a seat." Ahmi pointed her to the couch in her seating area. From the look of it, the crazy terrorist didn't entertain much. "Would you like some food or something to drink?"

Dee, the first rule of being a captive is to eat and drink if you get the chance, her AIC told her. *You never know when you'll get that chance again.*

Okay.

"I could eat. And I'm thirsty," she said. She made herself comfortable on the couch of the most wanted woman in humanity. Well, she wasn't really comfortable. In fact, she was shaking with fear and anger, and she just wanted out of there. But Dee was doing her best to stay brave.

"I'm having dinner sent up." Ahmi seemed more like a person entertaining a guest than a kidnapper talking to her victim. "What would you like? Do you have any allergies I should know about?"

"Uh, no, uh, allergies." Dee was almost bewildered by the way Ahmi spoke to her. Had she not been so frightening, she might have thought of the woman as nice. But Ahmi's reputation killed any such notions.

"Good. You should try our bison. It is amazing. Does that sound okay with you?" Ahmi asked her.

"Why am I here?" Dee blurted at her. She sat on her hands so they wouldn't shake.

"Well, you are straight to the point, aren't you? Good. Don't ever change that," Ahmi replied. Dee wasn't sure, but she thought the Separatist terrorist leader had just given her advice. "You are here because I wanted to meet you. And your parents and I have been at odds for so long, it is time we brought it all to a, well, a climax, if you will."

"What type of climax? You—you're planning to attack them, aren't you?"

"Oh, my dear, I guess you missed all the excitement today. You see, the Ross 128 system seceded from the United States today and joined me. Your father sent a ship to stop the secession, and today shall be the day that the Separatist Revolution is no longer considered a terrorist activity and will become the United Separatist Republic in the eyes of the rest of humanity," Ahmi explained. Then she zoned out briefly as if she were talking to her AIC. "Ah. Dinner is here."

That was fast, Bree thought to her.

Yeah. We don't get that kind of service in the White House.

Well, your dad isn't likely to shoot the chef in the head, either.

You never know.

The elevator slid up through the floor, and Elle retrieved the food tray. She rolled the cart over to the edge of the entertaining area of her office, next to one of the large windows, and uncovered it. Ahmi started setting the food out on a small two-person dining table butted up against the window. Dee hadn't noticed the little table before. It was very bistro-esque and actually, with the view, was probably one of the choiceest dining spots in the entire system.

"Come on, dear." Ahmi waved to her. "I haven't eaten all day, and I haven't had a dinner guest in, oh, six years."

"Uh, okay." Dee hesitantly joined the woman at the table. The complete experience was so surreal that Dee felt like she was having a very strange nightmare. She was frightened out of her mind, intrigued, entertained, and wasn't sure what to expect next.

"Oh hell, I forgot all about this thing." Ahmi reached up behind her head and fed her ponytail down through her mask and then pulled it the rest of the way off and tossed it on the love seat nearest the dinner table. She shook her head and ran her fingers through her hair, letting it fall on her shoulders. "I've worn that thing for so damned long, sometimes I forget I'm wearing it."

Dee looked at the woman's face closely and didn't have to study it at all to recognize her. The milky white skin, the long, straight black hair, her nose, her mouth, the dimples in her smile, her deep brown eyes, there was no better likeness of her mother other than her mother that she had ever seen. Dee felt faint, very faint.

"What the . . . ?" She had no words, and she wavered in front of the dining chair.

"Oh. I figured you'd already know," Ahmi said. "Sit down, child, before you fall down and hurt yourself. I just can't understand why they wouldn't tell you at your age."

"Who, who are you?" Dee didn't understand at all what was going on. Her mind spun wildly, trying to grasp at an explanation that made sense, but there wasn't one she could wrap her mind around. Why did Elle Ahmi look just like her mother, Sehera Moore?

"Why, I'm your grandmother, of course."

CHAPTER 19

July 1, 2394 AD
Ross 128, Arcadia Orbital QMT Facility
Friday, 3:13 PM, Earth Eastern Standard Time

"Goddamned déjà vu all over again, hey, Tommy?" Corporal Danny Bates told the gunnery sergeant. Tommy didn't think it was ha-ha funny. He thought it was funny in that "Oh shit" kind of way. They had yet to meet any human forces the entire time they had been on the surface. On the other hand, the resistance from the autosnipers and AA cannons had been a real pain in the ass.

"Yeah, Danny, if you consider there ain't nobody here, anywhere. At least last time Top and the colonel got to let go some rounds," Tommy told his longtime friend. The fact that they had met no resistance at the hangar entrance, or the corridor leading inward to the inner rings of the facility, or finally to the elevator leading up into the QMT control room, or anywhere, was just goddamned eerie. It was too goddamned eerie, and it gave Tommy the skin-crawls.

"LT? We got nothing up here. We found what should be the control room, but there is nothing here at all." Suez checked his suit's sensors again, and the only movement they could detect was each other and the occasional automated janitor bots.

"Gunny, just hold tight. The *Madira* is dropping in some engineers. Place a beacon on the ground and back off," Second Lieutenant Nelms ordered him. "I'll be up in a few minutes, when Willingham and I finish sweeping the lower decks. Top and the colonel are on their way up now."

"Roger that, sir." Tommy motioned to PFC Howser. "Drop a QMT locator, Howser."

"Roger that, Gunny." She pulled a QMT beacon out of a compartment on the side of her e-suit, popped the safety, and dropped it on the floor. The beacon flashed a red light on and off once about every two seconds. They all backed away and stood at ready.

The blinking red light flashed to green, and then a bright flash of light filled the room briefly. There was a sound of crackling and sizzling like that of bacon frying in a skillet. The next thing the marines knew, there were three Navy chief warrant officers standing in front of them.

"Gunny," the lead warrant officer, a CWO-4, nodded to Suez and then turned to his men and started jabbering about finding the membrane ripple controller and the wavefunction transfer initiator. The three men scanned every inch of the control room and then began pulling panels off of circuit boxes and searching through drawers and cabinets.

"Chief, if you need any extra muscle, just ask. Otherwise, we'll be over here standing guard," Tommy offered the technical specialists.

"Thanks, Gunny. I was hoping we'd have better luck, but this control room looks like it hasn't been used in months. You should see the one back at the Oort." The chief turned back to one of the men that had plugged a hardwire universal data port cable into one of the panel computer's readouts. The other end of the wire was in a box on his shoulder. "Anything?"

"You're right. This control room hasn't been used in months," the tech expert replied. "This room was locked out. Hell, as far as I can tell the entire facility has been locked out. It's being controlled from somewhere else."

"Somewhere else?" the CWO-4 asked.

"Looks like there is a QM wireless between the initiators and the planet below."

"Any idea where?"

"Yep. Got it."

"All right, pack it up then," the chief ordered the other two. They both unplugged themselves from various panels and stowed their gear in packs. "*Madira*, away party ready to return. Snapback beacon is on."

"Good day, Gunny." The CWO-4 smiled and vanished in a flash of light.

"What the fuck was that all about?" Bates asked.

"Damned if I know," Suez replied. "You'd think they'd at least have waited for the colonel to get here."

"So what now, Gunny?" PFC Howser asked him.

"We wait for the colonel and see what our orders are. I'd say for now, pop your lids and relax." Tommy twisted his helmet off and tethered it over his shoulder.

"CO! CDC!"

"Go CDC!"

"Sir, we've got a massive buildup across the EM bands. There's a QMT coming in."

"Roger that, CDC. Stay on top of it," Rear Admiral Jefferson said over the intercom to the Combat Direction Center commander. "XO?"

"Should be the *Lincoln*, the *Roosevelt*, and the *Jefferson*. It's time for them, sir," BG Chekov answered the admiral.

"STO, is it them?"

"Can't tell yet, Admiral. Hold on, sir." The STO tapped at his console and listened to his AIC briefly and then replied. "Aye, sir. I'm getting their squawk, sir."

"Good. The party was getting a little lonely." RADM Jefferson shifted the view of the main screen to the port side where the QMT throw forward had exited. In the middle of the viewscreen were three U.S. supercarriers. Wallace sent them all a greeting via DTM.

"CO, I've got the report back from the tech team that teleported down to the facility control room," the STO said without looking up from his station.

"Let me hear it, STO."

"Aye, sir. The facility is completely automated from somewhere on the planet's surface. There appears to be no possible method for overriding the lock-out codes. However, the location of the planetside control room was determined as the coordinates I'm sending you now, sir, along with the rest of their report." The STO paused for a breath.

"So we don't have to read a goddamned report, Monte, why don't you tell us where it is?" the XO snapped.

"Uh, yes, XO. I overlaid the coordinates on a topographical map of the planet. It is in the governor's mansion, sir," Captain Monte Freeman answered.

"Well then." The XO grinned. "Looks like we need to send some folks to visit the capital of this fine colony, Admiral."

"I couldn't agree with you more, XO. Get everybody off that rock, and let's get us a battleplan figured out five minutes ago. I want to hit that region in fifteen minutes." The admiral thought about his next move. They had to have control of the facility in order to get home. Their orders were to stop the secession by taking the government of the planet anyway. This way they got to kill two birds with one stone. "Start QMTing the personnel up and get the Starhawks out there bringing in the tanks. Let's just leave the fighter squadrons out. They can cover our approach in to the planet. Luckily for us, we only have to go straight down."

"Roger that, Admiral." The XO nodded in agreement. "Ground Boss, you heard the admiral. Get our tanks in here A-S-fucking-A-P."

"Yes, sir."

"Admiral, I've got an idea, sir," the STO said. "Why bring the ground mecha squadrons in and then drop them out again?"

"You have a better idea how to get those heavy beasties off the asteroid and down to the planet, Monte?" the XO interjected.

"Uh, yes, sir. We QMT the things one at a time from the asteroid, to the ship, to the surface in one QMT control algorithm. The QMT pad in the AEM hangar is big enough to handle one tank and a few troops at a time. With the help of the *Roosevelt*, *Lincoln*, and *Tyler*, it should go pretty fast." The STO pulled up a graphic displaying the speed they could do it and DTMed it to the bridge crew.

"Hmmm." The CO rubbed at his chin. "Might work."

"The only problem, sir, is we need to know where to send them."

"Larry! Get me a battlescape five seconds ago!" the admiral said to the XO.

"Aye, sir."

"CO! CDC!" The Combat Direction Center hailed the bridge.

"Go, CDC." RADM Jefferson adjusted his posture in his chair.

"We've got an incoming QMT, sir! EM bands through the roof!"

"Where, CDC!"

"Just inside the orbit of the second moon, about two hundred thousand kilometers off our port bow, sir!"

"Commo!" the admiral shouted.

"Sir?" The communications officer snapped her head up from her console and turned toward the CO.

"Get a command channel open between me and all the fleet ships!"

"Aye, sir." The comm officer turned back to her panel and then shouted back over her shoulder. "Channel open, CO."

"CO *Madira* to fleet! We've got incoming. Pull into a tight cover formation on the *Madira* and start teleporting my tank mecha from the QMT facility to the coordinates on the planet my XO is sending you now. My STO is sending the algorithm to automate the QMT process." Jefferson hit the mute button on his chair arm and turned to the XO and STO. "Get this done now, guys."

"Aye, sir!"

"Assume this is an all-out offensive folks, and we're likely to be outnumbered," he continued over the open channel. "Get your fighters out now! Good luck and Godspeed."

Wallace looked outside the ship in his DTM view and zoomed out to the QMT disturbance of the incoming. The light ball was just vanishing, and then eleven red blips appeared on his mind-view battlescape. He zoomed in farther and could tell that there were four ships like the one he had seen earlier that might as well be called supercarriers, five of what looked like Seppy battle cruisers, and two old Seppy rustbucket haulers.

Shit, we are so outnumbered, he thought.

Maybe we should jaunt away and come up with a better plan, sir, Uncle Timmy replied.

Negative, Tim. When under attack and outnumbered, the best strategy is always to strike first. But we have got to get our guys off that damned rock, fast.

Aye, sir. Then might I suggest we try to break them up as best we can and create two fronts for them to fight on?

I agree with that. Synchronize our blue-red force trackers with the fleet now.

Done, sir.

"Fleet, CO *Madira*! Focus all directed energy weapons on bogy two. Looks like a supercarrier, so treat as one. And assume they have personnel QMT, so keep your SIFs rotating or you risk being boarded."

The fleet vehicles had pulled into position over the QMT facility and had started teleporting the tankheads to the surface one tank—and as many AEMs or AAIs as they could pile on it—at a time. The tankheads, the AEMs, and the AAIs would have to fend for themselves for a while without air support. They should be able to hold their own against the Armored National Guard of the Arcadian Colony, providing the Arcadians didn't get help from the Separatist ships above them.

The fleet supercarriers began pouring directed energy beams onto the targeted Seppy supercarrier. The green DEG beams from the four fleet supercarriers washed the enemy ship from bow to stern. They kept pouring the energy at the vehicle continuously until the SIFs of the ship failed and hull plating began boiling off into space and secondary explosions burst out all across the vessel. The enemy ship listed to port into one of the Seppy haulers, and the rustbucket crumpled as the supercarrier tore into the side. Both ships listed together with explosion after explosion bursting from their seams.

"Those two ships are gonna need a shitload of duct tape," the COB remarked.

"Gunnery officer, keep pouring on the DEGs until we absolutely have to switch targets," the admiral ordered.

"Aye, sir!"

Then the rest of the Seppy vehicles spread out and began returning fire.

"All right, let's start the evasive maneuvers and keep the QMT algorithm going." Jefferson braced himself, expecting impacts from Seppy missiles and guns as soon as they were in range. They were already in DEG range. The speed-of-light limit, though, would make targeting tough at that distance. They had been lucky in that the Seppy ships were stationary. Hitting a maneuvering target at that range was difficult since there was a significant fraction of a second that ticked by between when the ships were targeted in the optical sensor and when the DEG beam actually reached the target.

"How do you want the Air Wing separated, Admiral?" the air boss shouted.

"I want them all to take it to the first Seppy supercarrier that gets in flight range! Navy and Marines both hit that ship as soon as we get in range. No fighters to the planet yet."

"Aye, sir!"

Two of the enemy supercarriers went into hyperspace and jaunted the gap in less than a second. They popped out of the hyperspace conduit at thirty thousand kilometers altitude orbit just beneath them and the QMT facility. They were right on top of them.

"All right, those are bogies one and seven. All mecha to one, all fleet vessels focus on seven! *Roosevelt*, hold back and cover our ass from those targets above."

"Roger that CO *Madira*. *Roosevelt* taking up the rear!" the CO of the *Roosevelt* replied.

"CO! CDC!"

"Go, CDC!"

"We've got incoming missiles and cannon fire, sir!"

"Roger that, CDC!" Wallace gripped his chair. "Brace for impact!" *Timmy, sound the warning.*

Aye, sir.

"All hands, all hands! Brace for impact! Emergency crews stand by! Multiple threats detected. Repeat, brace for impact and prepare for incoming fire." Uncle Timmy's voice boomed over the 1-MC intercom, shipwide.

"XO!"

"Aye, Skipper?" the XO replied.

"Larry, we need to report back to Washington. Get the first courier loaded with as much info as we can and snap him back to the Oort Cloud base." The admiral uploaded some thoughts very quickly to Uncle Timmy.

Timmy, get as much data as possible summarized for President Moore and get it on the courier.

Aye, sir.

He needs to know about DeathRay and about the size and strength of this new Seppy fleet.

Aye, sir.

"Quartermaster of the Watch!" the XO shouted. "You heard the admiral! Let's get courier one ready to snap-back in less than ninety seconds."

"Yes, sir!"

"Sir, another one of the Seppy supercarriers just went into hyperspace!" the STO announced. "I've got a conduit opening up behind us, sir. They'll be right on top of the *Roosevelt*!"

"Thanks, STO." RADM Jefferson adjusted his mindview to see the battlescape around the *Roosevelt*. If they played it right, they could get into a game of cat and mouse using the QMT asteroid as cover. "CO *Madira* to CO *Roosevelt*!"

"Go, *Madira!*"

"Jaunt behind the asteroid. I want to see if this Seppy bastard will pursue. If he doesn't, then jaunt back and press the attack! We'll focus on a crossfire gambit." The admiral knew that pulling the *Roosevelt* off their rear flank would leave the backdoor open and put them in a bad crossfire situation. But he needed to know if that was the Seppy battle plan or not.

Just how clever is their fleet captain, or are they fighting as individuals?

I see, Admiral. This will tell us how orchestrated their attack is.

Yes.

"Roger that, *Madira.*"

"Sir, the *Roosevelt* just jaunted out of the battle to a cover position behind the asteroid," the STO said.

"Doesn't look like he's going after the *Roosevelt*, sir." The XO added, "We're gonna be in a serious crossfire any second now."

"Good."

"CO *Madira* to Fleet! *Tyler* and *Lincoln*, take up point on the two lower bogies and give the *Roosevelt* and the *Madira* cover to take on the one that just jaunted to our backdoor."

"Sir! The *Roosevelt* is waiting for your order to jaunt back into play!"

"Tell them to bring it!" Wallace ordered.

CHAPTER 20

"Gotcha!" Karen toggled her mecha into fighter mode even as she passed through the debris field of the Seppy she had just splashed. She looked for her stand-in wingman, Dragon. The rookie was good, but Fish had flown as DeathRay's wingman for over a decade. Partnerships like that are hard to beat. Fish was as much a pro as DeathRay, and it was only a matter of time before they had new rookies that needed to be teamed up with more seasoned pilots. No matter, when DeathRay was away the Gods of War would notice the absence. Fish knew she'd just have to make up for it. Besides, wasn't nobody better than her anyway.

"Hard right, Fish! Hard right!" Dragon shouted. "Guns, guns, guns!"

"Ho, woo, shit!" She pulled back right on the stick, huffing and puffing against the g-load of her maneuver while adding throttle and slip. Her g-suit squeezed the hell out of her thighs and midsection, as her teeth clenched the mouthpiece, releasing oxygen and stims. A mecha-to-mecha missile passed way too fucking close to her plane.

"Dragon, where the hell are you?" She could see her wingman out there behind her in her DTM mindview but couldn't get a visual on the rookie pilot. The blue dot in her virtual battlescape displayed him bouncing around like a wild man. She hoped his physical stamina would hold up. Not pacing themselves was a big mistake that a lot of new pilots made in their first combat missions. Fish needed to get him to settle down.

"Fox three!" Dragon shouted as he barrel-rolled over Fish, going to his mecha-to-mecha missiles. "Ha! That's two of you mothers!"

"Great flying, Dragon. Try to pace yourself and don't make it harder than you have to," Fish ordered him.

"Got it, Fish," he panted back to her.

"We're getting pounded, Fish!" Lieutenant Commander Charles "Stinky" Allen complained over the net. "Just once I'd like to be on the side that has superior numbers. This shit is thick."

"Just another target-rich environment, Stinky," replied Fish.

"The best way to give us superior numbers is to kill a shitload more of them. Then we'll outnumber 'em and really give them hell," Lieutenant Denise "Crash" Fourier added.

"Roger that, Crash." Stinky grunted against a high g-load maneuver he was huffing and puffing his way through. "Damnit! Guns, guns, guns!"

"Dragon, you with me back there?" Fish scanned her DTM for more Seppy Gomers—there were plenty of Gnats and Stingers everywhere. She spotted a group of four Gomers moving in on Stinky and his new wingman, Lieutenant Junior Grade Song "TigerLady" Davis.

"Roger that, Fish," Dragon replied.

"Upstairs, angels ten, twelve o'clock high." She waited for Dragon to spot the bogies in his DTM.

"Got 'em."

The flight-wing missions were usually the same for the *Madira* pilots. The Gods of War typically kept the outer part of the ball clear and watched the backs of the Demon Dawgs. The Dawgs in turn watched the backs of the Utopian Saviors so the Marine mecha pilots could get in close with the objective, in this case an enemy supercarrier, and inflict as much damage as they could.

Fish pitched up ninety degrees and finally caught a clear visual of her wingman. Ensign Zeke "Dragon" Franklin was almost directly behind her, rolling around and around her line of flight, still wasting too much of his physical endurance. She pitched back over and then pulled in tight on his right wing, forcing him to settle into formation with her.

"TigerLady, Stinky, you've got four Gomers on your six. You'd better watch your ass before they get the drop on you."

"Roger that, Fish! I see 'em," Stinky replied.

"Stinky, these bastards are hellbent for us," TigerLady shouted. "We better do something quick to shake these motherfuckers! I'm getting pinged by a targeting tone!"

"Hold on for a few more seconds. We're coming."

Fish slammed the throttle all the way forward and pulled the stick to her stomach. Dragon stayed tight on her wing. They shot up into the higher altitudes of the engagement zone, in the direction of the QMT facility. They were already pulling six gravities, but anytime they had to juke or jink, the g-load shot up in the nine gravities range. Time was critical. If they didn't get up to Stinky and TigerLady in time to disrupt the Gomers on their six, the two pilots would be in serious trouble. Fish wasn't going to let that happen. DeathRay would kill himself to prevent that from happening. If that was what it took, that would just be what it took. Fish was beginning to realize the burden of being the squad commander. She couldn't imagine how it must feel to be the CAG.

"What's the plan, Fish?" Dragon said faintly against the added gravity.

"Okay, Dragon, we'll use DeathRay's favorite approach," Fish replied.

"Yeah, what's that?" the young ensign asked eagerly, hoping to learn some new wisdom and tactic of being a fighter pilot.

"DeathRay would say, 'All right, Fish, we fly in there, and we kill those motherfuckers.' So I think we should do that," Fish grunted.

"Uh, right. Good plan."

Spike, work the scenarios. Too bad Jack ain't here. He's missing all the fun, she thought to her AIC.

Roger that, Fish. He's probably goldbricking. A bunch of flight vectors jumped around in her virtual mindview, showing the flight paths of the Gomers, how they intercepted with Stinky and TigerLady, and where she and Dragon could converge on them and take them out. The red and blue lines twisted around and around each other in a confusing mess that looked like a sky full of multicolored spaghetti. The spaghetti was sinewy and tied up in knots with itself and was damned near indecipherable.

Remove the ones taking more than thirty seconds and all that require more than ten gees.

Roger that.

Most of the flight solutions vanished. There were three left that showed where they could get the drop on the enemy fighters if they did it right.

That one, Fish thought and made the other two go away. *Give it to Dragon.*

Done.

"Okay, Dragon, hold on to your ass and follow me in. Don't underestimate your kinetic energy or we'll overshoot them. We don't want to do that until we've mixed them up. Stay on my wing, but barrel-roll for the shot if you can get it."

"Roger that, Commander!"

Fish continued to push the throttle forward, but it just wouldn't go any farther. She jinked and juked through the attack pattern that Spike had laid out for her, sticking to it like a magic spell. A couple times it looked like if she stuck with the precalculated spell she'd turn into a frog, a dead bloody one at that, so she made up shit when that happened. She didn't turn into a fairy princess, but in a furball like this one she'd settle for "boat cute." If her plan worked, she was sure Stinky and TigerLady would think of her as at least "boat cute" and likely even queen of the fucking dance.

"I'm locked up!" Stinky shouted. The enemy Gnats had just about managed to drop in directly behind his six and put a bead on him and TigerLady. Seppy tracer rounds plowed through the space all around Stinky's mecha, and a few of them hit the rear portion of his empennage, rocking him pitch forward a bit, but he was lucky. His SIFs and armor plating held, and he managed to keep control of his fighter.

"You two wheel each other, damnit!" she ordered them. The two started barrel rolling in and out and around each other, hoping to confuse the enemy targeting systems. The constant barrel rolls made them look like a big wheel rotating in space out in front of her.

"They're too close, Fish!" TigerLady shouted.

"All right, goddamn it! Pull into the shortest downward bank you can stand, *now!*"

"Roger that! Banking down!" the two pilots shouted and grunted and cursed and grunted some more.

Stinky's mecha dove into a very tight downward turn. The g-forces on him would push him to the brink of blacking out.

Fish had done that maneuver hundreds of times and she knew that about then Stinky's seat would be several inches up his ass and his butt cheeks would be clenched as tight as he could get them. TigerLady, on the other hand, barrel-rolled over and around Stinky's mecha while staying with Stinky's vector. She continued in a wheel about him, and what she did next showed brilliance, superhuman stamina to withstand ungodly g-loads, and balls the size of the Jovian moons. She went to bot mode while keeping the same wheel vector about Stinky's downward roll-out.

"Damnit, TigerLady, what the fuck are you doing!" Dragon shouted.

Fish didn't think that the young pilot could take that kind of pressure for long. One of the enemy Gnats open fired with its cannon, and tracers lanced between Stinky and TigerLady, missing them both. Then another opened fired, but missed again. It was a good thing those Seppy Gomers weren't very good pilots, or things could have been a whole lot worse. As it was, a couple rounds pinged against TigerLady's hull plating, but they were glancing shots, and did little damage. Her bot-mode mecha yawed around to face her pursuers, and she opened fire with both forearm cannons.

"Aarrrrgggh! Guns, guns, guns!" TigerLady shouted. "Get off my ass, goddamnit!"

"Lookout!" Fish screamed through her bite block as friendly tracer rounds missed the enemy Gnats and flashed just past her cockpit. "Watch your firing solutions for blue on blue, goddamnit!"

"Fox three!" Dragon yelled.

"Fox three!" Fish followed up. Mecha-to-mecha missiles twisted out from Fish's and Dragon's mechas and both of them hit home on the Seppy Gnats. Two of the enemy fighters exploded almost simultaneously in a combining orange and white plasma ball. There was no time for the pilots to eject. Fish and Dragon plowed on through the fireballs where the two enemy fighters had been, passing the other three Gnats. They came into formation beside Stinky and TigerLady, who was still firing behind them at the remaining Gnats.

"Shit!" Fish banked and rolled while trying to swallow her stomach, then pitched one-hundred-eighty degrees and yawed forty-five. "Guns, guns, guns."

"Fox three!" TigerLady shouted. A missile screamed out from

the bot-mode fighter's midsection and twisted its way right into the cockpit of one of the pursuing Gnats. "Hot damn! That's one!" the young lieutenant shouted.

The two remaining Gnats continued to bank through the turn, trying to get a firing solution on any of the Ares. As the two Gomers pulled in tight behind them, their trajectories led them right across multiple firing solutions, and the four Navy aviators laid waste to the Seppies. But just before the last one crossed a firing solution, it did something that none of them had seen before. The Seppy Gnat transfigured into a bot mode and went into a Superman dive, going to guns with its forearm cannons.

"Guns, guns, guns!" Fish's railgun cannon tracers cut in across space in front of the transfigured Seppy Gnat and tracked its trajectory until it flew right through the forty-millimeter cannon rounds. The enemy fighter was ripped to shreds by a fusillade of baseball-sized, high-incendiary, armor-piercing tracer rounds, scattering debris and gas vapors from it.

"Guns, guns, guns!" Dragon followed up.

"Guns, guns, guns!" Stinky shouted.

"All wings, all wings! Be advised that the Gnats have a bot-mode! I repeat, the Seppy Gnats have a bot mode now!" Fish communicated wide, with full dispersion across all the flight-wing channels. She guessed that several others had to have seen the same by now and wondered why nobody had called it in.

"Fish, Fish, *Madira*!"

"Go, *Madira*!" Fish replied.

"We need air support dirtside! It's thick down there."

"Roger that, *Madira*. It's thick all goddamned over."

CHAPTER 21

July 1, 2394 AD
Sol System, White House
Friday, 3:26 PM, Earth Eastern Standard Time

"Yes, Mr. President, it would appear that the fleet ships in the Ross 128 system are severely outnumbered," the young courier officer said over the holoview communication from onboard the QMT facility out in the Oort. "The final information is encoded, and I was told by the admiral himself that you would understand this message. The message is, quote, Operation Bachelor Party is in play and has visual confirmation of missing package. Missing package is on enemy supercarrier that QMTed out that DeathRay pursued. DeathRay also confirmed via sensors that missing package was aboard said enemy supercarrier-class vessel just before he vanished with it."

Alexander Moore and his wife stood in front of the long mahogany conference table in the White House Situation Room, watching the holoview communication intently. The Situation Room had basically the same décor that President John Fitzgerald Kennedy had added back in the mid-twentieth century after the Bay of Pigs incident. President Moore stood grimacing with his arms folded at the head of the room where more than ninety-six other presidents had stood and pondered the heavy decisions of their time. As if the weight of the office bearing fully on his shoulders wasn't enough, now the fate of his teenage daughter was wrapped up in the decisions he would have to make. Was there some approach that his predecessors had used or some profound thought that had kept them on the right path that he could emulate? He wondered if other presidents thought the same things as they had stood there over the last couple of centuries.

How had President Alberts felt when he learned that the Separatists were attacking Mons City on Mars just twelve years earlier? How Nixon must have paced the room during the bombings of Hanoi. What of the "Great Communicator" President Reagan during the many Cold War incidents with the Soviet Union? What of the father and son Bushes during their respective wars in the Middle East? How had they felt? How had William Jefferson Clinton handled the stress of dealing with the fighting in old Africa? How did the several presidents that followed during the Global War of Muslim Extremism deal with those troubles? And how had the many presidents to follow the "Great Expansion" of humanity handled their various "situations" of slow economies, overpopulation, civil unrest between colonies throughout the Sol System, and political infighting for territorial control? Alexander thought about the great men and women of history that must have stood in the very spot he was standing, thinking what he was thinking. He thought of how the great general and—Alexander laughed to himself at the thought—President Sienna Madira handled the Separatist Secession and the creation of the Reservation in the desert of the red planet. *That crazy bitch probably had it all planned even back then,* he thought. He wouldn't be surprised if she had caused it to happen to put her plans into motion.

The one thing those presidents didn't have to deal with was the fact that their daughter had been kidnapped by the leader of the enemy forces. And the leader of those enemy forces wasn't the estranged mother of the First Spouse. *This goddamned mess has to fucking end,* he thought to himself.

Yes, sir, his AIC agreed.

"Are you sure that Captain Boland made it through the QMT jump to the other side?" Sehera asked the courier.

"Yes, ma'am. There was no sensor evidence of his fighter on this side of the jump."

"Only one place they could have gone, Mr. President," the secretary of defense said. "Tau Ceti."

"Yes, I agree." Moore ground his molars together so hard that it was audible. There was no way to know if his daughter was safe or not. That thought made veins bulge out and throb with each heartbeat. At least Boland and, amazingly, that CIA agent that had been presumed dead since the Luna City attack were there trying to get to her. But that just wasn't enough for Alexander. His face was red with the fiercest anger that he had felt in more than forty years.

"Alexander." Sehera put a hand on his shoulder and spoke calmly to him. "What do you think you are going to do?" Alexander could tell by the tone of her voice that she was being rhetorical.

"Thank you, Lieutenant, for this report. Send word back to the *Madira* that they absolutely must, and I mean must, carry this day to victory at Ross 128. We're going to send forward four more ships to help out. The *Blair* and the rest of the fleet are going to Tau Ceti to take that planet back. Lieutenant, you must tell Admiral Jefferson to expect no more help today and that he must under all costs be victorious. Good luck and Godspeed, son."

"Yes, sir. Thank you, Mr. President." The Navy lieutenant saluted, and Moore promptly and sharply returned it.

"Alexander?" Sehera said again, not letting go of his shoulder. "What are you planning to do?"

"Thomas!" Moore turned to his bodyguard, former AEM and longtime trusted friend. The man stood near the exit, blending into the woodwork.

"Yes, sir, Mr. President." The Secret Service agent stepped forward.

"Get Mr. Kudaf and our suits and be prepared to move out in ten minutes. Have Air Force One ready to teleport us up with jaunt coordinates prepared for the Mars QMT gate."

"Uh, Mr. President," Thomas started to respond, but Moore cut him off quickly.

"No discussion." Moore looked at Sehera and his bodyguard with that look that told them both that there was nothing they could do or say that was going to change his mind, so, they had just better get onboard and do what they could to help out.

"Mr. President?" the chairman of the Joint Chiefs interjected. "I'm not sure what you're planning, sir, but I don't think you should actually be in the middle of it. It would put you at serious risk, sir."

"Well, I am going. And that is that. Get the vice president in the White House in the event a transition needs to be made. Pick four supercarriers, get them loaded for war, and detach them immediately to the Ross 128 system. I want them QMTing in less than twenty minutes. Get Admiral, uh . . ." Moore was briefly at a loss. "Get the CO of the *Blair* to develop a battle plan to attack and hold the Tau Ceti system with the remaining fleet."

Rear Admiral Lower Half Sharon Walker, sir, Abigail told him DTM.

Thanks, Abby.

"Walker. Admiral Walker," he added out loud.

"Yes, Mr. President, but I'm not sure why you think you must go, sir. Mr. President, we've got Special Forces troops trained to—" The national security advisor, Frank Puckett, was cut off by Moore abruptly slamming his fists on the table.

"No, no, no!" He hit the table again. "Because, Frank, it is *my* daughter out there, and I'm going to by God go out there and bring her the fuck home!" Moore glared at the senior White House advisors and staff and his wife, daring them to defy him on this. If he had to, he'd get up on the table and kick all their asses right there. He'd put on an e-suit and go take over a ship himself and jump it there. He'd take on the entire goddamned universe if he had to, but he was going to help his daughter!

"Then I'm coming, too," Sehera added. "If you're going, I'm going."

Moore started to object, but he could tell from the look on her face that his objection would be duly noted and overruled. So he didn't respond. Instead, he turned to his staff.

"All right, make this happen." He took a deep breath and tried to calm himself. "I have grown so tired of dealing with these Separatists with the goddamned kid gloves on. I've tried being diplomatic, and every single time to no avail, no matter the approach. These people are waging warfare against our everyday way of life, and we have become so politically correct and bureaucratically corrupt that we can't seem to understand that we are standing in the middle of the goddamned forest staring at the bark on a fucking tree! I am so sick of seeing one good soldier after another killed in the endless skirmishes that are mainly the cause of *one person*. One crazy, evil person has used our own sedentary, benign, and I dare say, passive political personalities against us in such a way that we will not admit the obvious. WE ARE AT WAR! We have been at war for more than five decades. We have been at war ever since Elle Ahmi donned her ugly ski mask for the first time. Ever since I was tortured by that whack job in the Martian desert, we have been at war. Ever since she killed or had killed my entire platoon, we have been at war. Ever since she had tens and tens of thousands killed on Mars twelve years ago and ever since the Battle for the Oort QMT facility and the attack on Orlando, we have been at war. How many more good soldiers, America's finest, must we send to the grave because of our inability to accept the obvious? No, sir!" Alexander slammed his fists against the table again, jarring it to the point that coffee mugs jumped and pencils rolled onto the floor.

"No longer can I stomach this on my watch!" Moore hadn't felt free to do the right thing in so long that the emotions were flooding over him. The time had come to finally take care of business. "I, for one, am a soldier, and have always been a soldier, and it is time I stand up for what I believe in like a soldier and elections be goddamned! This is the last day that I will see the endless waste of the lives of one good soldier after the next. No, this will be the end of an old era. Possibly the end of my administration, but I don't give a damn. I'm going in there to get my daughter out and once and for all we will end this goddamned Separatist nonsense today! I'm issuing an executive order right now that the Separatist movement is to be eradicated from existence!"

When he finished his speech, the room was dead silent. He glowered around the room a couple of long, awkward moments. There were smiles on the faces of two of the Joint Chiefs and of the NSA. The others were more insider politicians and were horrified by the impact Moore's actions would have on the party and their careers. Alexander didn't give a flying fuck. It was time somebody did something that was best for the country and for humanity. He turned and marched out of the Situation Room with Sehera at his side matching him stride for stride. He didn't bother to ask the opinions of his Beltway advisors. He didn't need or want their approvals anyway.

"What do you think you are doing, Alexander?" Sehera asked him.

"I'm gonna end something that I should have ended forty goddamned years ago," he said.

Oorah! Sir! Abigail agreed with him. *I'm glad to see Major Moore back in action, sir.*

Fuck that. I'm promoting myself to general.

CHAPTER 22

July 1, 2394 AD
Ross 128, Arcadia, 10 kilometers south of the
capital city of Megalopolis
Friday, 3:26 PM, Earth Eastern Standard Time

The capital city of Arcadia was known as Megalopolis, with all the ancient Earth historical references intended. The governor's mansion sat on a hill in the middle of Capitol Park. The park was actually a forest reserve. The mansion was the only building in any direction for twenty kilometers, and surrounding it was a dense hardwood forest reminiscent of the oak trees that grow in the Appalachian Mountains of North America. There were three small rivers that met just south of the mansion, and there was ample Arcadian, as well as imported, wildlife living in the park.

Capitol Park was surrounded by four districts known only as Capitol North, Capitol South, Capitol East, and Capitol West. Capitol North was mainly a business and political district. Capitols East and West were manufacturing districts. Capitol South was the analog of the defense industrial complex district. A government building designed in honor of the Pentagon housed the leaders of the planet's Armored E-suit National Guard. Just to the west of the Capitol Pentagon was the armory for the National Guard as well as several airstrips and hangars. The planet had a small air force, but the ground forces were quite impressive.

Smaller city suburbs tied the four main cities together in a giant ring of humanity, pavement, steel, and streetlamps over forty kilometers in diameter. The local natural vegetation still

covered the region where there were no obvious signs of civiliza-
tion. In essence, Megalopolis was a giant ringed city about ten
kilometers in width surrounded both within and without by wild
natural forest land. There were roads that led into the governor's
mansion from each of the four main extensions, making the city
look like a giant wheel with four spokes when viewed from space.
The three rivers running through the forest were mostly straight
and formed a Y shape with the intersection on the south-sided
lawn of the mansion. The legs of the Y met the outer ring at the
five, one, and nine o'clock positions. The rivers added three offset
spokes to the wheel of Capitol Park and the Capitol Districts.

Colonel Mason "Warlord One" Warboys had been, just seconds
before, on the QMT asteroid forty thousand kilometers straight
up, looking up at four supercarriers of the U.S. Navy fleet being
pounded on by several enemy battleships. The U.S. fleet ships were
heavily outnumbered, and things didn't look too good for them
at the time. He was ordered to prepare for immediate teleport.
Rather than tac-nuking the capital city and risking large numbers of casualties, the plan was to drop ground and air forces to
take back Arcadia. After all, President Moore had promised to
minimize civilian casualties.

So Warboys prepared himself as best he could. He loaded as
many of Colonel Ramy Roberts's Robots AEMs onto the surface
of his tank as would fit and then told them to hold the fuck
on. For a brief instant he thought he saw a flash of the inside
of a supercarrier tank bay. Then the next thing he knew he was
in the middle of a forest staring at about fifty enemy tanks and
a line of Arcadian armored ground forces only two kilometers
away. The enemy troops detected his presence almost instantly
and started firing on his position. Small caliber railgun rounds
and larger caliber armor-piercing rounds with tracers filled the
air all around him.

"Holy shit! Roberts, get off my mecha!" Warlord One shouted
over the open tac-net to the AEMs. The armored e-suit marines
dove for cover almost as soon as they materialized from the
QMT teleport.

"Move it, Marines!" Warboys recognized First Sergeant Tamara
McCandless's voice. His DTM view showed the blue dots scrambling for cover behind trees and rocks. The trees didn't seem to
be helping the AEMs that much, as the larger rounds passed

through them like a knife through hot butter. The anti-mecha rounds from the enemy guns plowed through a ninety-year-old oak tree just to Warlord One's right like it was nothing more than balsa wood. The oaks splintered into millions of pieces as the forty-millimeter railgun rounds punched through them, leaving a splintered half-meter diameter trunk sticking up some three meters off the ground and another twenty meters of splintered tree raining down around him. Flames poured off both pieces of the tree, adding to the already hectic situation.

"Look out, Cross, that goddamned tree is gonna fall on top of your ass!" one of the AEMs shouted.

"Marines! Take cover and I'll see if I can draw some fire away from you," Colonel Warboys said. His heavy armor plating and SIFs gave him a much better chance of survival in the hailstorm of armor-piercing death than the AEMs. Their suits were tough, but not designed to take on anti-mecha armor piercing rounds like a hovertank was.

"Roger that, Warlord One! AEMs are digging in!" Colonel Roberts replied.

Warboys throttled his mecha up and moved the tank-mode metal through the trees as best he could, trying to perform some sort of evasive maneuvers. He took several low-caliber railgun rounds in the process. The rounds simply *twanged* against his tank, throwing sparks and ionized metal. The larger anti-mecha fire tracked onto him, which encouraged Mason to be more abrupt in his evasive maneuvers. The vegetation was so thick, however, that tank-mode wasn't very effective. He couldn't move around through the trees fast enough as a hovertank to avoid getting hammered by those large-caliber guns. His other choice while in tank mode would be to just ram the trees over, but that would seriously slow him down, cause unnecessary hazards to himself and the AEMs, and give him a serious headache after a couple trees. Warboys toggled his mode controls over to bot, and the tank flipped up and transfigured itself into a bipedal metal behemoth with a giant DEG barrel for a nose. The main railgun cannons of the mecha moved into position on the forearms of the standing armored bot.

Just off to the colonel's left and right two more tanks appeared out of QMT, each of them loaded with marines. A few seconds later, several more tanks popped in, loaded with either marines or Army infantry. The enemy line ahead of them was opening up with full force. There were almost enough U.S. troops teleported in to create an offensive line. Almost.

Cannon tracers and DEG blasts splashed all around them in a multicolored barrage of green directed-energy plasma burst and violet railgun ion trails. Another large thirty-meter-tall oak tree beside Warlord One suddenly burst in the middle from a cannon round, and wood chunks the size of a human leg were thrown asunder. Several of them ricocheted off his tank, making a loud *kathunk* sound against the armor plating. The large oak crashed down onto several of the marines just behind him. Flames engulfed the tree as the marines crawled out from underneath it. Their armored suits had protected them, but Warboys bet they had some serious headaches.

"Warlord One, this is Five!"

"Go, Five."

"Where the fuck are we, sir?"

"We are ten klicks south of the governor's mansion and ten klicks north of the Capitol Pentagon. We have to push north." Warboys panned the map in his head, looking at the terrain. It looked rough, and there were those damned rivers up ahead also. His lidar system took an extremely long integration time to find enemy targets through the foliage. His optical and IR sensors were marginal, but his QMs were working just fine. And what they showed was that there were more tanks and troops between him and the governor's mansion than there had been Seppy bastards that day of the Martian Exodus. It had been bad then, and he had had a squad of Marine FM-12s along for support, as well as air cover from the Navy. This scenario was probably really going to suck. It was probably going to suck big-time.

"Sir, if we were supposed to take that hill ten kilometers away, why the hell didn't we just teleport to there?" Warlord Three asked.

"According to my sensors, Three, it is way too goddamned thick with Seppies to drop in on them by ourselves. Plus, there so much goddamned EM noise around here that I'm not sure we could safely QMT any closer in. The Seppy bastards must have some kind of jamming fields around the Capitol. We draw them out, let fire and brimstone rain down from heaven, and then we punch a hole in the line and let the marines rush the end zone for a touchdown," Warboys replied.

"I see, sir."

"Besides that, it's our orders, Three."

"Yes, Colonel. But just what happens if that fire and brimstone doesn't come in time, sir?" Warlord Three asked.

"Well, Three, then we'll just have to improvise."

"Besides the fact that it is our goddamned orders, Corporal, my guess is that it is too fucking thick with Seppies up there for us to just drop in on them unannounced with no backup," Gunnery Sergeant Suez told Corporal Bates as the two of them dug in behind several large rocks. The landscape reminded Tommy of Tennessee more than any place he'd ever seen. Had he not known he was fifteen, or sixteen, or whatever number of light-years away from Earth, he'd have sworn he was somewhere just south of Knoxville. The steep hills covered with large oaks and white limestone rocks reminded him of that one time he had been to the Smoky Mountains when he had been a kid. He remembered being bored to tears as his parents drove around gawking at trees and waterfalls and bears and shit. This forest had enough going on in it, like enemy soldiers and tanks firing at them, that he didn't expect boredom to be a problem.

"Well, I was thinking that the governor might invite us in for tea," Bates replied.

"Gunny?" Colonel Roberts's voice came in through the net.

"Yes, sir, Colonel?"

"We need to dig in here for now and hold this spot. As soon as we see hell coming down from above, we'll make our push. Get your squad covered and do not let the Seppies advance on us. Watch out for those M3A16s. Those tanks are older than ours, but they're still tanks nonetheless."

"Yes, sir." Tommy checked his DTM mindview. Bates was right beside him. Howser, Willingham, and Sergeant Hubbard were dug in about fifty meters to his east, near the bank of the river.

Hey, where does this river go? he thought to his AIC.

Here is a map, Tommy. It goes right to the front lawn of the governor's mansion, where it Ys and strings outward to the nine and one o'clock positions of the Megalopolis beltway. In the other direction, the river crosses the beltway around five o'clock.

How deep is it?

The only records I have are from the local Internet connections.

It looks like it has a barge channel in it, so it must be at least ten meters deep.

That would be deep enough.

Deep enough for what?

"Top, got a second?" Tommy called to Tamara.

"Well, Gunny, other than ducking all this goddamned Seppy cannon fire and DEG plasma and watching out for these exploding fucking trees around me, I'm not that busy. I was considering taking a nap." It was the typical AEM joke. Tommy ignored it. Well, first he chuckled to himself, then he ducked and prayed as a tree just behind him crashed after it exploded about five meters up the trunk, *then* he ignored it.

"Well, Top, I'd hate to bother you while you're napping, but did you notice this river about a hundred meters to your east?"

"Uh, yeah, Tommy, what about it?"

"Well, Top, it has a barge channel in it, and it goes all the way to the front lawn of the governor's mansion." Tommy thought for a second, then added, "You think a tank can walk underwater?"

"Son of a bitch. Hold on, Gunny. I need to talk to the two colonels," Top said.

"What's up, Tommy?" Bates asked him.

"Danny, are you up for a swim?"

"I don't know, Mason, it might work. We might be able to go really quiet, as quiet as we fucking can, and slip right past them. Especially if there were enough resistance from the line here, it might just work. The Army armored infantry and some more tankheads could do that." Colonel Warboys listened to Colonel Roberts's wild-assed, harebrained, bat-crazy U.S. Marine scheme over the command net.

"Well, if we timed it with some help from above, I believe that might do. What do we do when we get there?" Warboys thought about it briefly as he ran his bot-mode tank through the forest, dodging trees and anti-mecha fire. He pulled up maps of the park and details of the rivers and was beginning to see a plan. "We'd be behind the lines, and they wouldn't be looking for us. A few tanks could cover you AEMs long enough to get inside and take the QMT controls. I dunno, Ramy. It's risky. But it might just work. It's a long shot your AEMs would survive."

"Hell, Mason, sitting around here like fish in a barrel ain't?"

"Good point. Shit! Guns, guns, guns!" He turned over backward to avoid incoming while returning fire in the general direction. He probably didn't hit anything but a fucking tree, but it might have at least made some Seppy bastard duck. "All right, Ramy. I'm getting tired of this shit. Our diversion strategy should still be our original strategy. The tanks and grunts on the line hold it until we get support from above. Then they try to poke a hole in the line and rush through to the mansion. By then we might be there, and we'd probably need somebody to cover our asses." Mason liked the plan. Well, it wasn't so much that he liked it as he liked it better than sitting around dodging cannon fire and exploding trees. The marine's plan was bold, daring, sneaky, and only a little bat-shit crazy. Only a little.

"I agree with that plan. We should shoot it up to the ground boss," Roberts said to the senior colonel.

"Yep. I'm a little busy over here. You want to take care of that?" Warboys dove his tank over a downed tree, taking cover from an incoming rain of anti-mecha fire. One of the tracer rounds passed just below his canopy and between the arm and torso of his mecha.

Shit that was close, he thought.

Too close, sir, his AIC agreed.

Warlord One's targeting system tracked the trajectory of the railgun rounds back to the generation-old tank that had nearly got him and then locked on with the DEG.

"Guns, guns, guns!" he shouted. The directed energy burst from the barrel atop his bot-mode tank and traced across the hillside, cutting through several oaks as it did. The DEG blast followed the enemy tank as it bounced through the woods up and down the slope until it finally hit its mark. The energy burst tore into the cockpit of the Arcadian M3A16 hovertank. The bot-mode tank exploded at the seams in an orange flash and then fell forward, sliding to a halt into an oak tree farther down the slope. Black smoke poured from the dead tank's joints and seals.

"Ground boss likes the plan, but can't be certain when we'll get top cover. Apparently, things are tough all over up there," Roberts communicated back to him. "I tried to convince them that things were tough all over down here, too. They said they would try to get us some FM-12s for backup."

"Air cover would be nice," Warboys replied.

"How long will it take you tankheads to walk ten kilometers underwater and against a current?"

"Uh, my AIC says eighteen point six minutes. Let's shoot for twenty-five," Warboys answered the Marine colonel.

"Got it. I'll work the plan. Assuming we get approval, let's be ready to move in five minutes. Pick your team and start moving them to the river without looking like you're moving them to the river."

"Roger that, Ramy. Let's do it."

"All right, folks, listen up!" Warlord One broadcast to all the tanks, AAIs, and AEMs. "Our mission is to take the governor's mansion. That is where the controls for that QMT facility are supposed to be, so we can't just blow it up from space. We have to march in there and take it away from the bastards standing there. Let's go show them how the United States of America plays king of the hill."

"Hoowah!"

"Oorah!"

The Warlords totaled twelve state-of-the-art M3A17 transfigurable tank mecha. There were two squads of AEMs and three squads of AAIs. Warboys's DTM view of the battlescape showed him at least fifty enemy tank mecha and more than a thousand ground troops, and that was just in the near vicinity. His long-range sensors showed a much larger mass of troops just beyond the main line between them and where the control center for the orbiting QMT facility was.

"Warlord Two, you and the rest of the even numbers will stay here and lead this attack. I'll take the odd-numbered Warlords and a few AEMs for a swim," Warboys ordered his second-in-command.

CHAPTER 23

July 1, 2394 AD
Ross 128, Arcadia Orbit
Friday, 3:38 PM, Earth Eastern Standard Time

The Utopian Saviors had been ordered to hit the Seppy supercarrier closest to the planet with all they had. The Demon Dawgs were backing them up and drawing the enemy ship's AA. Deuce and Goat, and Jawbone and Popstar had their FM-12s in bot mode, bouncing across the side of the hull of the giant armored spaceship that was presently facing the planet like fleas on a dog. These fleas were packing armor-piercing railgun cannons, DEGs, and a shitload of missiles, not to mention the hands and feet of their mecha. As they ran across the hull, they dropped HE grenades into any devices, protuberances, antennas, or any other parts of the spaceship that jutted beyond the structural integrity field that protected the hull. The strategy behind the battle plan was that the ship might be forced to die the death of a thousand cuts. The mecha attack on the one enemy supercarrier freed up the already overwhelmed fleet ships to focus their attack elsewhere. The problem was that the AA of the supercarrier was focused on the mecha, but the DEGs kept blasting toward the *Madira* and the *Tyler*. Deuce had already noted several hits. But that wasn't her mission right now. Skinny had taken several of the others around to hit the DEG battery. Deuce's team was tracking to the SIF-generator power conduits that ran along the underside of the supercarrier. And like any squad of good marines, they were creating mayhem and blowing shit up along the way.

Deuce clanked at over seventy kilometers per hour across the hull and flipped her mecha behind an AA box that was pumping out green tracer rounds into the fray around them. There was clearly some U.S. pilot in the targeting solution of the box. One of her buddies, most likely. She rose to her feet, bringing her DEG to bear on a Seppy Gnat that had been trying to lock her and Goat up. Goat flipped his mecha over her sideways and atop the AA box. Then he bounced to cover somewhere out of her visual several tens of meters behind her.

"Guns, guns, guns!" Deuce tracked across the horizon at the enemy fighter as it flew over the horizon of the ship's hull. "Shit, I missed!"

"Don't worry, Deuce," Goat said. "There's plenty more where that one came from! Fox three!" He let go a mecha-to-mecha missile that careened around a radome in front of him and twisted upward into the tail section of a Seppy Stinger that was pulling away from him. "Shit!" he shouted as the Stinger burst into a fireball.

"Goddamn, Goat, quit complaining. You got the Seppy bastard!" Popstar noted.

"I was aiming for the fucking radome! The goddamn sensor pulled off and locked up the fighter!" Goat replied.

"Don't worry, Goat," Deuce grunted. "There is plenty of shit to shoot at!" She ducked for cover behind an exhaust vent that jutted out of the deck behind the AA box as the Gnat that had vanished over the horizon of the ship screamed back up, going to bot mode. The Gnat hit the hull running at top speed and serpentined across the hull of the enemy ship toward her. The Seppy splashed her with DEGs but missed. The directed energy beam cut through empty space and kept on going and continued to track onto Deuce right up until she took cover. Then the Seppy Gomer cut the DEG off just in time to keep from blasting a hole in his own ship.

This Gomer has a hard-on for me.

Yes, ma'am! Her AIC started plotting possible trajectories for the enemy mecha.

And I still want to take out this fucking AA gun behind me.

Well, then, do it!

Right.

"Deuce! On your six!" her wingman warned her. Another enemy Gnat was starting to get a drop on her.

"I got it, Goat! Guns, guns, guns!" She leaped backward, firing both shoulder cannons and the giant DEG gun she held in her left armored mechanical hand into the AA box. She held the trigger in place until she saw the AA barrels stop firing, and then she carried her motion through a backflip with her feet thrusters at full throttle over the second enemy bot-mode mecha that had snuck up on her. Deuce went to missiles for it, and guns for his wingman that had been putting the pressure on her. "Fox three! Guns, guns, guns! Take that, you Gomer motherfuckers!"

She hit them both, but only took out the one in front of her. The Gnat that had been behind her managed to break out of her firing solution, and it got off a round of mecha-to-mecha missiles that were tracking in on Deuce's position way too fast at that short distance. The missiles arched upward from the mecha just as her guns had taken out the enemy fighter in front of her. As the missiles arched up and then back over, they acquired a radar lock on Deuce's FM-12, and the enemy fighter that had been behind her gave her the slip.

"Fuck! Goddamnit to fucking hell!" She rolled onto her back, firing at the incoming missiles with her DEG, triggered her electromagnetic countermeasures, burst some chaff, and then kicked her bot up into a full run using the ship's structural features for cover. "Eagle mode!" she cried as the missiles twisted and turned around the structural outcroppings of the Seppy supercarrier's hull. Deuce's fighter rolled over into eagle mode with the forty-millimeter cannons above and below the fuselage of the fighter and the DEG still in the left hand. The main drive of the fighter now was capable of flying the vehicle at top speeds and to outmaneuver the missiles. But just as she jinked around an outcropping on the ship's hull and was about to go full throttle and out of the missile's lock, an enemy Stinger twisted overhead and exploded, throwing fragments in her path that slammed into her nose. The impact of the unexpected explosion tossed her eagle-mode fighter tail over nose toward a sensor-array platform just ahead of her, and the missiles still had her locked up. Twice she managed to soften her tumble by putting her hands down, but the fighter was spinning beyond recovery.

"Hold on, Deuce! Fox three! Fox three! Guns, guns, guns! I got you." Jawbone's voice came through the net just as Deuce felt her eagle-mode mecha jerk into a completely different direction, throwing her against her restraints painfully.

Shit, I think that broke some ribs!

Stay with me, Colonel! Breathe! Hit the bite block! her AIC told her. Deuce chewed her TMJ bite block for a fresh load of stims and oxygen.

Jawbone had dived in between Deuce and the incoming while letting loose two missiles. Just as the missiles pulled out from her mecha, she gunned them down herself, creating a fireball of hot plasma and shrapnel between their mecha and the enemy missiles. The enemy missiles exploded behind them, as Jawbone then used the momentum of her jump and the force from the explosion to carry her into Deuce's path to knock her free of the sensor array.

"Shit! What the—" Deuce attempted to shake her head clear, but her mecha still spun wildly. Jawbone held fast to the right leg and arm of Deuce's eagle-mode mecha with both hands of her bot-mode FM-12.

"Just hang on. I'm spinning you down. Letting go in three, two, now!" Deuce could see Jawbone's mecha breaking off and bouncing back down on the deck, firing its DEGs into some other part of the spaceship.

"Fuck!" The Marine lieutenant colonel grunted and bit down on her TMJ bite block again, this time even harder, as the eagle-mode fighter steadied itself out of the spin. The effect of the stims washed over her, boosting her energy level from beyond exhausted to just really fucking tired.

Then suddenly she was thrown back and forth from incoming cannon fire—the goddamned Gnat that she had missed had managed to stay on her through all the shit. The armor and the SIFs held as Deuce shook the previous second's mess out of her mind and accepted her current predicament. That was what mecha pilots had to do. Forget the past and watch the present.

She had a Seppy Gnat trying to lock her up as she was climbing up into the gray area between the supercarrier's bowl and the bigger engagement ball. The enemy version of the Navy Ares fighter barrel-rolled around her trajectory line, trying to get a good shot at her. And she had pulled so far away from her wingman that there was no way he would get to her in time to help. She was on her own.

Deuce pulled the HOTAS back to her stomach and pushed full throttle forward, sending the FM-12 into a full-speed high g-load dive toward the enemy supercarrier and back into the bowl. She left her stomach somewhere at the top of her direction reversal, and she had to choke the bile back down as best she could. Her suit soaked up the rest fairly quickly. She managed the vector reversal just in time, as she was about to slip into a swarm of Gnats and Ares-Ts going at it above her.

She recognized several friendlies whizzing by as she pressed downward into her dive. A U.S. Navy Ares-T in bot mode passed by her so close she could read the pilot's helmet. It said "Poser."

"Watch out, Marine! You've got a Gomer on your six!" Poser warned her.

"I see him, Poser!" Deuce replied. She pushed down on the right foot pedal and pulled up on the left one, throwing a hard yaw into her flight path so she could target with her DEG as well as her cannons. She was flying backward and upside down, facing the Seppy fighter accelerating into her flight path. She rolled the nose around, trying to keep the enemy in view. No matter what she did, she couldn't seem to lock up the bastard.

"Warning, enemy targeting radar detected. Warning, enemy targeting radar detected," her Bitchin' Betty warned her. The cannon tracers flying by her in every direction were a bit of a hint as well.

There he is, Deuce! her AIC alerted her, already downloading the vector to her DTM.

Got it! Deuce yawed another thirty degrees and pitched up. Her missile-guidance sensor sounded a tone, and the yellow X in her mind turned red.

"Warning, enemy targeting lock imminent. Warning, enemy targeting lock imminent."

"Fox three!" Deuce shouted. "Not any fucking more! Aaaaaahh, woo, hoo!" She grunted through the bone-crushing maneuver, trying to force more blood and oxygen back into her brain. The missile flew out from under her wing toward the enemy fighter and into the thing's cockpit. Just before the missile hit, the canopy blew and the ejection seat launched into space. The Seppy Gnat exploded into a white and orange fireball, almost engulfing its pilot.

Great shot, Deuce!

Let's get back on the deck. Deuce toggled to fighter mode and corrected her flight path back into a strafing dive toward the enemy supercarrier's hull.

"Goat, where the hell are you?" she shouted out to her wingman as she pulled up over the hull of the ship. Her DTM mindview showed him close by, bouncing on the deck, but she couldn't find him visually.

"Great flying, boss. Now see if you can help me get this Stinger off my ass!"

"Roger that, Goat. I see 'im!" Deuce increased her acceleration to the deck until she reached the point that she wouldn't be able to flare out of the dive if she didn't back off. "Guns, guns, guns!"

Tracer rounds tracked out of the cannons and pounded against the SIF-reinforced hull of the Seppy supercarrier on either side of the enemy Stinger. The enemy fighter was in bot mode and chasing Goat around and about the hull. Goat was diving for cover as best he could and running about trying to stay ahead of his pursuer. Deuce kept pouring the rounds into the deck at the enemy bot but couldn't lock up on him. Her speed was such that she was going to overtake the bot and Goat in about two seconds. She'd have to bleed off most of her speed in order to get behind the enemy Stinger.

"Goat! Go to eagle mode now and pull out at full throttle!" She hoped the Stinger would take the bait. The Stinger's cannons started tracking at Deuce and firing.

"Warning, enemy targeting radar detected! Warning, enemy targeting radar detected!"

"Hell!" Deuce rolled about her flight path, still holding the trigger of her guns. She caught a glimpse of Goat's mecha launching from the hull out and up, away from the enemy bot. The enemy transfigured to fighter and took off after him while still firing its topside cannons backward at Deuce.

She rolled around and around the firing solution of the rearward cannon fire, taking a few tracers into her nose plating. Her armor and SIFs held. As Goat screamed away and the enemy pursued hot on his tail, it pulled their vectors out in front of Deuce's really hot approach. She pulled the throttle full back, slamming her forward into her restraints.

"Unh! Goddamned fuck!" she screamed at the negative g-load. "Faster, Goat! Faster!"

Deuce continued to roll and adjust her trajectory so as not to overshoot the enemy fighter. She managed to control her kinetic energy just enough that she pulled up right on top of the Stinger. As she rolled cockpit toward the enemy fighter, she could see him looking up at her only meters away. The two of them bounced around each other several times, the Stinger in fighter mode and Deuce's FM-12 in eagle mode.

"Fuck this," she muttered. Deuce pulled out away from the enemy fighter far enough to roll one hundred and eight degrees over, putting her eagle-mode talons and hands toward the enemy fighter. She stomped at the cockpit with her claws and gripped them. The two mecha locked together and pitched forward madly. The nose of Deuce's mecha slammed into the empennage of the enemy fighter. Then she used her right fist and punched it through the armor of the fighter repeatedly until she hit the power core. Finally, the cockpit tore free, and she spun off of the fighter, still gripping it in her talons. Sparks and air vented from the enemy plane, and then the ejection seat blew just as the fighter exploded from within, throwing the wings off in two different directions. One of the wings ricocheted off her canopy but did no damage she could detect.

"Savior Team One, we have got to get our focus back on to those SIF generators!" She straightened out her flight path and pulled her trajectory back around to the supercarrier. "Jawbone, Popstar? You with me?"

"Roger that, Deuce," Jawbone replied.

"I'm on Jaw's wing," Popstar added.

"Good. Goat, wing up with me, and let's get back down there and get those damned SIFs knocked out!"

Other than the enemy supercarrier and the hauler that the fleet ships had managed to knock out of commission at the start, the battle had not gone that great. The *Roosevelt* and the *Madira* had managed to catch one of the supercarriers in a cross fire just above the QMT facility and did overtax that ship's SIFs and armor briefly. The sensors had shown that they were ablating the hull and that atmosphere was venting from the enemy ship into space. Then RADM Wallace Jefferson realized that the damned Seppy bastards were pulling the same trick on him. The lone ship advancing on them from the rear was just bait.

As soon as the *Madira* and the *Roosevelt* pulled away from the *Lincoln* and *Tyler*, three enemy battle cruiser–class ships jaunted into position, splitting the fleet into two groups. Now they were in a mix of two enemy supercarriers at thirty-thousand kilometers altitude above the planet in non-Keplerian hover orbits. Just above them were the *Lincoln* and the *Tyler*. Above the *Lincoln* and *Tyler* were the three enemy battle cruisers that had just jaunted into position. Then came the *Madira,* with the QMT facility off to starboard. Above the *Madira* was another enemy supercarrier, and beyond that enemy ship was the *Roosevelt.* There were still two battle cruisers, a supercarrier, and one hauler that the enemy was holding in reserve, way out around two hundred and fifty kilometers or so. Wallace wasn't quite sure why they were waiting to swoop in for the kill. But at the moment he had too much on his mind to worry about the ships that were *not* engaging him and the fleet.

"CO! CHENG!"

"Go, CHENG!" the admiral answered from his captain's chair. The *Madira* was rocking left and right and up and down from the overwhelming punishment she was taking. Wally kept his seat belt pulled tight against his midsection.

"Admiral! We're gonna lose the SIF generators in three minutes if this pounding continues. They just can't take it any longer," Commander Joe Buckley Jr. warned him.

"Keep them running, Joe! If those SIFs go out, we'll get boarded for certain!" the admiral ordered. He turned to his executive officer off-mike. "XO, better get marines stationed at all critical systems of the ship, and I want everybody carrying a sidearm or an HVAR."

"Aye, sir." The XO turned and started sending orders to onboard security details.

"Sorry, sir," the CHENG continued. "There will be nothing we can do unless we can jaunt out of here and cool off for a few minutes. The DEGs and AA systems are running full bore and have taxed the coolant systems to the max. Which would you rather lose first, sir, the SIFs or the DEGs or the AA guns?"

"I don't want to lose any of 'em, CHENG! Figure it out!" the admiral ordered his new chief engineer.

"Yes, sir. But I just wanted to advise you, sir, that if the SIFs go, everything is gonna go quickly, sir!" Commander Buckley's voice sounded pretty certain. Wallace was fairly good at determining if his officers were exaggerating a situation due to fear, and he didn't think Joe was that type of officer. Hell, he knew Buckley wasn't. The kid had already damned near killed himself to protect the ship. Wallace figured he'd better take his advice.

"Very well, CHENG." Wallace thought for a second or two, trying to figure out what tactic to take. "Keep at it, Joe."

"CO!" the ground boss called for his attention.

"Go, James."

"Sir, we desperately need to get some air support dirtside. Our tanks and AEMs are taking a pounding. The Robots, the Warlords, and the entire AAI battalion are constantly calling for support, sir. Casualty rates are growing beyond acceptable rates, sir." The one-star Army general also sounded certain that things were getting rough downstairs. This battleplan wasn't working worth a damn, and Wallace knew he needed to make a change in his tactics quickly or shit was going to get even worse.

"Admiral, this might be a good time to do a strafing run and turn this damned space ball into a bowl," the XO suggested.

"Air Boss concurs with the XO on that, Admiral!"

As it stood, the battle was filling a three-dimensional sphere or "ball," and it was a common trick for fighter pilots to pull a fight down close to the surface of a ship or planet to take out half of the sphere, turning it into an upside-down bowl. That way bad things couldn't sneak up from underneath. Well, there were mountains, AA fire, and such, but another fighter couldn't get under you if you were hugging the surface. Another good aspect of going to the atmosphere would be that Seppy haulers were no good there. That would limit at least one of the ships that hadn't attacked them from way out in deep orbit yet. Since the other Seppy ships seemed to perform as well or better than the U.S. supercarriers, Wally had no choice but to assume they operated in atmosphere just as well.

"I think you're all correct." Wallace studied the mindview battlescape closely and then sighed. "I hate running from a fight just to get into another one."

"Yes, sir," the XO grunted. "We'll get back to them in good time. Or, hell, sir, they'll probably just follow us any damned way."

"Nav! Prepare for treetop strafing runs on the enemy positions near the governor's mansion. Gunnery Officer Hall, I want you taking hell to those enemy tank lines!"

"Aye, sir!"

"Fleet, this is the *Madira*! Pull out of the current engagement, and let's put this battle near the surface. If the Seppy bastards want to fight us, they'll have to come down to the atmosphere and do it. I want all ships to jaunt out of this fight in two minutes, to these coordinates. Starting now, I want all ships running the QMT site-to-site algorithm teleporting the fighter squadrons to twenty kilometers above the engagement zone below. If we haven't finished teleporting all the fighters, we still jaunt and will take back up the QMT effort as soon as we materialize back into normal space." He DTMed his battle plan to the other Navy supercarrier captains. "Once we are out of the fray and in normal space, we'll lick our wounds for two minutes, and then we hit the deck, blasting away. All fighter squadrons are to take it to the Seppy line in standard layered protection zones and cover the groundpounders and our strafing runs. Air bosses will be sending our flight plan soon."

"All hands, all hands, prepare for hyperspace jaunt in ten, nine, eight, seven, six . . ."

CHAPTER 24

"I never thought I'd see you again, Penzington!" DeathRay was so glad to finally do the twist and pull, taking his helmet off. Finally he could rub his neck where it hurt like hell. Penzington had dragged him into the Seppy Lorda that she had commandeered and was running the ship through a take-off cycle.

"Well, there have been times when I'd have thought that nobody ever would. You okay?" She looked over her shoulder at him from the pilot's chair of the enemy troop transport vehicle.

"Penzington?" DeathRay did a double take. "Is that you?"

"It's me, DeathRay. Had to have a little work done to change my look. Hazards of the job."

"Well they sure did good work." DeathRay was pretty sure he looked like hell warmed over.

"The ejection chair absorbed most of the crash landing onto the QMT moon, but my already broken tailbone, back, and neck from the previous crash into the ship hadn't quite healed yet. So it fucking hurt when I hit." Jack gritted his teeth and pulled himself into the copilot's chair. He snapped the safety cap off another shot of immunoboost and jammed it into his neck. He started feeling better almost instantly. "I'll be tip top before we hit the planet. What's our ETA on that? Do we have a plan?"

"ETA depends on where we are going, but we could be on the planet in five to ten minutes. A plan? Well, no. Intel? Yes. Deanna

211

Moore is being held in Elle Ahmi's penthouse suite. We have to get inside there to get her out," Nancy responded. "I can get in as Ensign Bella Penrose to the first or maybe second floor, but there is no way to get to the penthouse through the front door. And there are SIFs around the top floors, so we can't teleport in."

"What else do we know about the penthouse?" Jack rubbed his neck some more and then started pulling off the flight armor suit down to the second skin layer. He slid out a small bag about the size of a deck of playing cards and unfolded the contents from within it. The universal combat uniform top and pants he pulled from the vacuum-packed bag expanded as soon as they hit the air. He shook the no-wrinkle, fire-retardant, nanotube-armored compression materials out and set them aside as he pulled the organogel seal layer off his body. The seal layer *schlurrped* like pulling a suction cup from wet glass. Then he slipped into the UCUs and put his flight boots back on. He stretched his spine straight briefly and was certain that he'd be fine in five or ten minutes. He pulled an MRE bar from his gear and started crunching on it.

"Hungry?" he offered the CIA agent a bite. "Damned immuno-boost and stims make me hungry and thirsty as a horse."

"Uh, no thanks," Nancy said.

"Okay, so what'd we know about the penthouse?"

"There is only one elevator into it, and only Elle Ahmi has the key."

"Well, is it guarded with AA guns as well as SIFs? If not, I say we ram in there with this ship and just take her away. All I have to do is put this on her." Jack showed Nancy the forward QMT teleport device on his wrist. "I push this button, and she'll be teleported to the Oval Office. Well, after we clear the SIFs, of course."

"I don't know about the AA, but I'd imagine it has at least the same protections that the White House would have. And I doubt we could knock out the SIFs long enough to get through them *and* back out. I used a Lorda and a Stinger once to burst through the SIFs on a battle cruiser, and I barely had time to punch through before they closed back up." Nancy glanced over at Jack and shrugged.

"How are we not being chased down right now?" It had just dawned on Jack that they were in a Seppy troop/cargo transport vehicle—the counterpart to the U.S. Starhawk—and nobody seemed to be looking for them.

"After twelve years of being here, my AIC is really good at

negotiating with the Seppy flight-manifest systems. As far as anybody but us knows, we are doing just what we are supposed to be doing," Nancy replied quite confidently.

"Jesus, that's right. You've been here all by yourself a long fucking time. That's a hell of a sacrifice, Penzington." DeathRay had gone into the shit many times over in the past couple of decades, but he hadn't been in it twenty-four hours a day, seven days a week for over a decade. That had to be hell on your psyche. His respect for the CIA agent went through the roof as he made the realization.

"It's my job, Jack. I volunteered for it, same as you." Nancy shrugged. "So, what is our plan?"

"Can that AIC of yours figure out where the SIF generators for the penthouse are?" Jack finished off the food bar and swigged at some sports drink from a pouch in his flight suit. He was beginning to feel his normal self again.

"She says so. Here, I'll put her on speaker," Nancy said.

Candis, go audible also, he told his AIC.

Roger that.

"Hello, Captain Boland, my name is Allison," Penzington's AIC said. Jack was surprised it was a female AIC. Jack had long known that some women can talk to a female personality easier than a male one. Some couldn't. As fully female as Penzington appeared, he half expected some very male and suave voice. He was always surprised by the story he found inside the cover of books. He thought of Fish. Karen Fisher was more than "boat cute" by a long shot, but she was as much a tomboy as anybody would ever meet. Her AIC was as male as could be.

"Nice to meet you, Allison, Ms. Penzington. I'm Candis."

"Call me Jack, or DeathRay, Allison."

"Yes, Captain," Allison replied.

"So, what can you tell us about the SIF generators on the penthouse?" Nancy asked her AIC audibly.

"Here, I'm transmitting a DTM image of the Capitol Building at New Tharsis. The engineering components of the building are mainly in the basement area here," Allison pointed out in Jack's mindview. He could see the Seppy leader's building, and then it zoomed in and downward to an auxiliary equipment room beneath and behind it.

"Hmm, that is kind of stupid. There are no SIFs around the SIF generators?" Jack pondered out loud.

"Yeah, that seems a bit uncalculated for Ahmi, doesn't it?" Candis added.

"Well, if you take into account that there is a garrison of soldiers that usually stands guard there, I'm not so sure," Allison answered.

"Well, were I to attack from the air or space or even with tankheads, I'd go for the SIF generators first." Jack replied. That gave him an idea.

"Hey, that gives me an idea," Nancy said.

"Me, too. You go first." DeathRay turned to the CIA agent and pointed. He smiled at Nancy. She looked a lot different than he remembered her. Her hair was a different color, and shorter, her body was very tanned from what he could tell, she was in amazing athletic shape, or at least the enemy compression flight suit she wore suggested so, and she looked much younger. Jack was sure she had been rejuved fairly recently, maybe within the last four or five years.

"Okay. We see about commandeering some mecha." Nancy didn't seem to even flinch at the thought of stealing enemy fighters. Jack just figured that her time here must have really made her proficient at getting what she needed. "Stingers or Gnats would be fine. We autopilot the Lorda into the SIF generators, and then we burst into the penthouse with the fighters. There you teleport her out of danger. Then we fight our way out as best we can. Or not."

"Okay. That's more or less my plan. I figured you being a secret agent and all, your plan would be more sneaking around, breaking and entering, and getting out without being detected." Jack smirked at Nancy with his left eyebrow raised.

"I prefer the direct approach sometimes," she said. The tone in her voice almost sounded to Jack like an invitation to flirt with her. Some other time he'd consider it, but right now, saving Dee was the only thing on his mind.

Saving Dee was the only thing on Alexander's mind. He and Sehera and his two loyal Marine bodyguards had rushed across the Sol System to the QMT facility in the Oort Cloud. They boarded the USS *Anthony Blair* only seconds before the jump to Tau Ceti. Alexander and company were led to the bridge by the XO of the ship as the QMT teleport occurred. Before they reached the bridge, the entire remaining U.S. Naval Fleet had teleported to a three-minute hyperspace jaunt from the planet Ares. That put them about four-and-a-half astronomical units from the planet.

Their location was directly out of the ecliptic plane of the Tau Ceti system above Ares.

"Mr. President." Rear Admiral Lower Half Sharon "Fullback" Walker addressed him as he stepped onto the bridge of the supercarrier. The rest of the bridge crew stood at attention and saluted. Moore promptly returned the salute.

"Please, as you all were. Admiral Walker. Thank you for, uh, entertaining us today." Alexander smiled at her through thin lips. His sense of humor had left him about the time he realized his daughter was in trouble. Sehera stood beside him, and the other two marines stood behind him quietly.

"My pleasure, Mr. President. What are your orders, sir?"

"I'm not here to give you orders, Admiral. I know two things about running a supercarrier, and diddly is one of them. We are here to take this system back from the goddamned Separatists, and I am here specifically to find my daughter, who has been kidnapped by Elle Ahmi!"

Admiral Walker gasped. "My God, sir! We had no idea. We are at your disposal, sir."

"No, Admiral. Once we have found Deanna and gotten her safe, we'll get out of your way. My guess is that the Seppies must have detected our QMT by now. Shouldn't we be getting the battle plan under way?" Moore nodded to the admiral.

"Uh, yes, Mr. President. We have. I'll have the long-range sensors looking for your daughter." Walker turned to her crew. "STO, start looking for the First Daughter's AIC emergency beacon as soon as we get into range."

"Aye, ma'am!"

"As soon as you find her, Admiral, my team and I will be teleporting down as close to her as you can manage," Moore said, motioning to his wife and the two bodyguards with him. The four of them were wearing AEM skin suits. "We'll be in the QMT deck getting our suits on."

"Uh, sir, we need to speak . . . privately. If you'd join me in the briefing room."

The president was ready to cut the Admiral off on the spot but looked around the command deck and thought better of it.

"After you, Admiral."

With a nod from the admiral, the STO joined them, as did Sehera and their Secret Servicemen, Thomas and Koodie.

As soon as they were alone, both Admiral Walker and the president started to talk, but the admiral quickly ceded the floor to her commander-in-chief.

"—I know what you're going to say, Admiral, but I don't give a flying damn. I'm going down to that planet, and I'm going to find my little girl and bring her home."

"With all due respect, sir, you aren't. I know what you're feeling, but we will not allow it."

"We?"

"Sir, there's not a single senior officer in this fleet who would allow you to go down to that planet, even if you order them directly, even if you do have snap-back QMT wristbands." The STO had been nodding in agreement with his CO, until a withering glare from the president caused him to tuck in his chin like a plebe being dressed down.

"Knowing we have a way to whisk you away to safety is why I didn't object when you insisted on coming aboard. But it's one thing to know we have got some of the strongest armor and SIFs in the entire fleet between you and harm's way. It's quite another to let you go down to a hostile planet. Unless you're ready to relieve every officer serving in this fleet, you are not going down to that planet, Mr. President."

Moore looked about ready to explode. He glanced at his bodyguards, but they didn't flinch, nod, or wink. They'd been with Moore for too long and seen him do what he damned well had to and Secret Service be damned. Moore looked back at the admiral.

The STO snapped to attention, and spoke. "Mr. President, we cannot allow the enemy a chance to capture you. It is simply unthinkable, sir. It could completely compromise our attack."

President Moore looked ready to chew through a bulkhead until his wife laid a hand upon his clenched arm, breaking his intense glare at the officers.

"Alexander, they're right. And you know it." Something passed between the husband and wife, and President Moore relaxed ever so slightly. Sehera turned to the Secret Service men. "Thomas will get her for us, won't you?"

"Yes, ma'am." Thomas and Koodie stepped forward and nodded.

Abby, we expected this.

Sir.

Move out on our other plans.

Yes, Mr. President, his AIC responded and then added, *or is that General?*

"Might I suggest we send along a squad or two of AEMs or mecha?" Walker asked.

"No, Admiral," President Moore said. "That would draw too much attention. As long as you make a menace of yourselves elsewhere, that should provide all the diversion . . . they need."

"CO! CDC!"

"Excuse me, sir." Walker tapped a button on her comm. "Go, CDC!"

"CO, long-range sensors have picked up two friendly AIC handshaking signals." Walker turned to Moore inquisitively but said nothing.

"Might be DeathRay and that CIA agent, Alexander," Sehera interjected. "Talk to them!"

"Admiral, can you connect us?"

"Not sure. CDC, can you connect us to the two signals?" Walker asked.

"Hold on, CO." Moore and Walker passed glances back and forth during the brief seconds they waited for an answer. Walker didn't think they were close enough to get a connection with the AICs. Limits were usually about a light-minute with no large repeaters. The *Blair* had plenty of amplification, but the little AIC on the other end didn't. "Sorry, ma'am. They are too far away."

"Keep at it, CDC. I need to know as soon as you connect to them."

"Mr. President?"

"I say we start getting this attack under way."

"Agreed, sir. We'll jaunt in and attack in five minutes, sir," she said as she snapped a picture-perfect salute, trying to keep the relief from showing on her face.

"So, Nancy, uh, nice place here. And, where did you get these mecha?" Jack asked. They had landed just outside New Tharsis at a fairly nice farmhouse. The hangar in the back acreage of the farm housed two Seppy Gnats.

"Oh, well, I've squirreled away Seppy dollars for years, and I have several safe houses spread about the planet. This is one of the better ones. The mecha are actually part of a requisition error made on an order to the manufacturer. They delivered two more than they were supposed to down at the spaceport in New

Tharsis. I happened to be a shipping clerk by the name of Carrie Thomas there about five years ago. I needed to do some training in these, so I managed to get them here. There's also an Orca drop tank out back. The logistics was a little more complicated than it sounds. The point is, I have them. We can use them. Think you can fly one?" Jack tried not to laugh. Nancy had managed to infiltrate the Seppy acquisition system so well that she procured two brand-new Gnats without anybody ever missing them. She and her AIC must be real good at their day job.

Jack started slipping his flight gear back on, and Nancy followed his lead and pulled out some flight armor from a locker in the hangar. The two of them changed and climbed into the mecha.

"Hey, this thing feels almost just like my Ares-T. The controls inside the cockpit are identical down to the coloring," he shouted to Nancy.

"Yeah. They stole the blueprints from the manufacturer. They are as close to a real Ares-T as it gets," she replied.

Jack pulled his helmet down with a twist and lock. Air hissed into his face. Instinctively he started to pull the hardwire UDP connector out and plug it in to his shoulder harness port.

Jack, not sure about going hardwire. It would be harder to fire-wall attacks from the Seppy AIs, Candis warned him.

Fine with me. He let go the cable, and it reeled itself back into the panel.

"You read me, Nancy?" He spoke into the communications net link he created between his and her fighter. He started toggling through the weapons stores in the mecha. The enemy mecha was loaded for bear. Penzington was prepared. Prepared for what, Jack wasn't certain.

"I got you loud and clear, DeathRay. Try not to damage my hangar as you pull out."

"Roger that, Penzington." Jack thought about it as he cycled the landing gear up and went onto the hoverfield. "Have you filed a flight plan for us, or are we going to hit a bunch of resistance along the way?"

"We should be good right up until the last couple of kilometers. Then we should go thrusters full," Nancy said.

"Right. Good. Let's get on with it."

"Roger that, DeathRay."

Hold on, Dee, we're coming, he thought.

CHAPTER 25

July 1, 2394 AD
Tau Ceti, New Tharsis
Friday, 3:44 PM, Earth Eastern Standard Time

"It would appear that your father has sent a fleet of ships to rescue you, my dear." Elle Ahmi looked at Dee with what she would have described as a crazed look. "I had better take care of this. Don't bother trying to escape. And don't worry. You are perfectly safe here, Dee. I wouldn't want anything to happen to you."

"Then why don't you just let me go?" Dee argued with her terrorist grandmother.

"Ah, I wish it were that simple. But there are things happening here today that are bigger than all of us." Ahmi held her hand up to Deanna's cheek and touched it gently. "I wish we could have met under better circumstances. I'll return shortly." She turned and met the elevator as it rose up from the floor. Dee tried not to shudder from the touch. Ahmi donned her ski mask as the elevator dropped out of sight.

Several minutes passed before Dee decided to gather herself up and try to find a way out. She walked around and around the periphery of the terrorist leader's penthouse but couldn't really find anything of use. Every drawer, closet, door, or other moving part, blunt instrument, or sharp object was behind an AIC lock that probably only Ahmi's AIC could unlock. Dee was trapped in a very good prison, behind SIFs, and several stories up.

What do I need to do here? she thought to herself. If her father had sent a fleet to Tau Ceti, then she needed to contact them.

She decided to allow her AIC to handshake briefly with any so-called friendlies that might be out there.

Be careful, Bree, but see what you can see, she told her AIC.

Sure thing, Dee. I'm looking.

Well?

I don't see any fleet vessels, but that could just mean they are too far away to detect. I am getting a response from two different AICs. One from that supposed CIA lady again . . . and the other from DeathRay!

DeathRay! He's here!

Apparently so. All the security clearances check out, and it certainly appears to be Candis—DeathRay's AIC. The probability of the Seppies being able to forge such an exact replica of Candis, much less having known to do so, borders on nil.

Put me through!

Okay. Go.

DeathRay, DeathRay! Is that you? Dee thought frantically.

Yes, Dee. It's me. I have a CIA agent with me as well. We are on our way right now to free you. We'll be there in about thirty seconds.

Holy shit! I'm so glad to hear from you. Ahmi just left about five minutes ago from this penthouse, saying that my father had sent a fleet of ships. Are you with them?

No, Dee! I don't know anything about that. I'll check into it. In the meantime, if you can, go to the south side of the penthouse and take cover!

Roger that, DeathRay!

Dee looked out the window, trying to decide what south was on a moon orbiting a Jovian. She applied the same logic as she would on Earth. The rings of the Jovian planet had risen earlier, so she assumed that direction was east. She pushed the love seat over and dragged it next to the far window and then crawled under it. About that time, an enormous blast made the penthouse ring and rattled her teeth. At first she thought they might be explosions, but then she realized it must be AA cannon fire coming from the rooftop. Hell, she was practically on the rooftop, so that fire was coming from just outside. No wonder it sounded so damned loud. Then there was an explosion from somewhere down below her that seemed to shake the entire building. . . .

✧   ✧   ✧

I've got the fleet signals, Jack. I'm boosting them through the mecha's comm system, Candis told him.

Good, put me through.

"Fleet ships, fleet ships, this is Captain Jack "DeathRay" Boland, CAG of the *Madira* Gods of War squadron. Do you copy?"

"Roger that, DeathRay. This is CO, USS *Anthony Blair*. Please advise of your status and status of our missing package." DeathRay recognized Admiral Walker's voice.

"Admiral! It's damned good to hear your voice, ma'am. Be advised that Ahmi knows you're here. The package told me that herself. I'm engaging her location as I speak and hope to be in physical contact with her in seconds . . . at the coordinates my AIC is sending now!"

"Roger that, DeathRay! Be advised that we are about to hit this system with everything we have, as hard as we can. You had better get in there and get out."

"Yes, ma'am. I am painting two Seppy Gnats with the blue force tracker for you. That is me and a friendly operative code-named Bachelor Party, ma'am." Jack wasn't sure if Admiral Walker had been briefed on Nancy or not, but it didn't matter as long as she knew not to shoot her out of the sky.

"DeathRay! What is your plan?" Walker asked.

"Ma'am. We just rammed a Lorda into the SIF generators, and are now attacking the penthouse where Dee is being held. All due respect, Admiral, I really need to focus on what I'm doing at the moment." DeathRay twisted the enemy fighter through a corkscrewing trajectory around the firing solution of the AA boxes atop the Seppy Capitol Building. He grunted slightly; the maneuver wasn't that rough compared to others he was used to.

"Roger that, DeathRay. Keep us posted."

"Aye. DeathRay out."

Jack continued to draw the fire of the AA boxes until Penzington screamed over the top of the building at about mach two, blasting away at them. The boxes exploded into pieces, and the tracers stopped tracking his fighter. He toggled the Gnat into bot mode and grunted through full-reverse thrusters, coming down feet first through the roof of the penthouse armored windows. The windows cracked at the impact and absorbed most of his force. Then they gave way completely, sending Jack crashing through onto the floor below. The ceiling of the penthouse was no more than seven meters high, so he was stuck at his upper torso. He carefully tore out a large-enough chunk of the domed top and tossed it behind him, then bent over and reached a hand through.

"Dee!" he shouted over the loudspeakers. "Come out! Now!"

Jack could see her crawling out from underneath some furniture and running toward the fighter's outstretched hand. Jack gripped her gently and stomped the upward kick pedals and threw the bot-mode mecha in full upward flight. As soon as he cleared the penthouse, he covered Dee with his other hand to protect her from wind, debris, and any potential incoming fire they might get into.

"Hang on, Dee!" He skyrocketed with the mecha. "CO *Blair*! DeathRay! If you can lock on to Dee now, QMT her to safety!"

"Roger that! We've got all three of you, DeathRay!" Admiral Walker replied.

Jack could see out of the corner of his peripheral vision that Nancy was in trouble. The remaining AA fire from the ground tracked her still, and she was diving right at it. As far as he could tell, she was going to sacrifice herself to take out the box. Well, that would keep it from firing at Jack and the First Daughter.

Just as her fighter careened toward the ground and the AA box, her canopy blew and the ejection seat exploded out. Then DeathRay was standing next to a shivering Dee and a fast-panting CIA agent on a QMT pad inside the *Blair*. Jack couldn't believe his eyes: just off the pad were the president and the First Lady . . . in AEM skin suits. Jack helped Dee to her feet. She stood and rushed off the pad to the Moores.

"Daddy! Mom!" She reached out to hug them, and there was a flash of light and the sound of sizzling bacon as she vanished into thin air.

"Motherfuck you, Ahmi!" Moore shouted, grasping at the air for his daughter.

Jack and Nancy rushed to where Dee had stood and scanned around. There was no need to scan, because they all knew that it was Ahmi's backup plan. They should have expected such.

"I am going to kill that bitch!" President Moore's rage seemed uncontrollable.

"Sir! We'll get her back. I'm sorry, sir. I didn't think about a boobytrap." DeathRay wasn't sure what to say. "I'm at your disposal, sir."

"Me, too, Mr. President," Nancy offered. "Sir, the SIFs can't be back on line yet. There is no doubt she was teleported back to the penthouse. Send us now, sir!" DeathRay realized that Nancy was right—there was still a window to get to Dee. They'd just have to figure out a way to deal with that snap-back boobytrap that Ahmi was using.

"Right!" Moore and the First Lady started to climb into nearby AEM suits while the QMT techs started gibbering into their comms and the QMT CW rushed up to the president.

"Mr. President, I've strict orders not to allow you and the First Lady to—"

Moore ignored him, as he nodded to the First Lady and the other two AEMs, who stepped onto the pad. The First Lady twisted on her helmet, as did President Moore. Nancy reached over to her shoulder harness and pulled out the railpistol from her flight armor. The five of them stood at ready on the pad.

"Agent Penzington, send my AIC the coordinates," the president ordered.

"Sir?" DeathRay knew the president was one heck of a marine, but the CW was right: he *was* the president. "Agent Penzington and I will go get her, along with your men. We'll bring her back to you."

"Coming, DeathRay?" the president asked. Jack could tell from the expression on the president's face that he was talking to his AIC.

"In for a penny . . ." Jack sighed under his breath and pulled out his own railpistol, stepping onto the pad. "Wild horses and a repulsor tugship couldn't keep me away, Mr. President."

"But sir!" the CW protested.

Even as the CW was shouting for the techs to cut power to the pad, Jack heard the president quietly say, "Any time now, Abby—"

The room flashed, and Jack could hear that frying-bacon sound again. The next thing he knew, they were standing in the penthouse of the Seppy Capitol Building, looking up through a big hole in the ceiling. Dee stood just in front of them with a bewildered expression on her face.

CHAPTER 26

July 1, 2394 AD
Ross 128, Arcadia
Friday, 3:44 PM, Earth Eastern Standard Time

"Goddamnit! They know where we are!" Colonel Mason Warboys and the odd-numbered Warlords had their M3A17-T hovertanks in bot mode. The mecha splashed out of the water at the foot of the dam and into the enemy tanks with a vengeance even though they were outnumbered a little more than two to one.

"Watch out, One! Guns, guns, guns!" Warlord Three shouted.

"Shit! Guns, guns, guns!" Warboys maintained a constant bombardment from his DEG into the Arcadian tanks' line as they advanced on them and went to the smaller but more rapidly directed forty-millimeter gun on top of the DEG turret for in-close and rapidly maneuvering targets. The forty-millimeter gun usually ran in anti-artillery and anti-missile mode. Warboys had put the guns to use by giving his AIC control of them and telling her to shoot any enemy thing it felt necessary to shoot at. While in bot mode, the turret-mounted railgun looked like a half dome head atop the bot's cockpit, with the barrel sticking out for a nose. Below the tank torso two large metal feet thudded into the soil, squishing up mud and the underlying vegetation.

"There's another one targeting you, One! I got him. Fox Three!" Mason saw an anti-mecha missile scream out from Warlord Seven and twist out in front of them toward an enemy tank. The enemy tank dropped backward and fired his countermeasures, setting off the missile just in time to save his ass. Mason didn't like that.

"Stay on him, Seven! Guns, guns, guns!" Warlord One fired his main gun across the river at another rushing tank-mode enemy vehicle. A bright blue-green pulse of energy separated the turret from the main body of the Arcadian M3A16 tank. Mason turned and leaped across the river, running headlong at the exploding enemy mecha. As he jumped over the fireball and on top of the tank beside it, he rammed his heavily armored fist into the enemy vehicle and punched through to the inner workings of the linkage between the torso and the right arm. Infantry railgun fire *spitapped* against the armor plating of his tank, and a couple of larger rounds shook him violently. He looked up in time to see a third tank dive-tackling him.

"Watch out, One!" Warlord Five shouted. "Guns, guns, guns!"

Warboys could see the glint of a DEG blast digging into the back of the bot-mode tank that had tackled him. He rolled over, stood and stomped into the back of the enemy tank. The force of his foot stomping into the mecha broke through the armor plating. Sparks and steaming black and red hydraulic fluids spewed from within it. Warboys grabbed at the main gun turret on the dead enemy tank, ripped it free, and then tossed it like a hammer thrower at the enemy tank-mode tank chasing after Five. The turret bounced into the second tank, knocking it sideways just as it fired. The blow caused it to fire a DEG blast into the dam by accident. A crack formed in the dam, and water started pouring through it. Warboys spun to his knee, firing his main DEG through the pilot of the enemy mecha. Five fired his guns just over the colonel's shoulders at another target.

"Colonel, on your six!" Warlord Three burned a blue-green DEG bolt across the sky just behind Warboys, taking out a tank that had caught the colonel unaware.

"Thanks, Three. Son of a *bitch*, we are outnumbered here!"

"You got that right, Warlord One."

"Warlord One, it looks like the Seppy bastards have figured out that we are here," Warlord Nine noticed. "We gonna get some help anytime soon?"

"Just keep pounding at the fuckers, Warlords! Whether we get help or not, we kill as many of these Seppy motherfuckers as we can, until there ain't a one of us left. Just like that time on Mars! Got it? We've got to punch a hole through here and get these jarheads to the mansion!" Warboys had to go to guns and fired blindly behind him as he ran and leapt toward an outcropping of rocks for cover.

"Hooah! Colonel!"

"One, Duck!" Warlord Five shouted. Mason saw two Arcadian tanks trying to sandwich him and trap him at the edge of the river.

"Shit!" He took off running in an orthogonal direction while he continued to fire the forty millimeter behind him blindly. His AIC tracked on to one of the tanks with the auto-cannon and slowed him down some. He scanned to his left and caught a glimpse of the mecha glinting in the red light of the setting sun as it slowly dropped behind the hill to their left. The governor's mansion was less than a kilometer in front of them up the river, and the enemy tanks were heading them off in that direction, too. There were tanks behind them, to their left and right, and they were trying to get in front of them. Warlord One turned his gun toward the general direction of the glint and fired.

"Guns, guns, guns!"

Enemy cannon fire from his other side knocked him to the ground. Mason tried to roll his mecha over onto all fours and then up. Then he caught a quick glimpse of four of the Robots bouncing with HVARs firing just over his head. Warboys could see that one of them was Colonel Roberts himself. The AEMs kept firing anti-tank rounds from their suits, mixed in with continuous HVAR fire. Warboys bear-crawled out of their way as best he could and then came up into a trot toward the tank to his right.

The Robots and the odd-numbered Warlords had made it almost all the way up the river to the intersection of two other rivers in front of the governor's mansion before they had been discovered. Six tanks and a dozen AEMs had bounced underwater for nearly a half hour until they reached a dam that blocked their path. Their original plan had been to just lock through it, but they couldn't convince the AIC guarding the locks to cycle without a visual confirmation of a ship. No matter what they tried, they couldn't get the water level to fill the dam's lock so they could just swim through the dam. So the Robots had done what they do best. They crawled out of the water and took the fucking dam, which was a mixed blessing. Now they could cycle the lock, but there was no need because they had gotten in a shoot-out with a guard unit stationed to protect it. They alerted the other Arcadian National Guards that the AEMs were there, and then a squad of tanks and enemy infantry were on top of them in no time. There was no need to hide the Warlords at that point. Especially as Arcadian tanks started rushing the AEMs at the dam. The shit got thick very quickly, and the Warlords were getting pounded. They pounded back even harder.

The AEMs dove for cover as a bot-mode enemy tank with a missing leg tumbled to the ground where Mason had been knocked down. First Sergeant McCandless rushed out from the other side of the downed enemy mecha and tossed a grenade into the shattered cockpit, then dove for cover as it exploded.

"Thanks, Marines!" Warlord One said as he returned the favor and went to guns on the tank running for cover behind them. "Guns, guns, guns!"

"Warlord One, Warlord One! Colonel Warboys, are you okay?" Warlord Five rushed to the side of his leader and turned his back to him, laying down more cover fire with his DEG to give Warboys time to regain his composure.

"I'm all right, Five. We've got to get these AEMs to the mansion before those tanks ahead close us in! Let's keep moving north, Warlords. Faster! Let's move it! Let's pave the damn road."

"Yes, sir."

"Ramy! Get your AEM asses moving. If that squad of enemy tanks beats us to the front lawn, we'll be totally outnumbered and surrounded, and there ain't no way you're gonna get in there."

"Roger that, Colonel, the Robots are moving!"

Warlord One looked at the battlescape in his mindview and realized that the Warlords were not going to be able to outrun the enemy squad of tanks, but the AEMs might. It was a race through a closing gauntlet that they would just have to by God endure. The only thing he could do was to push against the enemy line as it closed around them, slowing them down enough to give the marines a chance. "Goddamn it, we have got to move! Lay fire on that enemy line, Warlords, with everything you have."

"Oorah, Colonel."

The AEMs spread out in front of the tank squad, bouncing in zigzags, firing their HVARs and anti-tank grenades as fast as they could manage. Warboys knew this was the last play of the game and the clock had run out on him. He had to push the marines through. The Army had to get the marines to the objective! Even if that meant that the Army was going to be surrounded and have to fight to their last breath once they got the AEMs where they needed to be.

Goddamn that support from on high would go good about now! he thought.

Roger that, Colonel. The air boss claims it is only seconds away, his AIC replied.

Hope we last that fucking long!

"First to fight for the right," Warboys started humming. And then he started singing to himself in a barely audible tone over his open tac-net tank channel. As his mecha's legs moved so fast they were a blur to the human eye, he pounded across the terrain, picking off targets with every bounce. "Guns, guns, guns!" he shouted. "And to build the nation's might, and the Army goes rolling along!"

"Guns, guns, guns, motherfucker!" Three shouted as he fired at a tank in the closing line. The enemy tanks from the rear were crossing the river faster than water pouring from a bursting dam.

Mason could see the tanks to the west going to bot mode to keep up with them, and the tanks to the north had beaten them. The enemy vehicles were in tank mode and firing DEG plasma bursts through the scattering AEMs and the six Army tanks. Mason pushed on as the railgun fire got thicker.

"Proud of all we have done, fighting till the battle's won, and the Army goes rolling along!" He'd found his voice, and let out a full-throated roar. Twice he leapt over AEMs so as not to squish them under his mechanized feet, and each time he went to his DEG or his auto-cannons to take on an incoming anti-tank missile or another tank. He locked onto two tanks with his lidar and QMs and went to anti-tank missiles.

"Fox three! Fox three!" The two missiles spiraled out through the air, leaving purple and white glowing ion trails in the twilight. The missiles crossed paths about seventy meters out and went in opposite directions into two different tanks. The tanks blew out at the turrets almost simultaneously. Then all the tankheads joined him.

"Then it's Hi! Hi! Hey!"

"Fox three!"

"The Army's on its way . . ."

"Guns, guns, guns! Goddamn, I'm hit!"

"Count off the cadence loud and strong!"

"Take that, you Seppy assholes!"

"Warlord Seven is down, Colonel!"

"For where'er we go,"

They charged into the sea of enemy tanks.

"Shit! Three, watch your ass!"

"Guns, guns, guns! Five's hit!"

"You will always know . . ."

"Look out, One!"

Mason could see the AEMs bouncing just ahead of them . . . and ahead of the closing enemy line to the north. The marines were only meters from the mansion. The Army had done its job.

"Fox three!"

As they were engulfed by enemy tanks, the remaining Warboys' Warlords bellowed, *". . . that the Army goes rolling along!"*

CHAPTER 27

July 1, 2394 AD
Ross 128, Arcadia
Friday, 3:45 PM, Earth Eastern Standard Time

"Break left, Goat! Climb, damnit, climb!" Lieutenant Colonel Caroline "Deuce" Leeland yanked the HOTAS left and back and clamped her teeth down on her mouthpiece, thirsting for that shot of stims to hit her system. The compression layer of her armored g-suit crushed against her at over nine gravities. Her grunts, muscle squeezes, breathing techniques, and rapid cussing were barely enough to keep her from tunneling out. She stomped both right pedals and spun her mecha around with a one-hundred-and-twenty-degree yaw, and then she added some pitch and roll that let her track across the bowl at the remaining Gnat. Her radar tracking X went from green to yellow then to red, and a tone sounded in her mind and in the cockpit. "Guns, guns, guns!"

The DEG locked on, and a wash of blue-green directed energy ablated armored hull plating off the right wing section of the enemy fighter that was on her eight o'clock. As the hull ablated away, plasma burst out of the fighter and then flashed bright as if it hit something that burned hotter. Then the beam cut into the power system and the enemy plane burst open into a million pieces along its trajectory. Deuce didn't have time, and she didn't really give a shit, to look if the pilot ejected or not.

"Warning, enemy targeting radar detected! Warning, enemy targeting radar detected!" The voice of her Bitchin' Betty rang through the cockpit.

"Deuce, we've got to pull out of this climb or we're sitting ducks!" Goat warned her over the pilot's tac-net channel.

Deuce's vision spun as she yawed back around into a dive, and then she killed the throttle briefly and stepped on the left upper pedal to yaw her around not so abruptly. Once her fighter was facing downward, looking at the enemy supercarrier, she pushed the throttle all the way down. She held her line toward the ship as both AA fire and tracers from a bot-mode mecha on the hull of the ship continued to try and lock her and Goat up.

"Shit! Watch the AA, Goat!" she grunted and tossed her mecha into a barrel roll over Goat's line. Bile rushed up her esophagus, and her stomach retched a bit, but she managed to force it down.

"Warning, enemy targeting lock imminent. Warning, enemy targeting lock imminent!"

"Look out, Deuce!" Popstar shouted as she and Jawbone strafed through the line of fire, but both of them missed the enemy bot. It did confuse the thing's radar briefly.

"Fox three!" Goat shouted. His missile went wide of the bot but hit the AA box, knocking it out.

"Shit! I'm locked up!" Deuce jinked and juked and did everything she could as she saw a missile fire out of the bot's torso missile tubes. "Fox three! Fox three!" she shouted as the unlocked missiles jumped out in front of her. She tracked the tailpipe of her own missiles with the upper and under forty-millimeter cannons. "Guns, guns, guns!"

Her tracers tore through the ass-end of her mecha-to-mecha missiles just as the enemy's missile began spiraling up at her. Her two missiles exploded into a fireball, confusing the enemy missile, which lost lock and spun out of control through the plasma in front of her. Deuce rolled her fighter, and the enemy missile tumbled centimeters past her. She yawed herself one hundred and eighty degrees and tracked the tumbling missile with her cannons, blasting it out of the sky. She pitched back over to orient her nose back into the line of travel and was now cockpit-to-cockpit with Goat as they barrel-rolled around and around each other.

"Guns, guns, guns!" Goat shouted. "Shit, Deuce, we're coming in too fast!"

"Prepare for QMT in five, four, three, two, one," the air boss's AIC voice chimed in Deuce's mindvoice.

"About fucking time!" Deuce killed her throttle and banked left and suddenly had a brief view of the inside of a ship and then was in very thin atmosphere about twenty kilometers directly above the Arcadian governor's mansion. Her blue-force tracker showed several other mecha all around her at safe distances, popping into space. Several were already at full throttle toward the engagement zone below. Then Goat spun into existence beside her with sparks flying from his mecha. From the looks of it, he had tried to go to bot mode and something had taken the left arm of his mecha off. His DEG gun was nowhere to be seen.

"Shit! Look out, Deuce!" he shouted, but the air boss AIC had put him in at a safe distance. Unfortunately, it hadn't brought him in fast enough to prevent that Seppy fighter from getting him. His plane was out of commission.

"Toggle to fighter, Goat!" she shouted at him. The bot rolled over and tucked its legs in and expanded its wings, spinning into a fighter-mode mecha. The thin atmosphere was enough for the control surfaces to kick in and dampen out his spin.

"Shit! I've lost my DEG, and I've got systems going out everywhere!"

Jawbone popped into space nearby, and then Popstar. Deuce started counting up the Utopian Saviors and sending them a signal to form up on her through DTM.

Bobby, get the message to all the Saviors as they QMT in.

Aye, ma'am.

"Do you still have SIFs and propulsion?"

"No SIFs, but I have propulsion."

"Shit, you're out of the game, Goat. They should've teleported you out first!" Deuce said it before she could stop herself. Hell, she knew that "should'ves" never do anybody a damned bit of good. "All right, Goat, you can't go back to the *Madira* from here. So you need to find a safe place on the ground to hang out and see if you can stay out of trouble."

"Damnit. Sorry, Deuce."

About that time another FM-12 spun in out of control. It was Skinny's wingman, Captain Michael "HoundDog" Samuels. The FM-12 was in eagle mode in a three-dimensional spin, and his tail section was spewing plasma and his cockpit venting air and smoke.

"I'm hit, I'm hit!" HoundDog screamed with real pain and fear in his voice. The right tailfin of his plane blew off and a fireball started to form. "Eject, eject, eject!"

HoundDog's ejection seat cleared the fireball of his exploding mecha. The plasma and debris tossed his chair into a mad, freely falling whirl. In full gravity now, his seat started to plummet. When the sensor found enough air pressure, it would pop his chute. Unfortunately, he would land right in the middle of the fight below.

"Hang on, HoundDog!" Deuce dove her fighter over and straight toward the ejection seat. She hit the mode toggle, pulling into eagle mode. As she pulled up into an even free fall with Hound-Dog, she backed off her throttle to match his speed precisely and then reached out with her right mecha hand and grabbed the chair gently. "I got you."

"Goat, I've got a mission for you now!" Deuce arced back out of the free fall and leveled off. "Get HoundDog down and check on his wounds. Form up on me and take him. HoundDog, you with me?"

"Barely. I caught something in my abdomen. My suit sealed it off, but I don't feel too good," Hounddog replied. She did a quick check on his vitals. They were stable enough. Deuce had seen a lot worse come out okay, if they got medical attention soon enough. She wasn't sure why the *Madira* hadn't QMTed him up to sickbay, unless the medi-AIC doing triage had a whole lot more wounded in worse shape than HoundDog. From the looks of the way things were going in space, Deuce was pretty sure that was the case.

"I'm on you, Deuce. Ready for handoff in three, two, one, drop," Goat told her. Deuce let go of the chair, and it gently fell into Goat's remaining mecha hand. Then Skinny popped into space.

"HoundDog, HoundDog, where are you?" Skinny shouted over the net.

"I'm here, Major," he replied.

"Shit, Marine, I thought I'd lost you," Skinny said. After a brief pause, she added, "You need to hit the immunoboost soon."

"My suit is handling it."

"All right, Saviors, listen up," said Deuce. "Several of the other squadrons are popping in and are starting to form up. We're all here minus Goat and HoundDog. Skinny, old girl, looks like you're with me."

"It'll be just like old times, Deuce!"

"Let's hit the deck and help out the tankheads. Use the DEGs as often as you like, but conserve the ammo on the cannons. Don't know about all of you, but my counter is getting pretty goddamned low. Blue-force tracker shows a small group of marines and tanks making a push to the governor's mansion. Let's help them A-S-fucking-A-P. Maximum velocity with maximum ferocity, Marines!"

"Oorah!"

Fish was glad as hell to get out of that space ball. It was too one-sided with Seppy Gnats and Stingers. They were every-fucking-where. Her squad had been whittled down to seven out of the initial ten. Those were very bad numbers for the Gods of War. Lieutenant Commander Penika "Hula" Moses was dead. Lieutenant Junior Grade Geoffrey "Fireball" Julias was out of commission with critical wounds. And Lieutenant Commander Charles "Stinky" Allen was barely managing to keep his plane in the air. He was also carrying Fireball's ejection chair with him.

She could see in her DTM that the Saviors and the Dawgs had taken some casualties, too. The Dawgs had suffered the worst, losing half their squad.

"Deuce, Deuce, this is Fish."

"Go, Fish."

"We're forming up, ready to help out. I see you're on the way down. We'll be right behind you."

"Roger that, Fish. Looks like Poser is the senior of you squid pilots."

"I heard that, Deuce!" Poser's voice chimed in. Fish could see her in the DTM, forming up near the Gods of War.

"Take her cues, Fish," Deuce advised her.

"Roger that, Deuce," Fish acknowledged.

"Poser, Fish, we need to clear out the enemy line on the south side of the governor's mansion and hold it. And, Fish, the fight is on the ground there for now, but you need to be my eyes skyward."

"Understood, Deuce." The FM-12s the Saviors flew were more suited to close-in fighting on the ground and other surfaces, like carrier hulls. The Ares-Ts were designed for top cover and fighting in open space, but that didn't mean that ace Navy aviators couldn't fight on the ground as well. That was the main reasoning for Navy procurement officials to decide on a new Ares model that could transfigure into bot mode.

"Poser, you got the middle ground if we get Gomers. Otherwise, both of you take it to the surface dwellers." Deuce said. "We didn't do too good turning the tide up top, but we have to turn the tide down there."

"Roger that."

"See you in the shit. Deuce, out."

"Demon Dawgs, Demon Dawgs, form up on the Gods of War! We are regrouping here," Poser announced.

Fish and Poser went through the losses and started pairing off pilots with missing wingmen. They ended up splitting into six fighters in each group. Fish was still the designated squadron leader of the Gods of War, and Poser kept the Demon Dawgs.

"Let's go shoot some tankheads," Poser ordered.

"Roger that," Fish said. "Okay, Gods of War, here we go."

"Look out, Warlord One!" Deuce dropped in first on the line, burning through three different tanks as she boomed overhead at treetop height. She passed the line at over nine hundred kilometers per hour causing the tall oaks to sway almost to the snapping point. "Guns, guns, guns!"

"Holy hell, I'm glad to see you mecha jocks!" Warboys replied. The screaming fighters overhead were enough of a distraction to the enemy troops that the Warlords managed to take a breath, regroup, and fight their way back to their feet.

"Fox three!" Deuce said as she rolled up into a long loop-over to bleed off some of her velocity. She hit the mode toggle as she came back around to the five o'clock position of her looping trajectory, going to bot mode. Skinny was right on her wing, following suit. The two mecha twisted and turned in midair like ballerinas.

"Fox three!" Skinny shouted. Her bot-mode mecha overshot Deuce slightly, but intentionally. Deuce could see her bounce to the ground, running and flipping over enemy mecha, slamming down on the Arcadian tanks with her armored feet as she did so. Deuce was right behind her.

"Guns, guns, guns!" Deuce washed the line with her DEG, blasting a tank off the back of Warlord Nine. After firing her mammoth handheld DEG, she turned and rammed the mecha's left elbow through the cockpit of a tank behind her. The enemy tank grabbed at her, pulling her backward and almost off balance. With right pedal and manipulation of the armature controls, she rolled off the enemy tank and took her bot through a handspring over the top of it, then tucked into one of her trademark judo rolls. She followed through the roll by putting the elbow of the forearm of the mecha down first and then the back, buttocks, legs, and then back up to her feet, firing away with the shoulder-mounted auto-cannons. Her DEG in her left hand waved back and forth, looking for targets to either shoot or smack.

"Warning, enemy targeting system is acquiring lock. Warning . . ."

Still a little dizzy from her roll, Deuce used her DTM targeting system, focusing on the vehicle that was targeting her. It wasn't a vehicle at all, but instead a mobile AA and anti-tank turret firing away at her. She kicked at two of the pedals on her left side and yanked the stick, sending the bot spinning like a figure skater.

She couldn't get a lock with her DEG, and she was way too close for missiles. She decided to go with the DEG anyway. "Guns, guns, guns!"

The DEG directed a plasma burst of energy that tracked across the AA box, burning away one of the barrels of the cannons. The missing barrel caused the box to misfire and explode on itself, destroying the box.

"Where are you, Skinny?"

"I'm behind you, Deuce." Skinny shouted over the net, and Deuce spotted her on the right and behind her. "Look out, Warlord Three! You've got one on your three-nine line!"

Deuce launched herself in the air with a giant leap, and she kept her mind on that damned tank. She rolled over at the crux of her jump and slammed feet forward into the upper torso of the bot-mode tank like a martial artist doing an aerial double frontkick. The two mecha clanged together briefly, but Deuce's forward momentum sent the enemy tank flailing over backward and through a middle-aged fir tree. The tree snapped off at the base of the trunk. Warlord Three pounced just in time to pick up the tree and stab it through the cockpit of the Arcadian mecha. Pieces of fir tree flew everywhere and erupted into flame in a ball of smoke and ash.

"Thanks, Deuce!"

"Welcome, Three." Deuce continued forward and out of the way as Skinny came in behind her, settling up to her mecha back-to-back fashion. The two of them scanned for more targets. There were plenty. It was more of an issue of which one to go after first.

"Two o'clock, Deuce!" Skinny shouted and pounced away toward another bot-mode enemy tank, her auto-cannons firing off forty-millimeter rounds as she launched over it in a full throttle leap. She pitched forward over Deuce's head, firing her DEG from the hip into the tank's wingman before it even realized what had happened. But the shot wasn't a kill shot, and the enemy wingman turned on Skinny and started to raise his cannon to track her.

"I got it!" Jawbone butted in as she landed on top of the bot, squashing the torso to the point that metal reached its elastic limit and gave way. The knees of the enemy mecha faltered, and one of the Army tankheads put a round through the cockpit of the thing just to be sure.

"That's what I'm talking about!" Jawbone said through the grunts and growls that the g-load had forced her into. "Popstar, watch your four o'clock, girl! Guns, guns, guns!"

"Great work, Saviors. Let's keep it frosty!" Deuce shook her head to clear the spins. More radar warnings pinged at her, and she tossed an oak tree down that she had been wielding in her right hand as a club. Cannon tracers passed by her on the left, and then something pushed her over. She started to fight back until she realized it was a blue-force vehicle that hit her.

"Look out, Marine!" Warlord One rolled off of her and onto his back, firing upward at two enemy tanks leaping on top of them. "Fox three, fox three!" He let loose two missiles that hit home dead center on the two tanks. They blew apart from the torso, scattering mechanical arms and legs in every direction.

"Thanks, Warlord One." Deuce rolled over and searched for her wingman in her DTM. Then she settled down and located the rest of the Saviors as they scattered around the Warlords. They needed a plan that was a little less random.

"Anytime, jarhead."

"Saviors, we need to fan out in a half moon, covering our flanks and leaving the moon open behind us to the north. That way we can work away from the mansion, giving the AEMs some cushion. Warlords, feel free to jump in there and give us what cover you can!"

"Roger that, Saviors," Warlord One responded over the net. "Get down, Nine! Guns, guns, guns!"

Three enemy tanks in bot mode came crashing through the trees. Deuce hit her thrusters, launching into a backflip. As her bot twisted over the scrambling Warlords, she pointed her DEG in the general direction of the Arcadian tanks. Her directed energy plasma bursts ablated some of the armored hull of the tanks, and her auto-cannons poked holes where the DEG didn't get. One of the tanks was crippled. The other two took on some damage but weren't out of commission.

Auto-cannons, Bobby! she ordered her AIC.

Got it! The AIC tracked the enemy tank on her left, but it was having a hard time locking it up.

"I got the third one!" Popstar burned it down in a mad charge, firing her DEG.

Deuce pursued the remaining wounded one, which then turned on her and one of the Warlords. The enemy tank tried to go to its DEG and shoot from the hip, but the Warlord grabbed the end of the barrel and tried to yank it away, which led to a tug-of-war between the two mecha. Their struggle was enough for Deuce to get the upper hand. She managed to get the end of her DEG pointed into the cockpit of the enemy mecha, and then she pulled the trigger.

Great move, Deuce!

"Watch your backside, Deuce," Skinny's voice buzzed.

Deuce dropped and spun as best she could manage, but a tree trunk caught her in the side of her torso, sending her flying across the battlefield and down. The enemy tankhead was good and managed to keep her too busy to go to offense. Every instant required her to make a new block or dodge.

"Jump up, Deuce!" Skinny shouted. "He's got help coming in on your seven!"

"Warning, enemy targeting lock imminent! Warning, enemy targeting lock imminent!" said her Bitchin' Betty.

"Shit, I'm locked up!" Deuce jumped and went full throttle, but she didn't jump away from the enemy tanks. Instead, she attacked the wingman of the one that had just locked her up. Her bot-mode mecha propelled full-force into the enemy tank as it fired its cannons at her. Several rounds splashed against her hull, and a few of them actually tore through her wing. She tackled the tank at the shoulders, spinning it around. His wingman hesitated at that point, which was just enough time for her to push off the tank she had tackled and run into the mix of Army tanks and Marine FM-12s to break up his lock. Or so she thought.

"Warning, enemy missile lock! Warning, enemy missile lock!"

The Arcadian tankhead fired a mecha-to-mecha missile that was locked on her. The missile twisted through the traffic and caught her square in the back as she pulled the ejection handle. Her ejection seat shot out of the explosion at a low angle up through the trees, pounding into them and flipping end over end. Several large tree limbs broke off into the seat and Deuce's body until the seat cleared the tree canopy on a ballistic trajectory that then fell right back through the trees. This time the tree limbs were a blessing, as they slowed her descent, but they weren't blessing enough. Deuce came to a stop against a giant boulder near the river, her neck broken and her heartbeat failing.

I'm a goner, Bobby.

Just rest, Caroline. I'm administering immunoboost, stims, and pain medication.

Oh, God.

I've triggered the beacon. Help will be here soon.

It was great serving with you, Bobby.

The honor has been mine, Colonel.

Deuce flatlined, but the suit managed to bring her back.

Stay with me, Caroline.

As she tunneled out for the last time, she was blinded by a brilliant white light.

CHAPTER 28

July 1, 2394 AD
Ross 128, Arcadia Orbit
Friday, 3:45 PM, Earth Eastern Standard Time

"We're all stop, CO! Approximately three astronomical units from Arcadia out of the ecliptic," Nav announced.

"Good job, Penny!" the admiral replied. "XO, COB, get my ship back in order."

"Aye, sir."

"Air Boss, how is the QMT of the fighters coming?"

"We'll be at one hundred percent within the minute, sir."

"Good. As soon as that is done, have the wounded QMT protocols sped up. I don't want to lose a good soldier because we couldn't get them to sickbay in time."

"Aye, sir."

Wallace scanned the ship in his DTM, trying to figure out his next move. It wouldn't take long for the Seppy ships to figure out where they were. The interesting thing would be to see if they attacked them there, or if they took the QMT facility back, or if they'd try to protect the QMT control facility on the planet below at Capitol City.

Whatever the Seppy bastards did, he needed a new strategy. Casualty reports from the first wave were huge. The *Lincoln* was dead in the water, and the *Tyler* had lost Aux Prop and several DEG batteries. The *Roosevelt* and the *Madira* were in the best shape, but they were limping a bit.

"CO! CDC!"

"Go, CDC!"

Shit, what now? he thought.

I'm detecting seven hyperspace jaunts, sir. I'm sure it's that, Uncle Timmy replied.

"Sir! We just detected seven hyperspace jaunts. Five from the previous engagement zone and two from the enemy vessels that were waiting in reserve out by one of the moons," the combat direction center officer explained to him. Wallace didn't like what he was hearing. That was seven ships; they were coming to finish them off.

"Roger that, CDC." Admiral Jefferson turned back to his XO. "Larry! We've got incoming. Let's get ready for it."

"Aye, sir!"

Sound the call, Tim.

Aye, sir.

"General quarters, general quarters, prepare for incoming attack. All hands, all hands, man your battlestations. Prepare for incoming attack. All hands, all hands, man your battlestations," Uncle Timmy announced again over the intercom and to all AICs.

The bosun's pipe sounded throughout the ship, sending a chill over the already overworked crew. Considering that the day started with wargames in the desert of Mars and then wound up across the stars in a real shooting war, the admiral realized that his crew were performing like superhuman heroes. Sometimes, that wasn't enough. But according to his orders from the president, it had to be.

"CO, the ships are coming out of jaunt near us at the following coordinates, sir. Uh, only one of them is coming out close to us. The others are a tenth of an AU off," the STO shouted over klaxons that started up. Wallace had his AIC turn the annoying things off.

"Roger that, STO."

"CO! CDC!"

"We've got the ships coming out of hyperspace, CDC."

"Uh, yes, sir. But, sir, we're picking up EM disturbances near the planet that would suggest QMT jumps."

"Keep me posted, CDC. I hope that's our backup."

"Aye, sir."

"CO! That Seppy hauler is on a collision course for the *Lincoln*!" the Nav shouted.

"I'm detecting activated gluonium, Admiral!" the STO added. They sure as hell didn't need to be around if the Seppies fired off a gluonium bomb that close.

"Shit! Kamikaze, Admiral!" the COB shouted.

"Helm, emergency jaunt away from here now!" Wallace sounded an alarm across the fleet ships and opened a channel. "Evasive jaunts immediately! Gluonium Kamikaze!"

"Emergency jaunt, sir!" Helmsman Lieutenant Junior Grade Cindy Lewis frantically punched in the commands for an emergency jaunt. It would take the hyperspace projector a few seconds to spin up the quantum vortex required to pass out of normal space. Who knew if they had time?

Wallace sat calm for the few seconds as they passed. The enemy hauler pulled in closer to the *Lincoln* and opened fire on it. All of its missiles, DEGs, and railguns poured into the wounded supercarrier's sections that housed the jaunt system. The Seppy ship moved closer and closer to the *Lincoln*, and Wallace could see that there was nothing he could do for them.

"Goddamn those bastards!" He slammed his fist down against his chair arm. Just as the hyperspace vortex whirled around them and they blanked out of normal space, the Seppy kamikaze ship exploded. The *Lincoln* was vaporized instantly.

A few seconds later, as the *Madira* popped out of hyperspace, the admiral managed to relax long enough to breathe. His DTM dinged in the updated blue-force tracking signals showing that the *Tyler* and the *Roosevelt* had managed to jaunt away before the hauler had exploded. The three U.S. supercarriers were battered and badly outnumbered. Or at least they had been. His blue-force system showed four new U.S. supercarriers: the USS *Ronald Reagan*, the USS *Barack Obama*, the USS *Zachary Taylor*, and the USS *Andrew Jackson*. There were still eight Seppy ships, but only four of them were supercarriers, and one of those supercarriers had taken a good bit of damage. The other four Seppy ships were battle cruiser class—about two-thirds the size of a supercarrier. Seven supercarriers to eight Seppy ships; finally some decent odds.

"CO *Madira*, CO *Obama*!"

"Goddamn, I'm glad to hear from you, Johnny!" Wallace answered Captain Johnny Practice's hail. He opened a channel to all the fleet ship captains. "I'm glad to see all four of you. Be advised. We just lost the *Lincoln*. She was totally destroyed. Her pilots and ground-pounders are on the surface of Arcadia near the governor's mansion in the center of Capitol City. Our intel has determined that is where the QMT controls are. So do not destroy that mansion! In the meantime, we're a bit surrounded over here and could use a hand. We also need to put a couple ships on the planet to support the fight there. Carla, you and Johnny take the *Obama* and the *Jackson* down. Felix, you and Kiana form up on us here and see if we can't keep the Seppies away from our attack long enough to get that QMT system under our control."

"Aye, Admiral!"

Now things are gonna get a little better, he thought.

Damn right, Admiral, Uncle Timmy agreed.

"Admiral, the Seppy fleet is forming up on us. Looks like they brought their fighters with them, sir," the XO said.

"Well, that will help out downstairs. All right, let's prepare to take incoming!"

"Admiral, with that in mind, do we want to continue our plan to jaunt in two minutes back to the planet?" Commander Penny Swain, the nav officer, asked.

"Good question, Penny." Wallace thought briefly. They were still outnumbered up here and in a ball. He still liked the idea of going to a bowl and being able to support the troops on the ground better. "Yes. Our men and women down there need us."

Timmy, DTM the plan to the rest of the fleet.

Aye, sir.

"Joe! The SIF generators on the aft of the ship are down. There just aren't any other cooling systems to bring them down," Lieutenant Mira Concepcion shouted. The noise in the Engineering Room was a little too loud to talk at normal tones, and the stress from the ship being rocked back and forth didn't help.

"Well, it sure as hell didn't take long for the Seppy mothers to find out where we jaunted to," Petty Officer Andy Sanchez added.

"If y'all wanted peace and quiet you shouldn't have joined the Navy!" Joe scanned the three-dimensional diagram of the ship, looking at all the systems at once in detail all the way down to the nuts and bolts, transistors and integrated circuits, and quantum-fluctuation exciters and spacetime limiters. His problem right now was the universal one, one that caused almost all systems to end up failing: thermal management. Waste heat was the hardest goddamned problem in all of physics and engineering to deal with. And now that one SIF generator was down, he was having to spread the structural integrity fields thin from the others to cover that section of the supercarrier. That meant that other SIF generators were now working even harder. It was an avalanche of disaster that only needed one or two more snowflakes to trigger it.

I should've taken up business or marketing, he thought.

Yeah, but then you'd be rich and would miss out on all this, his AIC, Debbie, replied in his mindvoice.

"Too bad we can't just jaunt over the ice cap of this planet and cool the thing off," Andy said sarcastically.

"I don't think that would work, Andy," the technology officer shouted over his shoulder. He had a flashlight between his teeth, power cabling draped across both shoulders, and a multitool in each hand, working away at an overloaded control circuit for the QMT power supply. The specialist warrant officers were the experts on the quantum-membrane teleportation technology, but those guys still needed good old-fashioned power, and all that came from Engineering. And, from what Joe could tell, the QMT had been working overtime since the battle started. That meant there were heavy casualties and/or a lot of troop movement.

"Why not, Lieutenant?"

"Well, you'd have to get the cold air in contact with the hot coolant somehow. Not sure how you'd do that. Oh shit!" A spark flew across the panel he had pulled out, discharging several thousand volts across his fingers. "That fucking hurt," he said, dropping the multitools and shaking his hands.

"Watch yourself, Lieutenant. Do I need to get Andy over there to show you how to handle high voltage?" Joe laughed. Then, as he panned the three-D image by the flow loops between the aft SIF generator heat exchangers and the main coolant reservoir one deck below Engineering, it hit him. "Son of bitch, Andy! That just might work."

"What will, Joe?"

"Cold air." Joe continued moving the mindview diagrams around rapidly, looking for the one that would work. Then he found it. "There it is! The main coolant lines of damned near everything flow through the exterior bulkheads that aren't pressurized. Any cooling along the flow lines is purely radiative. Hmm . . ."

Debbie, what if we pumped pressurized helium or air or something in there? he thought.

Well, the only thing we could do in a hurry is air, Joe.

Okay, let's do it. What about some water mist?

Yeah, we could do that.

Hell, we are about to jaunt into atmosphere. Let's just open up some panels and let it flow through.

That would work. With the flow speed, it would supercool the air as it was forced down the tube. My calculations show it would increase the cooling efficiency by ten percent.

That might be enough.

"CO! CHENG!"

"Go, CHENG!"

"Sir, we need to get into atmosphere. It might allow us to cool off the SIFs quicker. The sooner, the better."

"We're headed to treetop high in about seventy seconds."

"Great, sir.

"All right, we're hitting the air in about a minute. I want hatches opened to the bulkheads, uh . . ." Joe stepped toward a holoscreen and had his AIC display the image that was in his mind. "Okay, that's it. Here, here, here, and here. We open these hatches and route airflow through the exterior hull walls. We need to figure out how to pull the structural integrity fields in one layer hull or just turn them on and off rapidly enough to get some airflow in there. Any ideas on that?"

"Shit, at the rate we're going, the SIFs are gonna shut down anyway," Mira complained.

"Probably, but let's hope not! Shit, there has to be a way to get the air in the exterior dry hull without compromising our security." Joe was perplexed and running out of time. "We'll figure it out. Get those hatches open. Andy, be careful. You'll be outside the SIFs on the hull, and there are fighters and incoming out there. Armor up, but do it quick."

"I'm on it, Joe," Andy replied. He took off running across the room, underneath the hyperspace projector conduit, and into an antechamber where the e-suits were kept. Joe hated sending one of his team into such a dangerous situation. Before he would have done the dangerous bit himself, but now he was CHENG and had too many problems to deal with to do every little dangerous and shitty job. Part of command was sending good people into bad places. Joe would just have to get used to that.

"We need a sheer fence, Joe," the main propulsion assistant, Lieutenant Commander Keri Benjamin, said. "You know, a metal plate full of holes, or a grate."

"Maybe that would work," Joe thought out loud, rubbing at his chin. "Would that stop a QMT? Kurt? You're the tech officer."

"Hell if I know, Joe. That QMT shit is so new I barely even understand why it is possible," Lieutenant Kurt Hyerdahl replied from halfway inside the console that had previously tried to electrocute him.

"Okay, we'll ask." He had to ask his AIC for the names of the warrant officers assigned to the ship as the QMT experts. Then he got one of them on the horn. "CWO4 Ransom, this is the CHENG!"

"What can I do for you, CHENG?"

"Would a metal grate stop a QMT?"

"No, CHENG. You can QMT through walls, you know."

"Duh, right. But what about SIFs? Isn't there some interaction with spacetime or the vacuum fluctuations or something that confuses the QMT connection?" Joe asked.

"Uh, something like that, CHENG. Uh, sir, is this gonna take long, cause, well, we're kinda busy down here." Mr. Ransom seemed a bit uppity to Joe, maybe even constipated.

"Well, we need to flow air in from the outside without allowing enemy QMTs. Could we put small holes in the SIFs and do that?" There was no immediate answer, which meant that Joe had asked a question that the arrogant CWO4 QMT expert hadn't thought of.

"Damn, I never thought of that. Hell, you could just make the SIFs a screen instead of a solid field, and think how much energy you'd save on that," he replied.

Energy saved, hell—think of the heat we wouldn't have to dissipate if the field were half the size due to holes in it, Joe thought. *Since it is a surface-area thing, that will be a squared factor! We could increase the SIF lifetime in battle by orders of magnitude.*

We need to get on with this, Joe, his AIC warned him. Time was getting short, and the fucking Seppies were still outside, pounding away at them.

"Uh, how small do the holes need to be?"

"My AIC says a tenth of a millimeter in diameter with the same center-to-center spacing. And I bet that is conservative. Damn good idea, CHENG."

"Right, Mr. Ransom. Thanks for your help. CHENG out."

"You're welcome, CHENG."

Joe turned and noticed for the first time the bewilderment on the faces of his engineering crew. He wasn't sure if it was because they were confused or couldn't believe the brilliant idea they had just pulled out of their collective asses. He didn't care. Ideas did nobody any good if you didn't follow through with them.

"Okay, Kurt, get that damned panel fixed and get on to the next job. Mira, thanks for the sheer-fence idea. I'm reconfiguring the SIFs on the aft section and in nooks and crannies that are unlikely to be hit by enemy fire to have the screen geometry. I'm also doing that over the openings that Andy is making. We'll see how it works."

"All hands, all hands, prepare for hyperspace jaunt in ten, nine, eight, seven, six . . ."

"Goddamn, that's a sight," Engineer's Mate Petty Officer First Class Andy Sanchez clanked through the outer dry hull of the aft starboard section where the SIF-generator coolant conduits flowed. Even in his tech e-suit he could feel the radiant heat from the pipes. He looked forward and then aft. As far as he could see was the empty corridor between the outer hull and the next layer that the Navy had called the dry hull since the days of submarines. The corridor was poorly lit, and the white light from his helmet cast eerie shadows across the deck plating. The ship jerked downward fast, making him lose his balance briefly. Andy fell back into the coolant conduit and could feel the heat even through his armored glove and seal layer. "Goddamn it all to fuck, I'd better watch what I'm doing or that fucking thing might fry me."

Andy crawled up through the bulkhead to the outer hatch and clanked it a few times with the BFW he had brought with him. The technical term for the tool was a "big fucking wrench." After tapping the bolts on the outer hull hatch with the BFW, he placed it on the nuts, let it self-adjust to them, and then he torqued like hell to break them free. After a few seconds the bolts popped loose. He turned the safety latch and was almost sucked out of the ship. As soon as he had pushed the hatch panel up beyond the SIF, air—very fast-moving air—grabbed it and yanked it away. Twilight from the red dwarf shined through, and Andy could see the planet below.

"That's three. One more to go," he told himself. Then he dropped down to the deck and hurried to the last one of the exterior hatch panels, a good hundred meters away.

The bolts on the last hatch were more stubborn. Andy tapped them harder with the BFW and tried to torque them loose. No luck. He tapped them again, and this time he sprayed some solvent on them. He tapped them again, and then tried turning them again. One of them broke free, and he managed to get the thing off. The second nut was stuck.

"Stubborn bastard!" Andy pulled a laser cutter out of his pocket and started in on the bolt with it. About that time, something slammed into the ship above him with so much force the metal vibrated in his hands and made his suit ring.

"Ahh!" He reflexively grabbed at his ears, which were inside his helmet, of course.

Then another loud hit and the hatch blew free and the SIF directly above him blinked out for the briefest of instants. That was all it took as the atmosphere rushing over the hull at several hundred kilometers per hour sucked him right out of the blown hatch and into the evening sky. Large orange and green AA tracers zipped all around him, slamming into the ship's hull from the ground below. Andy spun with his arms and legs akimbo until he nearly passed out from it. One of the tracer rounds passed right between his legs and nicked his thigh. It burned for a brief second, but the suit sealed it off and killed the pain. Seeing the tracers pass between his legs scared him more than seeing one tear into his leg. His bladder and bowels let loose uncontrollably.

A few seconds passed, and then he realized that the impact of him hitting the air so abruptly had certainly broken several of his bones. A tech e-suit had minimal armor on it and wasn't designed to take that type of punishment. His right leg, not the one hit by the AA round, was definitely broken. His left arm had banged into the hatch as he was sucked out, and he was sure that the arm and the collarbone were snapped completely. The suit had administered meds to him, or he would've been in so much pain that he would have passed out anyway.

Andy spun out away from the ship's gravitational field too quickly to fall back to it. He was falling free. He looked down and could see the ground beneath him at about two kilometers. The *Madira* had already jaunted in to atmospheric entry height of about twenty kilometers and was decelerating to the treetops. The treetops were still a ways off, and now Andy could see the *Madira* almost a quarter of a kilometer away from him. At one point several mecha zoomed by, shooting at each other. Andy thought he could have reached out and touched the things, until the air wake hit him and sent him spinning again.

"Oh shit! I don't wanna die like this . . ." Andy closed his eyes as the treetops rushed upward at him. Just as he was bracing himself for death, his heartrate hit nearly two-hundred beats per minute. The next thing he knew, there was a flash of light and the sound of sizzling bacon.

CHAPTER 29

July 1, 2394 AD
Tau Ceti
Friday, 3:45 PM, Earth Eastern Standard Time

"Dee!" Alexander and Sehera rushed to her. The two of them popped their e-suit helmets and tossed them over their shoulders on the tether. He held his arms open and let her hug him. He couldn't really hug her back in the suit, but he wanted to very badly. He was sure that Sehera felt the same.

"Daddy!" Dee hugged the armored suit anyway. No matter how tough she was, she was still only eighteen, barely at that, and was daddy's little girl. Moore leaned down as best he could to kiss her on the head. "Mom! What happened? I was there, and then I was back here."

"Elle Ahmi," Sehera grunted. Sehera looked into her daughter's eyes and added, "Anything you might have learned here is classified. Do you understand that?"

"That's right, Dee. We'll discuss things later," Alexander added. Dee looked up at them and nodded that she understood. "Now, how do we get you safely out of here?"

DeathRay and Nancy gave the president and the First Family some room and started trying to find the QMT controls that would get Dee out of there. Thomas and Koodie bounced around the penthouse, looking for the best way out and getting the lowdown of the layout.

"How do you get in and out of here, Dee?" DeathRay asked.

"Well, the last time it was through the ceiling in the hands of a Seppy Gnat." She smiled at the pilot.

251

"Well, that does us no good now," Moore said.

Abigail?

Yes, sir. I'm hacking as best I can. If you don't mind, sir, the CIA agent has a very formidable AIC and I'd like to interface with her.

Whatever works fastest is fine with me.

Yes, sir. It would appear that the room is AIC locked, and there is an elevator.

"The elevator is right here. Only Elle Ahmi can open the damned thing. Bree and I have been trying but with no luck," Dee said.

"I see. Stand back." Alexander walked over to it and stood atop the elevator. He lowered his HVAR and started blasting the shit out of it until he fell through. He looked up. "I got the elevator unlocked. Come on."

"Your father sure likes the direct approach." Sehera shook her head.

"Ms. Moore, listen very carefully," the CIA agent said. "There must be a small QMT pad somewhere nearby. That pad has you tagged somehow and is not letting you travel too far away from it. That is why you snapped back to here after we QMTed before."

"I understand, uh . . . You are who, exactly?" Dee raised an eyebrow at the stranger with DeathRay.

"Sorry. You can call me Nancy Penzington." She held out her hand, and Dee shook it. "It is an honor to meet you."

"She's with the CIA, Dee," DeathRay added.

"Hmm. Thanks for helping. Uh, there is a pad like that. A small one just big enough for a few people at a time. I saw it on the second floor as they brought me in."

"Good, that's our way out. We destroy that thing, and the link to you should be cut," Nancy said.

Sehera dropped through the hole in the floor second. Then Dee, DeathRay, and Nancy. Alexander was listening to the conversation as his two Marine bodyguards helped the nonsuited members of their little band down the hole in the floor. Sehera and Alexander helped them on the bottom. Then the AEMs dropped down the hole.

"Okay, Dee, take us to this QMT pad," Alexander said.

"Somebody give me a gun," Dee said, putting her hand on her father's shoulder.

"Dee, I'm not sure that is—" Thomas started to tell her, but Alexander cut him off.

"Here, Dee. Don't use it unless you have to. We don't want to draw fire to you if we can avoid it. You don't have any armor on," Moore told her. He popped a panel on his left thigh armor and pointed out a railpistol designed for human hands, not suit hands. It was a standard survival component of the suit. Dee reached in and pulled out the gun and checked it as if she had seen it all her life. In fact, she had. She had trained in all things U.S. Marine since she was twelve.

"Right, Daddy. Come on. Listen—there are holowalls everywhere here with security guards hiding behind them. There is one on the second floor as soon as we get out of the elevator by a bust of some old guy."

"That's good to know," Thomas replied.

"Thomas, I'm sorry to tell you, but, Clay is dead."

"We know, Dee. Your AIC got the message to us before the long-range comms were knocked out. Sorry to hear. Clay was a good man," Thomas said.

"Thomas, Koodie, you two are closest to the door. As soon as it opens, get out and rush that bust. Dee, you stay put," Moore ordered.

"Yes, sir."

The elevator dinged, and the second floor light lit up. A second or two later the doors slid open. The hall appeared empty. Thomas and Koodie jumped out as best they could and pumped several rounds through the wall near the only bust in the room. There were some sounds of something falling, and then blood spilled through the holographic wall as it oozed onto the floor.

"Check it, Koodie," Thomas told him.

"Got it," he said and disappeared through the wall. He stepped back through. "Clear!"

The rest of the team poured out of the elevator.

"This way," Dee said, pointing the railpistol down the hallway.

Like father, like daughter, Abigail thought to Alexander.

Elle Ahmi stood on the QMT facility control bridge looking out the zoom-window at the Jovian's rings and at her beautiful planet Ares below. She took a deep breath and sighed, because she knew things weren't as peaceful as they looked. Only moments before, she had been warned that the U.S. had sent a fleet of ships to Ross 128, and so she sent hers there to stop them. Following that, what must be the remainder of the U.S. fleet, seven supercarriers, had QMTed into existence just above New Tharsis there in the Tau Ceti system. That goddamned Alexander Moore had balls. The only way those fleet ships could return to the Sol System would be to take over her QMT facility. And Elle Ahmi was not going to let that shit happen without a big fucking fight. She zoomed in on the planet to get a better look at the ships. They were already dispersing formation and firing on key targets around the capital city of the Separatists.

"Ma'am?" a tech called for her attention.

"Yes?"

"We have the QMT long range up and have Admiral Maximillian on the line," the tech said.

"Great. Put him through here on this screen." She nodded to the man. He turned and punched in some commands on a console across the room, and her screen faded out to solid blue briefly. She could see the reflection of the red, white, and blue ski mask in the screen. Then it blinked on, and there was Max.

"Admiral Maximillian." She smiled at her commanding general, or admiral in this case. "How is the battle going there?"

"Not as good as we hoped, ma'am. There were four U.S. super-carriers originally, and we were winning. We actually totally destroyed one of them. Seconds ago, four more U.S. ships QMTed into the system and have reinvigorated the U.S. fighting spirit." The admiral looked a bit haggard. Elle didn't like the sound of his voice, either. He sounded nervous.

"And the ground forces? How is the governor holding out?"

"They are holding their own for now, but the tide seems to be turning. The numbers are almost even here, ma'am. It could go either way," Admiral Maximillian replied.

"Not good, Max." Elle thought to her AIC for moment and discussed through her mindvoice some alternatives until she settled on a course of action. "Max. Tell the governor he'll just have to make do on his own. Ares is under attack. From the numbers you are telling me, we have split the U.S. fleet. The other half of it is here in the Tau Ceti system now. There are seven supercarriers here. I need you here. Now!"

"Understood, ma'am. We'll jaunt to the QMT gate and jump immediately."

"Great. Hurry, Max. Hurry," Elle said and motioned to the tech to cut the transmission. "Get me Captain Tangiers, now!"

"Yes, ma'am."

A second or two later, Elise Tangiers appeared on the screen. Elise had helped Elle fund the Separatist movement for decades. Her family had owned one of the largest shipping companies in the Sol System, and they had used those ships—the so-called Seppy haulers—for more than just cargo on a number of ocassions.

"Elise, Ares is under attack! I need you to scramble whatever ships you can muster to hold them off until our fleet returns from Ross 128," Elle ordered her.

"I seem to recall telling you that I didn't think we were ready to spread ourselves so thin just yet. We can't protect ourselves and the Ross 128 system," Tangiers said smugly.

"Stow it, Elise. Now is not the time. We couldn't have expected the U.S. to actually mount an offensive only minutes after the Arcadians joined us." Elle gritted her teeth. Saying I told you so never helped anybody and wasted time. She slammed her black leather–gloved fist into her hand and shouted back into the screen. "Elise! Get your troops moving! I want some ships in the air now! I don't care if they only have three people flying them, I want them in the air!"

"Yes, Elle. We're scrambling now."

"Good." She cut the transmission. Then she turned to the tech. "Put me on a systemwide broadcast channel. Make it fast!"

"Yes, ma'am. Ten seconds . . ." The tech fiddled at his console and then waved a hand at her. "You're on, ma'am."

"People of the United Separatist Republic, the Americans are attacking the Tau Ceti system as I speak. They presently have seven U.S. supercarriers over New Tharsis. We must fight them! We haven't had to fight like this in over a decade, and never here on our own soil. But this will be no different than our days on the Reservation on Mars or at Triton. We will fight, and we will prevail. Take up arms and defend your way of life against the evil oppressor! Defend your home!" She cut the feed.

Elle thought for a moment, trying to decide what her next move should be. Deanna was down there in her penthouse. Since those U.S. fleet ships attacked the city, they might hit the Capitol Building and Dee could be in danger. She needed Dee alive. Dee was the only thing she could use to bargain with Moore. She had to have Dee alive. There was something deeper down, she wasn't sure quite what it was. A memory or a feeling she hadn't had in years that compelled her to want Dee alive. It was the same she had felt about Scotty when she had to kill him. She loved Scotty more than any man she'd ever met. But something, logic, had forced her to kill him for betraying her plans. Dee made her question the plans as well. She felt strongly for her grand-daughter. But quickly those feelings were squashed by heartless logic and cold calculation. She needed Dee as a bargaining chip, nothing more.

Copernicus, we have to go get Dee and take her to safety.

Well, where do you want to take her?

Probably to our safe house in the outer-system moons.

In that case we will have to deactivate the snap-back alogorithm for her beacon. She can't leave the atmosphere of Ares or it triggers. The only place to deactivate it is the Capitol Building.

I know. Let's go.

Elle tapped her watchband, triggering her own snap-back, and vanished from the QMT facility. She reappeared a tenth of an AU away on the second floor of the Capitol Building in New Tharsis, where her personal QMT pad was.

The building shook from the explosions outside, and she could hear missile launches and some AA fire coming from the ground. There were no visible guards around the QMT pad, which was normal. The Capitol Building from the second floor up was hers anyway. Only the occasional VIP visitor or particularly strategi-cally important pieces of her plan, like Dee, were allowed to pass through her personal pad. Otherwise, they used one farther out in the city or shuttled in. She often met with her generals on this floor, but they should be out defending her empire from the Americans. Another blast wave made the building tremble, and the windows rattled.

Elle? General Fink wants to talk to you.

Put him through.

"What can I do for you, General Fink?" she said as she walked toward the elevator.

"I'm on the first floor, ma'am. I need access to the military protocols so I can help you defend your city. I came back as soon as I saw the mecha crashing into the penthouse."

"What? Mecha in the penthouse?"

"I'm sorry, ma'am. I thought you knew."

"I'm bringing you up now."

Copernicus, give Fink access to whatever he needs. But keep an eye on him. He's a slimy one. And teleport him up to my pad now.

Yes, ma'am.

Elle stopped and turned around. If there was mecha hitting the penthouse, then she might be outnumbered up there. She wanted to know what happened to her defense systems and SIFs, but that would have to wait.

Are we going back for Fink? Copernicus asked her.

I have an idea. Adjust the protocols and teleport Dee to the pad when I get there. Fink and I can keep an eye on her there.

Very well, ma'am.

As she rounded the corner to the pad, there was Fink in a full-body armored e-suit. His helmet was off and tethered over the shoulder as marines typically do while in an atmosphere. Ahmi looked at him curiously.

"Expecting trouble, General Fink?"

"Always, ma'am. That's why I'm still alive."

"It's just around the corner here," Dee said.

"All right." Alexander held up his armored hand. He and Sehera had redonned their AEM helmets and were both flanking their daughter. The other two in suits were behind them. DeathRay and Nancy kept their backs to the walls as they slunk through the hallway of the Seppy leader's house.

"It should be right—" Dee vanished right in front of them.

"Not again!" Moore lurched forward to grab her but got nothing but air.

"Are we too far from the penthouse, you think?" Sehera asked.

"I don't think so," Nancy replied in a low voice, almost a whisper.

"What the hell!" They heard Dee's voice no more than five meters around the corner. "Goddamned Fink, I'm gonna fucking kill you!" There was the sound of a struggle, and two railpistol rounds fired.

"I don't think you are in the position to kill anyone," Fink said.

"Fuck you," Dee said again, followed by more scuffling sounds.

"Stop it! Now! We need to get out of here." There was no mistaking that voice. It was Elle Ahmi. "On the pad, both of you!"

"Hold up!" Moore whispered, motioning them back against the walls. "We rush together in three, two, one, go!"

CHAPTER 30

July 1, 2394 AD
Ross 128, Arcadia
Friday, 3:46 PM, Earth Eastern Standard Time

"We go in three!" Colonel Roberts motioned to the rest of the Robots. The AEM squad had made it all the way through the tank line and across the front lawn of the governor's mansion. They were presently taking up a position outside the flower garden in a cover position behind some very large limestone and granite flowerpots. There seemed to be nothing more than a handful of infantry holding the mansion position. None of the enemy infantry were in suits. They had body armor and helmets, but a generation old and not powered. On the other hand, there were probably a hundred of them. There were only nine marines, and one of them had a hole where one of his knees used to be.

"Sir, we're ready on the east side," Gunnery Sergeant Tommy Suez reported. The squad was split into two by the driveway of the mansion. Tommy, Sergeant Hubbard, Corporal Bates, and PFCs Howser and Willingham were holding up behind a large ceramic fountain, across the driveway from the colonel, the second lieutenant, Top, and Corporal Cross.

"Good. Okay, Marines, in three, two, one, go!"

"Oorah, motherfucker!" Howser yelled as she bounced up and over the fountain, firing her HVAR from the hip into the Arcadian infantrymen. She bounced down and continued to run at over thirty kilometers per hour.

"Serpentine, Howser!" Tommy warned her. He zigged and zagged through the railgun rounds that were leaving purple ion trails all around him and fired his own weapon. A few times, he pumped grenades from the launcher in his forearm. The grenades lobbed out about fifty meters or so into the barricades and razor wire, exploding with a deafening report and flinging dirt and debris and body parts across the lawn.

"Take that, you motherfuckers!" Bates yelled. He ran at the suit's top speed, never letting off the trigger of either his rifle or his grenades. He crossed the fifty meters or so between where they had been and the barricades at the steps of the mansion in seconds. PFC Howser bounced in right beside him. The two of them were practically back-to-back behind the barricades, pumping railgun rounds out as fast as they could.

Tommy bounced fast, but a bit more cautiously. He could see the colonel, the lieutenant, and Top doing the same as they bounced in from his right. There was always a trap, or a second tier of troops, and they were trying to see if they were drawn out by the first round of AEMs that broke through the line. Tommy's caution had been well placed.

There were snipers in the trees and on the second floor of the roof that started peppering away at the AEMs with larger-caliber railgun rounds. Tommy picked them up in his peripheral vision as soon as they started firing. He tracked the ion trail back up through the air to the treeline and dove sideways, returning fire on them.

"Snipers on the second floor balconies and in the treeline to the east!" Tommy shouted.

"Roger that, Gunny!" Top replied.

"I got 'em," Second Lieutenant Nelms shouted. Tommy could see the lieutenant turn his bounce path and go top speed toward the trees. Railgun rounds chewed up dirt all around him, but the lieutenant just kept on running toward the trees.

"I have the second-floor sniper," Colonel Roberts said. He bounced up and tossed about ten grenades at once into all the second-floor windows.

"They're gonna need a shitload of new windows after that," McCandless called out as she pumped out railgun rounds to cover them.

Tommy had the best angle on the lieutenant's path, so he hunkered down behind a row of statues near the barricade and fired nonstop into the trees. The lieutenant bounced into the tree canopy and vanished from visual, but Tommy could still see him in the QM and IR sensors. Then the canopy exploded, and the sniper fire stopped. The second lieutenant was blasted out of the trees like a rocket, and he rolled and tumbled to a stop just south of Tommy.

"You okay, LT?" Tommy asked him.

"I'm good, Gunny. Keep moving."

"Yes, sir, LT!" Tommy bounced to his feet and over the barricade and joined in the rest of the squad as they mopped up the rest of the Arcadian infantry and security detail guarding the door—most of those poor bastards didn't have any weapons serious enough to do the AEMs real harm, unless they were willing to drop grenades into their own laps. And Ramy's Robots certainly weren't going to give them time to figure that one out.

They moved in closer to the door, and Bates popped it with a few rounds then kicked it open. They stepped back, then carefully charged in like a bunch of damned rhinoceroses—armored rhinos with big fucking guns and HE.

The interior hallway and foyer of the mansion had been blown to shit from all the grenades. The AEMs scanned the room and quickly cleared the first floor.

"So, if I were a control room to an orbital QMT facility, where would I hide?" Colonel Roberts asked.

"Not sure, sir." First Sergeant McCandless shrugged her armored shoulders.

"Well, Top, let's figure it out ASAP."

"Yes, sir."

"Sir, my QMs are reading a dead spot behind that wall," Tommy said. His sensors had plotted a three-dimensional map of the house in his head, but there was a spot just beyond the far wall that was blank. That meant his sensors were blocked.

"You know the only thing that can block the QMs, Gunny?" Nelms asked with a smile that Tommy could see through his visor.

"Uh, no training on the physics of QM tech, LT."

"Well, Gunny, SIFs are the only known tech that stop the QMs. You can jam the electronics and fool them, but if they are working right, the QM sensors can see through anything but structural integrity fields," the lieutenant informed them.

"Well, then, we should take a look," Roberts ordered.

"Tommy, give me a hand," Top ordered him. The two of them dug their armored hands into the wall boards and ripped them off.

"Hey, Marines, you off duty or something?" Tommy said to Bates and Howser. They joined in tearing out the wall, flooring, ceiling, wiring, plumbing, anything that was in their way.

After about two minutes of that the wall was gone, but there was an opalescent blue glow in its place. Tommy tapped it with his knuckles, and it felt as solid as armored deckplating from a supercarrier, or harder.

"Here." Bates pulled up his HVAR and started to fire a round into it. The railgun round vaporized into the field and splattered plasma back in his face. Had he not been wearing his visor, he would have been blinded and maybe even killed.

"Corporal, do you have a fucking death wish?" Top shouted at him. "Stand the fuck down!"

"Sorry, Top."

"Can we blow it with HE?" Tommy asked.

"No. We don't carry anything that would take out a field like that. And even the most precise strike from one of the carrier's DEGs could easily destroy not just the field, but everything inside it as well."

The lieutenant turned to the colonel. "Sir, my master's thesis was on the military application of SIFs for the infantry. I studied them considerably. It'd take a half kiloton or more explosive to take it out."

"Did you say a half kiloton, LT?" Tommy grinned.

"Oh shit," Bates said. "Here we go again."

"Well, Gunny?" Roberts laughed. The rest of the squad did as well—except the new second lieutenant. "Looks like you're up."

"Fire in the hole!" Tommy ducked behind the riverbank down into the water with the rest of the AEMs. But they were in suits. He was in his UCUs. All good marines carried a minimal change of clothes in the suit packs. He actually had a layer of light armor and his cover, too. He hated having to actually blow his suit, but at least he wasn't wearing it this time. And there was atmosphere to breathe, so he didn't have to have his suit to survive. But to an AEM, not being in his suit was damned near torture. Besides that, he had to duck under water and hold his breath for as long as he could once his suit's power core went critical. He hated not being in the suit.

They had tried to get an HE bomb from up top, but the QMTs

were all to busy moving wounded and fighting equipment around. Besides that, it would have taken too long to rig a small device for the job. Most bombs on the bigger ships were much too big for the job. So Tommy's suit was the answer, or at least his answer.

His AIC triggered the overload in the suit's power core. Three seconds later the quantum vacuum–energy storage unit overloaded and released almost a half kiloton of energy right on top of the SIF wall inside the governor's mansion. The mansion vanished in a giant fireball and mushroom cloud. There was no radiation because the suit overload was just a release of energy. Well, there was a blast of X-rays during the blast, but there was no radioactive fallout to worry about.

Tommy held on behind the bank of the river and Howser lay prone over him to give him more protection. The river was a good kilometer and a half away, but that put them right in the edge of the high-wind zone. The blast wave passed over them, throwing dirt, debris, and water everywhere. Tommy held his hands over his ears and kept his mouth open to prevent having his ears burst. The howling winds subsided, and they rose up over the bank to look at the result.

There was a smoldering crater where the governor's mansion used to be. There was a bump the size of a troop carrier right in the middle of it. The marines rushed it. Tommy humped it the old fashioned way. Willingham, who had a hole in his knee, stayed with Tommy.

About that time, nearly a hundred new FM-12s and Ares-T fighters dropped down from the sky. Drop tubes pounded into the ground, and tanks and other AEMs burst out of them. Two supercarriers tore through the atmosphere at several hundred kilometers per hour to the south and west firing DEGs into the enemy line.

"Did it work, sir?" Tommy and PFC Willingham were still a good forty-five seconds out.

"Damned right it did, Gunny. There's an elevator shaft here leading down two or three stories. The *Madira* is about to QMT some experts down, and we're going in to clear it first."

"Yes, sir." Tommy huffed out the rest of the run over the scorched terrain. He came to a stop where the rest of the squad gathered. Then Willingham vanished into thin air. "What the—?"

"That's a good sign that the fleet is getting ahead of the Seppies.

Willingham's injury was noncritical. If they are already getting the noncritical wounded up, then we must be finally winning this thing," Second Lieutenant Nelms said. Nelms started speaking quietly into his comm. Tommy decided that he liked the young officer. He was a good and smart U.S. by-God Marine. There was another flash of light, and the sound of sizzling bacon.

"Gunnery Sergeant Suez, you are out of fucking uniform for this type of AO, soldier," Top shouted at him.

"Uh, Top?"

"You better suit up if you're going down with us," Tamara said, pointing behind Bates at an empty AEM suit on the ground. Nelms must've had a spare suit sent via QMT. There was also ammo for the rest of the squad. Damn fine marine.

"Yes, First Sergeant."

CHAPTER 31

July 1, 2394 AD
Ross 128, Arcadia
Friday, 3:48 PM, Earth Eastern Standard Time

"Admiral! The enemy ships are disengaging, sir!" the CDC officer radioed up to the bridge.

"Yeah, I see that, CDC. STO? Any ideas?" Wallace watched in his DTM as the enemy ships pulled away from the planet, heading out of atmosphere.

"Sir, looks like their fighters are going with them. Do we pursue?" the air boss asked.

"Where are they going?" the XO asked. "Come back and fight, you chickenshits!" He waved a fist in the air as he growled.

"I got it, sir," the STO finally replied. "They are clearing the atmosphere and starting to jaunt. The first one is already popping out at the QMT jump sphere zone."

"They're leaving?" the COB asked. "Good damned riddance if you ask me. It'll give the CHENG and the firecrews time to get us back in shape, sir."

"Why are they leaving?" the ground boss asked. "Do they know something we don't?"

"Maybe they do. We don't care for now," RADM Wallace Jefferson responded. "Our orders were to take this system, and it looks like all that is left to do in achieving that goal is the mop up. So, let's mop up."

"Damn right, sir," the XO agreed in as much an enthusiastic manner as the old Marine mecha jock ever spoke.

265

"XO, get us a courier back to find out what is going on. Hopefully, soon we'll be able to control that facility and won't need the damned couriers."

"Aye, sir." General Chekov turned and in his gruff Marine voice shouted for the quartermaster of the watch.

"CO! The enemy ships just jumped. As far as I can tell, they are out of the system," the STO announced.

"Good . . . I think." Wallace studied the battlescape in his mindview for a few seconds, scrolled through the casualty list, glanced at the piling-up damage reports, and lingered on the intel. There had yet to be any sign of the Arcadian government officials. Well, he didn't expect they would find them on this trip anyway. He'd wait to see what the marines dug up from inside the bunker under where the governor's mansion used to be. He laughed to himself about that damned Ramy Roberts and his Robots. Then he focused in on how the ground campaign was moving along.

The tank numbers had been more than replenished from the new supercarriers in the system. Marine and Navy mecha had dropped on the ground in overwhelming numbers. AEMs and AAIs filled the gaps where they needed to. All said and done, there were over thirty thousand troops covering the planet in state-of-the-art military fashion. The first waves of mecha needed a rest.

"Air Boss, Ground Boss, pull back our guys to rear positions and give them a break for a while. I'm passing along similar orders to the *Roosevelt* and the *Tyler*."

"Aye, sir," the ground boss replied.

"Sir, it might be a good idea to bring in the mecha to reload them. Just in case, sir," the Air Boss said.

"Just in case of what, Michelle?" the XO interjected.

"Well, XO, in case they come back, sir."

"She's got a point, Admiral."

"All right. Order all the first wave mecha back in." Wallace unbuckled his seat belt. They hadn't been hit by a missile, DEG, or so much as a spitwad in a while now, so he wanted to get up and stretch his legs. "I'd say a seventh-inning stretch is in order. Good job, folks. Good job. COB, I think I'm gonna walk around my ship for a while. Care to join me?"

"I'd love to, Admiral." Charlie grabbed his coffee mug and released the magnetic base from his console. "Would you like one to go, sir?"

"Don't mind if I do, Charlie. Larry, you have the bridge."

"Aye, sir. I'll let you know when that courier gets back."

"Keep me posted if anything happens."

"Aye."

The COB handed the admiral a cup of his special coffee, and the two of them stepped out the bridge hatch into the foyer by the elevator. Wallace sipped at the coffee and tried not to make a face. Goddamned COB's coffee had been known to kill junior officers just from the smell. It took a tried and true boat captain to take a real swig of it. It took a fleet admiral to take a gulp of it and not keel over. Wallace took another hit of the stuff. And then hit the elevator button.

"Seven, sir?" the COB asked. Wallace didn't even think about it. The COB knew where they were going. He just nodded in agreement.

The three times they had survived bad scrapes over the last decade or two, the first place Wallace wanted to go was to the triage and see his wounded troops. He had done that back before the Martian Exodus, during the Seppy Reservation skirmishes, and the Battle of Triton. He had done that at Kuiper Station. As long as he sat in the captain's chair, he would do it.

The door opened to the mid level just outside sickbay that had been retrofitted with a QMT pad. Before the QMTs, the casualties would be brought in by Starhawks in the hangar bays. The QMTs had made a big difference in reaction time to extract the wounded, and Wallace hoped it would reduce the number of fatalities to zero.

"Admiral on deck!" an ensign near the hatch shouted through the room.

"As you were! As you all were!" He turned and saluted the young pilot standing near the hatch. He was in Navy pilot gear, and his left arm was gone from the elbow down. It was sealed in an organogel patch. His nametag said Wheeler. "What's your call sign, pilot?"

"Tarzan, Admiral. Ensign Francis 'Tarzan' Wheeler at your service, sir."

"Glad you're with us, Tarzan. You're a Demon Dawg, right?" Wallace double-checked with Uncle Timmy before he said it.

"Yes, sir."

"It was thick out there, huh?" the COB asked.

"If you don't mind my sayin', COB, it was thick as shit."

"Yeah, you did good, Ensign. Thanks." Wallace shook the ensign's hand and turned toward the next wounded soldier. By the insignia on his UCU top, it was an AEM. The PFC was missing his right leg from the knee down. The kid's name was Willingham. Wallace smiled at the marine and looked around the basketball court–sized triage area. This was going to take some time. He'd be there awhile, if there were no urgent calls from the bridge.

"All right, Gunny, there is floor about ten meters down. There's an elevator and a stairwell." PFC Howser shined her suit lights around the room, looking for signs of life or booby traps. She didn't see any. "Clear."

"Bates, go." Tommy told the corporal. Then he dropped in behind him. The rest of the Robots dropped in behind them.

"I've got an elevator shaft, Tommy," Bates called to him.

The room was pitch black. The explosion of Tommy's suit power core had knocked out every system in the place at that level. It had been strong enough to overload the SIF that was being projected around the control bunker. The AEMs had to keep their visors down and their QMs and IRs going. The visor and DTM displays were just as vivid as if they were standing in bright daylight on a perfectly clear day.

"I bet that ain't gonna work, Bates." The second lieutenant bounced in carefully beside Suez. "See if you can get it open."

"Yes, sir." Bates started fumbling around, trying to get a grip on the crease where the two elevator doors met. "Hell with that," he said and then kicked the shit out of it.

The door caved in, and he reached down and tore it the rest of the way off.

"Hey, look at that," Howser said. "The elevator car isn't here." She looked over the edge of the shaft and pinged it with her rangefinder. "Shit, the bottom of this thing is one hundred and fifty meters down."

"Get back, Howser," Top ordered the private. Bates and Tommy quickly dropped back from the opening, pulling their rifles up to ready.

"What gives, Gunny?" Howser asked.

"The last time we were at the bottom of an elevator shaft, we ended up in a firefight. Think about it, Howser. The elevator car is at the bottom. Elevator cars wait where they were last used until somebody presses a button somewhere else." Tommy had a feeling that the shit wasn't over for the day just yet. That was the life of a marine—always in the shit.

"What d'you think, Colonel?" Tommy asked Roberts.

"It's tight quarters, but there ain't but one way to do it," Roberts replied.

"Shit, I figured that. Looks like we'll need to be careful and climb a good eighty meters or so down. Tommy held his HVAR over the edge and pointed it down. He used the sighting-scope system to give him a zoomed view of the shaft. There was a ladder up the shaft, but it would be tough to climb in an e-suit.

"Colonel, wait. We should just get the *Madira* to QMT us down there," Lieutenant Nelms told him. The LT just kept giving Tommy reasons to like him.

"Fuckin' A," Bates whispered to himself.

"Second Lieutenant Nelms, that is a goddamned stellar idea," Roberts replied. "But first we'll have them send down a gas bomb or two. We don't want to damage the facility, but we may get lucky and catch them sleeping with their faceplates up. Stay alert, Robots, but chill while I set this up."

It didn't take long for Colonel Roberts to get the QMT approved. The QM sensors on the suits managed to generate enough data to create rough a map of the underground facility. At the bottom of the shaft was a very large chamber with other side chambers. The colonel decided to have the marines teleported to the center of that room.

"Okay, Robots, we're doing this from an outward-facing circle defensive posture," Top told them. "Visors down, form up." Howser, Bates, Cross, Hubbard, and Suez knelt in a circle and Top, the second lieutenant, and the colonel stood in the center back-to-back. One instant the AEMs were standing in the top-floor room of the blown-to-shit governor's mansion and the next they were in the middle of a room the size of a hangar bay. There were consoles lining the walls and equipment strewn about, but there were no signs of any kind of life.

"Fan out," the colonel ordered. "Recon. And keep those visors down—there should be plenty of residual gas floating around."

The team spread out in every direction, pinging away with sensors and being careful. They were alert, with all sensors and eyes looking for booby traps. The best they could tell, there were none. Tommy was pretty sure the place had been abandoned. That would mean that there was a QMT pad down here somewhere. He kept an eye out for that. And he was going to make damned certain to keep Bates away from any panels resembling a personnel QMT pad. The last one they found at the Battle of the Oort, Bates managed to teleport them into a room full of Seppy scientists.

"I'm getting no motion or hotspots. No bodies, either. Is anybody else getting anything?" Tommy asked.

"I've got nothing, Gunny," Howser replied.

"We're clear over here," Bates said.

"I think there must be a QMT pad down here, and they all went up to the facility or to those Seppy ships." Tommy offered his theory.

"Makes sense, Gunny," the lieutenant agreed.

"Here! I've got a pad over here, and there are lights on some of these panels, so there must be power coming from somewhere," Sergeant Hubbard announced.

"Everybody stay alert!" Top reminded them. "We make certain this place is clear before we call in the experts to start pushing buttons."

"Roger that, Top. I've got several panels and two doors here," Hubbard said.

It took another five minutes or so before Colonel Roberts and Top were convinced that the room was clear of booby traps, land mines, and assholes hiding in the closets. A generator and lights were QMTed down, and the marines went about setting it up. A couple more minutes and the place was lit up like noon, every door was opened, and there were lights placed in each exterior room. Then the experts came down. There were three of them this time, wearing their engineering armor. The highest ranking one, a CWO4, went right to work. As soon as he arrived, it was like he had seen the place before. He knew which panel to go to and which buttons to start pushing.

After a minute or two, he popped off his helmet and plugged a hardwire from the universal data port into a device that he stuck to his head behind his ear. The other two warrant officers did the same.

"We need to check this thing out," the CWO4 said. Tommy noticed that his name tag said Ransom.

"Colonel Roberts," he said. "I think we are ready to try our hand at controlling this pad. Would you and your AEMs be willing to teleport up to the counterpart to this room in orbit?"

"No problem, Mr. Ransom."

"Okay, sir. Whenever you're ready."

"Marines, circle the wagons," the colonel said as he stepped onto the middle of the pad.

CHAPTER 32

July 1, 2394 AD
Tau Ceti, New Tharsis
Friday, 3:48 PM, Earth Eastern Standard Time

"Don't you even fucking twitch, Ahmi!" Moore shouted as they turned the corner. He had his targeting crosshair on Fink's forehead, but the dishonored marine had his daughter around the neck in an armored grip and the forearm HVAR of his armored suit to her head.

"Too late, Alexander," Ahmi replied, and the three of them vanished.

"Goddamnit!" Moore said. "I should have shot the bitch!"

"No, Alexander, it would have put Dee at even greater risk," Sehera scolded her husband.

"All that is well and good, Mr. President, but we need to figure out where they went," DeathRay interjected. He and Nancy began reconnoitering the pad and control panels. "Nancy?"

"Give me a minute," the CIA agent answered.

Alexander was getting antsy. Next time he wasn't going to hesitate. He was going to put a bullet through Ahmi's brain the first chance he got. Fink had a railgun round with his name on it, too.

"Thomas, Koodie, keep our backs covered." Moore told the bodyguards.

"Got it, sir."

"Any ideas yet, Ms. Penzington?" Sehera asked, looking over Boland's shoulder. DeathRay turned to the First Lady with a solemn look on his face.

"Don't worry, ma'am, we'll find her," he said.

"Well, between the president's AIC and mine, we have figured out where they went," Nancy stated. "There is a pad somewhere in the outer part of this system. Looks like it is in orbit around a moon of another one of the gas giants farther out."

"Then we go there," Alexander said.

"Well, I have a better idea, sir." Nancy paused and conferred with her AIC. "I think we should send her somewhere else. The snap-back routine for Dee has been turned off so she could go to the other facility. I believe Allison and Abigail can hack this thing if they work together. Then, sir, I would suggest we use Boland's original plan. We send all of them to the Oval Office. We follow after leaving a charge on this thing to blow it to hell and gone."

"You think you can manage that, Ms. Penzington?" Sehera tried not to get her hopes up too high.

"Yes, ma'am. President Moore's AIC is very smart and mine is, well, even smarter. Elle Ahmi's must be somewhere on a level near the two of them but certainly not better than the two of them working together. We might even tap into all of our AICs if we need extra computational power. We'll see. They are already running the dictionary search hack on her control algorithm."

"Mr. President, if this is our plan, then somebody should go ahead to the Oval Office and prepare it for our arrival," Thomas suggested. The head bodyguard was right. Alexander needed to get in there, clear out his office, and get ready to turn on the office SIF. Maybe prepare a surprise or two for Ahmi and Fink. At the same time, he didn't want to leave the system without Dee.

"Okay, Thomas, you go. Snap back and set things up. If the vice president is there, tell him that he needs to vacate immediately. I'm having Abigail download you an e-memo now with my authorization. Then there are some other instructions she is giving you. Follow them to the letter."

"I was hoping you would go, sir." Thomas hesitated with his response. "It would make us all feel better about your safety, sir."

"Thomas, go," Moore told him.

"Yes, Mr. President." The bodyguard sighed, certain that no further argument would get him anywhere. Moore knew it wouldn't, because he came to this star system to find his daughter and bring her home safely. That is just what he was going to do.

"I'll see you soon, sir. Koodie, you keep an eye on things," Thomas said and then triggered his Oval Office snap-back. He vanished with a flash of white and blue light and a crackling hissing sound.

"We're in!" Nancy sounded excited. "Her passcode was a random string of digits two-hundred symbols long. Their beacons are quantum connected to this pad. I'm setting up a site-to-site algorithm from out there to here to Earth."

"We're gonna need HE, sir. Do you three have any grenades in those suits?" Jack asked.

"If we don't have enough, the *Blair* can drop us down more."

"Well, we need a pretty good charge for the pad. It is several meters thick. The control panels are just in here and is all soft circuitry, which shouldn't require a lot of HE. Ten grenades at once should do it for sure."

"We have enough then," Sehera added and started pulling out grenades from her suit's forearm launcher. She counted out ten and dropped them at her feet.

"I'll set them, ma'am," Michael offered.

"No thanks, Koodie. I've set a few grenades in my day," Sehera said. Everybody but Alexander raised an eyebrow at that. Sehera knelt down and put a fifteen-second timer on each of them. As soon as an electronic signal was sent from her launcher, the clock would start on them.

"Nancy, put this on." Jack handed her the wristwatch snap-back device he had intended to give Dee. "Dee won't need it. Maybe one day you can come back for your tank and any other planes and goodies you have squirreled away here."

"I won't miss them, Boland." Nancy laughed. "Okay, we're ready to trigger this thing whenever you are, Mr. President."

"The grenades are set. I say that Michael and I will pump a few extras into the walls and around here before we go. I've also sent a message to the *Blair* to blast this building off the face of this planet immediately upon my signal. She's waiting on ready with the crosshairs on us."

"Well, then, here we go. Is everybody ready?" Nancy looked at everyone to make certain they were. All responded with an affirmative nod.

"Everybody make certain your helmets are on, visors in place. Trust me, just do it," Alexander said. After everyone complied, he nodded to Nancy and raised his grenade launcher. His bodyguard followed suit.

"Triggering the snap-back in three, two, one, go!" Nancy said.

There was a flash of light as usual, and for a brief instant they could see Ahmi, Fink, and Dee standing surprised on the pad in front of them. Then they disappeared again. Hopefully, they had reappeared in Washington, D.C.

"That's it. Let's go!" Nancy said.

"Admiral Walker, this is Moore."

"Yes, sir?"

"Count to ten and then rain hell on my current coordinates and don't stop till there is nothing left but a crater."

"What about you and the First Lady?"

"We're snapping back to the Oval Office. Dee is already there."

"That's good news, sir. Sir, we just had multiple Seppy ships QMT into the system. We are outnumbered here now!"

"Get a courier to Wally to get over here and help you. Now start blasting!"

"Aye, sir!"

"Go, go!" Moore said. Sehera vanished. Nancy and DeathRay flashed out. Moore and Koodie pumped a bunch of grenades through the walls, computers, down the hallway, and into the ceiling.

"Let's go, Michael."

"Yes, Mr. President."

They vanished. Seconds later the room erupted into a ball of high-energy plasma and debris. Fire spread and engulfed the floor. Then the building began to shake and shudder as DEG and missiles rained down from above. The Capitol Building of the United Separatist Republic, the house of terrorist leader Elle Ahmi, was being razed to the ground.

CHAPTER 33

July 1, 2394 AD
Sol System, Washington, D.C.
Friday, 4:15 PM, Earth Eastern Standard Time

Moore appeared in the Oval Office just behind the *Resolute* desk. His HVAR was at the hip, and he was flashing crosshairs for Ahmi. Thomas had done his job. The office was cleared, and as soon as all of them reappeared, there was a SIF field put in place around the room. Nobody was getting in or out.

Unfortunately, Ahmi and Fink were still on their feet. Fink was now wearing his helmet, and while Ahmi seemed a bit unsteady, she was somehow still standing—probably immunoboost and stims.

"Don't fucking do it, Alexander!" Ahmi screamed at him almost in a pitch too high for dogs to hear. She had an unconscious Dee by the neck and a railpistol to her head. Fink was on her left with his HVAR leveled on them. He had his back to the window facing the White House lawn and waved the weapon back and forth cautiously.

"Let her go, Elle!" Moore shouted at her. He shifted the weight of his feet and readied himself. For what, he wasn't sure, since he didn't have a plan of action yet.

"Let her go," Sehera said. Sehera was near Thomas at the entrance to the office, and both of them were pointing their rifles at Ahmi, trying to get a line of sight where Dee wasn't in the way. Koodie, Nancy, and DeathRay were on the other side of the couch.

"You shoot me, and my AIC will fire this pistol. Dee will die," Ahmi said. "Now drop the SIF and let us go."

"Dee stays here," Alexander growled.

275

"Very well, Moore. You win, this time." Ahmi tightened her grip on Dee. Dee started to regain consciousness—they must've given her something as well.

"Don't move, Dee. It'll be all right," Sehera warned her.

"Ma'am, if we're gonna go, let's go," Fink said.

Dee was quickly regaining her feet. "Fuck you, Fink. I am so gonna hunt you down and rip your goddamned head off," Dee shouted.

"Easy, dear," Ahmi said.

Abigail! Ask Nancy's AIC if they can QMT Dee out.

No, sir, they cannot.

Can we track them?

Yes, sir. That was all part of Nancy's plan. Allison, her AIC, is quite brilliant, sir.

Then if we let her go, I can go right to her?

Yes, sir.

Now we're talking.

Yes, sir.

"Go, Ahmi, and don't come back. Your Separatist movement is over," Moore told her.

"We shall see, Alexander. We shall see. Now drop your SIF."

"Drop the SIF, Thomas." The Secret Service bodyguard triggered the SIF generator off.

"Done, sir."

"Let her go. I gave her my word." Moore motioned to the rest of them.

"Yes, you did. You are such an honorable marine, Alexander. I should have killed you long ago!" Ahmi pushed Dee forward and fired three rounds of the railpistol into Moore's chest as spheres of crackling light flashed around her and Fink. Dee dove for the ground, and DeathRay, Nancy, and Sehera pumped railgun rounds through the balls of light to no avail. Thomas and Koodie dove for the President. They covered him until the firing stopped.

"This is Thomas Washington. We have an emergency. The president is critically injured with three rounds to the chest. I repeat. The president has been shot."

"Daddy!" Dee rushed to his side. There was no blood, as his suit and organogel had sealed it off. Immunoboost had been administered, but the rounds were completely through him in three places.

"I'm alive, Dee. And most important, so are you!" Moore smiled as he tried to open his visor. Then he, the bodyguards, Dee, and Sehera vanished from the Oval Office.

They reappeared in a hospital room in someplace unknown to Dee. Sehera tossed her helmet on the floor and helped Thomas and Koodie pull Alexander Moore out of his armor.

"Leave the seal layer on." A team of doctors rushed in around them. "Stand back, we've got this."

"He was wounded pretty badly. His right lung was collapsed and torn asunder. His intestines were cut in half. And his heart had a hole in it big enough to put your thumb through. We did everything we could, ma'am." The doctor looked at Sehera and Dee. Then he looked over their shoulders at the bodyguards and politicians.

"No, Daddy!" Tears flowed down Dee's cheeks.

"Come with me," the doctor told them.

"Dee, shhh. It is okay, baby." Sehera held her daughter's hand and led her by the hand calmly as she followed the doctor.

He led them down a long white corridor to a double door where Thomas stood in his Secret Service–agent black suit and tie and dark sensor glasses. He nodded to them but didn't say a word as they passed through the doors.

The room they entered was a large private hospital room with a single bed in it. Moore was lying in the bed with a blanket covering him. The blanket had the presidential seal on it. They could only see the foot of the bed, as the head of it was blocked by a wraparound curtain that hung from ceiling to floor.

"It will be okay, Dee," Sehera comforted her. Dee was trembling and crying, barely maintaining control.

"Of course it will. Why wouldn't things be okay?" Alexander slid the curtain back. Dee's eyes widened.

"What! Daddy?" She rushed to his side and hugged him.

"Ouch, not too tight, princess, and not too loud, either." He hugged her back.

"Why? Why would you do this to me?" Dee looked angry.

"Shhh, Dee. Listen to your father before you say anything else." Sehera sat on the edge of the bed and rubbed Alexander's leg through the blanket. He smiled back at her.

"We have some very hard decisions to make, Dee," Alexander started.

"What do you mean, decisions?" Dee interrupted. "There are no decisions. We go and find Fink and my deranged grandmother and we put about ten bullets into each of their brains. No decision. It is simple!"

"Like father, like daughter." Sehera smiled again. She rubbed Dee on the back with her other hand.

"Well, yes, Dee, we will do that, if that is the right thing to do. And believe me, I agree with you. But Elle Ahmi controls and inspires millions of people. If she suddenly vanishes, there will be chaos and Tau Ceti will tear itself apart. The power-hungry assholes like Fink, Elise Tangiers, and many others will usurp resources and create a world of factions that will continue to be a war zone for generations." Moore paused for a breath and adjusted the tube in his nose. For the first time, Dee noticed it.

"Dad, what's wrong?"

"Ha, nothing. They haven't had time to finish printing me a new lung yet, so I'm still only using one of them. The doctors spent all the time so far printing me a new heart and then a new section of intestine. I'll be fine after my surgery in a few minutes, but first we need to talk. The lung will be printed by then, and the surgery is quite routine. With immunoboost, I'll be back to normal in two hours tops."

"Okay. I love you, Dad." Dee had never seen her father hurt before. He had tackled giant mechanical monsters with his bare hands and come out without so much as a scratch, but he seemed extremely mortal to her now lying in the hospital bed. The feeling scared the hell out of her. The fact that it was her own grandmother that had shot him just made her more certain that Elle Ahmi was nothing more than raw genetic material. If Dee got the chance, she'd kill Ahmi for doing what she had done to her dad.

"So, the decision we have to make, Dee," Sehera added, "is what do we do next? Ahmi can't continue to be in charge of the United Separatist Republic, as she calls it. The U.S. can and will forcibly take the system, but there would be terrorist activity for decades and decades, until every last Separatist is found and killed, if it isn't handled delicately. And who is to say that the next president will have the fortitude your father has had in dealing with them. After all, no matter how much *we* love him, no president will continue to get reelected forever. Nor should they."

"What are you two saying?"

"We have a plan in mind to take out the heads of all the cells in the Separatist movement and remove their desire and ability to resist the U.S."

"How?"

"It is our family that has caused this mess for humanity for so long. We are going to take on the responsibility to clean it up," Sehera added. "The Separatists are dug in much deeper in our society than the general public knows. There are moles in Congress and the Senate. There are moles here in the White House. There are moles in every colony and territory. There are CEOs and other officers of big corporations and conglomerates involved that will have to be removed from their positions of power."

"How?"

"The three of us, Captain Jack Boland, Nancy Penzington, and Thomas Washington, are going to end this thing covertly, quietly, and quickly. We'll do it in a way that history will never know about, but mankind will be the better for. We'll start with the Separatist cell leaders today. Over the next year, we'll deal with the others." Moore clicked the remote on his bed and raised the back of it a bit to make him a little more comfortable. "We can't and we will not do this if you aren't with us, Dee. And your mother and I are serious when we say that we will not do this if you don't want to. We can go on the way things are, and you can live your life as you have been. Although we will need to put more security on you."

"I'm in, Daddy. What do I do?"

"That's my girl. Your mother will talk with you about that while I'm in surgery."

"So, there is one thing I need to understand," Dee said. "My grandma was an evil twisted psycho nut batshit crazy bitch?"

Sehera let out a rueful chuckle. "Like father, like daughter."

CHAPTER 34

July 1, 2394 AD
Ross 128, Arcadia
Friday, 4:45 PM, Earth Eastern Standard Time

Admiral, I think you'd better get back up here, sir. The XO sent the message to Wallace directly to his mindvoice. *Our courier is back from the Sol System.*

"On my way," he said audibly. "COB, we'd better get back upstairs."

"Understood, sir." Charlie shook the hand of another wounded Marine pilot, call sign Deuce, as they made their way out of the postoperative ward. The marine would probably be paralyzed for days, until her new spinal column section that had been printed and implanted could heal and her brain could figure out which reconnected nerve went to what body part. It would take her weeks of rehab to relearn how to walk, run, fight, and fly mecha again.

"Hell of a mess, Charlie."

"Yes, sir. That QMT tech saved a lot of lives. We sure could have used it at the Oort or during the Exodus," the COB said. "Or back in the old days, or—"

"Didn't save them all, COB. We still have a lot of letters to write."

"Yes, sir." They turned the corner of the corridor out to the elevator. The COB depressed the button, and they waited patiently.

"Any word on the QMT facility controls, sir?"

"Uncle Timmy says that Ramy's Robots took it. It has been swept, and the warrant officers have it working. They've already

281

QMTed up and down between it and the orbital facility several times. We should be able to operate the QMT facility in a matter of minutes."

"Damn good news, Admiral."

"Indeed."

The elevator ride didn't take long, and after having been with the wounded for a while, neither of them was in the mood to talk a whole bunch. Seeing that many of America's finest maimed, dismembered, and disfigured was disheartening to say the least. On the up side, none of the wounded had low spirits and none of them felt bad about what they had done. That in itself was uplifting. The doors slid open, and it was time to get back to work.

"Admiral on the bridge!" The XO stood from the captain's chair and returned to his station.

"As you were." Wallace took his seat, and the COB took his. "So, what's up, Larry?"

"Sir, the courier just returned. The enemy ships left us earlier because Admiral Walker is leading the rest of the fleet against the Separatists at Tau Ceti. The president sent a message for us to get there somehow and help her out."

"Fullback is probably giving the Seppies hell."

"Yes, sir. I'm sure she is."

"I suppose we can't let her have all the fun." Wallace turned on the DTM battlescape view and ship readouts. His mind had been resting long enough. More information than could be understood visually, audibly, and through touch flooded his mind directly. The DTM mindview allowed for a completely different level of perception of massive amounts of data. "It's been a long day, hey, XO? COB, better mix up some more of your coffee."

"Aye, Admiral," Charlie replied. "It's been one of those fine Navy days, sir. Should I make it strong?"

"You mean there is a *strong* version of your coffee, COB?"

"Oh, yes, sir. I make the weak stuff because a lot of our junior officers can't take real coffee, sir."

"Then make it strong. And yes, Charlie, it *has* been a fine Navy day."

"I wouldn't know about Navy days, Admiral, but I don't think even us marines would want too many like the one we've had so far." The XO grinned.

"Do we have full use of the QMT facility yet?" Wallace asked.

"Yes, sir," the STO replied.

"How about that?" Wallace thought about it; things could have been worse. They had jumped into the Ross 128 star system not even sure they had a way home. They knew they were going to have to fight for control of the QMT facility. And fight they had. They had lost an entire supercarrier, with few survivors. "Ground Boss, how we doing down on the planet?"

"We've ground it down to a halt, sir. The fighting is done, unless we want to start taking it house-to-house to look for holdouts," the ground boss replied.

"That's not our call right now. Okay, we'll leave two ships here, and the rest of us will QMT to Tau Ceti and jump right back into the fight." Wallace paused, trying to decide which two stayed. The *Roosevelt* and the *Tyler* could hold down the fort in Ross 128 and lick their wounds. The *Madira* would lead the other four ships that had seen very little of the fighting on to Tau Ceti. He put out the orders to the fleet ship captains.

"Fleet ships, this is Admiral Jefferson. The rest of the fleet has engaged the Separatists at Tau Ceti and needs our help. The *Roosevelt* and the *Tyler* will remain here and maintain operations while the rest of us will rendezvous at the orbital QMT facility for the jump to Tau Ceti in thirty minutes. For the ships about to jump, send out the recall to all of your troops and start prepping for battle. I want us loaded up and ready to QMT into battle in thirty minutes. If that means we run the QMTs to get the tanks and mecha on board at the same time the hangar bays are running and the Starhawks are flying, then that is what we do. I hate to have to ask you to jump right back into the fray again, people. I know this has been a long fight already. But our fellow soldiers are in the thick and need our assistance. We will be there for them. So let us all get moving. Good luck, and God bless."

"Andy, you don't have to be here," Joe told the EM1. "You should be in your rack resting."

"Hell, sir, I'm fine. That immunoboost is good stuff," Sanchez replied. "Did it work? I mean, I'd hate to think I got sucked out of the ship and all banged up for nothing."

"Yeah, it did. I'm gonna have to put you in for some sort of commendation. Bravery or something—the kind of thing usually given to jarheads." Joe smiled. "When the air rushed through the dry hull, it was supercooled through a Venturi effect, and that cooled the overheated coolant big time. We also came up with a new way to run the SIFs that will reduce the heat exchange needs by a shitload."

"Just glad I could help, sir."

"I'm just glad we didn't lose you."

"Aw shit, I wasn't never scared of that, sir," Andy lied.

"You sure you're up for duty then?"

"Sir, EM1 Sanchez reporting for duty, sir." He saluted.

"Well, we're headed into the shit in just a few minutes, so find something that needs fixin' and fix it, EM1." Joe returned the salute.

"Aye, sir."

CHAPTER 35

July 1, 2394 AD
Sol System, Mississippi
Friday, 5:45 PM, Earth Eastern Standard Time
Friday, 12:45 PM, New Tharsis Standard Time

"Jack, you ready for this?" Penzington asked the mecha jock. She knew that Boland was probably revered as one of the greatest pilots in the fleet, but what they were doing was "wet work," up close and personal. She wanted to make certain that the pilot would kill up close as easily as he could through mindview targeting sights. The distance made it easier for some people, and for some it didn't matter. Nancy never trusted people who could easily kill. She just wanted them to be able to do the job when they had to.

"I'm good, Nancy." Jack slapped the ammo magazine into his HVAR and stepped on the pad with her.

"Good," Nancy said. "We'll take care of the Tangiers first. I know where Elise stays. If they are under attack, then she'll be in her safe house in the mountains. I was a member of the Tangiers inner circle for a while. I know them pretty well. I have her AIC's EM signature saved. As soon as we get near her, I'll be able to pinpoint her."

"Good. By the time you get back, I should be well enough to join you," President Moore said. He had squirreled away one of the original QMT prototype pads more than a year prior, as if he had been planning this all along. The pad was in an old abandoned airport outside Jackson, Mississippi, near where he had grown up. Nancy thought that he was a very resourceful and clever man. He would have made a good spy. He made a great marine, and not too bad a president.

"I've had my AIC train yours, Dee's, and Sehera's external AIC on the operation of the pad. All you have to do is tell them what you want, and they can get you where you need to be. We managed to put backdoors in all the QMT pads known to us. So we can operate any of them, anywhere, and bounce between the network of jump pads. From here, we can QMT through ships or Mars or out to the Oort, and from there anywhere forward and back with a snap-back algorithm. I think this must be what Ahmi was trying to figure out how to do, but she didn't have the advantage of having access to all of the QMTs everywhere. We'll see you in a bit."

"Good hunting, Nancy, DeathRay." Dee waved to them. Then the pad lit up and they were gone to Mars for a fraction of a second, then through the Oort Cloud facility to the big one at Tau Ceti.

A fraction of a second later they were in the northern mountainous region of the Tharsis continent of Ares, inside a hallway with hardwood floors and lavish interior décor. There were paintings on the walls that Nancy knew were priceless, and there were sculptures, suits of armor, and other artifacts aligned down the hall that were each artifacts of antiquity from human history.

"Look at all this shit." Jack whistled softly.

"Elise is a collector. If it is expensive, she wants two of them. You should see her antique cars." Nancy scanned each direction to get her bearings. "This way."

The two of them slipped through the halls until they came past several suites and then an elevator. The elevator had a stairwell to the right of it. Nancy eased the door to the stairwell open and poked her HVAR around the doorjamb.

"Clear. Come on. They'll be two floors down, in her shipping operations room."

"If you knew that, why didn't we go there?"

"I couldn't be sure I had the coordinates right. We didn't want to teleport into a wall or something. I had measured where we came in before because I was going to fly a bomb in there if I ever got the opportunity. I never got it. But what I did get is her SIF encryption sequence. Even though she changed it, she follows the same algorithm. Allison just cycled through the algorithm until she hit the right key code. Ergo, we're in."

"I see." Jack widened his eyes and tried not to grin. "What is this place, anyway?"

"Bunker, hideout, ski resort, spa, whatever she wants it to be. She has more money and power than God. The only person she answers to is Elle Ahmi herself. They are tight, apparently. I didn't find that out until six years ago, and it nearly got me killed then."

They quickly dropped down the stairs to the door into the operations room. There were no guards standing around that far inside the compound, because nobody could get through the layered defenses and security to that point—unless they had QMT teleport technology and the geospatial coordinate information to circumvent those layers.

Nancy motioned DeathRay forward until they came to the operations room entrance. Inside, they could hear people talking and rushing around. This would be the nerve center for the logistics tail of the Separatist army. Taking out this room and its occupants would stall the Seppies' ability to run their defense. The might of the U.S. fleet had been in-system for more than an hour and was pounding away at the mix of Seppy civilian-turned-military vessels, plus the seven Seppy supercarriers that had returned from Ross 128. The battle up top had become a stalemate. Nancy and Jack were about to change that.

Nancy, I've got a fix on Elise, Allison told her.

Where is she?

You're not going to believe this, but she is on the ski slope.

Skiing?

She's moving up the mountain at about two kilometers per hour.

Ski lift.

Probably, her AIC agreed.

Okay, calculate the jump to get us there as soon as we blow the operations room.

Done.

Wait for my order.

You got it.

"Now, Jack." Nancy motioned to him.

They burst into the room, letting loose nonstop railgun fire until nothing else moved in the room. Then Nancy pulled out an HE pack and armed it.

"Be ready, Jack."

"Like I'm not now," he said.

Now, Allison. Nancy pulled the pin on the HE and dropped it at her feet. They flashed out, and the room exploded. They reappeared atop a snowpeaked mountain behind a ski-lift shack.

"Goddamn, Nancy, you couldn't have found a colder place to go?" Jack laughed.

"Shh. Our target is getting off that lift in about sixty seconds." They hid behind the shack. There was nobody else on the peak or the slopes as far as they could see.

"You're telling me that this lady is going snow skiing while her planet is under attack?"

"She lives in a different world, Jack."

"She must."

"I've got this." Nancy leaned around the corner to see the lift seats coming up the hill. She raised her HVAR and opened the sight link in her DTM view. The targeting X appeared in her vision. She zoomed the scope and put the X right on Elise Tangiers's forehead. She breathed out softly and squeezed the trigger. She could see the back of the woman's head blow out, and then her body slumped forward.

"You got her," Jack said, looking through his sight. "Let's move on."

"Right."

Allison, Mississippi.

Done.

"Dee, you hold the fort down for now," Alexander told his daughter as he, Sehera, Thomas, Jack, and Nancy stepped onto the pad. From the QMT usage that Nancy's AIC had managed to download on their trip to Ares, she had figured out that there had been a QMT to the outer-planet moon pad that they had detected earlier. It had to be Ahmi.

"Okay, Daddy. I don't know why I can't go now, though."

"Because, dear," Sehera told her, "I don't want you around her ever again."

"Don't worry. We'll be back soon, Dee," Alexander reassured his daughter as they flashed out.

They popped into realspace on a small personnel transport QMT pad in the middle of a larger cylindrical-shaped room with a domed roof. The room was mostly transparent and looked right out into space. There was a blue-green Uranus-sized gas giant filling the horizon. There was a red, white, and blue ski mask lying next to a photograph of President Sienna Madira being sworn in on a desk nearby.

"What the hell!" Sehera said at the odd view. Elle Ahmi was sitting in a chair, staring blankly as if in a trance. She wasn't moving at all. "Ahmi! Elle Ahmi!" She poked at her with her railgun rifle.

"Ah, hello, dear," Ahmi's face gained color, and her eyes no longer looked vacant. "I figured this wasn't over with yet."

"It is now." Alexander stepped beside his wife and put the gun to Ahmi's head. "Sweep the place." He motioned to the rest of the team. They spread out and started searching the room.

"It looks clear, sir," Thomas said.

"There's a door over here, but it's locked from the inside," Jack added.

"Oh, Alexander, don't bother. I'm the only one here," Ahmi said. "So, you gonna pull that trigger or what, son?"

"We need to know the leaders of the cells, Elle," Sehera said. Tears started to form in her eyes.

"So, this is it, then. I tell you what you need to know just like that, and then you take me out?"

"Yes, something like that," Alexander told her.

Sir, her AIC is trying to hack me, Abigail warned him. *He's hacking into all of us, sir.*

Are you okay?

For now, sir! Allison is helping! But, sir, her AIC, is, is . . .

Abby? Abby!

Alexander slapped Ahmi upside her head with the butt of his HVAR very hard.

"Stop trying to hack my AIC! Now!"

"Mother! Tell me what I need to know. You have to help me." Sehera pushed the barrel of her rifle harder against her forehead. "Please, Mother. I can end this today! We must end this today! But we will need your help. Damnit, Mother, if you ever loved me, if you are even still in there, help us."

"Fuck this," Nancy said. "I owe this bitch." She walked over and started to put a round into Ahmi before her AIC could hack theirs. Nancy had never believed there could be an AIC stronger than hers, or even close. But this AIC was attempting to hack a top-secret AIC, a very, very brilliant one in Abigail, and a top-of-the-line mecha jock's AIC all at the same time, and doing a pretty good job of it.

"No!" Sehera turned to her. Alexander stepped in Nancy's way. "Not yet," he said.

"Elle!" Sehera started to cry. "Sienna Madira, are you in there? Help us. Help us!"

"Alexander," Ahmi looked over at him. "You . . . I— I'm sorry I tortured you, son."

"Help us, then."

"Sehera, I love you. Copernicus, stop it! Copernicus, no! I'm in control here!" Ahmi fell forward, holding her head and screaming. Blood started to trickle from her left ear, and then it poured. "Stop it!" She rose up, lunging forward into Sehera and taking the railpistol from her daughter's side holster.

"Mother! Tell us who the Separatist cell leaders are!" Sehera pushed her away, not realizing her pistol had been taken.

"Show, unh, Dee who her grandfather was." Elle stood, held the railpistol to the side of her head, and pulled the trigger.

"No!" Alexander shouted.

Sehera stood looking over mother's body. *There should have been more blood and gray matter,* she thought. She knelt beside the body of the one hundred eleventh president of the United States, of the most wanted mass-murdering terrorist in human history, of her daughter's grandmother. Sehera reached out and closed her dead mother's eyes.

"*You* two are the White House moles!" Nancy stepped forward and swept her weapon between Alexander and Sehera. Thomas instantly turned and raised his weapon on Nancy. DeathRay looked unsure of whom to point his weapon at.

"No, we're not," Alexander said. "Sehera is just one of many victims of her mother's schemes, and I'm the White House double-agent. Ms. Nancy Marie Bloomfeld, I would think a woman playing the role of somebody else for most of her life could understand the concept."

"But you *have* been involved with her. Your wife is her daughter? How can we trust you?"

"Before you were even an itch in your daddy's pants, Ms. Bloomfeld, I fought this woman with every fiber of my being. I watched her slaughter, capture, torture, maim, and kill my men. She tortured me to near-death on several occasions. I swore then I'd stop her no matter what it took. And believe me, it has taken a lot."

"Still, your wife is *her* daughter. How can we trust you?" Nancy repeated.

Sehera answered her. "Put down your weapon, and I'll show you. Plus, I'll save your AICs." Sehera wiped tears from her face. Then she rolled her mother's head over, revealing the exit wound. Sehera reached in and wrapped her fingers around something inside her mother's skull and pulled a gray and bloody deformed mass the size of an egg out. There were clear slimy tendrils extending into her head. Sehera continued to pull until she had extracted the thing from her. Her mother's neck twisted and popped a few times as she pulled. The plastic-coated device looked more like a jellyfish than it did anything else. She tossed it on the floor next to her husband.

"What the hell is that?" Jack asked, alarmed at the sight.

"The root of mother's evil," Sehera replied. Alexander stomped a boot on the thing, shattering it to pieces. He stomped it a few more times and twisted the ball of his foot over the plastic pieces until they were nothing more than a bloody stain rubbed into the hardwood floor.

"That was a prototype top-secret super AIC from over eighty-five years ago," Moore said. "And this used to be President Sienna Madira, until that damned thing went nuts and started taking over her mind. She became Elle Ahmi after that."

"And she *was* my mother," Sehera continued to cry softly. "As I grew up, I saw her go through multiple personality periods and wild mood swings and amazing periods of brilliance and amoral evil. I always knew something was wrong with her, that she was more than just a terrorist. Alexander and I figured it out during the Martian Desert Campaign, while he was in the torture camps. Being a student of history, he recognized who she really was from things she said and mannerisms she had."

"And it has taken us decades to figure out how to stop her." Alexander put his hand on his wife's shoulder. "How to stop *it*. And the crazy damned plans twisted around other plans within plans. There was always a glitch in the plans, though. Madira was still in there and was somehow fighting to hold the AI in check. And it looks like she finally won out in the end."

"What did she mean about telling Dee who her grandfather was?" Thomas asked.

"Sehera's father was former Supreme Court Chief Justice Scotty

P. Mueller, and Ahmi's partner until she killed him," Alexander said. "I guess she wants her to know who he was."

"Scotty? There was a Scotty who helped me escape on that kamikaze battle cruiser for Luna City six years ago. Was that him?" Nancy asked.

"He let you go?" Sehera asked.

"Yes,. he did. If it weren't for him, I'd be dead, and that ship would've probably hit Luna City. After Ahmi and this crazy doctor tortured me, he snuck in and cut me loose," Nancy explained.

"That sounds like my father," Sehera asked.

"You're why she killed him, then. She said he had betrayed her," Moore said. "And I bet I met that crazy doctor of yours forty years ago. I'd like a few minutes alone with that sonofabitch!"

"I killed him."

"Can't think of someone who deserved it more," Moore said with disdain for Ahmi's torture expert. That sadistic bastard had needed killing.

"Wait, wait. This is all too much. You talked to Elle Ahmi after the Battle for the Oort?" Jack asked.

"Yes, I did. We had to keep stringing her along until we found out how deep her Separatists were within the government. We've kept in contact with her and acted like we were part of her plans for decades," Moore said grudgingly. "I couldn't think of a better plan, DeathRay. We had a chance to stop her entire plan, not just her. We had to stay the course. And we had also simulated the outcome of just killing her. The colonies and Mars would have been thrown into a period where warlords fought each other for bits of the power vacuum that would follow."

"I was just asking, sir."

"Jesus, I've got a top-secret super AIC in my head, throughout my body. Could that happen to me?" Nancy asked.

"We've read your file, Nancy. The technology is decades ahead of what President Madira had implanted," Moore told her. "Besides, Abby really likes Allison and assures me that she is perfectly healthy."

"Ahmi, or Madira, whoever, didn't say 'tell Dee who her grandfather was,'" Nancy said as she lowered her weapon. Apparently, she believed Alexander and Sehera—or at least wanted to give that impression.

"What?" Sehera looked up at her sharply.

"No, Allison just played it back for me in my head. She said '*show* Dee who her grandfather was,' and her emphasis was on the word *show*." Nancy repeated the dead president.

"Abby says the same," Moore agreed.

"She never said anything or did anything without it meaning something else, or having design." Sehera rose to her feet. "She was trying to tell us something without giving it away to the AIC."

"Fan out. Look for a picture of Scotty P. Mueller," Moore ordered.

"I saw it earlier." Sehera walked over to the desk and picked up the ski mask. She held it in her hands briefly and then stuck it in her pocket. "Here it is."

She picked up the picture and examined it closer. It was in a very nice Mars cherry-tree-wood frame and covered with an antiglare pane of glass. The picture was of the newly elected Democratic president, Sienna Madira, shaking the hands of freshly congressionally approved Republican Supreme Court chief justice, Scotty P. Mueller. The chief justice had just sworn in the new president, and they were shaking hands. There was handwriting on the picture that read:

> The best minds are not in government;
> if they were, business would hire them away.
> Thanks, Sienna Madira,
> President of the
> United States of America

They all examined it closely but didn't see any double meaning. Sehera rolled the frame over in her hands a few times. They looked at the back of it and noticed fingernail marks on one side of the backing. Sehera pulled the frame open, and there was a piece of silica about the size of a microscope slide inside it.

"What is that?" Thomas asked.

"Thomas, my boy, I'll just bet you that there is data on that thing. And I'll bet it is data about who is who in the Separatist organization." Alexander smiled.

"Ma'am, we hadn't heard from you in a couple of hours. We feared the worst!" U.S.R. Fleet Admiral Sterling Maximillian said. "The battle is not going well, ma'am. The Americans have decimated our fleet. We have but a couple of ships still fighting."

"Put me on a systemwide broadcast, Admiral."

"Yes, ma'am. You're on, now."

"People of the United Separatist Republic, you have all fought so bravely and made such sacrifice. I love you, each and every one, with all of my heart. But the time has come that I must ask you all to lay down your weapons and surrender. There is no longer any need for us to continue the bloodshed. Our Separatist movement has been heard in history and throughout all of humanity, from Washington, D.C. to the deserts of Mars, to the Oort Cloud of Sol, and to colonies light-years from where man first crawled out of the muck. We have made our point to all of humanity, to our brethren. It is time now for us to make our amends with them. I ask you all to stand down. Thank you, and God bless you all."

"You are clear, ma'am," Maximillian said.

"Stand down, Admiral. Ahmi out." The holoscreen blanked out, and the view of the blue-green gas giant filled the horizon again.

"How was that?" Sehera pulled her hair out of the hole in her mother's ski mask and slipped it the rest of the way off.

"Perfect." Alexander smiled at his wife. "Let's go home."

EPILOGUE

December 14, 2396 AD
Tau Ceti, Ares
Saturday, 7:15 PM, Earth Eastern Standard Time
Saturday, 2:15 PM, New Tharsis Standard Time

Dee and her father sat on a park bench across from a row of condominiums, feeding the New Tharsis pigeons. December in New Tharsis was warm, humid, and more like May in Mississippi. It had taken Nancy months to figure out where their last target had slipped off to. It turned out that he hadn't slipped far. They had been finding the targets and eliminating them one by one for about fifteen months, and this last one had proven to be the most slippery of them all.

"Thanks for bringing me along on this one, Dad," Dee said.

"Like I would have ever heard the end of it if I didn't let you come." He laughed. "I just hope he shows up before we need to QMT to the embassy. I cannot miss the treaty signing. Finally reuniting all the human colonies—nothing is more important than tonight's ceremony. It'd be a shame to have to let Nancy finish this without us."

"We won't miss it. I'm sure Nancy's intel is right. So, are you going to run again?"

Alexander Moore knew he'd never get used to the way the gears were always churning in his daughter's head. "Well, your mother and I have talked about it a great deal, and—"

I've got our target in ten seconds. Nancy's voice rang in their minds.

"Saved by the belle. . . . We'll finish this conversation tomorrow." Alexander stood up and eased a modified railgun pistol out of his waistband, holding it casually against the side of his leg.

Dee stood up as well and turned toward her father.

"There's our target." Dee nodded toward the condos across the street.

A car pulled up and parallel parked in front of the condo just to the right of the only tree on the street. Dee and Alexander watched as the man got out of his car. He checked his mailbox and started to unlock his front door. Dee tossed the bag of pigeon food in the trash bin by the park bench.

"Time to go to work, Dad," she said a bit too eagerly.

Bree, QMT to target AO.

Roger that.

They flashed from the bench to the living room of the condo. As Alexander handed her the railpistol, Dee could hear the keys in the door. Then a shard of red and purple light from Tau Ceti and the Jovian's rings glinted through. Walt Fink stepped in and tossed his keys on the table next to the doorway and then turned and locked the dead bolt behind him.

"Well, hello there, *General*." Dee smiled at him and set the muzzle of her railpistol against his forehead. "Remember Clay Jackson and Jay Stavros? I do." Dee didn't blink when she pulled the trigger. One single tear rolled down her cheek as she stepped up and put a few more rounds into his head.

". . . a miraculous recovery," Gail Fehrer, anchor for the Earth News Network, said. "President Alexander Moore had the lowest approval ratings of any president since the twenty-first century, but between the decisive military victory over the Separatists and the historic accords that followed, his approval ratings have reached all-time highs. With less than a year of his present term left, will the Democrats be able to mount any sort of challenge?

"Moore's acceptance speech at the convention tonight is being viewed almost as a coronation. We go now, live to the floor of the convention center."

President Alexander Moore stepped out onto the stage and slowly walked up to the podium, surrounded by holo-images of his many triumphant moments as president. Many of the images prominently featured the vice president at his side.

When he reached the podium, the images ghosted away, and the lights dimmed down to two lone spotlights that lit up Moore and the presidential seal on the podium.

"George Washington once said, 'However political parties may now and then answer popular ends, they are likely, in the course of time and things, to become potent engines by which cunning, ambitious, and unprincipled men will be enabled to subvert the power of the people and to usurp for themselves the reins of government, destroying afterwards the very engines which have lifted them to unjust dominion.'

"I first took office nearly twelve years ago with a single goal—to end the Separatist threat and reunite humanity in common bond and purpose. With yesterday's signing of the Tau Ceti Accords, and thanks in no small part to the great courage, ingenuity, and sacrifice of many brave souls, we have finally succeeded.

"So the time has come for me to step aside, to allow a new vision, a new purpose, a new principle to lead this Grand Old Party and this great nation.

"Mr. Chairman, I hereby nominate Vice President Jacob Forest McClintock to be the next Republican nominee for the office of president of the United States—"

The tumultuous uproar that arose from the capacity crowd in the convention center was everything Alexander had hoped it would be.

Abigail, where are Sehera and Dee?

They are currently waiting to have dinner with you at Camp David. Dee and DeathRay are in the middle of a dogfight sim, while Nancy and Sehera are planning the wedding. I think Nancy and Jack make a very attractive couple, don't you?

Yes, I do. Take me to Sehera.

With a smile and a wave, the one hundred thirty-first president of the United States disappeared in a flash of white light and the sizzle of frying bacon.